SIEGE OF ARDON

HENRY EATON

COMING SOON BY HENRY EATON

The Inean Debacle

for Samantha, Heather & Matthew

Thanks to my sister, **Nancy Eaton**, **Professor of Physics**, **Wesleyan College**, for proofreading the manuscript to verify my science was as accurate as possible.

Manufactured in the United States of America

ISBN: 978-0-9852617-6-4

ISBN: (ebook)

ONE

ON THE WESTERN CONTINENT, more than a thousand zag (approx. 1300 miles) north of the planet's rebuilt capital of Delondra, a transport craft was preparing to launch from the newly built spaceport. The spaceport was named Udara after a former leader of the western continent, which angered people in the East. Udara would handle dozens of flights a day to all the colonies in the solar system and beyond..

Hundreds of people waited behind a barrier a few zag away from the tarmac as the transport ship *ShuBuré* prepared to ignite its engines. Armed soldiers patrolled the crowd because of threats from a local terror group.

The *ShuBuré* was a large ship measuring the length of a football field and half as wide. It had four large engines under the craft for thrust: two in the front and two in the back. Once off the ground, these engines would rotate the nozzles rearward to provide forward thrust as the ship headed for space. At the rear were three round engine ports in a triangle formation that utilized waste plasma from the star drive during solar system travel. The star drive utilized the tops of the main thrusters to house the high-energy plasma guns that would tear a wormhole in space that the ship would use to travel toward other star systems. This drive system slashed travel time to weeks and months instead of years and decades. The bottom of the ship had two large doors that swung open to access the cargo bay. On top of the ship were two long panels housing the inter-coolers for the antimatter star drive engines. The inter-coolers would swing down over the four rocket engines once the ship was in space. The crew and passenger compartments were in the ship's forward section and separated from the rest of the ship by a thick blast shield. This protected the occupants from any radiation the star drive produced.

The transport was heading to the third extrasolar colony on a planet called Silili in the Ubara system, dozens of light years away. The round trip would take them nine months to complete. It was just a routine mission to bring supplies and more colonists to their furthest colony yet.

The *ShuBuré* was commanded by Commander Gula and his first officer, Commander Puabi. Both came from the same village on the western continent, north of the base. They were experienced in interstellar space flight from an early age and were third-generation space pilots.

Gula and Puabi grew up together and were nearing the age of thirty. This was the age when Western women were to be married, and Puabi was constantly pressured by her mother to get married and spare her family the embarrassment of having an out-of-age woman in the family. A stigma would hover over them for years, and many would call her cursed.

Puabi loved Gula and felt they should be together, but Gula never seemed interested in being more than friends from the same village.

Puabi was running out of time.

Puabi and other women were also under constant pressure for their clothing. In the East, everything was acceptable, but in the West, which still embraced the teachings of Kur, it was quite differ-ent. Most women wore loose-fitting robes to cover any detail of their bodies, which conflicted with military requirements. Wearing a robe in a space suit or trudging through the mud or water during a military exercise was impossible. Their uniforms were designed to be as loose-fitting as possible and still conform to military standards. Many of the priests and teachers of Kur continued to fight the changing standards; some argued that the rise in immorality, especially in the East, was because of the lapse in standards. Then, people in the East argued the opposite.

The countdown began over a loudspeaker above the crowd. "Pur...nidi...amam...tulu...nadi." All four of the large engines began pumping fuel and fire and began to rumble from the large nozzles facing down. "Baur...gal...girse...kilu...tuam...zour!"

All four large vertical engines ignited with a thunderous roar, and the craft lifted slowly off the tarmac as the thrust from the engines blasted against the concrete platform. In the distance, people cheered despite the deafening roar, and they lifted their heads as the craft rose up and cleared the support towers. Once clear of the towers, the landing gear retracted. The engines rotated back slightly, and the *ShuBuré* headed off towards the thin clouds above. The ship passed low over a sports stadium and the game the game called Sabit had to be halted while the the spaceship flew overhead. Many waved at the ship as it headed toward space.

After the *ShuBuré* moved beyond the stadium the game continued

After a few minutes, the ship cleared the thin clouds and accelerated out of the atmosphere into space. Once away from the planet's atmosphere, the large engines rotated back completely and propelled the ship towards the inner moon Nisaba. Here, the transport would get a speed boost from the moon's gravity that would propel it out of the solar system. Once past Nisaba, the inter-coolers rotated down along the sides of the ship and began to glow with a green light as the antimatter engines warmed up. The *ShuBuré* exited the solar system in two days, and the star drive engines fired up completely. Four bright beams of energy shot out from the tips of the four engines and converged on a point in space well in front of the *ShuBuré*. A hole tore open in space large enough for the craft to enter.

Gula stood at the center of the bridge and got a nod from Puabi, who sat at the navigation console near the front of the bridge. All the indicators on her panel were green.

"Take us in," Gula stated as he sat back in his chair.

Puabi turned forward and slid the three levers on the side of her console forward, and the three large engines at the rear of the ship lit up. The *ShuBuré* flew quickly into the wormhole, taking the ship to Silili.

TWO

NINE MONTHS LATER, a dangerous race from another star system discovered Ardonnar. The Inean recon ships traveled more than a hundred light years to reach Ardonnar. Luckily for the Ardonnarians, they came from a direction opposite their colonies. The recon ships studied the planet for months and saw what the planet had for resources. After much debate among the Inean leaders, the decision was made to invade Ardonnar and strip it of its natural resources. It was a process the Ineans had used on several other planets in other systems. Their tactic was simple: attack swiftly and with overwhelming strength. Any inhabitants who survived would be killed off or sold as exhibits for their museums and zoos and as slave laborers. This eliminated any chance of a race returning to fight them, which concerned the Ineans. The sheer magnitude of the Inean invasions rendered many planets uninhabitable from the vicious bombing and stripping of their natural resources. The Inean home planet was becoming crowded, and the goal was to save this planet and inhabit it once the Ardonnarians were eliminated.

The decision to invade was difficult, mainly because the Ineans preferred overwhelming odds, but they did have the advantage of surprise. The Ardonnarians were more advanced than any other race they had conquered and were expanding into space too quickly. This prompted the Ineans to invade before the Ardonnarians posed a greater challenge later.

The Ineans were a nonhuman warrior race. They were taller and larger than humans, stronger but much slower. They had gray, blotchy, rough skin covered with minimal clothing made of leather-like material, sometimes made from the skins of races conquered. They had stubby, rounded horns protruding from their foreheads and a bony brow like a Neanderthal. Their tongues were long and forked at the end, contributing to the snapping in their deep, hissing voices, which boomed when they spoke. Their eyes were bright red and seemed to glow in the dark. They were a violent race and thought nothing of killing billions of inhabitants of planets they invaded.

The Inean warship, *Nikstra*, slowed as it approached the Ardonnarian system. The ship was here as the first step of an invasion fleet with Ardonnar as its target. The Ineans had planned a surprise attack that would quickly paralyze the Ardonnarians. The *Nikstra* was the first wave that would quickly knock out the planet's military and government. The full invasion would follow with dozens of ships that would kill all of the inhabitants. Once the planet was secured, larger ships would land and dismantle the rest of their infrastructure, stripping the planet of its valuable resources, which the Ineans needed to sustain their hungry society. The Ineans planned the first step around stolen technology, which was nothing new for them. Most of the technology the Ineans possessed was stolen from races they conquered or had helped fight other battles and then conquered. Either way, the Ineans feasted and expanded their society on their brute force and overwhelming numbers.

That was how they acquired the Star Disruptor. The Star Disruptor was a large device that took energy from a star and then used that energy to open a wormhole to a black hole in the galaxy's center. The black hole would then yank on the star violently until the wormhole could not sustain the energy surge and shut down. This would pull on the star, causing the star to erupt violently and blast a CME (Coronal Mass Ejection) in the direction of the device. If the probe was correctly positioned, the plasma burst could be targeted towards a planet or fleet of ships, where it could raise havoc. The Inean plan would target Ardonnar with repeated blasts and subsequent CMEs to disrupt the planet's power grids and weather patterns. The Ineans used this device with deadly accuracy on the last planet they invaded. By the time that race realized they were being invaded, it was too late.

The *Nikstra* had waited for activity to settle down in the Ardonnarian system as the autumn festival on the planet got into full swing. Few ships would go back and forth during the festival for two weeks. The *Nikstra* slowly started their way to Utui, Ardonnar's sun. The ship swung wide of Ardonnar to avoid detection and headed past the inner planets with their engines off, using the gravity boost from the inner planets and moons on their way. The Ineans had gone to the extent of covering the ship in absorbent foam that would absorb Ardonnarian scans. It was also painted black with the windows painted over, rendering the ship virtually invisible against the backdrop of space.

After a long flight, the *Nikstra* parked behind Utui and waited to ensure they had not been detected.

On the bridge of the *Nikstra*, the ship's captain, Damok-Sai, hovered over his communications officer, and both listened to the radio transmissions from the Ardonnarian ships. Damok-Sai was the son of Manava, the Inean leader Sankar's right-hand council member. He was conducting his third invasion and was highly regarded in Sankar's inner circle to replace his father, Manava when he retired from the Inean council.

The Inean government was set up based on family and class. Sankar had been the leader for nearly forty years, and his family had held power for over three hundred years. The next level was the parliamentary council, which included the next fifteen top family leaders, including Manava. The regional generals made up the next level, which Damok-Sai directly reported. One moved up or down based on the favor of the leader and his top council.

After several days of listening and scanning, Damok-Sai was satisfied that the *Nikstra* had not been detected. He turned to his weapons officer, who was responsible for deploying the Star Disruptor. "Akul! Launch the Star Disruptor," he said in a booming, deep voice, snapping some syllables with his forked tongue.

"Yes, Damok-Sai," Akul replied. He had waited impatiently for this moment. He hurried to his computer console and entered several commands into the computer. The bridge of the *Nikstra* erupted into activity as several Ineans ran about, preparing for the most critical part of their mission. Several more entered the bridge and took seats facing banks of computer terminals scattered about the command center atop the large ship. Beneath the five-mile-long *Nikstra*, several small explosions occurred between the hull of the ship and the long black cylinder beneath it. The cylinder floated away slowly, shedding its black cover, revealing a shiny silver, cigar-shaped cylinder. After the device cleared the *Nikstra*, Akul ignited the Star Disruptor's thrusters to take it toward the star Utui. Once it was at a safe distance, he parked it and began the startup sequence. Akul entered commands into the computer and watched his screen for the results.

The side panel bolts blasted off the Star Disruptor, and the panels swung outward. Four golden solar collectors unfurled and extended nearly ten miles in each direction. The panels unrolled sideways, two miles each, and ended up facing Utui. Akul watched as the power meter crept up from red into the yellow band and finally into the green. He entered more commands, and the lower panels blasted off, revealing a mass of pipes and equipment. Power cables as thick as a house. Magnetic coils as big as a skyscraper swung into place. The end closest to the star began to expand, going from a half-mile in diameter to nearly fifty miles. Large equipment swung into position, completing the fifty-mile-wide ring. Next, a long antenna extended out through the ring towards the star as lightning bolts crackled from the ball at the end to the ring. The antenna stopped just short of ten miles in length, and the energy was beginning to affect the *Nikstra*.

"Akul, move that thing away from us!" Damok-Sai bellowed with a glance towards Cakra, the scientist responsible for adapting the star disruptor to Inean technology. Cakra nodded as he monitored the interface between the ship and the star disruptor. So far, everything was working perfectly.

"Yes, Commander," Akul replied, and he ignited the Star Disruptor's engines. It moved towards Utui, a trip that would take a few days to complete under conventional rocket power.

A few days later, once the probe was a hundred thousand miles from the star's surface, Akul parked it. The energy readings were now solidly in the green, and he glanced up at Damok-Sai, who had walked onto the bridge moments before.

Damok-Sai, who was impatient, growled at him, "Do it!"

Akul nodded and pressed the final commands into the probe. The image of the Star Disruptor fluttered and shimmered, then disappeared. "The cloak is working. In three days, once the probe orbits to the other side of the star, we will have the first disruption, Commander."

"Excellent, engineer; get us back to the rendezvous point where the rest of the fleet should be by now."

"Yes, commander," Devavarya replied.

The ship's main engines came to life with a roar through the ship, and the ship shuddered and slowly pulled away from Utui. As the ship passed the innermost planet, one of the engines flared briefly and settled back down. Alarms sounded and then shut off as Damok-Sai turned towards Devavarya with a glare.

Commander Gula stood at the back of the *ShuBuré* bridge with Puabi as they talked about their plans for when they returned to Ardonnar. Gula had plans to attend the last days of the festival, which he was interested in unwinding from the long journey, while

Puabi planned to check on her sister's new baby and spend some time with her family.

The annual festival was a two-week-long, planetwide celebration of Kur, leading to the annual harvest. No work was done during this time, and no new flights left the planet. The festival culminated in a mass pilgrimage to Kurah, the temple of Kur, in the eastern city of Kurdash. The armies of both sides were well represented and on high alert following terrorist threats to kill the pilgrims as they made their way to the holy temple. It was a threat taken seriously, as over a thousand pilgrims had been murdered two years before. Many feared it would be the spark needed to ignite a planetwide war. Luckily, war was averted, but tensions remained high.

"Shall we take this conversation to dinner, commander?" Gula asked.

"Definitely, Commander Gula. I haven't eaten all day," she replied, following him toward the hatch. Gula had shown more interest in Puabi during this last mission, and she hoped that he was finally *coming around.*

As they approached the hatch, the door slid to the side with a hiss, and an alarm went off. It was the proximity alarm that warned them of something in the area. They both turned quickly and returned to their posts. His was in the command chair at the rear of the bridge, and hers was at the navigation console in the middle of the bridge, facing the main screen.

"Report!" Gula asked as he sat firmly.

"Sensors have detected an object in our vicinity, commander. Turning full sensor array in that direction," Ama-Anzud responded.

"What kind of object?" Gula asked urgently. His concern was for asteroids and comet fragments that could damage or destroy his ship. It was the annual season for the meteor showers, which raised the likelihood of such a strike.

"It is a ship, sir. Metallic and propelled."

"Whose ship is it? An eastern ship?" Puabi asked, knowing that the eastern continent had been slowly withdrawing from the annual religious feast for several years.

"I don't think so. It is way too big and is heading out of the system's orbital plane at a high rate of speed." Ama-Anzud replied.

"Can you track it?" Gula asked.

"Sorry, Commander. It has moved out of the sensor's range already."

"Save all your data," Gula replied.

"Already done, sir."

Gula walked forward and stared out the large view screen at Utui and the bright speck that was Ardonnar in the distance. He had a sinking feeling in his stomach that their lives were about to be changed forever.

Puabi admired Gula standing there, as most women did. Gula stood over six feet tall. His hair was cut in a typical military style, and his uniform was well-pressed and fitted to his muscular frame. However, she had the same sinking feeling. The feeling of doom. She watched him, wondering what was running through his mind.

Gula turned around. "Comm, contact Udara for me."

"Yes, commander," Puhrum replied. "Udara, this is *ShuBuré*; please respond," she repeated several times. Several seconds later, she looked up and said, "Commander, I have Udara on the comm."

"Thank you, lieutenant. Udara this is *ShuBuré*. We have detected an unknown ship leaving our system at a high rate of speed. Have you detected anything?"

"*ShuBuré*, we have not detected any other ships in your area. Please download all your data and check your equipment," the voice replied over the loudspeaker.

Gula turned to Ama-Anzud, who gave him the thumbs-up and replied, "All systems check out, sir."

"Udara, all systems check out fine. Data files are on the way," Gula stated, glancing at Puabi for any input. She didn't offer any.

"We have received your data, *ShuBuré*. We will analyze it and meet with you when you land. See you in a few days. Udara out."

"So that is it. We wait," Gula said, and he left the bridge.

Puabi followed him off the bridge. She wanted to be with Gula, even though it was forbidden for a woman to ask a man in their society. She hoped he would pick up on her interest and ask her for an official date. She knew he felt the same way but still would not take the bait. "Still hungry?" she asked.

"No, not anymore. I got a weird feeling about what that might be."

"Yeah, me too," she said, looking up at him with her dark eyes.

"I think I'll go to the gym for a while to think about this."

She stopped and watched as the elevator door slid open, and he walked away. She leaned back against the side of the elevator and sighed as the door slid shut. Puabi was tall for a woman. She had long dark hair pulled back in a ponytail. She had deep, well-tanned skin with dark, seductive eyes. She wore no makeup, as it was forbidden by the Priests of Kur.

On the *Nikstra* bridge, Damok-Sai and the rest of his bridge crew listened to the radio conversation between the *ShuBuré* and Udara. Then, there was silence. Damok-Sai turned and glared at Devavarya, his engineer, and growled. "Your incompetence has given us away."

"Commander, they don't know what they saw. They have no idea. They will just chalk it up as an anomaly and forget about it," Devavarya replied to his commanding officer. He knew the penalty for screwing up and feared for his life.

"For the last time, you have left me no choice. It was your engines that flared. It was your underestimation of our engines' needs to move the probe here. Delaying our emperor's conquest by six months. When my father retires, I am in line for the parliamentary seat, and you won't cost me that."

Devavarya got up from his seat and started toward Damok-Sai. "You blame me? Your impatience cost the emperor his precious months. I told you and many others, including Cakra, that the engines were underpowered for this mission, but you did not listen."

Damok-Sai lunged forward, growling loudly, bringing his large, jagged dagger down into Devavarya's chest. He pushed him back and drove the bloodied dagger down again as Devavarya stood his ground.

Devavarya reached for his own dagger as his heart began to falter, and he collapsed to the floor.

Damok-Sai pulled the dagger from his engineer's chest and put it back in his belt, with blue blood dripping from it. He wanted to show the rest of the crew that he would not tolerate dissent or mistakes. Everyone on the bridge went back to their stations and looked busy.

Damok-Sai grumbled and looked around his bridge, which was silent except for the computers' beeps and chirps. "Launch the EMP missiles towards the planet!" he shouted.

"Missiles away," a nervous technician replied as several missiles streaked away toward Ardonnar. Soon, their engines shut down, and the missiles drifted into position to avoid detection from the Ardonnarian sensors.

Damok-Sai looked down at the body on the floor. He growled and walked off the bridge, leaving the body of his dead engineer on the blood-splattered deck.

THREE

IN A CAVERN deep in Mount Laarsa, in the Humbaba
mountain chain, which runs north to south on the western side of
the western continent, dozens of Ardonnarian scientists staffed a
military base that monitored their planet and solar system. Several
large monitors along the walls displayed different views of Utui,
Ardonnar's sun, in one theater-style room. A few dozen people oper-
ated this part of the base, which acted as an early warning for the
planet should the star act violently. The Commander in charge,
Baltuti, had direct communication with the planet's president,
Aanepada, who could shut down the planet's power grid and
nuclear plants should a massive solar storm head toward the planet.

The day started off quietly, as they did just about every day.
Baltuti hovered near a terminal where an attractive woman monitored the temperature of Utui's corona. He had his hand on her
shoulder as he leaned forward and whispered in her ear. Enir
grinned and was about to say yes to his advances when her display
suddenly began displaying a stream of data. The screen flashed red
warning messages, and her fingers were a blur as she entered
commands into the computer.

Baltuti stepped back as all eyes turned toward her station. Then, all the other stations began to go wild with activity. Baltuti went from station to station, and the situation was the same: Utui had gone critical.

"Get me the president!" Baltuti yelled.

The big monitors switched to a scene of Utui belching a blob of fire directly towards Ardonnar. A dense Coronal Mass Ejection tens of thousands of times the size of the planet raced toward the planet.

"Baltuti! All of our readings are off the charts. This is thousands of times worse than our worst-case scenario. We must shut down the grid and reactors to avoid disaster!" Enir screamed over the loud chatter in the observatory.

Another technician turned his way. "Baltuti! Gamma rays are off the charts. I can't explain it!"

Yet another yelled out. "X-rays are spiking as well."

Enir turned to him. "Did a black hole hit Utui? Cosmic rays are spiking, and they shouldn't be right now!"

A young intern ran up to Baltuti, her lengthy hair flowing behind her and past her head when she stopped abruptly before him. She fumbled nervously with the radio and then handed it to him.

"Mister President, Utui has gone critical. You must shut down the power grid and nuclear reactors. All ships in flight must be grounded immediately!" Baltuti said with urgency.

"What happened, Baltuti? I didn't think the next solar cycle was due for years," Aanepada asked. He got up from his desk, where he had been working on a proposal to ease tensions with the East, and walked towards the large windows overlooking Delondra. It was a clear, cool day, and he watched the people going about their business below.

"It isn't, sir. I don't know what caused this. It is our worst-case scenario times a thousand. It is just short of Utui going supernova. All was quiet, and then all Tari broke loose, but the grid needs to be shut down," Baltuti said as he watched the screens on the walls. One after another, they turned to static as the large, fiery piece of the star destroyed the satellites between them and Utui.

"Nova? Can we survive this? How long do we have?" Aanepada

asked as he got tense. He turned his gaze to the sky, which was beginning to turn yellow.

"We can survive, but there are barely minutes before the dangerous radiation begins to hit our atmosphere. The storm is racing toward us at an unprecedented speed," Baltuti said as another large monitor displayed nothing but static.

"I will shut down the gri..." Baltuti pulled the transmitter from his ear and looked at it while all that came from the speaker was hissing. The connection was lost. Several other monitors shut down. The only one left active was one tracking the *ShuBuré*, turning towards its final approach to the planet. He had no way of warning the ship away, and there was no place for it to hide anyway.

Damok-Sai watched the solar burst head towards the planet, and he grinned. "Detonate the EMP weapons!" he growled.

Above the planet, the EMP bombs exploded, and Damok-Sai turned his head and howled. The rest of his crew did the same.

"It is a glorious day for Emperor Sankar," he bellowed, and his crew howled again towards the ceiling.

"The outer edge of the storm is already hitting our atmosphere, Baltuti!" Enir yelled as she glanced at the monitor, which had begun to crackle with electricity while tracking the *ShuBuré*. "There is a severe electromagnetic disturbance engulfing the entire planet. This is way too much for the solar storm to produce! I can't explain it."

"All ready? That is too fast," Baltuti said in disbelief. "And what is with the EMP?"

Enir turned toward Baltuti, "Sir, we must shut down."

"Is the grid still up?"

"It is, sir," another technician said from below Baltuti's level.

"Duga!" cursed Baltuti.

"Sir, we must shut down. NOW!" Enir yelled as she stared at her boss.

Baltuti slumped his shoulders in defeat. "Fine, shut it down."

Everyone in the room began to shut down their equipment when the storm hit. The lights glowed brighter and then began to spark and burn out. Terminals flared up, and a few wall monitors exploded, showering sharp glass fragments over the technicians below, who tried to take cover. The lights blew out completely, and the emergency lights flickered on. The room glowed red as they buzzed.

"Baltuti! The main relays are frozen," a technician yelled from the first floor. "The filters are melting!"

Baltuti turned and ran towards the main power cabinet, pulling the door open. Static electricity danced and cracked over the large breakers. He went to grab the handle of the breakers, and electricity cracked up his arm, sending him back a few feet. He pulled back and held his hand as the feeling went from his arm. He looked around for something to hit the lever with. He found a broom with a wooden handle, which he felt would be safe.

Others turned to watch, including Enir, who realized what he was doing. She stood quickly, held her hand out to stop him, and yelled, "No, Baltuti, don't do it..." but her words seemed to come in slow motion, too late. He jammed the broom's handle between the breaker and the lever and pulled down as Enir bolted towards him. The electricity crackled up the wooden handle and into his hands. He flew headfirst across the room into one of the large monitors on the wall. The monitor shattered, and Baltuti crumpled to the ground. Smoke rose from the remains of his hands and feet, which had completed the circuit when he opened the breakers. Glass crashed down around him, and the emergency lights went out.

President Aanepada stood in his office facing the large windows that displayed much of the capital city of Delondra. The sky had changed from a deep blue from the dry, crisp early autumn air to a bright yellow glow. The people below began to realize there was trouble as power transformers began sparking and exploding. People raced into homes and businesses only to rush out again as every-thing electrical began burning up. Smoke began to rise around the city beneath him, and then the sky turned orange and rippled as the fiery blob blasted into the planet's atmosphere. Soon, lightning bolts began crashing to the ground and across the sky, as the planet's magnetic field collapsed and tried to reestablish itself, funneling the Inean's EMP weapon's energy to the ground. Thousands of lightning bolts crashed to the ground in Delondra, forcing people to find cover that wasn't there.

The city was a combination of old and new. It was the capital of the West during the last war, and much of it had been leveled. Some of the outer parts were old, at least two hundred to four hundred years old, while much of the core of the city was relatively new. It overlooked Delondra Bay, which was crowded with hundreds of boats of all shapes and sizes. Many were fishing boats and pleasure boats with a few yachts. It was a sight to behold, especially this time of year, as the leaves changed color and reflected off the water.

The view from Aanepada's balcony was of the brick plaza below, which had statues, water fountains, colorful gardens, and small ponds that held various fish and waterfowl.

A younger woman came up beside Aanepada and held his arm. "This is terrible?"

He kept facing forward. "Yes, it is. Very bad. The whole planet will be affected over the next few hours."

"What will happen?" she asked.

"Well, I could not shut the power grids down, and communications went down quickly. So that means relays, transformers, and everything that requires electricity will be burned up. Soon, the planet's magnetic field will start stressing and snapping, which will induce many problems in the weather and allow dangerous charged particles into the atmosphere. Then it gets really nasty. This is all based on our worst-case scenario, which this blows away by a factor of about one thousand."

"We should get you to cover then," she said, tugging his arm as the lightning wave crept closer. Behind the wave was a wall of fire and smoke.

"Yes, of course," he said with a huff, more out of frustration that he could save himself while thousands below could not. He knew the death toll and destruction would be catastrophic.

She guided him from the room as a lightning bolt crashed through the large windows, blowing glass into the room. Kilar turned to see what crashed through, half expecting a transport to fall from the sky, but all she saw was a bright flash and a thunderous boom, and she stumbled.

Aanepada pulled her with him as she slumped in his grip. He stumbled and landed on the floor with her on top of him. He sat up quickly when he saw blood. He helped Kilar to sit up, and he noticed blood oozing from her chest. Then he noticed the large chunk of glass protruding from her chest. She saw it, too, and looked up into his eyes. "I love you, Father." With that, she convulsed and slumped against him.

Aanepada's hands shook as he held her. Tears rolled down his cheeks as he began to cry. After a minute, he began to chant to their god, Kur, as the building shook violently from the solar storm slamming into Ardonnar.

Aanepada's mind raced through his life, which was full of tragedy. His wife died at a young age from a rare cancer, and he raised his daughter, Kilar, and his adopted daughter, Dagan, from a very young age. His own father, Mituti, who was the leader of the planet, was killed with his mother shortly after he left office by an eastern terrorist who blew up their transport as it crossed the ocean from the eastern continent. Aanepada's brother died recently from a flu-like disease he contracted on one of the new colonies in another system. So he was surrounded by death, and his own daughter's death would prove to be his most difficult yet to deal with. He held her now lifeless body close as tears streaked down his cheeks.

The CME engulfed the entire planet in minutes as it blew past. Fires raged around the planet, transports fell from the sky, and the planet's power grid was soon a burned-up pile of copper, rubber, plastic, and silicon electronics. It would take years to bring power to the planet again and decades for some of the remote regions.

In the eastern capital of Ninki, the engines of a large transport shut down, and the craft crashed into the capital tower. The ship's fuel ignited an inferno that collapsed a tall tower into an adjacent tower, bringing them down on top of people trying to escape the disaster.

To the southeast of Ninki, in the city of Kurdash, tens of thousands of people swarmed into Kurah, the ancient temple of God for their culture and also the inspiration for the city's name. It was an enormous stone structure larger than a baseball stadium that had stood for nearly twelve hundred years and was the center of the current festival on Ardonnar. People rushed in, bowed down, and began chanting to Kur as an earthquake rumbled through the region. The quake was possibly brought on as the CME stressed the planet, and the magnetic field swung wildly about. The earthquake would be the largest on record for the region. The temple began to rumble. Dust and small pieces of stone rained down on the tens of thousands of people below, and they jammed the exits, trying to escape. Then, the ground heaved and crashed back down, and the temple collapsed on top of the people in a massive cloud of dust and smoke that swept across the city.

Large silver cylinders stood in the ultra-modern western city of Belit-Sheri, with glass and steel high-rise towers, above-ground monorail, and many exotic parks and gardens. The cylinders held millions of gallons of petroleum fuel from one of the last oil refining plants left on the planet. The fuel was used in remote areas, where it was impractical to bring nuclear power. People saw the waves of lightning coming their way and started to leave the area over fear if one of the tanks were hit.

Power transformers exploded off buildings and from underground power stations. Manhole covers launched hundreds of feet into the air, followed by fire and smoke. Several buildings erupted into flames as Ardonnarians ran from them into the streets. Cars, trucks, buses, and monorails rolled to a stop as their electrical systems overloaded, which was caused by the Inean EMP weapons detonating high in the atmosphere.

The people in the street looked up as a transport flew low overhead, flames coming from one of its engines. The transport spiraled out of control, crashed low into a high-rise building, and exploded. The building toppled over and crashed down on the Ardonnarians as they tried to escape.

The Ardonnarians breathed a sigh of relief as one of the petroleum tanks was hit by lightning and held, but it would be short-lived. Several bolts struck another tank; it split in two, and the fuel flooded the streets. A few minutes later, another lightning bolt struck a power station, igniting the fuel. The streets of Belit-Sheri were ablaze, and then the other tanks exploded, showering the city with flaming oil that ignited a city-wide fire. Rivers of fire swept along the streets, burning everything and everyone in its path.

There was no escape, as people of all ages were swept away into the sea by a wave of fire.

FOUR

PUABI WAS at the navigation console, entering the final approach to Udara. She typed away and plotted the course as the *ShuBuré* closed in on Ardonnar. "Commander, the final approach to Udara spaceport is programmed."

"Very well. All cargo and persons are secured. Take us down," Gula replied as he buckled his seat belt.

"Udara, this is *ShuBuré*. We are coming in," Puhrum said over her headset, which was mostly hidden under her long dark hair, which she wore down in defiance of military restrictions.

"*ShuBuré*, you are cleared for landing at terminal four."

A stifled cheer went up around the bridge, and Puabi began their descent, ending their long journey.

The *ShuBuré* entered the atmosphere at high speed. Fire scorched the hull as the friction with the atmosphere slowed the transport.

"*ShuBuré, ShuBuré* this is Udara. Abort landing; repeat, abort landing!" blasted over the bridge speaker.

"Udara, we are gliding in. We can not abort. Please redirect," Puhrum requested.

"Redir.. to ..dug..we..." then static.

"Get them back!" exclaimed Gula as he leaned forward in his seat in a feeble attempt to hear better.

"I cannot, sir. There is too much static."

"Static? From what?" Gula asked.

Alarms sounded throughout the bridge, and Ama-Anzud spun around to his sensors terminal. "What the tari!"

"What is it?" Gula asked.

"Oh crap, hold on!" Ama-Anzud yelled, and he grasped the side of his console.

The ship lurched hard to starboard, and more alarms sounded. Puabi fought the controls and tried to steady the transport while it began to spin out of control. The ship cleared the clouds as it spun towards the planet. The orange horizon was an eerie sight when they expected to see blue. They were now high over the eastern continent and spinning out of control.

Puabi reached for the joystick on the side of her console and began firing thrusters manually to pull the ship out of its spin. She fought the controls while the ship shook violently. After a few minutes, she regained control only a few thousand feet above the ground. She fired the main engines, which lifted the ship into the air and continued toward Udara. She could feel her heart pounding in her chest.

"Comm, anything?"

"Just static on all frequencies, sir, even eastern bands," Puhrum replied. She kept testing her equipment and searching for signals.

"How can that be?" Puabi asked.

"Sensors are picking up something in the atmosphere." There was a pause while Ama-Anzud studied his instruments. "This can't be."

"What is it?" Puabi and Gula asked impatiently in unison.

"A massive plasma cloud is slamming the planet from Utui. We must get down on the ground right now!" he exclaimed.

Puabi turned her head towards him, "We are over the ocean. We can't land, and we can't turn back either. We are low on thruster fuel."

"That CME is so strong it will fry our electronics, and we will fall into the ocean. We have to land somewhere," Ama-Anzud replied. As he talked, the ship's hull became polarized by the storm and began to glow and hiss from the charged particles.

"Navigation compass is swinging wildly," Puabi exclaimed as she began to fight with the controls again.

"That is because the planet's magnetic field is snapping for some reason that I cannot explain. We are not out of trouble yet," Ama-Anzud said as his monitors went to static. "Sensors are gone. We are flying blind." He tossed his headset onto the control panel in frustration.

Gula unbuckled and walked up to the main screen as the *ShuBuré* shook. The ocean looked turbulent below, and the horizon was bright orange. "Time until we land?"

"I don't know," Puabi said as she fought with the controls. "I think ten minutes."

Gula turned and went to her console, where he helped with the controls. He worked the joystick, which was hard to handle, and she returned to her calculations.

"What is that?" Puhrum exclaimed as she pointed to the main screen.

They all looked up, and a wall of fire extended to the ocean below. Lightning bolts crackled across the sky and into the water.

"Cushik!" Gula swore. He stumbled back, fell into his chair, and strapped in. "Puabi, get us out of here!"

Static electricity began cracking over several controls, and the main screen began flickering.

"I can't. The controls won't respond. We are going down!"

"Comm, shipwide," Gula yelled. "All hands, brace for impact. We are most likely going to crash into the ocean. Hold on!" He turned to his engineer. "Retract the intercoolers and dump the remaining antimatter containers! May a blessing from Kur save us!"

The *ShuBuré* slammed into the wall of fire and was struck several times by lightning bolts. Then, they cleared for a few minutes as the ship descended. They hit another wall of fire and lightning as the storm lined up with the planet's magnetic lines of force.

Another officer was calling out altitude readings. "One thousand pana, seven hundred pana, three hundred pana, fifty pana."

The *ShuBuré* hit the water and flipped end over end. The forward starboard engine broke off and exploded as the fuel pumping into the engine ignited and sprayed outward, followed by the rear port engine. The inter-coolers caught the water and tore off, tossing the ship high above the waves. The *ShuBuré* flew through the air and then slammed into the ocean. The cargo hold doors split open, and the supplies brought back from Silili spilled out above the ocean. The forward section with the crew and passengers breached along the blast shield, and water sprayed into the aft passenger compartments.

Gula and the others unbuckled and fell on the bridge's deck. "Status?"

"We have breaches everywhere, sir. We are going down," Ama-Anzud replied as he fumbled for his control panel.

"Get the rafts out and get the injured to them. How long do we have?" Gula asked as he finally got to his feet. He had trouble standing as the *ShuBuré* bobbed in the turbulent ocean.

"I don't know, Commander. Minutes, maybe less," Puhrum said as she helped Ama-Anzud up.

Gula went to the comm and pressed a button. "Abandon ship! Quickly. We are going down."

Gula looked at Puabi, who was leaning against the nav-con with blood running down the side of her head. "Puabi! Are you all right?"

"I think so," she said while blinking to refocus her eyes. "Let's get out of here."

She staggered towards the main hatch as Gula wrapped an arm around her to steady them both.

They went down one level and along a corridor as the *ShuBuré* began to list towards aft. It was sinking quickly. Gula found a red cabinet and pulled the handle. The contents spilled out and plastered him to the far wall. He cursed. The others pulled the supplies off him and then hurried to the external hatch with the blow-up rafts.

"Once we open the hatch, the water will rush in from below, so we must hurry or get sucked down with the ship," Gula yelled.

Everyone nodded, and he started to turn the metal wheel.

"Wait!" someone yelled from behind them, and they turned to see who it was. Ten crewmates staggered along the corridor, one foot on the floor and the other on the wall, as the ship twisted further to the rear, lifting the nose in the air. They had a young girl and a boy with them who were crying.

"Where are their parents?" Puabi asked.

An engineer with blood splattered all over himself looked at them and then at the children. "Not now," he said.

"Is there anyone else behind you?" Gula asked.

"No, Commander, just rising water and rising fast."

After the engineer spoke, the ocean water bubbled up behind the last group.

"Time is up. We must go!" Gula exclaimed as he struggled to turn the hatch crank. It finally moved as water flooded the corridor behind them. He spun the handle, and the hatch blew open from the built-up air pressure inside. "Get the rafts out!"

Ama-Anzud tossed the rafts out and yanked on the rip cords, inflating them in seconds. He looked out and saw that the water around the ship was ablaze from the spilled fuel burning on its surface. He hoped it would go out quickly. Luckily, below the hatch, it was still clear.

"Puabi, Puhrum, take the children; the rest of you go in the other rafts. Here, take the flotation vests!" Gula yelled over the roar of the ocean. He looked back at the ocean water bubbling up behind them. The water was now at his boots.

"Gula, take the rope," Puabi yelled. She then tossed him an end, which he wrapped around his hands, while Puhrum tied the other end to the raft. They paddled away quickly against the turbulent ocean. He was the last one out as the ship slid away, sucking him down with it. Puabi and Puhrum held the other end of the rope tight as their raft was pulled towards the sinking ship. They pulled and pulled, and suddenly, Gula popped through with a gasp for air as the rubber raft tipped into the water, soaking the occupants. He stayed in the water for a minute, catching his breath and mustering strength to drag himself into the life raft.

He collapsed into the raft with a splat. Puabi handed him a towel and a pack of dry, one-size-fits-all clothes. He dried and dressed himself the best he could in mixed company. He sat back in the raft and looked around. "Where are we?"

"No idea, but West is that way," she said, pointing. "I don't think land is too far away. That may be smoke, and the last time I checked, water is not supposed to burn." She stated that as the last patch of fuel burning on the water extinguished itself, leaving an oily residue on the water.

"Then we should go west," Gula said with a wave of his hand.

Puabi started the solar-powered electric motor, and the liferaft headed off with the others behind them.

Puhrum sat with her arms around the children on either side of her. "What is your name?" she asked the boy.

"Amar-Sin," he replied with a sniff. "Where are my mommy and daddy?" he asked, looking up at Puhrum.

"Your parents are in An. Kur has come to take them to paradise, where they will wait for you to join them," Puhrum replied. "They were good people, so they are not in Tari."

"I want to go now," he cried.

"Only when Kur comes for you. Until then, you must be brave," she said. "How old are you?"

"I am twelve. I was to take the entrance exam to Anunnaki," he said with another sniff.

"And you will take the test, and the priest will be pleased with you," she said. She turned to the girl. "What is your name?"

"Enhedu, I am eleven. Did Kur take my parents as well?"

"Yes, he did, and I need you to be brave as well."

Gula took over the motor from Puabi, who sat back with the children. They started to play a game to see who could name the most council members, then other cities and temples.

They traveled into the night with the marker beacons blinking on each rubber raft until they saw lights in the distance. They had found land. However, it wasn't the lights of civilization; enormous fires were burning. Gula checked his emergency radio, and all he got was static. Whatever caused the CME to strike the planet, the destruction was widespread. He shut down the electric motor as the batteries ran low and sat back with Puabi, taking her hand in his while Enhedu slept on her lap with her head against her chest.

"Do you think the ship we saw had something to do with this?" he asked her.

"Yes, I do. I don't know what angers me the most: Not knowing who they are or why they would do this," she said. "Who knows how many are dead? Maybe we are the last survivors."

"I hope not because if they are that powerful, then what chance do we have?"

"I don't know."

"Hello, Commander. Shall we tie the rafts together and get some sleep?" the engineer asked as their raft pulled up beside Gula's, and the last raft was behind them.

"Yes, we should," Gula replied, and he tied off his end of the rope. Soon, they all slept, but it wasn't a restful sleep.

Gula dreamed about the large ship they had seen three days prior, and his mind invented a reason for the attack. Human-like aliens assumed their colonization of other planets was an invasion of their territory and an act of war.

The next morning, they started for shore as Utui rose up in the East by paddling while the solar batteries recharged. The sky was still glowing between clouds of smoke and soot, blowing eastward away from the many uncontrolled fires on land. By mid-morning, the batteries were charged. Gula and the others switched to the electric motors and made it to shore hours later. They tied the rafts to the charred remains of a wooden fence along the beach. They looked around and got their first glimpse of the destruction. The beach was littered with debris and half-burned bodies. Gula led his crew up the beach towards the city, and when they made it to the top of the sand, the city was still in flames as the survivors wandered about in a daze.

Many people were injured and lying in the streets, calling out for help. Gula and what remained of his crew and passengers did what they could to help them, which consisted of just making them comfortable.

Not too far away from them, chunks of glass and concrete fell from the weakened buildings to the street below. One building, which had been engulfed since the day before, began to creak and groan, forcing Gula and his crew to take notice. They watched as one of the corners buckled, blasting concrete and steel across the street, and the tall building leaned with a groan while glass and burning furniture fell to the street below. Suddenly, the whole bottom three stories of the building exploded outward and gave way. It toppled into the street while flames and burning embers sprayed into the sky.

"We need to get these people to the hospital. Where is it?" Gula asked a man as he wandered by. "Hey! I asked you a question," and Gula grasped the man's arm, stopping the man who wore the robe of a local lower priest.

"It... it is gone. The hospital. It was three streets over. It's just a pile of rubble, you know." He pulled out of Gula's grip and wandered off, calling someone's name.

"What can we do for them?" Puabi asked Gula.

"Nothing. We must get moving to our village to see what is left and help them." He looked at a sign on the wall of a nearby building, which read "Belit-Sheri Theater," and turned to the others. "This is Belit-Sheri. I've been to this theater."

"This was a beautiful city. What kind of weapon could do this kind of damage?" Puhrum asked.

"Was," Ama-Anzud replied as he studied the destruction.

"I wish I knew," Gula replied as he looked about.

"Gula, we will stay and help these people as best we can," the engineer stated, and the rest of the crew looked about to see who would stay.

Puabi turned to Gula, "We should take the children to our village. They might be better off there."

"Perhaps you are right. Enhedu, Amar-Sin, come with us. The

rest of you can come with us or move on to your own villages as you see fit."

"Samuqan is over four hundred zag to the south. We should find a vehicle that still works," Puabi said.

"We may find one once we get out of the city. Let us walk for now." Gula said as he stepped over a half-burned, dead body. The children followed him, staring at the body on the ground with wide eyes. Puabi brought up the rear as she studied the children for reaction. She wondered what they must be thinking, being surrounded by death at such an early age. She was sure this was probably their first experience, and they had quieted. The children followed along, seemingly in a trance, which was how she felt now. All she thought was that this was a bad dream, and she would wake up at any moment on the *ShuBuré*, and everything would be normal.

FIVE

PUABI, Gula, and the two children walked along the road for several hours before coming across a roadside diner. One thing about the cities in the West is that they are condensed without much in the way of suburbs. Most cities were surrounded by farmlands, and there was not much in between cities and towns. The only things breaking up the view of the open pastures were the occasional roads and the monorails running between the cities. Now, they followed "the rail" towards Samuqan. Dust kicked up from their feet as they walked closer, and they noticed that several people had gathered. All had walked to the diner even though there were vehicles parked out front. People were bickering over the limited amount of food available. A fight would surely break out if it weren't for Gula and Puabi dressed in their messy military uniforms.

"We need food," several people yelled.

"I don't have enough for everyone, and look, more keep showing up," the owner stated as he glared at Gula, who stepped closer. Everyone can have a little bit or nothing. That is your choice."

A large man stepped forward, pushing his way through the crowd. "Give me that pie now!" the man yelled, pointing at the meat pie in the window while reaching into his pocket with his other hand.

Gula expected a gun to come out, so he pulled his from its holster and stepped between the diner's owner and the large man. "I don't know what is in your pocket, mister, but I would step away if I were you. The owner here said he has a limited supply of food. Everyone is welcome to a portion to get you to your next meal. I would suggest you take that offer."

"Leave it to the military to show up a day late," a woman yelled, followed by jeers from several others.

"Where were you when all this happened?"

"Yeah, where were you?"

The crowd was becoming unruly.

"We were trying to land the *ShuBuré* and avoid killing our crew and passengers," Puabi yelled at the loudest woman. She was easily angered when the military was criticized.

"Where is the rest of your crew then?" the woman asked as she stepped closer.

"The rest of them stayed in Belit-Sheri, which has been destroyed, to help the survivors," Puabi stated as she ushered the children behind her.

With that, the woman and others backed away at the news. Even the large man backed away and removed his empty hand from his pocket.

"Belit-Sheri is what?" the large man asked.

"It has been destroyed. There is hardly anything left at all," Puabi said as she patted the children on their shoulders.

"I was heading there to find my family," the large man said, choking back a tear.

"And they may still be there," Gula replied. "But fighting here is not the answer."

The man slumped his shoulders and stepped away. "Let everyone have a small portion," he said. I'm not hungry."

"Don't forget to pray to Kur," the girl, Enhedu, said with a glance to Puabi, who grinned back at her.

. . .

They ate and rested briefly, then continued south toward their village. As they walked, Puabi talked with the children to keep them occupied and not thinking about their parents until they came across a pub with several vehicles parked in front. There was noise inside, and Gula went in alone.

As he entered the pub, everyone stopped talking and turned towards him.

"Greetings. I am in need of a vehicle to go south to my village. I can pay for it," Gula said.

Everyone burst out laughing. "Your money is useless. The entire government has collapsed. We heard it on the radio earlier," one of them laughed while holding up a frothy brew.

"Radios are working? Can you call out? I need to contact Udara," Gula said excitedly.

"Can only hear, and it is very noisy and crackly."

"We tried to call out, but there are no tones and no signal strength," another added.

"Great!" Gula said with disgust. "How about the vehicle or a ride then?"

"None of them work; that is why we are here," as the man gulped his brew to the end. He slammed the mug to the bar. "Give me another," he bellowed.

"There is no more. You drank it all," the woman behind the bar said.

"What!" and the man lunged over the bar and bowled the woman over. He started beating her as several others chimed in.

Gula raced forward with his gun in hand and fired into the air. This brought several guns to his head, and he quickly holstered his weapon.

"Get out!" they exclaimed as the others continued to beat the barmaid.

"You are killing her! What has happened to you people?" Gula asked as one of the men cocked his pistol.

"She is already dead. The men are just frustrated, blowing off steam," one of them said.

"Now go."

"Kur does not approve of this. You must repent. Murder is not acceptable," Gula rattled off quickly as the others pulled themselves from the dead barmaid.

"Would you like to join her, then?" one of them asked as the group moved towards him.

"NO! I have others waiting for me."

"Then GO! Leave us," they shouted.

Gula turned and left the bar quickly. When he reached Puabi and the children, she saw he was scared.

"What happened?" she asked.

"They have all gone crazy. Come, we have to keep moving."

He ushered them down the road while continuing to glance over his shoulder. Gula saw several watching them from a window, and he expected them to come out after them. He was becoming concerned over the breakdown of their society. It had been less than a day, and already, people had abandoned their principles and morals out of fear of not knowing where their next meal was coming from or how to contact family across the planet.

After some time, Puabi caught up to him. "It is going to get dark soon. We should stop someplace for the night, Gula. Plus, the children are tired."

Gula grunted, looked toward Utui blazing low in the sky, then looked down the road and continued walking. After a few more zag, they spotted a house in the distance. "Looks like a house well off the road up there. Maybe they will be more hospitable."

They continued toward the house as the sun dipped behind the western hills, leaving behind a layered orange sunset. Gula pushed the iron gate open and led Puabi and the children up the winding brick path toward the main building. Gula was impressed by how well-kept the property was. The people who lived here must have had a staff to take care of the grounds and the buildings, which were meticulous. So far, they had not seen anyone.

Gula walked up the steps to the main entrance and knocked on the door. There was no answer. He looked in a window and did not see anyone inside. He knocked again and waited. He pulled out his pistol again and tried the door's lock; the door swung open with a slight creek. "Hello! Anybody here?" he yelled. There was no answer. "Anybody here? We are not here to hurt anyone. Just here looking for a place to sleep for the night."

No one answered.

Gula looked up at the stone fireplace, where two guns were proudly displayed. However, two appeared to be missing from their mounts on the stone face. "We are coming in," he yelled, expecting someone to fly around the corner with guns blazing, but no one did.

Puabi was next in the house, with the children behind her. She had her pistol out as well and was looking around. Gula pointed to the missing guns on the fireplace and held up two fingers; she nodded.

"Go check those rooms; I will check these," Gula said softly, pointing where he wanted her to go.

They searched several rooms and finally reached the kitchen area. "I have something!" Puabi yelled. "Keep the children out there."

The children stopped as Gula held up his hand, and then he entered the kitchen.

There were three bodies on the floor. All had been shot in the head, execution style. Two appeared to be maids, and the third was the cook. Had to be a wealthy council member's house, but where were the owners?

"Any food left in the pantry?" Gula asked.

"Some scraps. It will do for tonight," Puabi said. "Someone was here recently and cleaned the place out pretty good."

"Yeah, the blood is still fresh and has not coagulated yet. Whoever did this did not go far," Gula said while checking for a pulse and the maid's body temperature. Hmm, still warm."

"Whoever did this might still be here then," Puabi added as she gripped her pistol tighter.

They both jumped when Enhedu screamed. They swung around, and the girl was there staring at the dead bodies. The boy was behind her, covering his mouth but staring.

"Well, if they didn't know we were here before, they do now," Gula said as he ushered the children out of the room.

"We should feed the children and then bury the bodies. Then we can eat," Puabi said as she gathered what little food remained.

"We should sleep in shifts tonight," Gula said as he went out the back door towards the building, where he found a couple of shovels. Then he searched around and found the family monument on the other side of the house where family members, staff, and sometimes animals were buried. He marked off three squares and began to dig three shallow graves while Puabi took care of the children, and then she joined him to finish digging. Once the children were asleep, Gula and Puabi carried the bodies out and placed them in the graves. They chanted the burial rituals and tossed dirt on top of the bodies.

It was now very late, and each took a turn bathing in the small pond on the property while the other kept watch for predators and people roaming about in search of food. They dressed in clothes they had found in the closets and chests on the second floor.

"You should get some sleep, and I will keep the first watch," Gula said, and Puabi went to the second floor to sleep with the children.

Gula roamed from room to room. He took the guns down and checked them. They were hunting rifles, but they would do. They were not loaded. He searched for bullets and eventually found several boxes tucked away in a closet. One box was empty. He loaded the weapons and tucked the rest in a shoulder pack to take with him.

He sat in the main room, staring at the fireplace and then towards the kitchen. Whoever took the guns either had bullets with them or knew where they were in the house. Either way, the killer knew what to find and where. There was no sign of a struggle either. So, the murdered maids and cooks probably knew the killer. This disturbed him a little, and he started to nod off. He caught himself and got up to walk around some more.

Early in the morning, Gula woke Puabi and passed her one of the rifles. "Keep a lookout. I heard noises outside recently, and we may have company."

"Yeah, okay," she replied with a yawn. She gripped the rifle tightly and went to the first floor.

Gula fell asleep right away between the two children.

Puabi raced up the stairs at daybreak and shook Gula's shoulder. "A large group of people is heading this way, and they are armed to the teeth!" she said nervously.

"We should slip out the back and across the field. We don't need a confrontation with children here."

"Right. Come help me with the little ones."

They gathered their belongings, ran out the back door, hid behind an outbuilding, and waited. No one saw them. They crept into the tall grass and slipped away while the mob entered the house. Gula and Puabi could hear shouts and glass breaking as the mob trashed the place. Gunshots rang out, and people ran from the house in all directions while Gula, Puabi, and the children hunkered down in the tall grass.

They watched the spectacle from a distance as someone lit the house on fire and others smashed glass and furniture to pieces.

SIX

IN DELONDRA, thousands gathered outside the presidential tower to demand answers. They demanded food, clothing, and power, and they demanded the president resign for letting the disaster happen. Troops entered the plaza to keep order, but the crowd got angrier and angrier by the minute.

Aanepada, who had been dwelling on the death of his daughter, Kilar, composed himself as he was consoled by a tall woman in a hooded brown robe. She hugged him, and he pulled himself together. He stepped out onto the balcony just above the angry crowd and held his hands out for them to quiet down, and they did. "Fellow Ardonnarians, we have before us a crisis of enormous magnitude. The entire planet has been ravaged by a solar storm no one saw coming or could have predicted. Nothing in our history suggests that our sun, Utui, had ever done such a violent act before. The army will soon begin distributing food, water, and other supplies. Remember, the entire planet is in the same condition as Delondra. Billions are without power, water, or food and are in danger. We need to pull together if we are to survive this and take steps to not let it happen again." He paused a moment. "Ardonnar-ians have a resolve and proven history of excelling when faced with uncertain and dangerous times. Now is one of those times. We must put aside our differences and help one another in the truest of Kur's values."

Many cheered, but many others booed and tossed bottles, bricks, and whatever else they could find at the president.

He continued, "I know many of you have lost family members. My own daughter, Kilar, died yesterday in my arms." With that last statement, he broke down, and many in the crowd began to cry as well, as Kilar was like a goddess to them. She had been young, beautiful, and available for marriage.

Aanepada could not continue and left the balcony as a few rocks flew by him.

The top priest in Aanepada's government came out next and lectured the people about duty and responsibility to their friends and neighbors. No one dared to lob a rock in his direction. He spoke for some time and ended with a prayer, and the crowd dispersed.

SEVEN

DAMOK-SAI STOOD on the bridge of the *Nikstra*, monitoring the data scrolling down on the main view screen from the probes placed over key cities of Ardonnar. He was pleased at how much damage the star disruptor and EMP weapons had done to the Ardonnarian infrastructure with the first attack. Eighty percent of their power grid was gone. The military on both continents was in disarray, with little or no communication with one another. The people were starting to fight among themselves over the rapidly dwindling food supply in the cities, while grain remained in silos on most farms across the planet.

Damok-Sai grinned at his sensor's officer. "It is a glorious day to be an Inean," he said in his booming voice. Then he turned towards Cakra, who was monitoring the star disruptor, and asked, "Time for the next disruption of the star?"

"Eighty minutes, commander. This one will be the last one we will need. I timed it so it strikes their eastern continent head-on. What little electricity they have will be gone by tomorrow," Cakra explained.

"Both moons are currently behind the planet," Maraal said as he studied the data on his screen, which displayed the planet and its two moons.

"Recall all of our recon ships and probes. Then, move the fleet behind the furthest moon. They will be shielded from the solar blast behind the moon, and then we can strike quickly," Damok-Sai stated as he headed to the center of his bridge. He lifted his head towards the ceiling and began howling in his deep voice. The others on the bridge also stood, turned their heads to the ceiling, and howled. It was a victory howl, and victory would be theirs.

A few minutes passed, and they went to their stations and began retrieving their probes from orbit.

Adhik-Sai, the *Nikstra*'s communications officer, turned to his console, "This is the *Nikstra*; all ships in the emperor's Bakustra set course for the outer moon of Ardonnar and take up a position behind the moon."

A series of responses came into his console from all the ships, and he turned to Damok-Sai, "Fleet is on the move, commander."

"Glorious! Launch the next wave of EMP rockets and set them to explode when the star ejecta hits the planet," Damok-Sai growled his order. Soon after, several rockets streaked away from the *Nikstra* and towards Ardonnar.

The *Nikstra* rumbled as it slowly turned and ignited its large engines. In the distance, a bright dot took the form of a planet, and then two lesser dots grew into the two moons of Ardonnar. Off to the side of the screen was Utui, Ardonnar's sun. A huge fireball blasted away from the star and raced towards the planet.

On the outer Ardonnarian moon, Anaru, a technician, was monitoring the sensors when he detected several ships heading their way. "General! General!" he yelled excitedly.

"What is it?" The general asked as he turned and started walking towards the technician.

"Ships, a lot of them, heading this way!"

"What ships?" the general replied as he picked up his pace.

"Nothing of ours. These energy readings are nothing I have

seen before," the technician replied while pointing to one of his screens displaying the Inean engine signatures.

The general arrived and stared for a minute. "Shut the base down. Close the outer doors and turn off all tracking lights. Shut down external communications. I want stealth mode now!"

The lights dimmed, and several stations shut down on his orders. An external camera showed the large opening in the side of the crater closing as artificial, rock-faced doors slid across it. Several explosive charges ignited, kicking up rock and dirt, which settled along the seam of the door, hiding it.

The first Inean ships arrived and parked just above the base. The general was afraid that they knew about the base and were going to bomb it, but they didn't. His sensors terminals displayed page after page of data about the Inean ships.

"General, those are huge ships, and they are armed to the teeth. I am detecting nuclear weapons, a lot of them."

"Gather everything you can. We may need it," the general replied, leaning closer to the technician, "but DO NOT give us away."

"Understood, sir."

Several people, including military personnel, gathered around the station and watched the data streaming on several monitors as each ship was scanned.

As they studied the Inean ships, the second solar storm struck the planet and blasted by the moon towards the outer reaches of the solar system. Some of their data was scrambled as the monitors flickered from the overload.

On the *Nikstra*, Adhik-Sai turned towards Damok-Sai. "Commander, all ships of the emperor's Bakustra are safely behind the outer moon."

Damok-Sai walked forward and stared out his front view screen. He admired all the ships in his fleet that were in a close cluster behind the moon. He then stared at the moon and noticed something metallic. He stared at it for several minutes before turning towards his sensors officer. "Maraal, anything on this moon of interest to us?"

"Scanning Commander... Nothing sir. Some scraps of ships litter the far side, but nothing here interests us."

"Are you sure?"

"The solar flare is affecting my sensors, but I can compensate for some of the distortion. There is nothing here that could be a threat or mineable. It is just a big rock," Maraal replied.

"Very good then. Time until the solar storm passes?" Damok-Sai said as he turned away from the large view screen.

"About thirty minutes. This should be the last disruption we will need," Cakra stated.

"I know you want to retrieve your precious probe, Cakra. We will in a few days and return it to the science base on Adhideva to be readied for its next deployment."

"Thank you, Damok-Sai. I will shut it down and move it away from the star," Cakra replied.

In a chamber buried deep inside the moon, Anaru, several military personnel scoured the data.

"We must let the president know," one said.

"If we break radio silence, those ships up there will know we are here and perhaps destroy this base. We know..." he was interrupted, and he cleared his throat. What I was saying is that we know that our defenses on the planet are nonexistent right now. We may be the only line of defense, and to give ourselves away would be a disaster."

"I agree, we cannot break radio silence. We must watch from here and look for an opportunity."

"We must contact them!" another said with an agitated tone.

"NO! We will wait and study them. We have reams of data in front of us. Stop bickering and start looking for holes in their defenses."

"I agree," said the general in charge of the base. "What do we have to work with?"

"Each ship carries approximately fifty nuclear warheads along with several hundred high-yield conventional warheads. Each ship has over two hundred individual energy signatures within. I am going to call them fighters or other craft. Their hulls are thick but could be breached with nukes. Their engines must be powerful to have brought them from another star system."

"I see. Prepare the crews for our ships, but do not open a hatch until I order. Keep the hangar depressurized for now and the power off until those ships move away," the lead general said.

"Understood, General," the others said in unison, and they scattered, leaving the general behind.

The general stood staring at the computer monitors. He had just fifty ships. None of them had the armor or weapons of the invading fleet hovering a few zag overhead. He could not even turn a light switch on, fearing the invaders would notice and maybe destroy his base. Maybe they were peaceful, he thought, but why would they be armed with so many nuclear weapons and their ships armored to resist just about anything. No, *he was right,* he thought to himself. They *were* hostile, and he would wait for the proper moment to launch his ships. He would launch for no other reason except to get them out of the moon base and into open space. He knew their other base on the moon, Uggae, had just as many ships, and perhaps they could launch a surprise attack between the two bases. He kept thinking of a plan as he studied the data. The loss of life would be high either way.

Damok-Sai paced his bridge and waited for the solar storm to pass as one of his lower officers approached. "Commander," he said as Damok-Sai turned to face him.

"Go ahead."

"We were reviewing the data from our probes orbiting the planet, which picked up throngs of people protesting in the streets. We suspect they are about to overthrow their own government," the lower officer said.

"Are you suggesting that we wait?" Damok-Sai growled.

"They may do the bulk of the work for us and render more of the planet usable without having to use nukes like we did on Kir'iath-se'pher. The radiation will take a hundred years to clear so we can access much of the planet's resources."

"Are you criticizing our approach? Thousands of Inean soldiers were spared by our tactics." Damok-Sai growled as he got close to the lower officer.

"Not at all, Commander. I am grateful that our losses were minimal, and they can be here as well, and we could have the benefit of the whole planet," the lower officer said without a flinch of intimidation.

"I see. We will wait and watch how this plays out. However, the instant it begins to turn, we will pounce with full force," Damok-Sai said, turning back to the view of the moon, Anaru, below his ship.

"Very good, Commander. Our leader will be proud of the riches he is about to reap."

"Keep the fleet behind the moon for now. Cakra, your probe stays for now. Keep it on weekly cycles while we monitor the unrest on the planet." Damok-Sai stated while continuing to stare out the window. Something was not right about the moon below, and he didn't know why he felt that way.

"Yes, Commander, but if the probe stays too long, it will burn up, and it is the only one we have."

"I have noted your concerns. Now do as you are told."

EIGHT

SEVERAL WEEKS HAD PASSED since the first CME blasted the planet, destroying much of the planet's power and communications infrastructure. The people of Ardonnar had become reliant on their technology. They were now confused about how to go about life without the ability to press a button and have it done. Another CME ravaged the planet, but this one produced minimal damage compared to the first. The situation had become grim for billions of Ardonnarians, as the food supplies in the cities had now run out, and winter was approaching in the northern, more populous hemisphere. The people were restless and angry at the ineffective solutions the government had proposed. President Aanepada had come under fire from Ur, the eastern continent's leader, and Shulgi, the western leader. Both were in Delondra to meet with Aanepada and military leaders to find a way to bring food and warmth to the millions of people in the larger cities.

A half million people protested outside the capitol building as the meeting commenced. The people were angry, cold, and hungry. They carried signs denouncing the government. Many shouted obscenities, and many threw rocks, bottles, bricks, and anything they could hurl at the building. Riot police surrounded the building and prevented the masses from storming inside.

Aanepada stood at the head of the large table, flanked by Ur to his left and Shulgi to his right. Each leader had his own military leaders on his side of the table, facing the others. Behind Aanepada were a dozen of his own advisers who sat with notebooks and flip charts.

On the table were several hurricane lamps for light, which burned a kerosene-like fuel soaked into a braided wick. The light was soft but adequate. Aanepada cleared his throat. "Regional leaders and honored military leaders, we have a crisis of global proportions. We need to get food into the cities as quick as possible and to bring power to the people for heat this coming winter. We need answers, and more importantly, we need actions. I'm going to open the floor for any ideas on how we are going to do this," Aanepada pleaded.

Ur was the first to speak, "The military has been slow on both sides getting food into the cities, and frequently, it does not make it at all."

A general stood from Shulgi's side and pointed at Ur. "We have been limited by the number of trucks running and the ambushes. We have lost many soldiers to people setting traps to steal supplies. We need fully armed battalions escorting these caravans until we get the cargo ships flying again," he stated in frustration.

Ur stood and was about to yell at the general when Aanepada stood and banged on the table. "I understand the frustration, really, I do, but us fighting will not solve anything. We need to think clearly and in one direction if we are to survive this with minimal loss."

"Sorry, Mister President," the general said, and he sat back down.

Ur stood again. "I agree; the convoys roll virtually unprotected. I will issue a decree in the Eastern continent to sign up infantry soldiers to protect the convoys."

Shulgi nodded, "I agree also with the general. We need better protection."

"Then protect the convoys and get more of them rolling. We need many convoys into each city just to take the edge off. Then, we need several more to bulk up supplies. I am not the only one in this room that is in trouble politically. I don't care if we need to sign up militia to get the job done, but do whatever it takes," Aanepada said.

"When this is over, I propose each city should have a stock of essential supplies, say a month's worth," one of Aanepada's advisers said from behind him.

"Agreed," many in the room echoed.

"Now power. It will begin to get cold in the northern latitudes in another month. Even if we can centralize some power to give people places to go, it would be a start," Aanepada said.

One of his advisers stood behind him. "We can have limited power in Delondra and half a dozen cities in less than a month. The only major city that won't is Belit-Sheri. That city has been utterly destroyed, along with its entire infrastructure. We should try harder to get those people out of there and maybe down here to Delondra for the winter." The woman stated and then sat back down.

Outside, several top-level cabinet priests held prayer services with the people for any who would take part. Slowly, people were attracted to the bearded men in black robes and black pointed hats. They chanted familiar verses and got the people involved. The rock-throwing slowed as the small groups grew.

Across the great ocean on the eastern continent in the capital city of Ninki, a hundred thousand plus-sized crowd stormed the temporary capitol building, which replaced the tower brought down in the first attack and set it ablaze while workers inside scrambled for their lives. The leader's staff was cut down in a shower of bullets as they exited the building. The few that got away ran back into the burning building, never to be seen again.

The angry crowd moved on to Ur's palace. There, they were

met with troops who blocked their path. Inside, Ur's wife and daughters watched the angry crowd growing outside their windows.

Ashusikildigir, Ur's wife, took her oldest daughter, Kanpar, who was in her twenties, away from the windows. Kanpar was known to be a party girl around Ninki, and many of her friends were now tossing rocks at her palace. Enanatuma, the youngest at sixteen, refused to walk away and watched the crowd hurling rocks and other debris at the soldiers that stood between her and the mob.

"Mother, how come we do not help them?" Enanatuma asked while staring out the corner of the window.

"They are just the working class, Enanatuma. If we feed them, then we do not have food to eat," Ashusikildigir said as she tried to pull her daughter away from the window. "Come, we must go to a safer place."

Enanatuma pulled away, "But if they die, then we will have to do the work, making us the working class. Then we won't have food."

"That is foolishness. Now come away from there. I insist!" the mother said with an angry edge.

Kanpar, her older sister, stood between her and the window. "You are being an idiot. If they die, there will be millions more to take their place. We are the elite; we do not work," she stated as the window shattered and a bullet buzzed by her head and buried itself into the ceiling, which showered the women with chunks of plaster and dust.

The mother yelled and grabbed both girls and pulled them away from the window. "See, they are animals. They do not appreciate us or that they serve us. Why won't you get it through your head that you are above them in every way! Now, come away from here before you get killed."

The mother pushed them toward the door, where a maid waited to take the children to the bunker in the palace's basement. The maid glared at the mother but turned away when the mother looked up at her.

Ashusikildigir looked at the maid with concern and watched her take the girls away. It was inappropriate for a servant to make gestures towards the elite. She would be cast out of the house and blackballed, which meant she would not be able to work anywhere.

Across the city of Ninki, several people stormed the temple and grabbed the priests. They yelled and screamed at them about how Kur was not there for them, and they dragged the priests out to the street as the priests tried in vain to convince the mob that it was they who had abandoned Kur and that they were being punished. The priests continually warned people throughout the continent to repent for their evil ways, but the people refused to listen. The people chose instead to indulge in the luxuries of their society rather than serving Kur and the less fortunate. The priests were stoned and beaten by the angry crowd.

All across the eastern continent, word spread about how the priests were brutalized, and many more gangs went about killing the priests and stealing their food. Word reached the western continent, and there were a few isolated outbreaks, but more anger towards the eastern people for killing the Priests of Kur. The people of the West cried out to their priests and leaders that Kur would surely kill them all for what the others had done. Even though they were hungry and cold, the outrage festered.

Several days later, the first trucks rolled into Delondra with food, and the people cheered. The army distributed the food to the families, and the people returned home.

Aanepada continued his conversations with Ur and Shulgi via shortwave radio as the trucks brought food to the cities. The Western people quieted down, but the Eastern people continued their protests against Aanepada and Ur. Both leaders stayed in their offices under heavy guard until those protests quieted.

NINE

NEARLY A MONTH HAD PASSED since their transport crashed off the coast of Belit-Sheri. Gula and Puabi continued their trek towards their village, which was a long way south of the crash site. They had taken Enhedu and Amar-Sin with them and picked up several stragglers on the way. They ate what they could when they found it, mostly old food preserved and abandoned by people who went south searching for warmth for the coming winter. Gula and Puabi became very good at hunting the smaller animals since, as winter approached, many of the larger animals had gone into hibernation. They had come across stray bodies along the way. Some were shot or beaten, and some looked like they just dropped from lack of food. Either way, as they got closer to their village, the bodies were more frequent. They passed through a village the day before that had nearly twenty thousand people in it before they left. Now, all they found were ransacked homes and businesses and bodies, thousands of bodies scattered about in various forms of decay. Some had become food for wild animals and insects, prompting Gula, Puabi, and the children to cover their mouths and noses with scarves to block out the stench and possible diseases caused by the insects buzzing around. They saw that most had been murdered, and they were not sure what happened to some of the others, but the question that remained was: where did the other thousands go? There was no one left alive to answer that question. They certainly did not go north or would have come across them. So, Gula and the rest guessed they had also gone south, towards the warmer climate for the winter, which did not bode well for their village.

They saw in the distance hundreds of black birds known as Bulkrah flying in circles and crying out in their screechy yells. Bulkrah are similar to vultures on Earth, but these have sharp, razor-like teeth to rip at the flesh of animals that are not quite dead yet. Puabi walked up to Gula, leaving the children with a few of the others in their group. "Kur warned about such large numbers of those birds," she said with a weary look.

"I know. It means death," Gula replied as they continued to walk.

"It's a sign of the apocalypse," Puabi stated.

"How can you say that?"

"In the seventeenth book of Kur, Kur says, through the Prophet Seru, that in the end, fire will come from the sky and ravage the planet. Then, the Demons of Nergal will come down after the fire and consume all non-believers. Only a select few would be saved," Puabi said while watching the Bulkrah circling and screeching in the distance.

"I don't think we are in that time," Gula replied.

"I believe it. Kur says it will take forty years for it to all happen. It has only been about a month, and look at the destruction we have encountered. And the people, look how crazy many people have gone."

"Okay, so we are in the end times. What can we do about it?" Gula said with a trace of frustration.

"We need to pray to Kur that he finds us worthy," she said.

"Oka-a-a-y, you start. The rest of us will follow," Gula said with a grin. He was a religious man, but he was skeptical when anyone discussed the end times.

"Don't make fun of me, I am serious," she huffed. She slowly drifted back to be with the children.

Gula watched her fall back and knew she was angry with him. It upset him that she was mad. He really wanted to be with her, and they believed the same things. He was not good at verbalizing his feelings and frequently said things before thinking them through. She was more passionate about religion than he was. He wanted to apologize, but then, he was distracted by the sight before him as they crested the hill and looked at the valley below.

Dozens of Ardonnarians hung from trees naked for the birds to eat. They were hung by their hands, and over time, their joints would give out, usually about the time the Bulkrah had their fill, and they would die. Gula and the others walked down the hill, leaving the children and a few of the women behind. They walked briskly, being alert that there might be an ambush waiting for them. As they got closer, they drew their weapons and walked up to some of the people.

Some pleaded for help, and Puabi pulled out her knife. She climbed the tree and cut the rope. The woman dropped to the ground and landed on a thin coat of colorful leaves that had fallen from the trees. She cried out in pain as her shoulder, which was separated, took the brunt of the impact. The others helped her dress from the many clothes scattered about. One of the men who had some medical experience popped her shoulder back in place, yielding another scream of pain.

They cut down others who were still alive and then cut down those who had died.

"Some of these people have been here for a while," Gula stated with a grimace as the odor of the dead made him nauseous. It didn't help that the dead had stiffened from rigor mortis and creaked and cracked when their bodies fell to the ground.

"How did this happen?" Gula asked.

One of the men they saved cleared his throat, "We came from the West and came across these people hanging and started doing what you did for us, and then several dozen people wearing red robes jumped out of the bushes and grabbed hold of us, and now you know what happened. It was so fast. We had no chance to fight back." He finished talking and studied an open wound on his forearm from a Bulkrah that had taken a chunk of skin from him. Many people had bites all over their bodies, which would need attention. Still, Gula and his band of travelers had no medical supplies left.

The man looked at Gula and then his arm again.

"We ran out of supplies. You and your people will have to make do until we get to Samuqan," Gula said.

"I heard that Samuqan is where the people that did this to us came from. They must have headed back," a random woman said as she pulled on a dress and found some shoes to wear.

"How can you say that. We are from Samuqan. I can't think of anyone who would do such a thing!" Puabi said as she spun around to face the woman.

"All I know is what they said."

"Well, they must have been lying," Puabi huffed and helped find clothes for the others.

"What about the dead?" one of the men asked.

"We should take the time to bury them and honor them," Puabi replied as she looked around at the dozen or so bodies lying on the ground. Then she looked at Utui. It was a few hours from setting. "Gula, we should bury these people so the Bulkrah will fly away," she said while studying the large black birds perched on branches, waiting for them to move on.

"They won't eat something dead," Gula said, "but we should bury the dead anyway."

"Then what are they waiting for?" she asked, as a few of the birds kept watching her, turning their heads in short twitches as she walked by the tree. She was spooked by them and went along the edge of the road, picking up some rocks to use to cover the dead bodies.

Several hours later, Utui had set, and they had finished burying the dead. Gula stood up and looked around. "I know everyone is tired, but our village is only a few hours away. We can make it there tonight, and I hope there is food."

Everyone nodded and got to their feet. Some struggled but managed. They gathered the few supplies they had and began walking. Only one of the moons was out, Anaru, the smallest and most distant of Ardonnar's moons. The moon reflected only a small amount of light, barely enough to walk by, and the walk was slow. The dim moonlight produced eerie images as the light breeze swayed the trees, forcing a rain of leaves. The children were spooked by the imagery and clung to Puabi's sides.

Gula fell back to Puabi's position. He leaned towards her and said, "I'm sorry about what I said earlier. You are right about the times we live in. I just did not want to believe it."

"That's okay. I don't want to believe it as well, but it is all around us," Puabi replied.

He wrapped an arm around her and squeezed lightly, then patted her shoulder. She grinned at him, and he walked back to the front of the group.

In the distance, they could hear the howls of the Awah, hungry howls. The Awah were wolf-like but had claws on their paws for ripping their prey and for climbing trees. The Awah also had darker fur in the summer months and lighter fur for winter. They would be lighter by now as winter was just weeks away. Their tails were shorter and stiffer, and their teeth were finer and sharper for ripping up small animals. It feasted more on small rodents than larger animals. Still, when it was very hungry, it would attack anything or anyone. Awah traveled in packs of twenty to thirty. The howls and yips grew louder from the West, which only meant that a large pack was coming, and they could smell food. Gula spread the word that everyone should keep quiet and have their guns ready.

In the distance, they could see the glow of lights, not electric lights, but the softer, yellow glow of campfires and torches. It was Samuqan. Puabi caught up to Gula and smiled at him. They were almost home. Gula held up his hand, and everyone stopped. He turned and looked around.

"What is it?" Puabi whispered.

"The Awah are quiet. They have caught up and are stalking us," he paused momentarily, "we must be careful." He paused again to look around. "They might attack if they are hungry enough," Gula said. He started walking more carefully and slowly as he looked around. He expected one or more of the Awah to fly out of the shrubs and tall grass. They walked softly without speaking while listening to the rustling in the tall grass, which seemed to get closer. Gula and Puabi kept their guns pointed toward the tall grass as they passed by the field.

Awah typically attacked their prey in large numbers to ensure a capture and a meal. They would even attack groups and target a single animal in a pack or a single person if hungry enough.

The lights grew brighter as they approached Samuqan. Everyone was tense, expecting the Awah to come flying out of the tall grass with teeth bared and claws outstretched, but they never did. They were hungry but not hungry enough this time.

A little past midnight, they entered the outskirts of Samuqan and were greeted by armed sentries. They quickly recognized Gula and Puabi and lowered their weapons. One of the sentries ran back into the village and into a house. Seconds later, an older woman and man emerged in their sleeping attire, which consisted of long white robes, white cloth caps on their heads, and slippers. They rushed towards the travelers. Puabi saw them and holstered her gun, sprinted towards them, and hugged them.

"We thought you were dead!" her mother cried, hugging her.

"Mom, you are choking me," Puabi answered and kissed her mother and then her father.

"What happened?" her father asked after composing himself.

"We were landing when the solar flare hit, and it fried our electronics. We ended up crashing into the ocean near Belit-Sheri. We have been walking since."

"Belit-Sheri? We heard it was gone?" her father said.

"It is nearly destroyed. It looks like it just blew up; the whole city went up in flames. We didn't stick around to find out why," Puabi answered.

"Well, at least you are safe. Looks like you lost more weight.

How are you going to attract a husband if you are so skinny? Come, eat some food," her mother said, taking her by the arm.

Puabi rolled her eyes at this and quickly changed the subject. "How is Barra and the baby?" Puabi asked.

"Mother and baby are fine. We saw them yesterday, and we will take you there tomorrow," her mother said while entering the house.

Gula watched her go away and then ran back out of the house. She raced up to Amar-Sin and Enhedu, saying, "Come with me and get some food and a warm bath." The two children ran after her.

Other people were running toward them, and it was Gula's family. They surrounded him and took him away. The remaining travelers stood as several others from the village came forward. "Where are our manners? Come, you must be starving, and it looks like some of you are bleeding. What happened to you people?" a woman asked the man closest to her.

"We were ambushed by people claiming to be from this village. They hung us by our hands in the trees for the Bulkrah to pick at our flesh," the man said.

The woman put her hand over her mouth in horror. "What kind of animals would do such a thing? Bring your people to the community building. We will help you and feed you." The woman took him by the arm and led him to the large building across from the stone temple. "Bullu! Set up more guards. There are dangerous people out there that tried to kill these people."

Bullu, a rugged, bearded man holding a large caliber shotgun, nodded and began rounding up more people to protect the village.

"They killed dozens of others. Them in their red robes. Who wears a red robe?" the man asked no one in particular.

"They had red robes?" the woman asked.

"Yes, why?"

"I have heard of a cult that worshiped not Kur but Nergal and his demons. They wore red robes to signify the fires of Tari. I have never seen them, though," the woman said.

"Diyah, you will not speak of such things." Bau, the village's high priest, said as he approached from the stone temple.

"Sorry, Curate Bau. I was only talking with this man about what happened to him and his group." The woman apologized with her head bowed.

"That is all right. These people need to be bandaged up and cleansed before sunrise. Then we can purge the affliction of Nergal from them." He started to walk away.

The woman spoke after him, "Where are you going?"

"I need a male calf no more than two years old to sacrifice," he said while walking towards the stockades on the far side of town.

The woman guided the man and several dozen others into the community building while some young boys lit the candles. She turned to the boys and said, "Go fetch me some help and have Assara bring a pile of medical supplies back with her."

The boys ran off, yelling for Assara.

Assara and a handful of others from Samuqan treated the injured and gave them fresh clothes. When it was nearly sunrise, Assara and Diyah led the injured down the main road to the West of the town. There, they climbed the tall hill where Curate Bau had lit a fire in the large stone altar. He had the calf tied to a post, and he was chanting as he prepared for the sacrifice to Kur.

The air was cool, and there was heavy dew on the ground. The first frost of the season was just a few short days away. The group closed in, stopped before the altar, knelt on the damp ground, and waited. No one spoke except for Bau, who continued chanting with his hands held outward from his sides, palms up. His head was raised, and his eyes were closed. Soon, he finished, and he retrieved the calf. He pulled it up onto the altar and forced it to lay down. The animal struggled to get free, but Bau had it pinned. He brought the ax up in the air with his other hand and swung it down on the calf's neck, and its head fell and rolled off the altar into a golden bucket on the ground. He hung the calf by its back legs above a pan that collected the blood that drained from the animal. He then skewered the animal and placed it above the fire to roast it. He did not clean the animal or prepare it. This was the ancient way of performing the cleansing ritual. Until this was done, none of these people could enter the holy temple. He then dipped a straw brush in the blood of the calf that had collected in the pan and sprinkled it on the altar. It sizzled when it hit the coals and the iron grate inside. He then turned towards the group of people chanting the cleansing verses with their faces just above the dirt. He sprinkled blood all around the altar and around the people as they finished and stood up to face Curate Bau. He then dipped the brush into the blood again and sprinkled it on the people until it was all gone. When it was gone, the sun crested the low hills to the east.

The group dispersed and returned down the hill to the village, where a feast was cooking. Many took their time because they were exhausted from not sleeping for days.

After the morning feast, Puabi went with her mother and father to her sister's house to the south of town. It would be a day's journey, round trip, on foot, so they started quickly.

"Your sister will be so happy you are home for good," her mother said.

"You are staying home, right?" her father pried.

"Well, I am a pilot in the military. Technically, I am absent without leave, so I better get back to a base as soon as possible to check in."

"That can wait. Stay home for a few days, be with us," her mother pleaded.

"Maybe. Let me get at least one more good night's sleep before I decide."

The conversation turned to her mission to Silili and how the colonies were now more advanced than they were. They talked for hours until her mother brought up marriage again.

"Mother, Gula has not asked me. I can not ask him. It is forbidden. I will just have to wait until he is ready."

"And if he is never ready? Then you won't be honoring Kur by being childless into your old age," her mother huffed.

"I think we have bigger problems to deal with right now. That can wait a while longer."

Her father continued leading the way and had no desire to get involved in this conversation. It was a no-win, and he didn't want to argue with his wife about it.

After walking for several hours, they turned onto a different street and walked to her sister's house.

Her sister's husband was out chopping wood for heat and cooking. He stopped when he saw them coming and went to greet them.

Her sister, Barra, looked out the window and saw them, and she raced for the door. She threw the door open, ran down the steps, and tossed her arms around Puabi, sobbing. "We thought you were dead."

"If you keep choking me, I will be," Puabi gagged.

"Idiot!" her sister said, playfully shoving her back; Puabi hugged her firmly.

"So, where is this bundle of yours?"

"Oh, come. He is sleeping right now, but come see him." She took Puabi's hand and brought her into the home. They had a small dinner and visited for a short time. After a few hours, Puabi and her parents returned to Samuqan.

It was dusk when they arrived in Samuqan, and there was a commotion. Army troops were walking around the streets with guns in hand and more guns hanging from their shoulders. Puabi and her parents were stopped by two soldiers.

"Where are you going?" one asked.

"We live in this village. Our house is two streets over," her mother said, cautiously glaring at the questioning soldier.

"You may pass," he said to the parents but lowered his gun to block Puabi's path. "I know you. What is your name?"

"I am Commander Puabi of the *ShuBuré*," she huffed.

"Can't be. The *ShuBuré* was lost during the solar storm."

"Yes, it was. We crashed into the ocean off the coast of Belit-Sheri. We made it to shore and walked here," she replied. "Now, may I go, sergeant?"

"Belit-Sheri? There is nothing left of that city," the soldier said as he studied her.

"Yes, I know. It was on fire when we came through," she said, and now she got angry, "NOW, may I go?" Puabi said with an edge in her voice.

"Yes, Commander," and he saluted and let her pass.

The troops unloaded crate after crate of food and medical supplies while the trucks continued to run. The old-style diesel trucks had no functioning electrical systems; they were purely mechanical and could only operate during daylight. If a truck were shut off, it would have to be pushed down a steep hill to get running again. No one wanted to push one of these up the hill to begin with, so they chugged along.

"Commander," the soldier who had earlier questioned her ran up to her. It would be an honor to have you go back with us. We have a few transports that can fly but no one to fly them," he said. I knew this about you, but I just thought of the transports. It would help get supplies to the cities faster."

"When are you leaving?" she asked.

"In the morning. It is too dark to travel with these trucks and no lights."

"Let me find, Gula. He may want to go as well," and she wandered off after saluting the enlisted soldier.

Puabi wandered back to her parent's house and found her mother talking with Gula at the dining room table. He was sipping a cold glass of water while her mother was talking. They hushed when she entered the main room. Her father pretended to look busy when he saw the look on her face.

"Mother, what are you doing?"

"Just talking with your friend Gula."

"Mother, he is my commanding officer. Don't start trouble."

"What kind of trouble?" Gula asked Puabi after turning to face her.

"Nothing. I'm hitching a ride with the army troops at sunrise. They have working transports, and they need pilots," she said. She walked to the table and poured herself a glass of water.

"You can't leave so soon. You just got back," the mother pleaded.

"Mother, it is my job. People are suffering out there. This is the first village we have encountered with food and water since we crash-landed. Millions of others are dying, and it is now coming on winter."

Her mother got up and hugged her, "I know. Just wish you could stay."

"I know, me too, but I have a job to do."

Gula glanced up at her. "I'll gather up my stuff. I will go, too. They can probably use another pilot," Gula said, thanked her mother, and left the house.

"I need to ask you a favor, a big one?" Puabi asked her mother.

"What is it?" Shubad asked with concern.

"Can you care for these two children while I am gone? Their parents were killed in the crash, and they have nobody we know about."

"Yes, don't you worry. We will take care of them," she said and bent down. "Come here, children," they went to her, and she hugged them. You will stay with us until this crisis settles down."

The children sobbed, but they accepted yet another change in their lives, which seemed to happen on a daily basis.

They talked more into the evening, and when Utui rose the next morning, Puabi and Gula hopped on one of the troop carriers and rolled out of Samuqan with the empty trucks between the troop carriers.

TEN

"COMMANDER, YOUR FATHER HAS SENT A MESSAGE," the comm officer said as he handed Damok-Sai a video player.

"Send back to Manava of the emperor's high council that I have discovered a more valuable commodity on this planet, so our plan has changed. We will start gathering this commodity today and send as much back home when we can free up a ship."

"Yes, Commander. I will send that right away."

"I will be in my chambers," he stated and quickly left the bridge.

Damok-Sai went down to his chambers, which were located a level below the bridge and walked in. The ship's doctor was there examining a couple of Ardonnarian women. They had been tied to a support pole in the middle of the room. "Leave us," Damok-Sai growled.

As the doctor left and the door closed, Damok-Sai growled and walked over to the women. He snarled in their faces, which made them pull away from the beast. He gripped the first woman's face with his paw and turned her to him. She trembled and cried as he grinned at her.

"I must say, you are a very special species," Damok-Sai stated.

The women's screams could be heard halfway across the ship, it seemed, but there was nothing the doctor could do. Either they would bomb the cities and kill them or do what Damok-Sai had in mind. Either way, there was no fighting the Inean invasion fleet and surviving.

The women had been taken during a recon raid on the eastern continent of the planet along with dozens of others after the Ineans discovered sexual picture books in one of the houses they raided. The raiding party felt that Damok-Sai would be very interested, considering his past interactions with Inean women.

A short time passed, and Damok-Sai went back to the bridge and stared out the window at his fleet hiding behind the moon Anaru. He then turned towards a lowly worker. "There is a pile of garbage in my chambers that needs to be cleaned up. Go do it." The worker scrambled off the bridge quickly.

"Get the lander ready. I think it is time to visit with their leader and negotiate a transfer of this rare commodity they have," Damok-Sai said with a grin that showed his sharp teeth, which had pieces of human flesh still between them.

Pavak, the weapons officer, glanced up from his station. "Negotiate? Commander. Since when do we negotiate? We take their lives and then their planets," he stated while reaching for his sharp dagger, which was tucked in his belt. If Damok-Sai was going soft, then he would have to be replaced, he thought to himself.

"I said negotiate. These females of their race are wild. We can not kill them. We must send them back to Inea for our emperor's collection. Then we can kill the rest of them and take the planet," he growled. "Now, prepare our landing craft."

A short time later, the Inean transport ship, which was docked at the rear of the bridge, separated from the *Nikstra*. The transport floated away to a safe distance and ignited its engines. The ship flew towards Ardonnar and was in orbit a few hours later. They set their course for the city of Delondra and flew low across the countryside. A few minutes later, the transport slowly approached the city and landed outside the president's tower, sending thousands of people scrambling for cover from the debris blown about as the ship landed. Soon, the pads touched down and sunk slightly into the pavement as the engines wound down. People stayed quite a distance away and waited. Nobody had ever seen a craft like this before.

After a minute, the large hatch slid to either side with a hiss, and steps slid out from under the hatch to the ground. Several heavily armed, huge alien soldiers stepped down first and took up positions on either side of the hatch. Several more raced out of the craft and took up positions all around the transport. The Ineans wore heavier armor than usual and wore black helmets with a dark shade over their eyes. Their boots pounded and shook the ground when they walked. The people backed further away from them when they spoke in their deep voices, which hissed and snapped loudly.

Several armed Ardonnarians emerged from the palace and confronted the Ineans. Many were literally shaking in their boots. Both sides pointed guns at one another until Damok-Sai stepped down out of the transport with a small box in his hands. He spoke in Inean, which was just a loud noise to the Ardonnarians. Still, his voice played again from the box in the Ardon language, and many soldiers ran back towards the entrance to the tower.

"People of this planet, I am the emperor's emissary, Damok-Sai. I have come to your planet to offer help for what has happened to your planet from the unfortunate storms from your star. I am willing to trade."

One of the Ardonnarian generals walked forward with his gun lowered. "I am General Nanna," he said as he faced the large Inean. Nanna was a big man himself, but he had to look up at the Inean, who was much broader and taller than he.

More noise, and then, "General, are you the one I need to talk with to negotiate a trade?"

"No, you would need to talk with our president."

More noise. "Take me to him."

General Nanna held out his hand and guided the Inean toward the entrance to the president's tower.

Many of the Ardonnarian soldiers cowered away as the Inean passed them, and he hissed his pleasure at their fear.

Once inside, General Nanna guided Damok-Sai to the elevator as the two guards stepped aside and stared at the Inean. "How many ships do you have with you?" the general asked.

Damok-Sai spoke softly into the small box, and out came. "We travel as a fleet because there is safety in numbers to protect us from hostile races out there who would wipe us out, and your planet as well, in no time at all."

"We have never met anyone from outside our own system before," the general replied.

"That is probably why your planet is still here. Lucky for you," Damok-Sai replied. *Lucky for us*, he thought to himself.

"Have you fought with these other races? What do we need to know about them?" General Nanna quickly asked as the doors slid open, and the two guards looked up and backed away.

"Yes, we have. It has not been easy," Damok-Sai's voice boomed even though he was talking softly. "We have fought many bloody wars over the years. Costing millions and millions of lives."

"You will have to discuss this with our president as well."

"I will."

Aanepada stood facing the recently replaced, large window facing out over the crowd. A sea of people extended far beyond the square below where the Inean ship had landed. Ineans swarmed around the ship, maintaining a secure zone. He looked down and saw his own troops holding a position between him and the Ineans. Beside him was Dagan, a lower priestess whom he had asked to help him get through his daughter's death when the first wave struck the planet.

Aanepada was dressed in black with a hood pulled over his head. He would remain in mourning for another sixty days. She wore the standard, lower priestess attire, which consisted of a long brown robe tied at the waist with a frayed length of rope. The robe was hooded to cover her head so only her face was visible, with slight wisps of blond hair poking out around her face.

"Aanepada, it is normal for you to feel this way," she said in her soft voice.

"Kilar died in my arms, protecting me. It should have been the other way around," he replied, wiping a tear from his eye.

"I understand, but it is not your fault. No one saw this coming. You could not have done anything different to prevent this from happening," Dagan replied as she watched the activity outside.

"I know, but it still does not make me feel better."

"Have you been sleeping?"

"Not really. I get a few hours here and there but not a full night since Kilar died."

"I want you to chant to Kur the sacred verses five times before going to sleep tonight. After that, I want you to clear your mind for fifteen minutes and then sleep," she instructed as they watched General Nanna guide one of the large aliens toward their building.

"What is your take on this?" Aanepada said with a gesture towards the alien ship.

"The books of Kur don't talk about beings from other planets. I suppose it leaves the possibility open. I should consult with the elders before, I guess, at an answer," she replied as they both turned away from the windows. "It is safe to assume that they are coming up here to see you." She handed him a small cloth to wipe his eyes. "I should go now."

"No, please stay. I want your opinion on this creature after he leaves," Aanepada said.

She stopped on her way towards the door.

"Why?"

"I have a bad feeling about this creature."

"And you want me to put those concerns at ease," she replied with her back towards the door.

"Or confirm them."

"I am not qualified to make those judgments, Aanepada."

"You are more qualified than most of my council," he said while fixing the loose items on his desk.

"You put too much faith in my limited knowledge, but I will stay if you wish."

He was fixing the water pitcher and glasses. "Thank you," he replied while concentrating on the look of his office. He looked around. Two chairs faced his desk. One wall had shelf after shelf of ancient books, mostly history and the books of Kur. On the other side were portraits of his family and the previous president. On the far wall was another portrait of the first president of the global government. Along the lower portion of that wall was a countertop with glasses and fine china, as well as cabinets below.

"It looks fine, Aanepada," Dagan said with a grin.

"Huh? Oh, right," and he sat in his chair.

There was a knock at the door.

The general knocked on the large double wooden doors; Dagan turned the handles, pulled the doors open, and backed away at the sight of the Inean towering over her. She was tall as well, but this creature could snap her in two with little effort, she thought. Dagan shuffled back on her open sandals with her head bowed slightly. She stood to the side as Damok-Sai walked into the president's office and stopped while Nanna closed the doors behind them.

Aanepada stood facing the alien, and he looked up discreetly, but he still had to look up.

Nanna presented their guest, "Mister President, this is Damok-Sai from..."

"I am from a planet called Inea, and I am here to offer assistance," Damok-Sai said impatiently.

"We welcome the assistance, but what do you want in return?" Aanepada asked as he studied the Inean, who seemed too eager to help. It was their first encounter with an alien race, and Aanepada wanted to be cautious.

"We need supplies for our fleet as we pass through your system," Damok-Sai said as he studied the president.

"What kinds of supplies do you need? Do we have them?" Aanepada asked with a glance towards the general.

"We need food, water, and fuel."

Aanepada studied the Inean. He knew by watching the alien that he was not telling the whole truth. It seemed that the body language of lying went beyond his world. "How did you happen across our planet at such a time?"

Damok-Sai, sensing the president did not trust him, shifted to a softer approach. "We are explorers. We are exploring along the habitable plane of this spiral arm for planets to expand our race to. We studied your planet, but it is inhabited, so we are passing by." He paused for a few seconds to gather his thoughts. "We were amazed at how violent your star is and are curious as to how your race has survived for so long under its wrath."

The general piped up, "This is the first time in our history that Utui has exploded like this."

Aanepada held his hand up towards the general. "General Nanna, I will discuss the details with our guest. Would you like a drink, Damok-Sai?"

"No, I am fine," he replied.

Aanepada was curious why an alien who claimed to be hungry and thirsty would refuse a drink. He filed it away in the back of his mind for now. "How many planets have you inhabited so far? I find it very strange that Utui, which has been quiescent through our long history, would suddenly explode unexpectedly and with such violence. Must be a coincidence that you were just passing by."

"We have settled on two worlds other than our own. But let us discuss how we can help you, and you can help us," the large Inean growled. "We had nothing to do with your star exploding like it did. If we had that technology, I would not be standing here asking for a trade," he stated with a slight edge in his voice. He tried to control his anger at the accusation, but Aanepada picked up on his tone.

Aanepada sensed the Inean was getting impatient. Either he was more desperate for food, or he was under a deadline of another sort. His body language suggested he was lying again. He did know something about Utui that he would not admit to. "Why the rush? I think we are in a good position to help ourselves, Damok-Sai. Supplies are finally reaching the people who need them. However, we will consider giving you some things you need to keep on going."

Damok-Sai tensed. Aanepada saw it and continued. "Over time, our two races could establish relations and trade agreements, but for now, I think this should proceed slowly. This is our first time dealing with people from another world." He paused a second. "I want to make sure it is done correctly and fairly for all involved."

Damok-Sai grinned at him, "I understand, Mister President. I look forward to long-lasting relations between our peoples. Still, I am also willing to offer assistance in moving supplies to your people in exchange for food. I will have one of my junior officers compile a list if you would like."

Aanepada was leery of the Inean but agreed to part of this agreement and held out his hand. "Compile your list of items you would want in trade while I meet with my council to get their response." The Inean grasped his hand and easily shook hands with Aanepada. "Leave the general a means of contacting you," Aanepada finished.

General Nanna glared at Aanepada, and then he escorted the Inean from the president's office.

Dagan closed the doors and wrinkled her nose at the foul-smelling alien who was now gone. She walked up to Aanepada, who sat at his large desk. He rubbed the hand the Inean shook while he considered his first impression of the Inean.

"I don't trust him," she finally stated, and he glanced up at her.

"Why do you say that?"

"For the same reasons you feel. He is holding something back regarding Utui. It is not a coincidence that he arrived at our people's worst time of need," she replied while watching Aanepada.

"So, we need proof of his lies, and what are his true intentions?" he said as he got up and went to the windows again with Dagan coming up beside him.

"He wants something, and it isn't food or water, or fuel for that matter. He wants to help us, so we lower our defenses and then strike," Dagan said as they watched Nanna guide Damok-Sai out toward his ship.

"We need to find out what it is before it is too late."

"It might be. Look how your general is swooning all over this alien we know nothing about."

"Hmm," Aanepada sighed as the craft fired its engines and lifted off the ground slowly. The craft then spun around and moved away with a deafening roar that shook the building.

"Discreetly notify some of our loyal members for a meeting. Do not include General Nanna."

Dagan bowed towards the president, "Yes, Aanepada." She bowed again and left the room.

Aanepada met Dagan several years before when she was a young girl close to his daughter's age. He was drawn to the young girl and took her in. She had been abandoned when her parents had been killed in a bizarre accident on a mining asteroid, which, to this day, had not been solved. Her parents were working deep in one of the mines, analyzing a deposit of ore that would later be used to power the Ardonnarian spaceships, when a robotic vehicle started up and crushed them into a rock deposit. Scientists were unable to duplicate the incident, and it was ruled an accident.

Aanepada took her off the streets and raised her as his own. Soon after coming of age, she attended the prestigious prep school Anunnaki, which was hailed as the most difficult prep school to enter. A few years later, she went to one of the finest universities for engineering but dropped out after two years when Aanepada's wife died of cancer. It was at that point that she began asking about the afterlife. Even though she had spent hours and hours studying Kur's writings, she had never given much thought to the subject until then. She decided to study at the great temple in Kurdash, but was turned down because her bloodline was not of priestly descent. It took an extensive campaign by Aanepada's father, Mituti, who was the leader at the time, to get her enrolled in the temple of Kur. Her time there was difficult, at best, as she had to prove herself daily to the monks and fellow students who knew she didn't belong. Dagan made it through the ten years and eventually excelled, leaving the rest of her class behind. After her training in Kurdash, she moved back to Delondra soon after Aanepada became president. She continued her studies at the local temples until Kilar was killed, and Aanepada requested her to assist him during his grieving time.

The next day, the bulk of Aanepada's council arrived by midday and assembled in the large chamber. Some knew about the aliens. Most did not, but the few that did wasted no time informing the others. The chatter level continued to rise even as Aanepada entered the room. He stepped up to his chair at the center of a long table, which was up on a platform facing the council seats. The council seats were in semi-circles, with each row slightly elevated over the next like a theater. To his left was Ur, the Eastern leader, and Shulgi, the Western leader, was to his right. Below Aanepada was a podium, and one man stood there in his gray robe. Inanna, who was the leader of the council and also of the majority party, was shouting to bring the meeting to order. However, no one paid any attention to him. He began banging a gavel harder while yelling, and after several minutes, the room finally quieted, and the members took their seats. In the first row were the military leaders, including General Nanna, who was eager to work with the aliens. In the second row, the judicial council was positioned in the middle, and to either side of them were various religious leaders.

Aanepada rose to his feet and walked around to the podium. Lead council member Inanna bowed to him and went to his seat off to the side. Aanepada cleared his throat. "Fellow Ardonnarians, yesterday, as some of you know and the rest will today, we were contacted by an alien from space who said he was from a planet called Inea."

The chatter picked up again, and Aanepada banged the gavel several times and waited for the room to quiet. "This alien offered to help our people during our crisis in exchange for food, water, and fuel."

Aanepada was interrupted by several shouts of "Let them help!"

He banged the gavel again. "People, please, we must consider this. I find it very strange that in our greatest time of disaster, these aliens show up."

He was interrupted again by people yelling, "Maybe it was your beloved Kur! He sent them to save us because you have failed the people of Ardonnar." Many from the Eastern Continent yelled.

Others stood and shouted back at the Eastern members, "There is no way we could have prepared for this!"

"Your beloved Kur is a farce! You waste so much time bowing down to a stone carving!" The Eastern group yelled back.

"It is your turning away from Kur that has brought his wrath upon us!" The Western member yelled in return, and soon, there were a few cases of shoving.

The shouting went back and forth as Aanepada banged on his gavel. Again, several minutes passed before order was restored. "I know we have our differences, but we must put them aside for the moment."

"Coward! You can't sweep this under the rug, Aanepada! We demand a voice and change to our archaic way of running this planet!" some others shouted.

"It was YOUR ways that caused the last great war!" the Western members shouted back.

Aanepada banged the gavel several more times. "These aliens concern me. I think the best approach is the cautious one. We should allow dialog between us for some time before we enter into any agreements with them for anything." He paused a moment as more shouting erupted between sides. He was beginning to realize how divided his people had become. He was beginning to blame himself for this. His inaction on critical issues, rather than taking a stand and guiding his people down a particular path, was a sign of his weakness as a leader. He needed to correct this starting now. He banged the gavel several more times, and the room quieted. "I know in the past we have had difficulty reaching joint decisions, but as a people, we need to stand firm and together in the approach we take today."

More shouts. "It's about time!" several yelled. They were voices from his own people.

Aanepada continued, "I don't trust this alien who calls himself Damok-Sai from Inea. I think he is lying, and I think, from listening to him, that he has a hidden agenda. He grew impatient quickly during our first meeting, which I find strange. His ship was bristling with weapons and heavily armed troops. Someone who shows up looking for food and fuel does not do so with a whole fleet of warships in orbit."

Loud murmurs echoed throughout the seated members as they talked about what he had said. He gave them a minute to digest his words, and then he banged the gavel. "In conclusion, I would like to call upon Ninhursag, who has information from the Eastern Continent."

Ninhursag walked up to the podium slowly. He wore a black, hooded robe with gold collar and cuffs, which signified that he was a high-order priest of Kur. He bowed to Aanepada and faced the podium as the president stepped aside. He pulled his hood back off his head, which revealed his face was burned red and peeling, like a bad sunburn, and he stroked his graying beard. "Mister President, honored council and military leaders, I have come here as a testimony of what I have seen. By the glory of Kur, I tell you the truth." Many mumbled on the Eastern side of the room while the Western side sat up straight to hear his words. He continued. "Four nights ago, during an unusual rain storm in the Shuruppak plains near the river Tiamat, there was a roar from the sky, and a ship identical to the one which landed here yesterday settled in the mud outside the village. There were no lights, and it was dark. The only noise heard was the roar of the engines. The door on the side split and slid to the sides, and two dozen huge beings exited the craft. I saw this as I walked chanting towards the village, so I took cover behind some shrubs and watched them. They were armed and wore plated uniforms, possibly armored. They talked in this loud, booming voice, but their words I did not understand. They split into four groups and entered the village. While they were gone, I peeked into their ship as the doors closed and saw weapons stacked against the far wall of the craft. A short time later, I heard this random crackling noise, and soon after that, the aliens came back dragging dozens of women who were kicking and screaming and threw them into the open door of the craft. I watched as two who remained behind began to tie the women up with magnetic cuffs while the rest piled back into the craft. It soon roared back to life, took off, and went straight up into the sky. My face got burned from the blast from the engines because I was too close," he paused for a drink and continued. "I went into the village and saw all the men were dead. They had burn holes through their bodies, and the children cried over the bodies, but all the women were gone. I tell you this in support of the president's concerns that these beings may have an agenda other than what they tell us. By the glory of Kur, I was able to be here today to witness this truth to you." He bowed and pulled his hood back over his head. He then bowed to Aanepada and went back to his seat.

"Thank you, Ninhursag. I submit this testimony as evidence that we should be very cautious with the aliens," Aanepada stated and banged the gavel.

General Nanna stood and bowed towards the president. "Mister President, I request an opportunity to speak as well."

Aanepada looked towards him and nodded. "As you wish. The floor recognizes General Nanna, who was the first to speak with Damok-Sai."

Nanna walked up and bowed to the president and turned towards the podium and the five-hundred-plus people in the room. "I partially disagree with the president on his stand. While I do agree we need to be cautious and take this slowly, I do not see the harm in having them shuttle food and supplies to the people in the cities while we work on getting our infrastructure back up and running. What they ask for is food and fuel. Their ships must run on something we have in abundance, or they would have passed us by. I know they are larger than we are and have superior technology. They are quite intimidating when you come face-to-face. However, if they chose to invade, I would think they would strike while we were in disarray instead of helping us to build back up. I say let them help us, and we can provide them with the necessary supplies, hopefully getting them on their way quickly. That is all I have to add." He bowed to the council and then to Aanepada and left as the majority of the members stood and cheered.

"I have one more person who would like to speak," Aanepada said, knowing he was going to lose the vote if it was held right now.

"No more. We have heard enough. Vote now!" various members yelled out.

Aanepada huffed, "Let us see a show of hands. All in favor of voting now?"

The hands went up. It appeared to be a vast majority.

"All in favor of more discussion? Raise your hands."

A definite minority.

"Looks like we will vote. I will remind everyone present that only the council is allowed to vote and that a two-thirds majority is needed to pass the question at hand and the question is: do we allow these aliens, which we know nothing about, to land on this planet en masse and shuttle food and supplies to our people who are in need in exchange for supplies that we do not know what they require yet. If you are in favor of this, then vote yes. If you have too many questions still, like I do, then please vote no." Aanepada stated as the members began arguing amongst themselves. He banged the gavel several times, and the room came back to order. "Each of you has a ballot in front of you, circle the appropriate response, and then come forward. I would ask Shulgi and Ur to count the ballots. I will put a time limit of one hour to complete this task from now." He glanced at Inanna. "Start the timer."

Inanna started the clock, and the council members began arguing as some filtered down and cast their votes. Soon, a steady stream of council members lined up to cast their votes as the arguing and fighting continued.

At the end of the hour, Inanna stepped back to the podium and banged the gavel. "The voting is now closed." He glanced at Shulgi, who handed him a slip of paper, and then to Ur, who did the same. He did some quick calculations. He then looked up and banged the gavel again. "The vote is in. There were 410 total votes. A two-thirds majority is required to approve the assistance from the aliens, and the final tally is...two hundred eighty-four in favor and one hundred twenty-six against. The proposal is approved by a two percent margin."

Everyone on the Eastern side stood and cheered, and some on the Western side. The rest sat and bowed their heads.

Aanepada stepped up to the podium, "I do ask one thing, and that is we need to monitor the aliens. I am requesting an independent panel be set up right away to oversee this travesty and report back to this council daily their comments and concerns." He turned to Inanna. "See to it that it gets done."

"Yes, Mister President."

Aanepada walked away from the podium and exited the room without looking back. He was followed by Dagan.

Damok-Sai returned a day later with two dozen ships. Nanna instructed him where the food depots were and where they needed to go. Over the next week, the Inean ships began distributing food supplies to the cities around the planet.

Word spread around the planet about how aliens from space had come to help them, and people began cheering the Inean ships when they brought food and supplies around the planet. General Nanna and his Inean friend, Damok-Sai, traveled the planet denouncing the current government. They told the people that Aanepada and his council saw this crisis coming and did nothing to prevent the deaths of thousands of people and the destruction of their society. Soon, dissent began to grow towards Aanepada and his government over their inability to solve this problem. A few weeks after the Ineans began distributing the food, millions of people descended upon Delondra, calling for the resignation of Aanepada and all the top-level officials.

Aanepada looked out the window of his office at the enormous, angry crowd below and decided it was time. In a matter of hours, he assembled his closest cabinet members and discussed the future of the government.

"Our planet and society have been confronted with incredible challenges and changes in recent months," he began with a glance around the room. "The people have fallen at the feet of these aliens, as well as several of our military leaders. It is time for us to withdraw for the sake of maintaining the peace of our people and for saving their lives as winter settles in. I hope in the next few weeks these aliens will be on their way and life as we know it will return," Aanepada said to his loyal cabinet of more than one hundred council members and judicial court members. There was no cheering during this speech because many of them were quitting and leaving right behind him.

An hour later, Aanepada walked out on the balcony with General Nanna and Damok-Sai. The crowd booed and hissed at him when he appeared. He held up his hands to quiet the crowd as he prepared to speak. He went through their history; there was only one other president who had quit the office, two had died in office of illness, and two others had been murdered. He weighed the historic value of what he was about to do. "People of Ardonnar, it gives me great sadness to stand before you today to announce that I will be joining a very small number of people from our history in taking a leave from leadership of this planet before my term expires." The crowd cheered as he continued. "This decision was not made lightly and comes with a warning as I hand control over to General Nanna for the short term, pending new elections. We have allowed an alien race to help us with this unprecedented disaster in exchange for a trade, the details of which we still know nothing about. They have come to us in our time of need based on the unexpected instability of Utui. I ask you to be wary of these strangers." More jeers from the crowd as they began to chant their praises of General Nanna and the Ineans. "In conclusion, this transfer of power takes effect at sunset today." He waved to the crowd and abruptly left the balcony as General Nanna stepped forward to speak.

. . .

Aanepada had assembled his closest, most loyal political and military leaders. They packed up their families and had most of them head for the mountains, where they would regroup. He did this in small groups, hoping not to draw attention to their movements. He gathered his family, which now consisted of Dagan and no one else. The group exited from the secret tunnel that took them away from the presidential tower. Several military vehicles loaded and headed towards the southern city of Nnazu, which was Aanepada's home city. Further outside the city, other nonmilitary vehicles waited inside an enclosed building. Aanepada wasn't taking any chances and used the first convoy as a decoy, which continued towards Nnazu. A few hours later, when they were safely away from the city, they stopped in a small village and loaded into several camouflaged military vehicles, which took them out towards the western mountains nearly two thousand zag away. The journey would take them a week if they traveled nonstop to the Antum military base buried deep in Mount Laarsa.

Aanepada could not sleep still because his concerns for his people grew with each report coming in. It turned out that more and more women were disappearing from the eastern continent and now in the West. There was no indication that the Ineans were behind it, but the trend was troubling. There were more and more reports that the Inean presence was growing on the planet. He was becoming depressed that his planet was being invaded without a shot being fired, and only a select few were bothered by it.

The convoy entered the base at night with their lights off, hoping that the Ineans were not watching for them. Aanepada was led down the long, sloping tunnel and into the main chamber where his loyal followers had gathered. From here, they were able to monitor conditions around the planet and in space. They had isolated twenty-five enormous ships orbiting the planet and dozens of small ships going back and forth.

"General Asar, it is good to see you. How are we coming with organizing personnel around the planet?" Aanepada asked while grasping the general's hand firmly, holding it for a few seconds longer than usual.

"We are slowly putting troops in place. The reports coming in from around the planet are disturbing. Thousands of these aliens are in our cities, and they are heavily armed. We fear it is a takeover," Asar stated.

"How is Utui?" Aanepada asked.

"That is strange. We are reviewing the data streams that Enir has provided us from the multiple CMEs that have blasted our planet," Asar said.

Enir, who was nearby, heard her name and walked over to the general and president. "General, Mister President, it is an honor to meet you. I am Enir."

Aanepada shook her hand sincerely and held it for a moment as well. "Pleased to meet you."

Asar looked at her. "Describe your findings for the president, Enir."

"Yes, sir," she said. "We have compared all of the data from the six CMEs so far. They are coming regularly and without warning, which is impossible with what we know about solar storms."

"Why is that?" Aanepada asked.

"Each storm appears to be directed at Ardonnar, which is statistically impossible. Additionally, the data appears inconsistent with a typical CME. The various radiation we are seeing leads us to think there is a black hole affecting Utui, but only sometimes, which is very strange."

"Why is that strange?" Asar asked.

"Well, because a black hole orbiting Utui would be a constant threat to the star and to our planet as well, but it only manifests itself when the star blows off in our direction. This looks more and more like an invasion tactic than a random storm." She watched the president digest what she said and continued. "It is impossible for this to be random, sir. It fits the invasion formula in that you blast a planet and wipe out their electrical grid and send the people into disarray."

Aanepada looked at her. "When is the next one expected?"

"Day after tomorrow."

"You know this with certainty?"

"Yes," she replied. "Because they will move their ships behind the moon Anaru about six hours before Utui blows."

"You are certain?" Aanepada asked.

"Like clockwork," she said.

"Thank you, Enir. General?" Aanepada's stomach was churning with the news.

"We are studying the aliens and their ships, trying to find weaknesses we can exploit, but our forces are thin and scattered. We are not ready to muster a counterattack."

"Get the word out quietly. I don't want these Ineans knowing what we are doing or that we know what they are doing."

"Understood, Mister President." the general stated as he bowed and left the room.

"Good job, Enir. Help us find the source of these CMEs, as you call them, so we can stop them," Aanepada said as he gripped his abdomen.

"Are you all right?" Dagan asked.

"I need to sit down for a moment."

She guided him out of the room and to the mess hall for a drink and a seat. "You have to stop blaming yourself for this. There is nothing you could have done to prevent it from happening; no one could."

"I know, but still. I fear millions could die before they realize what has happened," Aanepada said, and he hunched over and vomited into a trash bin.

ELEVEN

IT WAS the height of winter in the Northern Hemisphere, but it was warm in most areas. Snow did not fall except in the mountains, and even then, it was nothing like a typical winter. The snow had been replaced with violent rain and wind storms that ravaged the countryside. The northern ice sheet was melting at a rapid pace due to warmer temperatures, causing a shift in ocean currents as millions of gallons of fresh water flowed into the salty oceans. The constant solar bombardment altered weather patterns and threatened to flood low-lying areas in just a few years if this weather persisted. In the grain belt, crops began to grow, only to be flooded by the rains. Lightning storms swept the planet, igniting wildfires that burned out of control. The fires swept over small villages and towns, sending the residents fleeing from town to town in a frantic race to escape the blazes.

The Ineans now had over twenty thousand soldiers on the ground, and people started to question when they would leave. Many confronted General Nanna on this, and he said they would be leaving soon. Many cited the disappearance of women and now men all over the planet. He shrugged it off as a coincidence, and he now kept two Ineans as bodyguards out of fear for his life.

He realized now that it was too late; he was wrong about the Ineans.

Nanna landed in one city to help distribute food and to rally the people. However, an angry mob was waiting for him. He started to help distribute food when a woman approached him. "General, may I have a word with you?"

He turned around as she pulled a gun from her robe and emptied the clip into him. He flew back into the Ineans, who were there to protect him. The Ineans turned on her, pulled their lasers, and aimed. She held her hands up in surrender, but they fired anyway. A half dozen laser blasts pierced through her body into the crowd behind her, killing her and a half-dozen others. The Ineans retreated to the safety of their ship as pitchforks and rocks flew by them. Others took to stoning the already dead general and dragged him to the center of the square, where they propped up his dead body for the crowd to hurl stones at. The Ineans took off with a ship full of food and supplies and did not return.

Reports of the attack spread around the planet, polarizing the people against the Ineans and prompting Damok-Sai's soldiers to take a stricter approach toward the Ardonnarians. People were stopped, questioned, and harassed daily by the Ineans while trying to go about their daily business. Many people were pushed, shoved around, and beaten up if they did not yield to them or answer their questions.

Deep in Mount Laarsa, Aanepada met with his generals, loyal council, and their head climatologist, Enlil. Enlil worked with Enir to create a model of their planet based on the effects of the solar explosions. Enlil stood before the group, and he was nervous about facing the gathering with his news. He cleared his throat and turned on the projector, which had a graph on it. "Mister President, loyal staff. What you see on the chart is the normal temperature scale for a year here on the Western continent. The red line displays the temperatures as measured since the first solar storm struck our planet."

"As you can see, the temperatures are spiking. We could see baking highs when summer arrives and expect crop failures as the grains and cattle roast on the fields." He took a nervous sip of water. "This next slide shows the altered jet streams in the atmosphere in red with the normal stream in blue. The yellow line is the normal ocean currents, and the green line is the change in ocean currents. Between the two changes, you can see that storms are tracking too far south here in the West, causing flooding of the farmlands and cutting straight across the ocean into the east before rising up over the eastern mountain range. This leaves the northern, more populated areas of both continents dry. Rain has not fallen in Ninki in two months. It should be their wet season. This next chart shows what to expect this summer. The brown-shaded areas indicate drought, the green areas represent wet areas, and the blue areas indicate flooded areas. Suppose these conditions continue, and there is no reason to expect them to change. In that case, you are looking at a complete planetwide crop failure. Famine, disease, and mass death could ensue. We should be rationing food now and hope to get through it."

Aanepada stood and walked forward slowly as he pondered what he had just seen. The room was quiet as he held out his hand towards Enlil. "Thank you for your report."

"I'm sorry, Mister President, I wish I had better news," he said softly, and he stepped away.

"General Asar, I want you to take Enlil to a radio transmitting station and get him on the air. Have him repeat this message around the clock so people know what to do." He stared off into the distance, and Dagan was concerned for him. He still had not slept a full night in months, and the pressure of reclaiming power and fighting the Ineans was taking a toll on him. She had suggested that he take sleeping aides and something for his blood pressure, but he refused.

"Yes, Mister President. I will get right on it."

"I am no longer the president," Aanepada said as he began to walk away. A tear rolled from his eye.

"You are still our president, sir, and we have received news that

General Nanna has been killed by a woman. She and several others have been murdered by Ineans. Sir, the Ineans are starting to take hold of the cities."

"Then the time has come for us to react."

"That is not all, sir. The people are calling out for you to come out of hiding and lead them again. They admit you were right," Asar replied.

It might be too late for that but make the broadcast. Let the people know that I am still the president, and it might instill hope in our people. I will work on an inspiring speech, but for now, get this climate information out there."

"Yes, Mister President," and the general bowed and left the room with Enlil.

"Are you up for this, Aanepada?" Dagan asked as she walked up to him and studied his frame of mind.

"I have to be. Come, we need a speech to rally the planet and boot these aliens out."

"Yes, Mister President."

Dagan bowed and followed him out the door.

Two days went by, and the Ineans secured the cities and began making life difficult for the Ardonnarians. Food was rationed as long as they swore allegiance to Damok-Sai. Some were required to turn their wives and daughters over to him for food, and some did. The women would never be seen again.

General Asar and a small group of soldiers stormed a broadcast station several hundred miles from the base in the mountains with little effort. He brought the climatologist, Enlil, who went on the air and broadcast their message around the planet. He told the people about their climate and informed them that a message was coming from President Aanepada. When he was done, he turned the micro-phone over to a woman who gave a report about the theories regarding the CMEs while Enir stayed in the mountains working on finding the source of the deadly solar storms wrecking their planet. Then, General Asar gave a stirring speech hailing President Aanepada, who is still in control and working on securing the planet. They placed the station on automatic, which kept the messages repeating over and over. They quickly left the station and hid in the nearby town that had been deserted. Asar and his group waited to see if the Ineans would come to stop the broadcasts. They didn't have to wait long. Two Inean fighters swooped down over the village with a roar. The buildings shook, windows shattered, and other items fell from shelves from their sonic boom. The fighters flew towards the radio station and fired missiles. The station exploded, and the fighters turned towards the village and circled it, looking for any trace of movement. They could not see any recent activity and flew off.

"Good thing we swept our tracks, general. We should get going to the next station," Enlil said.

"We are not going anywhere yet. We are going to wait and make sure they don't come back."

"They flew off, sir," Enlil stated.

"Yes, but they could be waiting for us to fall for that and pounce on us while we are in the open. We will wait a day and then move on. I would like to get into Delondra if possible. Draw attention away from the mountains."

"Yes, sir," Enlil said.

It irritated Asar when people acted like they were in the military or tried to tell the military what to do when they were not. He let it go for now, and they waited for night.

TWELVE

DAMOK-SAI VISITED one of his ships, the *Pavitra*, which had been converted for transporting people after sending all of its fighters, transports, and troops to the planet below. He toured the flight deck, which featured rows of beds and numerous food supplies. He praised the ship's captain on a job well done. "Fill this ship with the Ardon slaves and bring them back to Inea," he said while flipping through an Ardonnarian magazine. He passed it to the ship's captain, who began examining the pictures.

"What is this?" the ship's captain asked in amazement. "Of all the places we have overtaken, I've never seen this before."

"Oh yes, they are an amazing culture," Damok-Sai replied with a thunderous laugh. "It's too bad they are so fragile and die quickly." He looked around the flight deck. "We need to fill this room, and while you are en route to Inea, we will fill another ship to leave when you turn around."

"Understood, Commander Damok-Sai. We will have this filled in hours and be on our way later today," the captain replied. "May I have some of these slaves for myself?"

"Yes, just leave the majority for my father, Manava, and the Emperor, Sankar," Damok-Sai said, and he walked towards his transport, which had docked to the outside hatch of the ship. His transport headed back to Delondra, where he had taken over Aanepada's office and ran his operation from there.

Damok-Sai met with the Ardonnarian leaders who had elected themselves to office. "I think it would be prudent of you to start sending women and children to another planet we discovered on our way here. It's a little cooler than we like; however, your race won't be able to stay here much longer, as your star is working up to exploding. When it does, it will destroy your planet and all life on it."

"How is it possible to move billions of people across the stars?" Ur, the self-appointed leader of the planet, asked.

"You can not. So pick the cream of your society, and we will move them for you. At best, you could save tens of thousands of your people before the star renders the planet uninhabitable," Damok-Sai said in his booming voice.

Ur was going to mention their colonies in other star systems but held back. He did not trust this Inean, and, for all he knew, the Inean might not have been aware of the colonies. If he did, why would he move them to another system? He came back to the present as Damok-Sai bellowed at him. "Yes, Damok-Sai, I will send my family on the first transport to safety. I will contact them to be ready."

"What of the men?" another leader asked, looking to save himself.

"Once we get as many women and children off the planet, then the last transports will take you away as well. Do the right thing," Damok-Sai replied. "Now, there will be twenty transports to load, and we have a small window to load the ship for evacuation. Bring no belongings. They must be ready or be left behind, and there will be no guarantees that they could catch another transport. Understood?"

"Yes, Damok-Sai. We will spread the word at once."

· · ·

Ur contacted his wife, Ashusikildigir, in Ninki and told her to be ready to evacuate and to leave everyone else behind, including the staff. "I understand you will be separated. Kanpar is here with me, and I will make sure she is on the transport that leaves here."

Ashusikildigir pleaded with her husband, "You make sure Kanpar is on that transport. I must go now. I have to find Enanatuma to make sure she is on our transport."

"Alright, but make sure you contain that one. She has a habit of putting up a fight and that mouth of hers," Ur said, and he closed the connection.

At a home on the outskirts of Ninki, Ur's other daughter, Enanatuma, was helping a friend plant food in the dry soil when an Inean ship landed with a loud thud that shook the ground and the buildings around her. She stepped out from the barn and watched the dust settle around the ship. She slipped back into the barn and tried to get the attention of her friend, who was mesmerized by the craft landing. Several Ineans spilled out of the craft and grabbed the girl as Enanatuma hid behind a pile of straw used for animal bedding. They tore at the girl, ripping her clothes, while roughly tossing her into the transport while laughing at her. The transport quickly took off.

Enanatuma was frightened and went into the house and told the girl's mother what had happened. The mother cried out, and there was a loud boom from the center of the town. They both turned and watched Ineans falling out of a different craft that had landed hard. The Ineans began seizing women and children as a cloud of dust and smoke settled around the craft. They dragged them to the ship and tossed them in with little regard. Soon after, the craft labored as it took off, carrying hundreds of women and children on board. Enanatuma fell into the arms of her friend's mother as the communicator on the wall chirped. The mother picked up the communicator. "Yes?" she asked in a shaky voice. "She is right here. Do you know what just happened?" A pause while Ashusikildigir spoke. "You what! No way. They are animals. I will not put your daughter on that ship. We will never see her again."

Ashusikildigir was speaking again when there was a commotion outside. The woman looked out the window and tossed the communicator against the wall. She then grabbed Enanatuma and took her from the home as a pair of Inean soldiers walked towards the house in search of the girl.

Back in Delondra, Ur met with Damok-Sai and brought his oldest daughter, Kanpar, with him. "Damok-Sai, this is my oldest daughter, Kanpar. I want to make sure she is on the next transport out of here."

Damok-Sai sized up the young woman and decided she would do nicely. "Yes, of course, Ur, I will see to it myself. She may stay here. Now I need you to go and organize a search for the local women and children you wish to send along with her," the alien said with a fearful grin.

"Yes, yes, of course, Damok-Sai. I will do it now." He hesitantly left Kanpar behind and closed the door.

"What should I do?" Kanpar asked.

Damok-Sai grinned at her, "Why don't you lock the door and come close these curtains for me. The harsh light hurts my eyes."

"Yes, certainly," she replied, and she stepped back and locked the door and walked over to the curtains and closed them. "Anything else?"

Damok-Sai pondered this for a few seconds, and he pulled out one of the magazines he had been given and studied a picture on the page.

"Yes, there certainly is," he said.

He got up from behind the desk and clamped his hairy paw over her mouth. "Explain this for me. If you cry out or scream, I will kill your family."

Soon after, there was a knock on the door, and Damok-Sai looked up at Kanpar. "Open the door and let them in," he growled.

She got off the edge of the desk and wiped the tears from her eyes. Kanpar hobbled toward the door while holding her lower back, and she opened the door. One of Damok-Sai's officers entered the room and saluted. "The transport ship will land in about twenty minutes, sir. Should I take this one to the transport?"

"No, she is with me. I will make sure she is transported separately."

"Understood," he replied, and he left the room. Kanpar closed the door and locked it. She contemplated running for it, but instead returned to Damok-Sai's side.

She trembled from fear and the pain she endured.

He swiped everything from the desk and grabbed Kanpar, sitting her roughly onto the desk.

A few hours later, Damok-Sai sent Kanpar to the *Nikstra* to be patched up for their next encounter while he stayed in Delondra.

One of his generals entered the room. "Sir, what should we do with the old and feeble ones. Our Emperor would want nothing to do with them."

Damok-Sai turned from the large windows as the heavily laden transport struggled off the ground and headed for the *Pavitra*. "Kill them. Make them go away. Stack them in a pile and burn them. I do not care. However, here is a list of names from the city of Ninki. Find them and send them to the *Nikstra* for me. Some of them may be on the *Pavitra* already. Make sure you check and find them before that ship heads back to Inea."

"Yes, Commander, I will find them right away before the *Pavitra* leaves orbit for Inea."

"Very good. I want an advanced message sent to parliament leader Manava that his gifts are on the way, and I want you to issue these instructions while underway," he said, handing the general a memory stick. "I also want Manava to know that these children are tough and should work the mines and fields for years to come, saving us the grueling tasks that are meant for slaves."

"Excellent, Commander. I will take care of it," the General said and then stopped by the door. "I can't believe these people allowed us to take over their planet so easily. How did you know?"

"I had a hunch that this race was stupid. They have spaceships ferrying people around to different planets, but their infrastructure is weak and susceptible to simple solar flares that crushed their society in the first wave. They will believe anything we tell them without question. They are not worth wasting our bombs on."

"Hmm, alright. I will take care of these tasks," the General said as he exited the door. In the corridor was Ur, and he overheard what Damok-Sai had said.

He composed himself and walked into Damok-Sai's office. "I trust my daughter made it to the transport?"

"Yes, she did. Why do you ask?"

"Just making sure. They cannot find my other daughter, Enana-tuma. She has run off with the mother of her friend."

"My people will find her, Ur. Now I need to get this done, so go away." Damok-Sai said, and when Ur had left, he withdrew another magazine from the drawer and studied it well into the evening.

Several hours later, the Inean ship *Pavitra* turned away from the invasion fleet and ignited its large engines. The ship sped away quickly and was soon out of sight.

On the flight deck were thousands of Ardonnarian women packed in with no place to go and no room to move about without stepping on others. Many had bruises and cuts from being tossed about by the Ineans when their villages were raided. Several had worse injuries and lay about the deck moaning in pain.

The Inean soldiers stepped onto the deck in full armor and began separating the Ardons into groups. Once the injured had been separated, the Ineans herded them away to be bandaged up for the trip to Inea. The rest were stripped of most of their clothing, which was taken away to be shredded, packed in large containers, and sold on Inea as raw material to make a variety of products. After a long while, the Ineans returned with buckets of mushy food and buckets of water. They forced the women to eat with their hands, and the Ineans quickly took the buckets away.

The trip would last about four months, and many would die under the brutal conditions the Ineans forced on them.

On Inea, news spread of the *Pavitra*'s return, and crowds quickly descended upon the coliseum facing the Emperor's palace. Soon, Sankar would step out onto the podium and address the hundreds of Ineans standing around the central stage, and he would open the auction. Sankar liked to observe the crowds and gauge their enthusiasm, which was often worked up to a frenzy by the auctioneer. He liked to watch the fights outside as the Ineans fought to get inside, hoping to win a bid for the Ardon slaves. Many would spend a month's wage for just a few hours with them and then go hungry for the rest of the month.

The crowd was standing in the bright, warm day as a rumble emerged from the sky. The crowd jumped up and down, howling as the first transports from the *Pavitra* descended upon the Inean capital of Sabitta. The transports circled the coliseum and then set down on an enclosed, heavily protected landing pad just outside the coliseum. The ship's engines wound down, and soon, the side doors opened. Two Inean guards carried a chain in their hands and guided a hundred Ardons out of the transport. They were chained around their necks and winced at the intense sunlight and the heat of Inea. The guards hooked the chain to a far post and forced them into a straight line, then tied off the other end. Several other Ineans with hoses blasted the slaves with high-pressured, hot water to clean them off from their months in the cramped flight deck of the *Pavitra*, which was refueling for a return trip to Ardonnar. Many fell to the ground from the water pressure and intense heat. Soon, it was over. The Ineans dragged them up and guided them into the coliseum, where the Ineans inside jumped up and down, throwing money at the auctioneer.

Sankar grinned from his balcony and knew this would be a very profitable group for him while the guards circled the stage once and dropped the chain. The Ardons were frightened, and many cried as they were paraded around before hundreds of bloodthirsty aliens. There was nowhere to run, and if someone tried, he or she would have to drag ninety-nine others with them. Their fright turned to shock and horror as what happened next unfolded.

A woman on the end was unshackled and brought up on stage. Two large Ineans towered over the woman as they held her, facing the crowd of excited Ineans. They displayed the woman to all present, and then the auctioneer opened the bidding. In the rough language of the Ineans, he started the bidding high, and there was no shortage of Ineans driving the price up and up. Sankar's grin widened as he was joined by Manava, Damok-Sai's father, who was responsible for halting the slaughter on Ardonnar and bringing them here. Both enjoyed swelling profits, which ensured Damok-Sai took over for his father as a lead council member when Manava retired.

Soon, the bidding was between two Ineans who began fighting as they bid for the woman. One of them produced a knife and stabbed the other repeatedly until he alone was left standing. The auctioneer concluded the bidding, and the Inean faced the crowd around him as he held up his knife with blue blood dripping from it. He put his knife back, walked down to the stage, and tossed a small bag of money at the clerk, who dumped it out and counted. Once he logged it in his book, he waved off the Inean, who jumped up on the stage, grabbed the woman by her hair, and dragged her from the coliseum, never to be seen again.

The others were auctioned off in the same way until all one hundred were taken. The crowd thinned, and more were let in to fill the stadium, and the next transport was unloaded. A dozen more would offload their cargo and return to the *Pavitra*, which would return to Ardonnar for more. There were millions to take as long as the market held up, and, as Sankar watched from his perch above, there was no shortage of buyers.

. . .

Several other transports landed in a vast field thousands of miles from the Inean capital, Sabitta, and soon the children were taken out. Many fell back from the heat, but eventually, they were dragged from the transports and out into the fields, where several Ineans sat under shades. They guided them to the fields and hovered over them with whips while the children cultivated the plants. By the end of the first day, many had dropped from heat exhaustion and dehydration. The Ineans whipped them until they stopped moving. Then, the Ineans would drag them off to the pit. This weeded out the weak ones, and the rest were fed at the end of the day.

THIRTEEN

CAPTAIN ZUTTARA TURNED and faced Commander Gula as he approached. "Commander?" he said, his tone stern. Zuttara was a chiseled military leader with a strong build and crisp uniform. He had a short-cut beard to match his haircut.

"Captain Zuttara, I have received orders from General Asar. We are to head to Antum as soon as possible," Gula said as he snapped to attention.

"Antum? Is there anything else?"

"Yes, he wants us to remove the nuclear warheads and bring them there. We are to use several camouflaged vehicles and split up, taking multiple routes. He is concerned about the Ineans tracking movement on the ground," Gula said.

"I see," Zuttara said as he studied the piece of paper Gula handed him. "We ship out in the morning. Get all the teams moving on securing the warheads."

"Yes, sir!" Gula stated sharply. He snapped to attention, saluted Zuttara, and went off to organize the exodus from the Idimmu military to the Antum base, fifteen hundred zag northwest of the planet's capital, Delondra. The army worked well into the night, removing the warheads from the missiles and bolting them down in the trucks. They packed supplies and organized the three convoys. Each group would take a different path to the Antum base, buried deep in Mount Laarsa, in the western part of the Humbaba mountain chain, where Aanepada set up his base of operations.

Gula made sure he kept Puabi with him. He had made a promise to her father to keep her safe, and he wanted to be with her anyway. He still had not asked for her vow of betrothal yet, which was a problem he had with women. He was afraid of rejection, even though the signals she sent were perfectly clear. She was waiting for him to commit. He vowed once this invasion was under control, he would ask her, but for now, he would keep her safe. He watched her in the distance, laughing with several other army personnel as they finished loading the trucks. He watched the men talking with her, and Gula realized if he waited much longer, he might lose her if it wasn't too late already. He started walking towards them as they walked towards him. "Status?" he asked firmly.

"All trucks are loaded and secured, Commander," one of the men said.

"Very good. Get a few hours of sleep. We ship out early in the morning," Gula said as he studied the men.

"Yes sir," they all said, and they dispersed towards different barracks.

"Puabi, come with me," Gula asked.

"Yes, Commander?"

"I wanted to talk with you about something that has been on my mind for some time now."

"Yes," she said, hoping she knew where he was going, finally.

"I wanted to ask you..."

"Commander Gula, Captain Zuttara wants to see you right away," an infantryman said, out of breath as he raced up to Gula.

"Just a minute."

"The captain said without delay, sir."

Gula huffed, "We'll finish this conversation later," he said to Puabi, and then he ran off with the infantryman.

Puabi stood there and watched him go away. Her shoulders slumped while thinking about how close he came to asking her the all-important question. At least, she hoped that was his question. It was a question she had been waiting for more than a year to hear. It was a question she had rehearsed the answer to many times in her mind. She then glanced towards the barracks and headed off in that direction for a rare shower due to the rationing of supplies. They were all guaranteed a shower, a fresh uniform, and extra rations for the start of their mission.

The next morning, just as Utui rose above the rolling hills in the east, the first two convoys headed out. Each caravan had dozens of trucks and troop carriers. Hundreds of troops in each group with supplies slowly rumbled away. The first went south, and the second went northward, which, under normal conditions, would be a frozen, snow-covered, and frigid journey, but not this year. With the constant barrage of solar blasts from Utui, the planet's climate was changing rapidly. Storm patterns shifted, and planetwide temperatures soared.

Captain Zuttara readied the third convoy, which would head due west and hopefully arrive at Antum a few days before the other two groups, as long as the Ineans did not catch on. He, Gula, and Puabi climbed into the lead truck. Puhrum joined them as their radioman. She arrived the day before, having given up on Belit-Sheri because the Inean presence grew there. She fought her way to Idimmu while conditions across the upper continent deteriorated as quickly as the climate. She was the perfect choice for communications, given her experience on the *ShuBuré*, and, with Gula's recommendation, she was a shoo-in.

Zuttara went through his checklist one last time and then ordered the convoy to move out. He sat in the front seat while Puabi drove the lead truck. She shifted the gears and pulled away with a jolt. Their first destination was the town of Utuk. Rumors had been circulating in recent weeks that the Ineans had turned the town into a slave labor camp. While that was disturbing in itself, a new rumor was going around that the red-robed followers of Nergal were involved. Captain Zuttara was under orders from General Asar to investigate if these rumors were true.

The trucks rumbled along the paved road through the day and into the evening until the caravan stopped in a wooded area for the night. They ate their rations cold and kept the lights and heaters off to avoid detection from the Ineans. Even though the temperature still dipped below freezing, they were prepared with their thermal sleeping bags and extra layers of clothes.

Zuttara woke everyone up early and got them moving before sunrise. It would be two more days before they reached Utuk.

FOURTEEN

ACROSS THE OCEAN, Eridu, who was the mother of the girl abducted in Ninki while she worked in the gardens, hid under a pile of brush with Enanatuma, along with many others. They waited while several Ineans patrolling the road heading south to Akhkharu moved beyond the next hill. The Ineans had been tipped off that people were heading out of the cities and wanted to cut them off on their way. The travelers huddled under the brush until dark, and then a few slipped out to see if the Ineans had moved far enough down the road. The others waited until the all-clear signal was sounded. A whistling sound, like a bird, was the signal, and several others, including Eridu and Enanatuma, headed out from the brush pile and crossed the road. Once on the other side, they waited to see if they drew any attention to themselves, and then the signal went out again. There were forty in their group, and as each group crossed the road, the previous group headed out into the high field towards Akhkharu.

One last group was poised to cross when there was a rumble from over the hill. They looked at each other and decided to run for it instead of waiting. As they raced across the road, two Inean jeeps crested the hill and opened fire on the runners. Several were cut down in the road while some escaped into the field. The jeeps turned into the field and chased them down, capturing four of them, three women and one younger boy. The Ineans took them and stripped them to humiliate them into talking, but it did not work. One of the Ineans took the boy, placed a jagged knife to his throat, and turned to the women who huddled, trying to cover themselves, "Where are you going?" he asked in his rough voice.

"Just across the field for food," one woman said.

"You lie! Where is the rebel base you are going to?" he asked while pressing the knife to the boy's throat as he whimpered.

"NO! We are just looking for food," another woman cried out.

"You know the punishment for lying to us," the Inean said, and he pressed down hard on the boy's throat, breaking the skin. "Last chance, where is the base?"

The boy made choking sounds as the knife pressed on. The women cried but did not answer the Inean. They wanted to tell him but knew he would kill them anyway. It was the same tactics from which they were running. No one was spared Inean torture, even if they cooperated. The Inean sliced through the boy's throat and let him drop to the ground in a cloud of dirt and dust. He then turned to the first woman, who stood in shock and murdered her while the others watched. The whole time, he asked them where the secret base was. None of them answered, and he killed them all, leaving their bodies along the road as a warning for others to see.

Hiding in the tall grass, a dozen others watched in horror as the Inean killed the four captured. Some wanted to help them and had to be restrained, while others turned away and cried. Soon, the Ineans were finished and quickly studied the grassy area and left.

The Ardonnarians made it through the tall grass to the treeline and camped for the night. They had no food, and all went to sleep hungry. The next day, they pasted leaves and branches all over themselves for cover. They continued through the trees to a river, which was significantly lower than its normal height due to the severe drought plaguing the upper eastern continent. They drank the water and ate the undersized fruit from the trees at midday and quickly raced back under cover at the sound of Inean transports flying low just above the tree tops. The transports circled around, and the Ardonnarians suspected they had been found. The transports eventually moved upriver and then out of sight. Eridu and the others breathed a sigh of relief and continued their journey cautiously and quietly through the thick forest.

A week passed, and they finally arrived at their destination after playing cat and mouse with the Ineans the whole time. They looked off towards the ocean at smoke rising up from several buildings. Many buildings had been destroyed and were still smoldering. The streets were littered with debris and bodies. The group huddled in the trees as an Inean fighter flew low over the town and moved on.

Many in the group argued over heading into the large town right away, while the rest decided to wait until dark. The second group prevailed, and they all waited in the thick brush for dark.

When it was finally dark, a half dozen of the men ventured out of the thorny brush and worked their way across a dried field of melam, which is a type of wheat plant. They passed several fenced-in pens littered with dead sahu, which were very much like pigs, only these were very thin and most likely starved to death. Several other smaller animals skittered about pecking at the ground in search of food but scurried off as the men walked into town.

Most of the buildings had been damaged in some way, primarily due to blast damage that had destroyed the larger structures. There were some people present, mostly men and the elderly, but no women or children. One of the men walked up to a man sitting on the curb. His clothes were torn, and the edges were burned. He was splattered with blood and dirt as he sat staring at what little remained of his house.

Anzillu knelt beside him and asked, "What happened here?" He already knew but still needed to hear it.

"Those animals landed here, right there, and on the other side of town." The man pointed with a shaky hand. "They just grabbed my wife and daughter and all the other women and children in town and threw them in their ship with no regard for them and took off." The man sobbed.

Anzillu patted him on the shoulder, "I am sorry."

The man sniffed. "About ten minutes later, these long pointed ships flew low over the town and just started bombing the town. They had no reason to. They got what they came for."

The man broke down and sobbed while the others huddled around him.

Anzillu knelt closer, "I have to ask you a question."

The man nodded.

"Where are the resistance fighters located? We are trying to get to their base, which we thought was here," Anzillu asked.

The man composed himself and looked up at Anzillu, "It is. The base is underground, which is where we would have been, except we came out to gather what little food remained. Those animals knew it. They were waiting for us."

"So the Ineans know the base is here?" Anzillu asked.

"I would assume so. Maybe now they will leave it alone since they have bombed the town," the man said.

"How do we get in the base?"

"How many are you?" the man asked.

"About thirty of us," Anzillu stated.

"I will show you," he said, getting up slowly to his feet. With wobbly legs, he guided Anzillu and his men across the town towards a building that had been toppled. Bricks, stone blocks, glass, splintered wood, and other debris were scattered in piles that had been a library, but now the books were scattered with pages blowing about in the light breeze. They picked at the debris, clearing a path to a pair of steel double doors. They pried them open and were greeted by several marines with guns. The marines had been clearing a path from their end and had reached the doors at the same time.

"We are here to join with you," Anzillu said to the lead marine, who wore a black uniform with his face painted black.

"How many?"

"We have about thirty, including the younger daughter of Ur," Anzillu said.

"Everyone has to train to fight, no exceptions, including princesses. Understood?" the marine stated sternly.

"Yes, they are all prepared to fight," Anzillu said.

"Go, get them and bring them back here."

Anzillu dispatched two of his men to gather the others and bring them back while the marine led them into the tunnel that took them at least a hundred pana underground. They entered a long, wide corridor made of concrete reinforced with thick steel girders. Along the corridor were several doors, each guarded by two heavily armed marines who snapped to attention as they passed. No doubt the marine they had met was in authority. All of them wore black with no insignia or rank showing. They walked for quite a distance and then came to two large steel blast doors. The marines standing guard saluted and swung the heavy doors open. Inside was the Eastern Command Center. Dozens of people sat at computer consoles tracking the Inean movements and displayed the information on large screens along the walls. Up above on a balcony was their leader, General Rhanna, watching the displays on the walls, which showed the Inean ships in orbit, along with cities taken by the Ineans in red and colored charts showing Inean presence in each city around the planet. Anzillu and the others looked around in awe of what they saw.

General Rhanna walked down to the lower level and greeted the newcomers. He was a stocky man in his fifties with a graying short-cut beard. He extended his hand to Anzillu. "I am General Rhanna. This is the Eastern Command Center Akhkharu. We welcome all who wish to fight."

Anzillu saluted and then shook the General's hand. "Pleased to meet you, General. I am Anzillu. I was in the army several years ago, and remember who you are."

"Army? Well, we need everyone who can pull a trigger, including ruling party princesses," he said as he walked up to Enanatuma.

She could tell by the tone of his voice that he did not like her or what she represented. "I am Enanatuma, and I do not agree with my father on anything. If I did, then I would be on one of those transports going Kur knows where," she said while staring at the General.

"Good, that is good. The last thing we need is a prissy pants little princess..."

"I – AM – NOT – A – PRINCESS!" she stated firmly.

He grinned at her. "We will need to toughen you up some," he said while poking her in the shoulder, causing her to step back. "Yes, we will." He walked about and studied each person. None of them were up to his minimal standards, but they were all he had. He turned to one of his other officers. "Captain, take these people and clean them up. Get them some food and a dry place to sleep." He turned back to the group, "Tomorrow, you start training to fight these animals that have taken our world." He waved them off and went back up the steps. "Anzillu, come up here."

"Yes, sir!" Anzillu went up to the second level with the general and discussed how they had escaped the Ineans.

The next day, right at daybreak, Anzillu and his travelers were issued black uniforms and weapons. Then, they were taken outside and taught how to use the guns. Enanatuma was the first up, according to the captain. She picked up the gun and removed the safety. She aimed at a target set up against an abandoned house and pulled the trigger. The recoil from the gun knocked her on her rear end, and everyone laughed.

"Ha, ha, ha. Go ahead, laugh," she huffed and got up from the dirt while brushing the dirt from her pants.

"Here, you need to plant your feet like so," Anzillu said. He turned to the others. "This way, you won't fall over, and you will be able to hit your target. Try again. And I do not know why all of you are laughing. Half of you would still be on your backs."

She planted her feet and pulled the trigger. This time, she sprayed the target with dozens of bullets.

"Very good, you have a good eye. Who is next?"

Later that day, the captain pitted them against one another in hand-to-hand combat. He watched Enanatuma closely as she got knocked down quickly every time. It did not help that he pitted her against one of the larger men. He had enough and stepped between them. "Watch how this is done. When someone twice your size attacks you, you cannot rely on conventional tactics as you would on the playground. You need some moves to nullify your opponent's advantage. Like this." The captain waved the man to attack him, and as he did, he quickly kicked and hit him repeatedly in key spots, dropping him to the ground. "Now you try. Come at me," he said to the girl. She got up to her feet and dusted herself off. She went at him. He knocked her down, and while down, she kicked him as hard as possible in the groin. The captain fell to his knees.

"Like that?" she said while dusting herself off again, trying not to grin too much.

"Yes, perfect," he replied with a pained voice. "Time for dinner."

FIFTEEN

ZUTTARA COMMANDED his convoy to stop as they approached Utuk. He studied the area, which was densely wooded, and decided it was a good place to set up camp. "We will camp here for the evening. Once it gets dark, we will climb up Ziusudra hill and study Utuk. From there, we will come up with a plan to take the town."

"Take the town?" Puabi asked.

"Yes, General Asar wants us to capture an Inean and see what it takes to make them talk."

Gula spoke up, "I look forward to giving them a taste of their own medicine."

Puabi pushed her door open and grabbed her automatic rifle. "Yeah, me too," she replied.

"You may get your chance, but first, we need to see how many there are and what we need to take them out," Zuttara said. He opened the door with a creak as he slid out of the truck. "Spread the word to keep quiet and set up camp."

A few hours later, the camp was set, and it was getting dark. Zuttara gathered Gula, Puabi, and three others and headed for the tall hill between them and Utuk.

"We should get a good view of Utuk from the top of Ziusudra. We can count the Ineans and find out where they are," Zuttara said while they walked in full gear with their automatic weapons ready. The journey took a few hours, and they settled just below the crest of the hill. Zuttara motioned for them to pull the camouflaged net over them, and they crawled the rest of the way. Zuttara was first, and he pulled out his binoculars. He moved some brown grass out of the way and began to study the town below. "What the Tari?" he mumbled.

"What is it?" Gula asked, and Zuttara handed him the binoculars. "Oh, my An. Are those people in cages?"

"Yes, they are," Zuttara said, and he set up his camera to record the town into the night. "I don't see anyone wearing red robes."

"Let me see," Puabi asked, and Gula handed her the binoculars. "Those Ineans are so much bigger than we are. Hope we have enough bullets. What is he doing with that woman? Cushak!" she swore softly.

"What is it?" Gula asked her.

She handed him the binoculars, and he took a look. "Is he? Oh, how is it possible?"

"What? Hand that to me!" Zuttara insisted, and he grabbed the binoculars from Gula. "He's raping her. That is what the Ineans do," he replied matter-of-factly.

"But in front of everyone else?" Puabi said in disgust as the years of training she received from the village priest came back to her. She instinctively clutched at her own clothes at the thought. "I want to kill that one."

"You will get your chance. How many are there?" Zuttara said as he panned across the town.

"Why do they do that?" Puabi asked. She was having trouble accepting what the Inean was doing. It was an activity that was nearly unheard of, at least on the Western continent, as it brought public shame and humiliation to rapists who were caught. There were very few jails and prisons on the Western continent because of the way certain crimes were handled. Many would wish to die rather than endure the public humiliation by the priests. Puabi could not imagine what the woman was going through. She assumed the woman was praying to Kur to swiftly take her from this torture; at least, that is what she would do.

"We don't know. It is one of the questions the general wants answered. He wonders if they do this every time they take over a world or just ours," Zuttara said as he studied the scene below. "I count about a dozen of them so far. Napahu, how are your heat signatures coming?"

Napahu was several feet below Zuttara with his portable computer open, which was linked to the camera Zuttara had mounted at the crest of the hill. He studied the data the camera sent the computer. "Pan to the south a few degrees, please."

Zuttara turned the camera a few degrees as he visually studied the village.

"Can you pan to the other way? Now to the north?" Napahu asked as he studied the heat signatures, and the computer began to separate the Ardonnarians from the Ineans. "I count twenty-one alien heat-sigs, sir. Several are in the buildings."

"Can you tag them and track their movements through the night so we can download it to our handhelds for the morning?" Zuttara asked.

"Yes, programming it now. I would need a slightly wider field of view so none fall off the grid."

"Adjusting camera. How's that?"

"Good, let's bury this stuff so no one finds it," Napahu said.

They remained on the hill for a few hours into the night, watching the Ineans and how they interacted with the people down below. All were disgusted. Puabi wanted to vomit at what she had witnessed, and she was visibly shaken.

"Let's head back down to the camp and get some shuteye so we can take the town in the morning," Zuttara said.

They slipped away and headed back to the camp.

That evening, they slept, except for Puabi. All that ran through her mind was the woman getting raped by the alien. She began to doze off, but then she would bring the image back to the front of her mind. Eventually, she slipped off to sleep, and she was reminded of her father telling her and her sister scary stories about the devil, Nergal, coming in the middle of the night to take bad little children for a visit to Tari to give them a taste of the afterlife for bad people. Nergal and his evil Mullas would scare the children. She remembered him laughing after telling the story, which was meant to scare children into behaving. There was nothing to laugh about with these devils, as they tortured and murdered people for their amusement. That was it! She awoke to the realization that what the Ineans did was for their pleasure and amusement. It didn't fit any rule of war that she could comprehend. They were not tortured for information. They were just tortured for fun and left to die in the dirt. She slipped out of her sleeping bag and exited the camouflaged tent to sit by the truck. She laid back in the dry grass and stared at the stars in the moonless, above-freezing night. She pondered what other alien life was out there? Were they like the Ineans or more like her own people? She had a sudden fear for their colonies, especially the ones that relied on frequent deliveries from Ardonnar to survive. It had been over a year now since their transport went down in the ocean, and, to her knowledge, no other missions had gone out to them. The local colonies needed supplies every six months to survive, and there were minimal stockpiles to fall back on. She was concerned about them. She was concerned about the buried base on the moon Anaru. Had they been attacked, or had they escaped the Inean invasion? She stared at the stars and found two of the stars which had their colonies. The third was below the horizon. She finally fell asleep and dreamed of the *ShuBuré* crashing into the ocean.

She awoke to Gula shaking her shoulder. "Puabi, what are you doing out here in the cold?"

"Huh? What?" she said as she rubbed her eyes.

"Why are you out here in the cold?" he asked again.

"I was having weird dreams and came out here to get some fresh air."

"I see. Well, Zuttara wants us to get ready to head into town," he said, holding out a hand for her.

She took his hand and pulled herself up. She brushed herself off and walked with Gula to the command truck. They entered the truck and stood around the table with all the other officers.

"Glad you could make it, sleepy," Zuttara said with a smirk.

"Can't say it was a good night's sleep," she replied with a yawn.

"Are you up for this?" he pried.

"Yes. Let's go kill the Mullas."

"Good name for them," Zuttara said, and he returned to their battle plan, which involved hitting the Ineans from two directions, hoping it would confuse them long enough for them to take the town. "Gula, take your team and come in from this direction here," he pointed at the computer monitor, which displayed a topographical map of the town. "Use the tall grass to hide your approach. I will take the other team and come in from the north here and over the ledge," he stated while pointing at the display. "We should both be in position before midday. We will strike at high noon," he concluded.

"How is their security?" one of the officers asked.

"They don't have any that we can see. They seem fairly lax. I don't think they are expecting our people to put up a fight," Zuttara said. "Your handheld mini-computers are linked to the cameras we placed on the hill, so you will have the positions of the *Mullas,*" he said with a glance toward Puabi, "and our people. Use gas canisters whenever possible, and don't forget the flash-and-bang grenades. We need to see what works and what doesn't, so this is a test that General Asar needs feedback on. Let's get going."

The officers exited the rear of the truck and gathered their teams. Both groups headed out towards the town of Utuk from two directions. Puabi walked with Gula. They were followed by two dozen men as they circled around the hill. They weaved their way through the trees to the valley below while Zuttara took his team around the other side of the hill towards the ledge, which they would have to scale down undetected.

Gula walked beside Puabi, "What kind of dreams did you have?"

"I don't want to talk about it right now," she said as she clutched her automatic in her gloved hands.

"Okay, what do you want to talk about now?"

"Nothing," she said

He shook his head and walked away. He knew there was no prying information out of her. She would talk when she was ready.

Utui rose up from the east amid thin clouds, but thicker clouds were approaching from the west. Rain was coming. After a few hours, Gula's group neared the treeline, and there was a snap of a tree branch ahead of them. Puabi threw her clenched hand up, and everyone stopped, getting down low behind trees.

Gula looked forward, and there was movement ahead. He got down to his stomach and crawled forward to get a better look. Suddenly, a wild sahu rushed out, squealing at them, and one of the officers leveled a gun at the animal. Gula waved him off, and Puabi brought the butt of her automatic down on the animal's skull as it went by her. It squealed in pain and turned on her, and she hit it again. It staggered for a few steps and collapsed.

"Duga!" Gula cursed softly, and he checked his handheld. No Ineans heading their way. He got up, and they resumed their course towards Utuk.

One of the soldiers tied the sahu to a long stick and carried it with help from another soldier. It would be dinner.

Zuttara and his team walked along the open road as it went around the northern side of the hill. Soon, they would head into the trees and towards the town.

They came across several bodies strung up in the trees lining the road. Most likely a warning for whoever would come this way. It was a sign used by the followers of Nergal. Mostly elderly and women hung here. All had been stripped and beaten; all were dead. Some had been hanging for weeks and had succumbed to rot, insects, and Bulkrah. Several of Zuttara's men debated whether they should cut them down or not. Zuttara put an end to the discussion, "We need to focus on our mission. Once we take the town and gather what we came for, then we can cut them down before we move on." They agreed and continued on as they passed the woman who had been raped the day before. Her bloodied body hung from a high branch. Zuttara was glad Puabi did not see this.

After a few hours, Zuttara looked at his handheld display and counted the Ineans. They were all in place. He saw the green dots descending the other side of the hill and knew his other team was making good time as well. They pressed on as the sky clouded over. A slight breeze kicked up from the north, which normally meant snow for this time of year, but not likely this time; it was too warm.

After several minutes, Zuttara's handheld chirped. He held his hand up, and his company stopped while he checked the mini computer. Two Ineans were heading their way. Zuttara motioned for his troops to take cover quickly behind the trees and shrubs off to the side of the road. They watched as two Ineans dragged another bloodied nude body from the town. One had a length of rope coiled over his shoulder, while the other had two large guns hung over his shoulder. They trudged along, dragging another body in the dirt, kicking up dust. One of the Ineans pointed, and they both stopped, dropping the lifeless body of a woman on the road. They saw the boot prints in the dirt and began looking around, both checking their weapons.

Zuttara motioned for two of his men to check their silencers, and he counted down on his fingers from five to zero and the three opened fire on the Ineans with the slightest pop, pop, pop of their quiet automatic guns. The Ineans took several hits, and one managed to fire a shot with his laser, which missed Zuttara by a fraction of an inch. Finally, one Inean went down, and then the other landed on top of him. The shooting stopped, and Zuttara checked his handheld and waited. No more activity heading their way. He exited the bushes with his gun trained on the Ineans, followed by the others. It was their first close-up contact with the aliens.

"They smell bad," one of his officers said softly.

"Make sure they are dead," another said, and he pointed his gun at one of the Ineans head and fired several rounds into the thick skull, splattering his brains on the ground.

"Huh, their blood is blue. Don't Mullas from the fables have blue blood?" one of his other men asked.

"They do," Zuttara said as he knelt down beside one of the Ineans to examine him.

"Thought so," the man replied as he shot the other Inean in the head. "Shouldn't we drive a wooden stake through their hearts instead," he and some of the others laughed.

"Get these bodies off the road in case they come looking for them," Zuttara said as he grabbed an arm. It took several men to move each of the heavy alien bodies. After several minutes, they had cleared the path and headed back towards the town.

Both teams got into position on time, but Zuttara noticed activity in the town. The Ineans knew something was wrong, and several began checking their weapons. Four of them started along the road towards Zuttara, most likely looking for the two Ineans who had not returned. Zuttara had an idea. He flipped open his secured radio, "Gula, come in?"

"Go ahead," Gula whispered over his headset.

"I want your team to attack the town on my command. I'm just waiting for these four to get by us so we can separate them from the main group and take them out," Zuttara said.

"Copy that."

The four Ineans walked past Zuttara and his men and got about twenty pana away when he gave the command. "Go!"

On the other side of the town, Gula and his team had crawled between the buildings and started lobbing grenades at the Ineans. Several others who had positioned themselves in the tall grass opened fire, spraying the Ineans with bullets. The Ineans were confused and did not know which way to fight back.

Zuttara ordered his men to attack as the four Ineans turned to run back to the town. Zuttara's troops opened fire on them as they ran by, dropping the four Ineans in their tracks. Then Zuttara led the charge into the town while the Ineans turned to fight Gula. Many Ineans were dropped from behind and did not know which way to turn. After a few minutes, it was over. All the Ineans were down except for one who crawled on his hands and knees towards a discarded laser rifle. Puabi, who had killed four of the Ineans herself, ran up and kicked the gun away, pressed her gun to the Inean's head, and began to squeeze the trigger.

"No! Not yet," Zuttara yelled as he ran up to her.

The Inean sat up to his knees as blue blood oozed from his leg, arm, and abdomen. Dust and dirt stuck to the blood as it began to dry on his body.

"I need answers from this beast," Zuttara said as he caught his breath from running halfway across the town.

"I will not answer," the Inean grumbled, "kill me now."

"You will answer my questions because I won't let you die until you do."

The Inean spat at him, and Zuttara shot him in the foot.

The Inean howled in pain and fell back.

"Where is your transport craft?" Zuttara asked.

Gula and a few others ran towards Zuttara and Puabi.

The Inean rambled in loud, booming gibberish that was incomprehensible nonetheless.

"So I can understand you!" Zuttara yelled as he kicked the Inean in his injured foot.

The Inean howled again and turned to Zuttara as Gula and Puabi leveled their guns at his head.

"It is hidden in a warehouse in the next town," he replied in a pained voice.

"Which town?" Gula asked.

"I don't know its name," The Inean grumbled from the pain.

"Which way then? How far away?" Zuttara asked.

"That way, maybe a day's walk. But it will be of no use to you," the Inean said as he sat up straight with blood pooling in the dirt around his foot.

"Why is that?" Zuttara asked.

"It requires fingerprint recognition to fly."

"No problem," Puabi said as she withdrew her knife from its holster.

"You really wouldn't do that, would you?" Gula asked.

"Hold out his hand, and I will show you," she said as she gripped the knife firmly.

A woman officer walked up to Zuttara and handed him an Inean book and PDA. "Sir, this might be of interest to you."

He studied the book and PDA with their Inean scribbles, which resembled Chinese. "Where is Gisiga? Someone find him," Zuttara said while he held out his hand to stop Puabi from dismembering the Inean. "Now, just wait a minute," Zuttara said, and he turned back to the Inean. "What are your real plans for our planet."

The Inean laughed. "It is too late for you. We plan to kill all of you and strip mine your planet. The large ships are already on their way here, and when they arrive, we will dismantle your cities and take what we want. If you are lucky, some of you may live as exhibits in our zoos or as slaves for our Emperor, but I doubt it. We are very thorough in our takeovers."

Gisiga joined the three officers. "What is it, Zuttara?" he asked.

Gisiga was a tall, bearded man with longer hair pulled back and tied into a ponytail. He had his automatic slung over his shoulder, along with a portable computer and a host of other scientific instruments. At any other time, he would be surrounded by computer monitors in some locked-away secret facility cracking the latest security codes. However, he now worked for General Asar in the field, cracking Inean codes with the hope of stealing a ship.

Zuttara handed him the book and PDA. "Can you interpret these?"

Gisiga flipped through the book, "I think so. I have new software that Antum transmitted to my portable that is supposed to translate this crap into Ardo."

The Inean growled at him.

"Fine. Get on it," Zuttara stated.

Gisiga saluted and walked away while flipping through the book.

Zuttara turned back to the Inean. "What do you mean by 'it is too late for us?'" he asked as his stomach turned.

"We occupy every major city on your planet, and as you can see here, we occupy many smaller towns. Your military is fragmented, and your leadership is nonexistent. There is no hope for you. Each one of us you kill equals a million of your people."

Puabi struck him in the head with the butt of her gun. "Liar!" she screamed.

"Puabi, stop!" Zuttara yelled as she struck him again.

"That one has fire. Let's make a trade. I will give you the information you want in exchange for her," the Inean laughed as blue blood trickled down the side of his head.

"Why do you rape the women?" Puabi demanded while she fought the urge to kill him.

"For our pleasure. If you knew what someone like you would bring at the auction on Inea, I'm sure your Commander would sell you the first chance he got," the Inean then laughed.

"Is that where all the women have been disappearing to?" Zuttara asked.

"I've lost count of the thousands that have been sold as slaves back home." The Inean laughed again. "It has been very profitable for our emperor."

"We have what we came for. Kill him and cut off his hands," Zuttara said, and he turned away.

"How's this for fire?" Puabi said while gritting her teeth. She pulled the trigger of her automatic, and his head splattered everywhere. His body thumped to the ground in a cloud of dirt. She hung the gun over her shoulder, pulled out her knife, and severed his hands. "Get me a bag to put these disgusting paws in."

One of the other officers handed her a clear bag, and she dropped the severed hands in the bag. "Let's go find this ship," she snarled while kicking dirt on the Inean. He was the one she wanted. He was the one that raped the woman Zuttara's team found hung in a tree dead earlier, and now a woman had killed him. Justice, she said to herself.

"We will head out in the morning," Gula said. He went to say something else to her but decided not to. It was likely that she might shoot him in her frame of mind. So he walked away to free the people in the cages and find clothing for them to wear. Puabi followed him, and as she looked up, she noticed that many of the people they were saving looked at her with wide eyes. They were afraid of her, and then she realized why. Her hands were covered in blue blood. The front of her uniform was covered in blue blood along with bits of his skull, brains, and clumps of coarse hair. In her hand was the bag with the Inean hands. She thought she had become one of them. It did not bother her one bit, killing them until now. She went and washed her hands, and helping the people cleared her mind.

Zuttara sat with the leaders of the town and told them about the bodies hanging in the trees just outside of town. The townspeople said they would cut them down and bury them. That evening, they all feasted on the wild sahu as hundreds of people who remained thanked Zuttara and his teams for saving them. Several children sat with him while he was toasted by the town's leader. "Small victory in a much larger war," the leader said.

They clinked the glasses of wine.

Puabi sat off to the side, poking a stick into the fire and watching the sparks fly into the sky. Gula kept an eye on her. No one from the town would talk to her as she had crossed the line with the Inean. A few hours later, a young girl walked up to Puabi and placed her hand on her shoulder. "Why are you sad?" the girl asked.

Puabi looked up at her as a tear streaked down her cheek. She sniffed. "I've become one of them."

"Don't be sad. Look, you saved us. If you did not come when you did, those beasts would have killed all of us," the girl stated. "Or worse."

"I don't like what I did. I don't think Kur does either," Puabi said, and another tear rolled down her cheek.

"Kur said, 'Anyone who hurts one of his children deserves death and to spend eternity in Tari,'" the girl said. She sat beside Puabi, took the stick from her, and poked at the fire as well. It began to sprinkle.

"Yes, but..."

"You saved us, and that beast is in Tari right now. You did the will of Kur," the girl said.

Puabi threw her arms around the girl and hugged her. "How do you know so much at a young age?"

"My father is the priest of the town," the girl said. "Come, meet him." The girl tossed the stick on the fire, then took Puabi's hand and guided her back to the celebration. She introduced her to the priest.

The next morning, Zuttara and his platoon continued west in search of the Inean transport. Along the way, Gula approached Puabi. "Are you all right?"

"Yes, I have never killed with such hatred before, and regardless if they were animals or not, it did bother me," she replied.

"But today?"

"I'm fine. Don't worry. When it comes time to do it again, I still would not hesitate. The little girl was right. The Mullas need to die and go to Tari."

Gula patted her on the shoulder and walked up to the truck. He slid in and waited for her to slide in as well. Once inside, Zuttara gave the order to move out, and the trucks drove off.

SIXTEEN

ACROSS THE PLANET, word spread about how the Ineans had taken control of nearly every city and the government. Horror stories of slave camps and murderous rampages made it around the planet via the airwaves, underground print, and word of mouth. Small rebellions erupted around the globe as the Ardonnarians chose to fight the Ineans for their planet. Most of the rebellions were quickly put down, but some were well-organized and were able to push back against the Ineans.

Damok-Sai sat in his office in Delondra, overlooking the public square, as his top advisers scolded him for the changes in his plans over the past year. He was beginning to wonder if he had made a mistake.

"Commander, our troops grow weary of these rebels. They strike in the middle of the night, they strike during foul weather, and at times when we are most unprepared. It seems like they know when to strike. We need to make an example of them soon before his Emperor's finest fighters start dying in large numbers," one of his field commanders stated.

A different field commander spoke up. "They *are* dying, Commander. We lost over twenty a few days ago in the town of

Utuk, which is northwest of here. Rumor has it that they are massing and planning a bigger attack on Delondra itself."

Damok-Sai turned and faced them. "The Emperor has made it clear he wants us to cultivate this treasure and send him and the council thousands more before we destroy these people. The few lives lost is a small price to pay for the Emperor's pleasure."

"We have sent over twenty thousand back to Inea. How many more does he want?" the first field commander asked with a snarl.

Damok-Sai faced him and growled. "To be blunt, the Emperor stands to make a mighty large profit from them. Once word got out on our home world about the Ardo females, we can't ship them quick enough. Besides, the children of this race are working out well in the fields and mines back home. No Inean needs to suffer in those mines again."

"But Commander, we understand that, but we are wasting time waiting."

"Wasting *your* time, not the Emperor's. These Ardon slaves are bringing in over ten thousand denars each!" Damok-Sai emphasized.

"That's more than a month's wage for many of our people!" exclaimed one of the field commanders.

"That is right. Many have considered setting up an outpost here, where our people can come for sport. Kill the men and capture the women. Several in the council are pushing this plan, and the Emperor is considering it," Damok-Sai stated harshly to his underlings.

"That is not consistent with our mission. My warriors are dying while you propose a tourist colony. That is ridiculous, Commander!" another field commander exclaimed.

"I don't care what you think. It is the Emperor's call right now, and the call is to send him a loaded ship a day to satisfy the cravings back home," Damok-Sai snarled while reaching for his knife.

"To satisfy the Emperor's deep coffers more likely," said another.

Damok-Sai lunged across the table and grasped the field commander, pushing him out of his chair. The chair went flying as they landed on the floor. Damok-Sai pushed himself up and glared at the field commander as he sat up as well. Any concerns he had about his decisions to hold off leveling the planet were gone now. "We will have no more denigration of our Emperor!" He growled while pressing his jagged knife to the Ineans throat. "Understand?"

"Yes, Commander," the field officer hissed back.

Damok-Sai pushed him away and looked around the room. "This goes for all of you. You have your orders. Fight them off while filling your quotas. Now get out of here."

The officers got up and left the room in haste. Several minutes later, the transports lifted off from the pavement outside the glass building with a roar that shook the building and took them to their bases on different parts of the planet.

SEVENTEEN

ZUTTARA and his team entered the town of Magam, which appeared to have been deserted in haste. Doors flapped in the light breeze while trash blew about the streets as the wind and cold, light rain continued to blow in from the northwest. Gula took a team into a few of the homes on the way. One home still had a meal set at the family table. The insects were having a feast now, but he wondered what chased these people out of town with apparently no warning. Another home still had laundry blowing in the backyard on rope lines running from the house to a pole on the far side. They held their scanners out and detected only small animal life but no people or Ineans.

Gula turned to Zuttara. "What do you think happened to them?"

"Hopefully, they got away, but I suspect the Ineans got to them," Zuttara said while scanning another building.

"Usually, they take the women and children and leave the men, but there are no bodies," another in their group stated.

"Then I hope they got out in time," Zuttara said as he began walking deeper into the town.

Gula spoke while he looked at the clouds thickening from the northwest. "There is no evidence to support either."

"We don't have time to investigate. We have to stick to our mission before the Ineans get wind of what we are doing," Zuttara stated with firmness in his voice that ended the conversation instantly.

They entered larger buildings in search of the Inean transport but did not find anything on this side of town except supplies: cargo container after cargo container of food, clothing, portable generators, and every other imaginable necessity. Gula studied the labels and turned to Zuttara, "These were destined for Belit-Sheri."

"What is the ship date?" Zuttara asked.

"These were to be shipped the twelfth of Alme last year," Gula said.

"Six months ago. At that time, it may have helped," Puhrum said while leaning in to read the label.

Gula turned towards Zuttara. "We should take as much of this as we can to Antum."

"On our way out."

They reached the Akkad River and stopped. The Akkad River flowed from the western mountains twelve hundred zag away to Delondra and emptied into the ocean there. Zuttara looked upriver and then downriver; all bridges crossing the river had been collapsed into the raging water. Water flowed through and over the debris at a fairly good clip, even though the river was much lower than normal for this time of year.

Puabi winced at the icy cold rain hitting her in the face, prompting her to flip up her collar to block some of it. "Why would they blow the bridges?" she asked, gripping her automatic rifle while walking with her team to the edge of the river. They all looked upriver at the remains of the largest bridge.

"We don't know who blew them; it could have been the towns-people for all we know," Zuttara said. He tried to scan for heat signatures on the other side of the river. "If that ship is here, it has to be in one of those buildings."

"As long as the Inean was telling the truth," Puabi mumbled, but loud enough for Zuttara to hear.

"Oh, it's here all right. We need to get across this river before dark," Zuttara stated, and he turned to Gula. "Back in that warehouse," he turned and pointed to the large brick structure, "I saw some portable floating boat docks. We could string them together and get back and forth."

"I'll get right on it." Gula then turned to one of his officers, "Dingar! Take your men and bring the open trucks to that warehouse."

The men raced back up the hill to retrieve the trucks for Gula, and Gula turned towards Zuttara, "When we are done here, make sure we load the trucks and carriers to their limit with these supplies."

Zuttara stared into the cold mist blowing from the northwest. "Yes, we should. Let's find that Inean ship first before they find us. There is no doubt the Ineans know what we did to them in Utuk and are probably looking for us."

Utui was a faint glow through the clouds as it inched towards the western horizon while Gula and his men finished the rickety bridge. The first team, walking single file, went across carefully while the makeshift bridge swayed and creaked from the water flowing against it. The next team tightened the bridge and crossed it while the other two teams stayed behind to guard the vehicles.

Puabi joined Zuttara, Gula, and Gisiga as they walked along the street. Zuttara was studying his scanner, which he held up at eye level and swept from side to side. He was looking for the distinct signature of an Inean power supply. He got a blip, and then it was gone. He could not make it do it again. Puabi looked at Zuttara. "It beeped when you held it that way." She said while pointing up the next hill to a large building halfway up the street, which was littered with abandoned vehicles and other debris.

"Has to be a half zag away," Zuttara replied.

Puabi began to lean towards the direction of the large building. "I'm sure it was that direction. It did beep only for an instant, though,"

Zuttara looked at Puabi. "All right, let's check it out."

They walked towards the warehouse while Zuttara held out his scanner. He was beginning to have doubts until the scanner beeped again. Now, he was sure they were heading in the right direction. After about twenty minutes, they approached two large doors, big enough for an Inean transport. Dingar walked up to the door and cut the lock off with large bolt cutters. The lock and heavy chain clinked to the ground. Each of them turned on their handheld lights and entered the dark building. Soon, they stood in awe of the ship before them. It was not a transport. It was a sleek-looking, long-range craft, judging by its engines.

Zuttara turned and faced his people, "Gisiga, Gula, and Puabi, get on that ship. The rest of you set up a perimeter in case the Ineans show up, and they might once we get tinkering."

Gula walked towards the ship first, looking for the hatch, while Gisiga studied the writing on the craft and compared them to his notebook.

"Where's the door?" Gula asked.

Gisiga studied the words on the side of the ship, which were displayed on his handheld computer. "I think this is it," Gisiga said. "I think you press this."

When he did, a touchpad on the side of the hatch lit up, defined by a thin green line that now outlined the hatch. The pad had a dozen Inean symbols, which resembled Chinese symbols, arranged in four rows of three. Gisiga consulted his notes and pressed six of the buttons. There was a hiss, and the door swung open.

Puabi walked up first. "How did you know what the code was?"

"Stupid Inean wrote it down on the inside cover of his instruction manual."

"Good for us. Ooh, *what* is that smell?" She exclaimed as she wrinkled her nose while stepping up into the craft.

Gula sniffed and gagged on the Inean stench. "I don't think I want to know."

They entered the craft. The lights came on in their bright yellow, and then the heat started with a puff of steam from the vents. Other systems turned on and began humming as they walked forward. Zuttara entered the ship while looking around as his scanner recorded everything it could.

Puabi sat in the large hard seat meant for an Inean's large body. Her feet did not touch the floor when she sat, and this made her feel like a child sitting in her parent's chair. It was metal and uncomfortable as she tried to fit herself into it. She gave up and began studying the controls when Gisiga showed up. He removed a roll of paper tape and a marker from his backpack and began ripping small strips of tape, sticking them to the control panel. Then he consulted his computer as he entered the words on the display. "This one is thrust," he said as the marker squeaked on the tape. "This one is lift. These controls are the vertical thrusters. These are the steering thrusters. This is the guidance system." On and on he went until everything on the control panels was labeled.

Zuttara stepped on the craft and went forward. "We need to get this craft off the ground as soon as possible. There is another CME coming in from Utui, and we can use it as a screen to get this out of here."

"And take it where?" Gula asked.

"Anaru base."

"You want me to fly this in space?" Puabi asked while spinning around to face Zuttara. "I thought we were going to Antum?"

"No, Anaru base. You have about an hour to learn this craft and get it off the ground. I received a message from Antum that the Ineans have moved all their ships behind the planet. We have a clear shot out of here. In one hour," Zuttara stated.

"You have to be kidding me. It will take more than an hour to learn this craft," Puabi muttered.

"You have your orders. One hour, I want this ship out of here," Zuttara said.

Zuttara turned his back to her and left the ship.

"This ought to be fun," Gula said to Puabi.

Gisiga leaned forward. "It won't be bad. All we have to do is program the guidance system, and it will take us there."

"Oh, is that all?" Puabi said sarcastically.

"Watch," he said. He pressed a symbol on the panel, and a

menu opened on the screen. He entered some Inean commands and pressed another button, and the screen lit up in their language.

"Wow! They had our language programmed in here all the time?" Gula asked.

"Yes, I think this was an advanced scout ship that studied us before the invasion. There may be a wealth of useful information stored here. But our scientists will have to get that. Our job is to deliver this craft to Anaru."

They worked for their hour while the craft was loaded with numerous supplies taken from the town's warehouse.

Zuttara returned. "Time is up. The storm is about to strike, so it is now or never, Commander Puabi."

"Get everyone away from here just in case," Gula said, and they buckled in and began their preflight checklist, Inean style.

One of Zuttara's officers raced onto the craft. "Sir?" he said, out of breath. "Ineans coming this way. More than a hundred of them," he panted.

"How soon will they be here?" Zuttara asked as he walked towards him.

"Ten minutes at best," the man said, recovering his breath finally.

"We will fall back a hundred ima. Start your launch in six minutes." Zuttara raced away with several officers after him. "Relay to the troops to set up in those buildings to ambush them when they get here," he said to his officers while he studied the handheld scanner displaying the Ineans coming their way.

Gisiga instructed Puabi on programming the Inean flight computer, and after six minutes, she fired the engines. The craft lifted slowly and floated a few feet above the ground. She entered the following commands, which sent the ship crashing backward into the rear wall of the large building.

"Cushik!" she swore and entered in new commands. "Duga sa Tari!"

"Easy. Here, try this," Gisiga entered a few more commands, and the craft lurched forward and crashed through the large doors and then floated outside. They were now in the open. She pressed another command, and the craft took off toward space at incredible speed, pressing them against the seats. After a few minutes, they were engulfed in the fireball that was striking the planet. Then, the craft turned and flew towards the outer moon Anaru. The craft raced outward from the planet and closed in on Anaru. It entered orbit in just a few hours. The tail end of the fireball began to pass the planet. It was hot on the Inean ship as the cooling system struggled with the conditions they were flying in. Soon, they flew close to the moon and circled around to the back side, which was partially lit by the star. Puabi manually set the craft down while Gula contacted the base to open the doors. There was no verbal reply, but the large doors slid open enough for the craft to enter. Puabi then guided the ship into the military base, which was buried in the side of a deep crater. She brought the craft to a stop while the large doors closed and the flight deck pressurized.

Several minutes passed as scientists in pressure suits walked around the Inean ship, taking notes. And then one took his helmet off and gave them the thumbs up. Puabi was first out of her seat, followed by Gula and a rather ill Gisiga. Gula patted him on the back, "Good job, first time in space?"

"Yes," he moaned.

Gula helped Gisiga to his feet. "You will get used to it soon enough. Let's go."

"I'm not sure if it was the flight or the stench of this ship?"

Gula laughed. "Good point."

Puabi fumbled with the hatch controls, and the hatch finally opened with a hiss of its air controls. All three stepped out onto the cold flight deck of the moon base. They looked around at the immense facility. Dozens upon dozens of ships parked here of several varieties each: short-range fighters, long-range fighters, transports, cargo ships, and science ships. All parked in rows, stretching into the deep cavern hollowed out in the moon.

General Innin walked up to them, and they all snapped to attention. "Commander Gula, Commander Puabi, Specialist Gisiga, welcome to Anaru. The people of Ardonnar owe you a great debt right now. I sense a turn in this war by bringing us this craft."

"I certainly hope so. I hope there are no tracking beacons on this craft," Gula stated while getting accustomed to the lighter gravity of the moon. "Were we detected by the Ineans?"

The General glanced at the ship. "We don't think so. The solar storm raises Tari with both our sensors and theirs. Lucky for us."

Gisiga leaned in after his stomach settled down some. "I turned the tracking beacons off. I hope!"

"Praise Kur," Puabi stated, and she bowed down to the deck. The others followed her lead and then got back up.

Holding out his hand to guide them off the flight deck, Innin said, "Let me take you to our command center while our scientists take this thing apart."

"What is the plan now, sir," Gula asked the General.

"We hope to study their high-speed engines and adapt them to our ships. Then, we hope to send our ships to their planet and destroy it."

"Destroy their planet? Why don't we fight them here?" Puabi asked.

"Good question, but not practical. They control everything, and our forces are scattered. If we bomb them back home, then they may withdraw troops to deal with that and give us a chance to gather our troops in the field and fight them here," the General said while walking towards two guards blocking a door at the far end of the corridor. They snapped to attention as the general and his guests arrived at the door. Then, the guards stepped to the sides to allow the general to enter the room with Puabi, Gula, and one other guard. Gisiga remained at the craft, with the scientists still complaining about the stench and their stomachs.

"Bold plan, and it assumes a lot," Gula said while looking around the base control room.

"Too many assumptions if you ask me. Way too much can go wrong, or we run out of time, but it is what we have right now," the General said. "Here is our control center. From here, we have been studying the Ineans for several months and have learned an enormous amount of information."

"Impressive," said Puabi. "And they don't know about this place at all?"

"Either they don't know or don't care. They are quite arrogant about certain things, and they are lax in security," the General stated as they watched the CME exit the area. "Silent mode people." And the lights dimmed. "They are careless, and some would even credit the Ineans with being reckless."

"That's because they don't consider us a threat, General," Puabi said.

"I hope that changes," Gula said while he studied the information scrolling on one of the computer terminals.

"We all do, but not yet. I want those ships retrofitted and loaded with our latest urukii bombs."

Gula lifted his head at that and looked at the General. "Are those the multi-warhead ones?"

"Yes, and they each pack quite the punch."

"Those are the planet busters, right?" Puabi asked.

"Yes," replied the General.

"I want to pilot the first ship there and deliver one myself," she added.

"You might get that chance, Commander."

"Great. I can't wait," she said.

Puabi began studying another computer terminal while Gula walked over to join her.

EIGHTEEN

ON THE EASTERN CONTINENT, Anzillu crouched behind a loosely stacked pile of cut logs as he swept his scanner from side to side. He signaled to the rest of the group how many Ineans were patrolling around the transport that had landed several hours before. He would wait for dark to attack. The Ineans hated to be attacked when it was dark. Rumor had it their star was brighter, and their eyes could not adapt to the nights here on Ardonnar, especially when the two moons reflected minimal light from Utui. He hoped it was true.

He heard a noise and glanced through a hole in the loose pile of logs. An Inean soldier was walking his way. Was he spotted? He did not know, but the Inean was focused on the woodpile. He slid his gun through a space between the logs and waited. The Inean made it to the pile and looked towards the trees not too far away. He looked down as he began to urinate on the logs and saw Anzillu. The Inean went to point his gun, but Anzillu fired several shots into the Inean's groin. The beast howled out in pain and slumped. Anzillu fired two more shots into his head, and the beast collapsed the rest of the way to the ground.

However, the Inean's howls got the attention of other Ineans working on the transport. They placed their tools on the ground, grabbed their laser rifles, and started towards the woodpile. Anzillu waited. Then, there was gunfire from the trees behind him as a few of his group opened fire, cutting the Ineans down before they could get a shot off.

Anzillu checked his scanner and ran back towards the trees. He crouched down next to two of his team. The young girl, Enanatuma, had a grin on her face while a light smoke rose up from the barrel of her gun. "Nice shooting," Anzillu said as they watched the area for any more activity.

Enanatuma fixed her camouflaged netting and crouched back down in the leaves while pointing her rifle toward the Inean ship. "Thanks. It felt good to kill them after what they must have done to my friend."

Anzillu studied her as she crouched down, wondering if vengeance would lead her to do something reckless and put the lives of his team in jeopardy. He laid in the leaves and pulled some over him. "I know you want to kill them, but you scare me."

"I scare you?" she said softly while turning to him.

"Yes, you are a loose cannon. Likely to go off at any time and possibly at the worst time. I need you to control your anger if you want to help us," Anzillu said.

Anzillu turned from her when he saw movement by the Inean ship.

"I won't get you killed if that is what worries you," she whispered as she glanced forward again.

"It is what worries me, and I worry about the others." He tapped her shoulder and pointed. "Hush, others are coming," he whispered.

Anzillu and the others in his group quieted. They watched as a half dozen Ineans walked towards the transport. They spied the bodies and took cover behind a couple of crates of food supplies, which they had no intention of delivering to the city. Others crouched behind the landing gear of the transport and looked around for the attackers. After a few minutes, half of the Ineans broke away and circled around the transport. Anzillu knew what they were doing. The Ineans were trying to circle around and hit them from the rear, so he sent half of his group, eight people, in the opposite direction to come in behind the first group of Ineans still crouching by the building. Anzillu lobbed a grenade in the direction of the Ineans, and his people were off when it exploded. He opened fire, as did Enanatuma and Eridu. More grenades were tossed. The smoke and noise ensured the eight people got away and took up a position behind the Ineans and began shooting at them from behind. Anzillu and the group he had left with him turned around and attacked the Ineans, who were attempting to surprise Anzillu's group from behind. The Ineans ended up being the ones surprised, and all fell in a shower of bullets and shrapnel from the grenades tossed by Anzillu. The noise died down, and Anzillu looked around and then checked his scanner. He accounted for his people and two Ineans barely alive. He crawled out and checked the three they shot. One was reaching for his laser rifle. Eridu held her rifle to his scaly gray scalp and pulled the trigger. Blue blood splattered about with bits of bone, hair, and pieces of his brain. He dropped into the dirt, dead. Enanatuma did the same for the others to make sure they stayed dead. He heard gunshots from behind him, and the rest of his team finished the Ineans on the other side.

They regrouped by the transport and studied it.

"Urbat, get the urukii and mount it to this craft before others come back," Anzillu stated.

Urbat bowed and waved to his men, and they followed him. After several minutes, they rolled up in an old, open diesel truck that puffed smoke. In the back was a coffin-sized object wrapped in a tarp. They uncovered the device. It took eight of them to drag it out from the truck and to the Inean transport. They struggled to drag it under the rear of the transport. Then, Urbat drilled holes into the hull and bolted the straps to the hull. Once all the straps were in place, he tightened them, which lifted the device tight against the hull.

"Ineans are coming!" Enanatuma yelled.

Anzillu took the scanner from her to confirm. "She's right. Quick, cover that up with leaves and get these bodies out of here."

They hurried away, diving behind the trees and covering themselves with leaves and their camouflaged nets. The Ineans returned and looked around. One was speaking into a radio, but it appeared there was no response. They growled among themselves and entered the transport.

Several minutes passed, and Utui was beginning to set when the transport's engines ignited. The craft lifted off the ground, blowing leaves around, and it flew off with the nuclear bomb strapped securely to its belly. Once it was out of range, Anzillu sent a short text message to General Rhanna at the base in Akhkharu. "Package delivered." They waited until he got his confirmation. His PDA beeped, and he glanced at it. "Received" was what it said. He cleared it and guided his troops away to their next destination.

NINETEEN

DAGAN RACED down a long corridor with dozens of people running ahead of her. She had an automatic rifle in her hands, and several loaded magazines clipped to her belt. She flipped the hood of her robe down and spun around, firing the gun at several Ineans chasing after them. Several of them fell while more charged after her. She turned and ran as a laser blast sizzled by her head and blew a hole in the rock not far from her. Bits of rock flew out at her, and she had to cover her face for a second. She quickly turned and fired several more blasts blindly at them as an Inean caught her and tossed her against the rock wall of the tunnel. She slid to the ground as her gun tumbled away. The Inean grabbed her with one hand around her neck and dragged her up to her feet. He pinned her against the side of the tunnel and began to tear at her robe as she choked. He stopped suddenly as she jabbed a large knife into his abdomen and began lifting the knife to his ribs. He released his grip on her neck, and she slid back down to the floor. The Inean staggered away and collapsed. She had no time to catch her breath as more Ineans charged down the corridor. She lunged at her rifle, rolled on the floor, and began shooting until the clip was empty. She fumbled with another clip and clicked it in place as two Ineans were just about to grab her. She fired several rounds into them as a hand gripped her collar and pulled her away as the Ineans fell where she had been.

General Asar wrapped his arm around her and guided her down the corridor as they both fired over their shoulders. She could hear the engines of the transports winding up, and she was out of time. Smoke floated off the barrel of her rifle, and a red light was flashing, which meant it was overheating. Suddenly, the gun jammed, and she tossed it aside. More laser pulses snapped into the rock wall, spraying her with rock and dust. She reached into her pocket and pulled out a grenade. She pulled the pin and tossed it over her shoulder. Then she woke up, turned on the light in her room, and looked around. She thumped back down in the bed as her heart pounded.

President Aanepada sat at the head of a large table with Dagan beside him. General Asar described their plans to destroy the Inean home world.

Asar was standing. "The scientists on Anaru believe we can adapt the Inean technology from the interstellar transport we stole from the warehouse in Magam to our interstellar transport ships and use them to deliver multiple urukii warheads to the planet of Inea."

"What purpose would that serve?" Dagan asked as she sat with her hood down, exposing her long, blond hair. It was unusual for a priestess to be out in public with her hood down, but she had been bending the rules a bit here and a bit there to the annoyance of the higher priests at the base. Some thought, including Aanepada, that she did it intentionally for that purpose. Many of the priests were the same ones who tried to keep her out of Kur's training in the Great Temple of Kurah in Kurdash years before. Now, she had surpassed them in understanding the teachings.

Asar looked at her. "We are hoping that the Ineans will fall back to their home planet to aid their own people. This would give us time to reclaim our planet and prepare for their return."

Aanepada nodded. "Makes sense. From what we have gathered from listening to their radio transmissions, their society is very structured with a sense of loyalty at all levels we have identified."

"Don't they have other colonies to draw resources from?" Dagan asked with a glance toward Aanepada, who placed his hand on hers in a silent plea to let the military people ask questions.

"We have limited information on their colonies. We have identified three of them with a significant number of Ineans on them. And there are several others which are mainly mining colonies, much like what they want to set up on our planet. Based on the information available, the mining colonies have no military presence, with protection provided directly by Inea. The three main colonies don't appear to have much to offer back to the home planet, but we don't know enough about them yet."

Dagan continued to quiz the general. "What are we looking at for a time frame? The Ineans have control of almost everything here now. This would have to be a plan implemented very soon to have any hope of success."

"That is correct," Asar stated. "It will take us nearly two years to outfit our ships for this and to train crews to fly them. We have many warheads already on Anaru and Uggae, plus whatever we send them from here. It will also take us time to gather and transport the required supplies to the moons. We need to bomb them with everything we can to inflict the damage we think we need to draw them away."

"Can our people hold out for that long? Thousands are dying with each report we receive. There may not be enough of us to fight when the time comes." Dagan drilled on as Aanepada tightened his grip on her hand.

There was a murmuring around the room about Dagan asking questions, and Asar looked about the room. "These are very good questions, people." He glanced back down at his notes. "It will have to do. I can't think of a better plan," and he glanced at Dagan and wondered if she had one. This time, she met his stare and said nothing.

"What do you need from us, General Asar?" Aanepada asked.

"We need both sides working towards this goal. I have been in contact with General Rhanna in the east, and they are working to disrupt the Ineans as best as possible on the ground. They are working on taking out some of their large ships in orbit as we speak by planting urukii warheads on their transports, which are set to explode when returning to the large ships in orbit."

There was a knock at the door, and a lieutenant entered the room and walked up to General Asar with a nod towards Aanepada. "Excuse me, sir, Captain Zuttara and his group have arrived from Magam with supplies. They have several injured with them."

"Thank you, Lieutenant, we will be there shortly," Asar said.

The lieutenant bowed and exited the room.

"Are there any other questions?" Asar asked with a glance and winked towards Dagan.

She smiled slightly and turned from his gaze.

"Then let's tend to our injured and get Zuttara's report."

Dagan then stood and pulled her hood over her head, and spoke the words of Kur to dismiss the meeting.

Dagan went with the high priests to say the final words over the dead, but she was not allowed to speak. She was only allowed to assist, albeit minimally. This irritated her. However, she managed to find the strength to keep her mouth shut this time.

Aanepada walked with General Asar and wanted to make sure it was their best plan.

"It is, Mister President. I wish we had another one."

"I want to apologize for Dagan," Aanepada said softly.

"Don't, sir, she has fire and a desire to see us succeed. I don't see that in our other priests, which I am guessing is why she is turning many of their rules upside down."

"You've noticed?"

Asar stopped and looked him in the eyes, "Many have noticed

and side with her. They see her as the spiritual leader they refuse to be."

"I see."

"Don't be threatened by her. She looks up to you and follows you. I'm the one who should be afraid of her," he laughed, and they continued walking to the command and control section.

TWENTY

DAMOK-SAI STOOD with his back to the large windows as he snarled to his local commanders. "What took you so long to get to our transport in Magam?"

"Damok-Sai, we can explain," one of them said.

"Explain! There is nothing to explain about your failure in this situation. I gave you orders to secure all ships on the ground, and these weak little animals still managed to steal one of our finest crafts!" He spat on the ground. "I should kill all of you for this, and I still might do so. For now, I want one hundred of their men and children gathered and chained together in the square in two hours. Then, I want you to broadcast their execution for all to see as a warning about stealing from us. Now get out of here!" he said with a slam of his fist on the fine wooden table that once belonged to Aanepada.

In two hours, there was a knock on the door to Damok-Sai's office, and one of his commanders walked in. "The prisoners are ready, Commander."

"Very good, let's kill them," Damok-Sai said, and he guided the commander out of the room. Once outside, he walked up to several of his soldiers. "Go. Douse them in fuel, light them on fire, and let them burn to a crisp. If any one of them should try to help them, burn them, too," he said with a wave towards the thousands that had gathered to plead for their lives.

Damok-Sai walked to a central platform and faced the people gathered, especially the ones with cameras. He sniffed in the warm air as the seasons were changing, and then he glanced up at the bright sun overhead. "We are here today to remedy a problem. A few days ago, some of your soldiers stole one of our transport ships. If you have any information that would lead to their capture and the return of our ship, then I will let them go." He held his hand out towards the hundred men and children chained across the public square. He waited, and then a woman pushed her way forward.

She walked up on the platform and faced Damok-Sai, who towered over her. "I have information for you."

He smiled at her. "Please tell us what you know of this?"

She smiled back at him while staring up at him. "I hope you rot in Tari. We will not help you, and we all know you will kill them anyway!" she yelled at him.

He howled at her and reached for his jagged knife. He pulled the jagged knife out and brought it above her head, and she closed her eyes while chanting to Kur. This made him angrier, and he brought the knife down into her skull. She screamed, and he pulled the knife out and thrust it into her chest, and he let her fall to the ground. He then looked up as the crowd was chanting to Kur to kill the Ineans. Rage flowed over him. He took the torch from his officer over to the line of people and lit them on fire. He stood and growled at them while they screamed out in agony. Many fought to break loose as the fire consumed them. Soon, the screaming stopped, and the crowd surged forward until shots rang out from the Inean guns. Then, the crowd fled. Damok-Sai's commanders knew this was a bad idea, and Damok-Sai was now realizing that he had just polarized the Ardonnarians against him.

He threw the torch down as the bodies burned and walked towards the presidential palace with his field commanders behind him. The crowd dispersed quickly ahead of the Inean lasers firing at them. He went up to his office and to his desk as the commanders entered the room. He then opened the drawer, removed his laser pistol, and shot all three of them before they could react. He walked over to the bodies, stared down at them, and growled. "You have failed us for the last time. Your stupidity has polarized these people against us."

Damok-Sai stepped over the bodies and went to his transport. Once inside, he growled at the pilot, "Take me to the *Nikstra*."

A few minutes later, Damok-Sai's private transport lifted off the ground with a loud roar and headed for space.

On the Eastern Continent, General Rhanna watched the large screen from deep in the Eastern command center in Akhkharu, which showed a small blip heading towards one of the large Inean ships. "Once that ship gets inside the open doors, trigger the urukii."

"Yes, General. Almost there... In three... two... one... warhead is set, sir. Detonation in ten seconds," the technician said from below.

"Now we wait to see if it works," Rhanna said as he watched the image being sent from a telescope mounted on the inner moon, Nisaba.

As Damok-Sai's transport flew toward the *Nikstra*, there was a blinding flash of light near one of the ships. Damok-Sai came forward to see what it was, as the windows tinted automatically. He saw his worst fear come true. One of his large warships was disintegrating among other ships that were in a tight group. Then, another ship exploded as one of its antimatter tanks was pierced by a large piece of the first ship's hull. The fireball threatened to engulf more ships as they struggled to get away from the nuclear fireball. Large chunks of the two ships flew about, striking the Inean warships and causing them damage. A large piece of hull flew past the transport, and Damok-Sai howled at his pilot to land on the *Nikstra*.

A third ship was now disabled from the debris flying about and rammed into the side of the *Nikstra* as Damok-Sai's transport landed, sending his craft sliding into the side of the landing bay. He was tossed against the side of the transport and then back to the floor. Damok-Sai howled out in pain, jumped to his feet, and waited for the deck to pressurize.

Once the light turned green, he limped from the transport and towards his bridge for answers while warning alarms screeched.

Zuttara sat facing President Aanepada and General Asar when Dagan entered the room. She sat to the side of Aanepada and kept to herself while Zuttara gave his account of the battles they fought on their way to the base.

"You are certain the Ineans did not follow you?" Asar asked.

"I am certain. We killed them all, and there was no trace of them for several hundred zags until we got here," Zuttara said.

"That is good. What is your take on these aliens? Can we defeat them?" Aanepada asked with a glance toward Dagan. He saw that she was studying Zuttara but not in her usual manner, which led her to question General Asar or the scientists. It was more a look of attraction.

"I think so, but we must do it now while they try to figure us out. Once they do, it may be impossible."

"Explain, what is their weakness?" Dagan asked as she pulled her hood down to her shoulders.

Zuttara looked at her, unaccustomed to being questioned by a priestess about military issues. "Um, they don't have any security. They are very lax in the basics. I think it is because when they take over a planet, there is very little resistance by the time they put boots on the ground."

"We can use this to our advantage?" Dagan asked.

"We have so far. They also lack any in-depth military training. They can't think beyond the basics, it seems," Zuttara said while making eye contact with Dagan. Aanepada watched the exchange, and he saw a sudden connection between the two, who were roughly the same age. He was handsome, and she was very attractive, especially when she pulled her hood down to reveal her face and long blond hair.

General Asar looked at Zuttara. "Thank you, Captain. Starting tomorrow, I want you to begin training the recruits that keep trickling in. Most lack even the most basic of skills, much like the Ineans."

"Yes, General, I will put a program together. Where will I set up?" Zuttara asked.

Dagan looked up, "I can show you the facilities below if you have a few minutes."

Zuttara was unsure how to answer the priestess, so he hesitantly nodded. "Um, okay then."

Asar exchanged a look with Aanepada. It was a look of wonder at what was going on.

"Thank you, Captain, that will be all for now," Asar said.

Zuttara stood and bowed to the general and president and went for the door. He was followed by Dagan, who caught up to him.

"Zuttara, I have one more question for you," she said, and he stopped in the middle of the corridor as people went by them and stared.

"What is it, priestess of Kur," he said while turning to face her, and then he bowed slightly.

"I want you to train me how to fight," she asked.

"Excuse me? That wouldn't be appropriate," he said, taking a step away from her.

"Why is that? There is nothing in the books of Kur that says that. It is our society that has added words and beliefs to Kur that are not there. I request of you to train me because you are the best, and I feel it is my calling." She gripped his arm and stopped him in his tracks.

"Are you certain of that? I was always taught differently. Like this conversation should not even be happening."

"I am sure of it. That is why the older priests do not trust me all that much. I raise questions they can't or won't answer for fear of crossing their beliefs, which many are not found in the writings of Kur," she said while staring into his eyes.

He hesitated a moment.

"Zuttara, General Asar says you are one of the best. What better person to train me."

He exhaled. "All right, show me to the gym then."

They talked briefly as she guided him to the training rooms buried deep in the mountain. He hesitated to talk with her, especially when people walked past them. Some gave a questioning look, which made him feel even more nervous. He never felt this way with a woman before, but she was a priestess of Kur, and any conversation frightened him.

She showed him the shooting range on the way out of the gym. "That is about it for now. There are other large training rooms as well, and I can show you those if you would like?"

"That won't be necessary today, but thank you."

Zuttara glanced about, hoping she would leave. She didn't. She just seemed to be hanging around. "Okay, then. Well, I will see you in four hours then?" he asked nervously. He wasn't sure what scared him more. What if she was right or if she was wrong, and the higher priests got wind of their activity? He wasn't sure what would be worse.

"Thank you, I will be here," she said with a smile that made Zuttara melt a little.

"Okay. See you then," and he walked away with a glance over his shoulder, hoping she did not follow him.

She watched him walk away until he turned a corner. Finally, she turned back towards the main complex deep in the mountain.

Dagan sat in the middle of the floor of her room with her legs crossed, head tilted towards the ceiling, and her eyes closed. She studied the books of Kur and chanted the verses for several hours. It was something she did daily like the rest of the priest, but when she studied, she looked for the true meaning of what Kur was trying to say. She did her best to block out what her society wanted to believe. Frequently, she came to different conclusions, conclusions that all too often put her at odds with the higher priests. It was this constant friction that nearly got her thrown out of Kurdash on multiple occasions. The priests accepted what they were taught and did not ask questions. She asked questions, questions that would turn their religion upside down if truthfully answered by the higher order. This was why she was not liked and why they discredited her every chance they could. Her only saving grace at this point was Aanepada, but even his influence had limitations.

Aanepada was in the command center conversing with General Rhanna about their successful attack. He watched the video feed from the moon, Nisaba, and he was uneasy about the destruction of the Inean ships. "General, we applaud your success, but we must prepare for the inevitable revenge by the Ineans. You have to realize they won't take this without getting even."

"I understand, Mister President, and we cringe at the thought of what they will do next."

"Make sure you move your operation as soon as possible because they will come looking for you," Aanepada stated as General Asar and Zuttara both nodded.

Asar leaned towards Aanepada and stared into the camera. "We should upgrade our security as well."

"Yes, by all means," Aanepada said. "What would be the likely targets should the Ineans strike?"

"We have pinpointed a few cities here that are of little value to them but would yield a high casualty count. So, we have taken steps to move as many people as possible out of these potential strike zones. I want to add that our facility here can withstand a five-hundred megaton urukii strike, so we will remain where we are and run our operation from this location as long as possible."

"Be careful, General. We are greatly outnumbered right now and can not afford to lose a major facility with your capabilities," Aanepada said.

"We won't take any chances, sir. We must go now," General Rhanna said.

"Very well, and may the blessings of Kur guide you to victory," Aanepada bowed slightly.

"And to you, Mister President."

The connection closed with a crackle.

Aanepada liked hearing people calling him president once again. He also knew that his actions would dictate how long it would continue. Any sign of weakness and the people would quickly replace him.

Damok-Sai burst onto the bridge of the *Nikstra*, which had the image of the third ship with flames blowing off its engine room. "Turn that noise off!" he yelled, and the sirens stopped. "What is the status of our fleet?" he screamed.

"Sir," Maraal, his sensors' officer, spoke up. "We have lost the *Zikaar* and the *Shukka*. The *Belleti* is on fire, as you can see. Over three thousand of the Emperor's finest warriors murdered! Two other ships are damaged. The *Chanak* and the *Okya*."

"Commander, Looks like the *Belleti* is going to explode soon. We should evacuate the crew while there is time," Adhik-Sai stated from the communications station.

"Do it, get them off that ship and move the fleet away from all ships that are damaged!" Damok-Sai growled as he watched the fire growing on the critical ship. "What caused this to happen?" he screamed as he stared at the transports leaving the burning ship.

Zammani, who arrived on the last ship from Inea, stood at the Engineers console and growled at Damok-Sai. "You know what caused this! Your incompetence allowed these people a chance, and they took it. Now, over three thousand of the Emperor's finest are dead."

"That is enough out of you," Damok-Sai yelled as he spun around to face the new engineer.

"You know it's true, Damok-Sai. That is why General FarQue assigned me to this ship."

"Enough!"

"He has concerns about why these people are still alive, and now our ships are under attack!" he bellowed, stepping from behind the console while Damok-Sai stepped towards him. Soon, they were nose to nose and screaming at each other.

"The general knows why we have not killed these people!"

"He wants them destroyed! The mining ships are on the way and should be here soon." Zammani yelled as spit flew from his mouth.

"You were sent here to spy on me!"

"If I may interrupt?" Maraal asked. "The Belleti is about to explode.'

Damok-Sai growled at Zammani and turned towards Maraal. "Move us away!"

"The transports are not far enough away yet. We have to get between the ship and those transports to save them," Maraal stated.

"We can not put the *Nikstra* in there. Then this ship will be destroyed!" Damok-Sai yelled as he stomped to the front of the bridge and stared out the main screen at the white dots heading their way from the burning warship. "I said move the *Nikstra* out of the area now!"

The helmsman grumbled but moved the ship away while the communications terminal lit up with the transports calling for help. Then the *Belleti* exploded and engulfed the transports, killing all aboard.

"You can add their deaths to your list of casualties to support your father's craving for their women," Zammani stated.

"Get off my ship."

"I have been assig.."

"I said, get off now!" Damok-Sai's voice rumbled while reaching for his jagged knife.

The rest of the bridge crew watched and waited to see who would win. Zamani finally walked off the bridge, and Damok-Sai turned towards the main viewer again as the fireball began to dissipate.

"I will ask one more time. How did that first ship explode?" Damok-Sai asked while staring out at the debris expanding outward from the destroyed ships.

"Damok-Sai," Maraal spoke up. "Sensor logs show a transport

entered the Zikaar just before the explosion. I am reconstructing the image of the transport and its flight path to determine if it was the cause and where it came from."

"Make it quick."

A few minutes went by, and Damok-Sai was growing impatient. He growled at Maraal, who finally put the grainy image up on the main screen.

"Damok-Sai, here is the transport approaching the Zikaar. The image is a reconstruction, so it is of poor quality, but it looks like something hanging underneath the craft as it enters the Zikaar."

"Where did this ship originate from?" Damok-Sai growled.

"The computer is calculating the course. While we wait for that, the radiation readings from the Zikaar indicate it was a large nuclear device that was detonated," Maraal said while the bridge crew digested what it meant. They had not done a thorough enough job of securing the Ardonnarian weapons as they had thought, and now, over four thousand troops were dead. It was the worst loss ever encountered under Damok-Sai's leadership.

"Our ships can withstand a nuclear attack!" Damok-Sai howled.

"From the outside, Damok-Sai, but from inside, there is no protection. None at all, and someone down there knew that, and there is only one possible way for that to be," Maraal said. His tone suggested that one of Damok-Sai's warriors could be helping the Ardonnarians to make Damok-Sai look bad.

"Where did that ship take off from?" Damok-Sai yelled.

Maraal looked up at Damok-Sai. "Sir, the transport took off from a small town outside Ninki on the eastern continent."

"Send a full contingent to that town and get answers for me," Damok-Sai stated. "I also want our ships spread out around the planet so they can't be destroyed so easily." He turned towards the main screen again, which had switched back to a view of the debris field. "I also want each and every transport inspected before leaving the planet for the fleet. Make sure all ships and crews do this." He started walking towards the rear hatch. "Turn those emergency lights off while I contact General FarQue."

"Damok-Sai, we should strengthen our security. It is quite

possible that one of our own is helping these animals," Maraal stated.

"Why would they do that?" Damok-Sai growled.

"Sir, there are some who want to see you fail. It is that simple," Maraal said.

"Then I want a list of these people, and I will take care of them. And I want it now."

"Yes sir," Maraal stated, and he sat down again to compile his list. He pondered if he should put his own name down as well, which would mean a death sentence unless Damok-Sai could be done away with.

A few hours later, a pair of Inean transports set down in the small town outside Ninki from where the transport that had destroyed three Inean battleships had taken off. The Ineans spilled out of the transports and began looking around. They found a few dead Ineans that had been killed by Anzillu when they had planted the bomb. That was all they found. They got back in their transports and began circling around, looking for clues as to who had done this.

TWENTY-ONE

DAGAN WALKED along the corridor toward the gym and pushed open the door to a darkened room. She felt around for a switch along the wall as the door closed, engulfing her in total darkness. She felt something brush by her. "Is someone here?" she asked. Then, a hand clamped down around her mouth, and she was tossed to the ground, which was covered in soft mats. Then, she was rolled over and held down to the floor as the lights came on. Her look of fright was replaced with a look of recognition, and the hand lifted from her mouth. "What was that all about?" she asked sternly.

"That was your first test: always be prepared. Always keep your senses on alert for anything and pay attention to every detail." Zuttara said as he got off her and extended her a hand to help her up.

"So I failed then?"

"Was that a question?" Zuttara asked.

"Fine, what is next." She huffed.

"Let's work on some basic hand-to-hand for today. By the way, it might not be a good idea to train in your robe," Zuttara stated as he picked up some punching pads he slipped on his hands.

"I have nothing else to wear," she said.

"What do you have on besides the customary robe?"

"Um, this is all I wear. It is all that is required," Dagan replied as her face turned red with embarrassment.

"Then you should keep the robe on then."

"I intend to."

"But find something else for the rest of our training," he said while planting his feet. "I want you to punch the pads as hard as you can."

She stepped in front of him and swung and punched the pad with everything she had, and his hand did not budge at all. She swung with the other and got the same result.

"Are you sure you really want to do this?" Zuttara asked as he sized her up. She was nearly as tall as he was, but all those years buried in books and prayer chants did nothing to build up her body.

"Yes, I do."

Then he had an idea. "I want you to get on a weight-training program and an exercise program. You won't last half a second with an Inean the way you are right now."

"So we should get started on it," she said as sweat beaded up on her forehead as she kept punching his hands.

"Okay, stop for a moment," he said, and she did.

He walked over to his gym bag, pulled out some paper and a pen, and sat on the bench. He started writing her instructions. "Come and sit," he said while patting the bench beside him.

Dagan sat beside him, and he went over the notes he had written. When he was done, he guided her to the gym, located in the next room, and showed her how to use all the equipment.

Their session lasted for two hours, and at the end, she excused herself. They bowed slightly to each other. Dagan then walked to her room and showered while Zuttara spent another hour in the gym. Afterward, she went in search of regular clothes that would fit her.

Their training sessions lasted for two hours a day, every day for several months, and Dagan advanced quickly in hand-to-hand combat, firing and cleaning a varied assortment of weapons with the most seasoned military officers. She was even becoming well-versed in advanced fighting, and Zuttara considered calling in an expert to train her further. All this occurred in secrecy from Aanepada and the male priests, who would have her head if they knew what she was doing. She knew in advance that, even though there was nothing in the writings of Kur, the higher priests had their own rules that she still needed to follow. Her dreams of leading the people against the Ineans still occurred regularly. She was convinced it was Kur who was speaking to her in her dreams. She had recently dreamed of an event that had not yet happened, and when it did, the details were as she had seen in her dream days before. This was not the first, but it was the most vivid and well-detailed vision she had.

TWENTY-TWO

WHILE THE INEAN ships were being destroyed by the Ardon nuclear bomb and Damok-Sai was formulating his retaliation, the Ardonnarian scientists swarmed over the stolen Inean long-range transport. Much of the ship was disassembled and scattered all over the flight deck hidden deep in the moon Anaru. Several scientists congregated around the engines with cameras and test equipment as they studied how the engines worked. It would be the key to their plan to strike Inea while the Ardonnarians still had a chance. If they failed, then Damok-Sai's bold promise that their race would be extinct would come true.

Gula worked with this group of scientists, having previously served as an interstellar transport engineer before commanding the *ShuBuré*. He had one of the Ardonnarian transports wheeled over to compare the designs and how to integrate the Inean technology with as little modification as possible. He stood at a large, tilted architect's table with the transport's schematics spread across it while instructing a pair of engineers on removing the engines.

At another table surrounded by computer consoles, other scientists studied the antimatter containment system and designed a system to produce enough antimatter for dozens of ships. On the computer screen was a large particle accelerator that would smash atoms together and produce the antimatter fuel, which would be contained in electromagnetic containment cylinders. Their task was to upgrade this machine deep inside the moon with shielding to prevent the Ineans from detecting it.

An atom smasher would require an enormous amount of power, and multiplying that by the size that would be needed to produce enough of the volatile fuel for twenty-five ships in a month's time would be easy to detect from several planets away. The scientists shook their heads and walked over to General Innin, who was in command of the Anaru facility.

"General Innin, we have come to the conclusion that we cannot upgrade the particle accelerator here on Anaru," Faursag stated while stroking the whitening beard on his chin. He was an older man in his late fifties, his uncombed hair long turned white from the stress of recent months. He had the look of a typical scientist, with an IQ at the top of the charts and the demeanor to match.

The general studied him for a moment. "I was afraid of that," he paused for a moment as he thought about his options. "I suppose I won't be court marshaled for this after everything we have faced. We have an accelerator already in operation deep inside the outer moon, Uggae, which orbits the gas giant Idpa."

"I was unaware of any base with that capability on the outer moons," Faursag stated.

"It is a secret base, and due to the highly explosive state of anti-matter, especially in the quantity we need, it was best kept as far away from Ardonnar," Innin said while staring at a transport being readied across the hangar. "Gather all of your things, plans, and people, and be on that transport for the next solar blast, which is expected in a few hours."

"Yes, General, we will be on that transport," Faursag saluted, as did the rest of his group, and they scattered to gather their belongings and designs.

With the Inean warships surrounding Ardonnar and its moons, it was necessary to utilize the Inean-induced solar storms, which produced various radiation, to conceal their transports. Luckily, the storms occurred at regular intervals, which hid the transports from their sensors, allowing for supplies and people to be ferried about the different colonies and moons. It was not easy to bring them back, however. This created an overpopulation problem on these colonies, which meant that more and more supplies needed to be shipped out. If the solar blasts stopped or the Ineans intercepted one of the ships, then disaster would soon follow on the fragile colonies on the other planets and moons in their system.

Gula and the scientists swarming over the Inean engines along with several machinists. The machinists measured and tested each component, logging the information in portable computers running advanced CAD software. The components took shape on the computer monitors, while other computers connected to specialized scanning equipment tested the metals used. It was a long, tedious process that needed to be completed quickly and with exacting detail.

In another part of the base, away from the hangar, several other machinists input the dimensions, loaded stock into their milling machines and lathes, and began duplicating the Inean design. Under normal circumstances, they would have redesigned the engines to Ardonnarian specifications; however, time did not allow for that. Each day, thousands died, and thousands more were taken from their planet to be sold as slaves on Inea.

Puabi joined Gisiga and another group as they compared guidance systems and began making changes to the Ardonnarian ships. This turned out to be an easy task, which involved loading the Ardonnarian computers with the Inean navigational files, which comprised all the obstacles between there and Inea. The Ardonnarian gyroscopes were vastly superior to the Inean and would not be a problem. One other problem did crop up, and it was the hull designs. The Ardonnarian ships were not designed for such high speeds, and welders began reinforcing the prototype bombers. Bright blue lights sparkled all around the ships as the welders fused the various plates and ribs to the hull, which showered the flight deck with sparks and fragments of metal.

· · ·

Damok-Sai exited his quarters while pulling on his pants with bloodied hands. Behind him were the remains of three Ardonnarian women that he just finished brutalizing to death. There was not much left of them as their broken bodies lay in a pile on the floor in a growing puddle of red blood. He stormed onto the bridge of the *Nikstra* and bellowed his next command, which his crew was waiting for. "Target these two cities with our nuclear missiles. If these people want to play with such weapons, then maybe they would like a taste of what they can do."

A map of the planet appeared on the main screen, and he walked up to it and pointed to the two blinking lights with Inean writing beside them, which were the coordinates of the cities: one on the eastern continent and one on the western. The eastern city was Anshar, located five hundred zags south of Kurdash. It currently had a population of three million and was the port city responsible for shipping grain around the planet from the southern farmlands. The Western city was Suen. It was about the same distance to the south of the capital city of Delondra and was a major port city on the Kibrat-Ati, also known as the Gulf of Kibrat. It had a normal population of nearly seven million but had been ravaged by the Ineans to the point where more than half had escaped to the countryside.

The *Nikstra* fired its large engines and headed toward the planet. The launch tubes slid open, and the tips of the nuclear missiles extended outward. Soon, the ship was in position above the first target, which was Anshar.

"Launch the missile!" Damok-Sai yelled, and Pavak, his weapons officer on the bridge, launched the nuclear missile. Several minutes later, there was a flash on the planet's surface, and then a fiery gray dot expanded outward from Anshar. Then, the ship fired its engines again and headed around the planet.

On the ground, the large city with its tall, steel-and-glass skyscrapers was engulfed in a blinding flash and then a deafening roar as the fireball expanded outward, blowing the tall buildings apart as it did.

On the ground, people began to run, but it was too late as the heat from the detonation vaporized them in their tracks, and the shock wave blew them away. The large mushroom cloud slowly rolled into the sky, blowing the thin clouds away into a doughnut shape as it headed for the upper atmosphere. The fire rolled outward, consuming the city and the people who lived there.

At the main ocean port, dozens of cargo ships were blown over by the shock wave and sunk as the fire rolled outward, consuming everything for a twenty-zag diameter. There was nothing left. On the outskirts of the city, people watched the mushroom cloud rising up and knew what it was. They began to run away and take cover as the shock wave hit, blowing trees and rickety buildings over.

The situation was the same in the city of Suen. In a matter of minutes, the city was gone, along with over one million people. Most of the ones who survived died within days from burns and radiation. Many more would die from diseases caught from the rotting, burned corpses and the lack of clean water and food.

Word traveled around the planet about what the Ineans had done, and anger toward them was growing. Many who supported the Inean's help in the beginning now turned against them. They joined militias and organized independently. Those with military training took charge and trained others. Many of the military bases were raided by the people and stripped of every hand weapon there was. Handguns, grenades, automatic machine guns, shoulder-mounted grenade launchers, and shoulder-mounted rocket launchers were the most significant prizes taken.

In the following weeks, Damok-Sai was informed of the growing militias and their raids on military bases. He sat with his planetary commanders, who were growing concerned about the mounting threat. He got up and stared out of the large windows of the president's tower at the large brick square below. Then he turned to his field commanders, whom he had recently appointed to replace the ones he had executed weeks before. "I want the bases secured. I don't want these people getting their hands on the nuclear warheads that are scattered around this planet. Send troops into each facility and take all of their big weapons out. Destroy them if you have to, or obliterate the bases. Don't be the incompetent fools your predecessors were. Just get it done!" he growled. The field commanders agreed with him and left the room. They boarded their transports and went to gather their troops for the mission.

Over the next few weeks, the Ineans located and raided many of the Ardonnarian military bases, where they met some resistance but managed to take control of the bases. Some were small. Others were large complexes with airstrips, squadrons of fighters, and rows upon rows of tanks and rockets, but the Ineans found very few nuclear warheads. Most had been taken or hidden away from them. There was no way of knowing who had the warheads or how many there were. Once Damok-Sai was informed of this, he grew increasingly concerned. He wanted to level the planet right away, but his father, Manava, wanted more and more of the slaves shipped to Inea. He was becoming one of the wealthiest members of Sankar's cabinet and, thus, one of the most powerful. Sankar was reluctant to destroy the planet as well because he made millions of Denars off the sale of slaves, which funded his own enterprises. Sankar also wanted the children to work in dangerous mines, where many died instead of Inean workers.

Damok-Sai ordered the mining ships to land and begin stripping the planet despite the militias. The large container ships settled on the planet in the middle of the cities, and armed troops swarmed around with large automatic laser rifles in hand. Workers, mostly slaves chained together from other planets taken over, began disassembling the cities of their precious metals. Once underway, the buildings came down easily with the use of high-powered lasers mounted on the mining ships. Everything was sliced up, and many of the materials were loaded into the container ships. Anything not wanted was left in piles of rubble where buildings once stood before and burned. Some of the ships settled down near the nuclear power plants, which sat idle now as the Ineans shut them down, denying the Ardonnarians of power. More ships landed every day.

There was very little resistance from the militia groups, as most of them had found a way to contact the higher generals and were now under their control. The word from above was to train and organize and wait for the orders to attack which would come.

General Asar led the western militias, and General Rhanna led the eastern rebels. Rhanna had a way of keeping the Ineans on their toes with subtle, quick raids and murders of Ineans that the Ineans could not defend against. The rebels would sneak in and kill one or two and then escape before being detected. This drove Damok-Sai and his field commanders crazy.

The prototype bomber was nearly complete after two months of around-the-clock work on the moon, Anaru. It was a four-person craft with nuclear missiles mounted in a row of six cylindrical tubes in the center of the craft facing down. The bomber had two large engines mounted in the rear with two large pylons, one on each side, that housed the antimatter fuel cells, regular fuel cells, air tanks with purification systems, and water tanks. The bombers had fore and aft-mounted missile launchers for defensive use against the Inean fighters, which they hoped to avoid. The ships were rebuilt long and sleek compared to their boxy predecessors. They were also coated in an absorbent material and painted black to confuse the Inean sensors. There were no external markings or windows, with the exception of the forward shield, which had a sliding shade to prevent any light from escaping when needed.

General Innin was satisfied with the design and ordered the immediate construction of twenty-five more on Anaru and twenty-five on Uggae. He wanted them completed, fueled, and armed in six months. He was concerned that there was no way to test the ships until they went into service, and no one knew with total confidence that the converted Inean engines would work. It was their best hope, and even if it didn't work, it was still possible to pull the Ineans away from Ardonnar or use the missiles to destroy the Inean ships in orbit. It was their plan B.

Puabi sat in the mess hall, picking at her rations while studying the programming code for the navigation computer. There was a flaw in the code that no one could find that caused the system to crash during simulated runs at Inea.

Across the room was one of the fighter pilots lazily eating his basic rations. Bel was a middle-aged man with a scraggly short beard and longer hair than what was required for pilots. His uniform was fitted perfectly, and he was a muscular man who worked out whenever he got the chance. He had a spiral-bound tech manual open in front of him, but his attention was drawn to Puabi. He was attracted to her but hesitated because of her relationship with Gula. He had noticed that Gula had not made any moves while on Anaru, and there were plenty of opportunities for him to do so. He finally closed the manual and gathered his dishes and trash. He got up from the table and took the dishes to the window, where the dishwasher was waiting for him. His path brought him toward Puabi, who sat marking the printout with a red pen. He glanced down at her while walking by; she did not take notice. He delivered his dirty dishes and started back. On his way back, she looked up at him and grinned as he approached. For some reason, he didn't know why, but he pulled out a chair and sat across from her. She put her pen down and rubbed her eyes.

"Hi, I'm Bel," he said with a grin.

"I'm Puabi," she replied with a yawn. She rubbed her eyes and looked at him.

"I know. I have admired you since you were piloting the *ShuBuré*," he replied.

"That seems so long ago now." Her grin went away as she thought back to those carefree days before the Ineans invaded their planet.

"I know, it has been, what? Two years now," he replied.

"Yeah, almost."

"I have to ask you a question," he said and waited.

"Go ahead," she said hesitantly.

"Are you involved with anyone?"

"Oh. Um. No, not really. Why do you ask," she stumbled.

He hesitated a moment as he digested her answer, which was guarded. He knew her defenses were up now for some reason. "I was hoping you would like some company, that's all."

"Sure, why not," she grinned back at him. "I have to warn you that...oh, never mind," she stumbled as Gula walked in with several of the engineers.

"What is it?"

"Nothing. What would you like to talk about? Where are you from?" she asked as she watched Gula, who paid no attention to her.

"I'm from Suen. Was from Suen."

"I'm sorry. Is there any word from your family?" she asked.

"No, there hasn't been any since before the attack. I can only hope they got out of there, but it doesn't look good," he said carefully, not wanting to look weak and have a tear roll down. "Where are you from?"

"Samuqan, just north of Delondra. Last time I was there, everyone was all right. It has been several months since then, and no word," she said while looking up at the monitors hanging from the ceiling.

"Touchy subjects. Why don't we talk about something lighter?" He asked.

"That would be great."

They continued talking for some time. Gula finally looked over and saw Puabi and Bel laughing and talking. He was going to walk over and interrupt. However, he could not muster a good enough excuse for doing so. So he returned his dishes and left the room.

TWENTY-THREE

OVER A HUNDRED INEANS marched along the streets of Ninki on the eastern continent. At the same time, another mining ship landed in front of the remains of the now abandoned Eastern leader's palace. Several Ardonnarians scattered into other buildings at the sight of the Ineans, who had raided the city several times before. The women and children knew what it meant to be captured, and the men were murdered instantly. The Ineans began knocking down doors and grabbing people. The men were tossed to the side and chained around their necks and chained to one another in work lines. Once chained, most of their clothes were stripped off to humiliate them and to prevent them from hiding weapons. Then, they were tossed harshly into wagons pushed by short, hideous aliens who were chained together. Obviously, slave workers from another planet were taken over by the Ineans. The short aliens had greenish-smooth skin. Their feet were webbed, with four toes each, and their hands were webbed as well with four fingers. They had long ears, and behind their ears were slits for breathing in water. They also had sharp fangs for ripping animals. They growled at the Ardonnarian men and bared their teeth in disgust. The women were tossed into the large buses that followed the Ineans and were taken to a transport that had landed several streets over. Their clothes were tossed out the rear of the bus for the hideous aliens to retrieve. The children were tossed into other buses and taken to another transport for delivery to the Inean mining camps for immediate work.

Once the men were prepared, a few Ineans walked up and down the lines and began whipping them to make them stand and began barking orders at them. They marched away toward the mining ship to gather tools and start tearing down their city.

It only took a few hours for the Ineans to gather everyone who chose to hide instead of run. Soon, the transports lifted off the ground with great effort and headed for space. Several other Ineans began setting up defensive positions in the city while another transport landed with reinforcements who kept the workers busy and on Damok-Sai's schedule. They worked around the clock, and many collapsed from exhaustion and lack of food and water. They got whipped until they returned to work or until they died, which many did.

General Rhanna watched the ships landing on the monitors and knew the eastern capital was being occupied. He picked up a portable radio and pressed the button on the mic. "Anzillu, come in."

A few seconds later, Anzillu's voice crackled over the tinny speaker. "Go ahead, sir."

"Ninki is being occupied. What is your status?"

"We are undercover, probably six hours away, sir."

"What do you have for resources?" the general asked.

"We have thirty trained troops and over two hundred local militia at our disposal," Anzillu said over the handheld radio.

"I want you to raid the city and get us some up-close recon. Engage the Ineans only if you have to."

"Understood, general. We will be heading out once it gets dark," Anzillu stated.

"Very good, Anzillu. May Kur be with you," the general said, and he placed the radio in the cradle on his desk.

The general then went down to the lower level and leaned over the shoulder of a woman who wore a headset. "Contact General Asar for me, please."

"Yes, sir," she said and began pressing buttons, making a secure connection to General Asar halfway around the globe without tipping off the Ineans. After a few minutes, she glanced up at Rhanna and said, "Connection established, sir," and then handed him the headset.

Rhanna discussed the situation with Asar at length, and then he handed the headset back to the woman.

The next morning, Anzillu was crouching behind several barrels on a street corner with one of his officers, who was recording all of the information he could. They watched the Ineans whipping workers as many stumbled from the beatings, and most were bloodied with open wounds. Two other troops raced up to an open doorway with scanners in hand. Once inside the door, they gave Anzillu a thumbs up. Anzillu crept up the sidewalk while keeping low against the wall until he made the next door opening. He then watched the Ineans further up and then pulled a portable radio out of his pocket. "Next group, move up."

"Confirmed," came the hissing voice, and he placed the radio back in his pocket.

After several minutes, his radio beeped, and he pulled it out of his pocket. "Yes?"

"We are in position," the speaker hissed.

"Confirmed. Next group, make your move from the north, and group three, start coming in from the south," Anzillu stated, and he waited for confirmation. These were the militia groups he was waiting for, and he knew some of them would not make it. Most of them were poorly trained, if at all, and out of shape, as well as having no military structure. They were unreliable at best and a liability at worst. He waited and waited until both groups checked in. Both radio operators sounded nervous and out of breath, but so far, they had not been detected. Anzillu chalked it up to more Inean arrogance, stemming from the fact that they did not expect anyone to attack such a large ground presence. He hoped they would be wrong. "I now want all groups to enter buildings and set up positions high up so you can take out as many of the enemy as possible."

Anzillu headed into the building and had to step over the body of an older man who had a burn hole in his skull. He headed up the stairs with his radioman. He had his scanner in his hand, which was programmed to detect Ineans. So far, none were in this building as they climbed the littered stairs to the top floor, hoping to gain a good vantage point. After climbing ten stories, they pushed a door open and found more murdered people with burn holes in their heads. Most were old and of no use to the Ineans. The flies had already found them, even though it had been less than a day. They exited and tried a different room and found a woman hanging by her hands in the middle of the room. She had bloody bite marks all over her body. She had obviously been tortured by the Ineans but was still alive. She lifted her head as the door opened, and her eyes went wide.

Cen-Dirig went to help her, but Anzillu grabbed him. "No!" he yelled softly as the woman shook her head, trying to tell him to stop. Her mouth was gagged, and she could only muffle the sounds.

"What! We have to help her," he struggled against Anzillu's iron grip on his arm.

"It's a trap," and with that, the woman began nodding, and Cen-Dirig finally saw what she was doing.

"How so?" he asked.

"She must be wired, or something," Anzillu said, and the woman nodded again with a gesture to her left hand.

Anzillu looked closely and saw the fine wire twisted in with the rope. He followed it behind a cabinet. He pulled the cabinet out slowly and saw the bomb with the blinking light on it. He moved the cabinet away, and Cen-Dirig knelt beside it. "If we cut her down, then the circuit is opened, and that triggers the bomb. If we can somehow short it away from her and hope it isn't resistance wire, then we should be okay," he said as he studied it some more. He moved the thin wires about, which made Anzillu nervous, but he stayed in the room. Then, he pulled an electronics meter from his backpack and began testing the circuits. "Crap, it is resistance wire. I can not cut these and short them."

"It relies on a specific resistance?" Anzillu asked.

"Yes, and she is part of the circuit."

"Will the bomb reach the window?" Anzillu asked.

"I think so. You want to push it out as we cut her down?"

"Do you have a better idea?"

"No, but those animals will know we are here," Cen-Dirig stated with a glance at the naked woman and then at Anzillu, who removed the short piece of rope gagging her. She started to cry.

"They will in a few minutes anyway. Let's do it," he said as he grasped the cabinet and dragged it out of the way even more.

Cen-Dirig carefully lifted the bomb, carried it to the windowsill, and set it down while watching the fine wires. He then lifted the window open just enough to push the bomb out. Neither of them knew just how powerful it may be. It could topple the entire building, but Anzillu didn't think so.

Anzillu pulled out his knife and held it to the rope, tying the woman's hands. He stood between her and the window to protect her from the blast. He started to cut the thick rope away from the wire and stopped when the rope began to creek. "Now!" he said firmly, and Cen-Dirig pushed the bomb out the window and ducked down as Anzillu cut through the rest of the way. The bomb exploded with a thunderous boom as Anzillu pushed the woman to the floor, and he covered her. The building shook violently as plaster from the ceiling rained down on them. Flames flew past the window, and the glass blew into the room, showering them with shards of sharp glass. The wall cracked, the floor buckled, and the worst had passed.

The woman crawled out across the glass, which cut her hands and knees until she found the remains of her clothes across the room. As their hearing returned, they could hear the loud, shrill of an Inean warning siren. Suddenly, their soldiers and militia opened fire on the Ineans. Anzillu and Cen-Dirig stumbled towards the blown-out window and saw dozens of Ineans heading their way. They quickly removed their automatic rifles from their shoulders and leaned out the window. Anzillu and Cen-Dirig began cutting down the Ineans until the majority took cover.

The Ineans found themselves trapped as they took fire from four different directions. The bodies piled up and fell into the street as others used their fallen comrades for protection. That was when Anzillu started shooting again from his perch above. He saw several other Ineans starting to shoot back at the warriors, and then he saw them reaching for grenades. He pulled back while pulling Cen-Dirig with him. "Time to go!"

They got to their feet and grabbed the woman on their way out of the room as a grenade was hurled through the window and landed on the floor. A second later, it exploded, engulfing the entire room with fire and debris. The two men and woman stumbled and fell down the stairs as the building shook. They got up slowly and looked back up towards the room they had come from, and it was now a raging inferno.

Anzillu made it to the first floor and saw Enanatuma and an older woman firing their automatics at the Ineans surging up the street. The girl's gun started clicking, and she pulled the clip out and tossed it on the ground. She quickly pulled another clip from her vest pocket and clicked it into the gun. She settled back down and began shooting again while the Inean lasers buzzed by her and the woman.

Anzillu crept up to the other side of the door frame and began shooting as well. Cen-Dirig helped the injured woman out of the way, and he joined the others in shooting at the Ineans. Enanatuma saw an Inean reaching into his pocket and pulling out a baseball-sized device, and it was blinking. "Grenade!" she yelled, and they all ran back as the grenade bounced onto the floor and then exploded as they raced deeper into the building. The room exploded, and a fireball chased them down the hallway, blowing them down as the fire roared over their heads. A few seconds later, they crawled into a side room and caught their breath.

Enanatuma was trying to speak but could not hear herself. The blast had caused her to go deaf, for now at least, as she kept hitting her ears with her palms. She had a scared look on her face as she looked up at Anzillu while she drove a glove-covered finger in her ear. He mouthed the words, "Don't worry about it." She nodded and followed him out the door with her partner. Cen-Dirig and the injured woman followed behind them.

Soon, laser shots whizzed by them as the Ineans stormed the building after them. The woman was hit in the back and fell, pulling Cen-Dirig down with her. He tried to get up and was hit as well. Anzillu turned and started shooting at the Ineans as he fell back through a doorway, following Enanatuma, who opened the door. Several Ineans were hit, allowing Cen-Dirig to stagger to the room and in the door.

"Where is she?" Anzillu yelled because his hearing was still not restored.

"Dead! Shot through the back."

"I'm okay!" Enanatuma piped up as she got up off the floor after checking the woman militia fighter with her. She pulled her scanner out and checked the screen. "Company coming!" and she scrambled back behind a table and flipped it on its side. Anzillu wondered how she knew to do that as he took cover with Cen-Dirig. The other woman dove behind a cabinet. The Ineans turned their guns into the room and began firing. Then they stood in the opening and entered the room. Anzillu stepped out and fired several times, dropping one Inean, and he ducked back. Then Enanatuma did the same. She sprung up, fired off several rounds, and ducked back down as several laser blasts struck the table and burned holes into the thick wood. One kept firing in the same spot, and soon, it would burn through where she was. The woman militia fighter saw what was happening and knew the girl was going to die. She stepped out and emptied her clip into the Inean and was shot by another in the abdomen. She dropped her gun and looked down at the hole burned through her body and fell to the ground. Enanatuma screamed and popped up again with bullets flying. Anzillu did the same, and they dropped the last remaining Ineans. A laser pulse struck Enanatuma in the shoulder, and she flew back, tumbling over the overturned table.

Enanatuma went to the woman and pulled her helmet off with shaking fingers. "We'll get you help!" she said with a wavering voice.

The woman looked up at her and brought her blood-soaked hand to her face. "It's too late for me. At least I got to kill a few of them before they got me." Her hand dropped across her chest, and she was dead.

Enanatuma cried while Anzillu pulled her off. "We need to keep moving and get to the rendezvous point before their reinforcements come after us."

They went back into the hallway. Cen-Dirig led the way while Anzillu helped Enanatuma from the room. She was not injured badly, as the laser grazed her skin. It would hurt for some time. Anzillu was beginning to like this girl. She was a scrappy fighter, a vastly different girl than the first time they met when she did not even know how to hold a gun.

They encountered minimal fire as they escaped from Ninki. Several hours later, they met the rest of their group in an abandoned warehouse well outside town. Anzillu took a count, and they had lost eleven fighters and had over thirty injured, some of whom were seriously hurt. He also took a rough count of killed Ineans and came up with well over one-hundred dead. A good ratio, if you could call it that. They licked their wounds and headed out under the cover of darkness.

TWENTY-FOUR

ON THE WESTERN CONTINENT, several Inean transports settled down around the town of Samuqan. Dozens of Ineans raced into the town and began killing the men and grabbing the women and children. They entered one home, and the place exploded, killing the Ineans. A girl and boy raced across the street to get out of the way, and the girl was captured by the Inean. It was Enhedu who was left behind by Puabi over a year ago. The Inean grabbed her, decided she was of age, and tossed her towards the woman's group. The boy, Amar-Sin, who was also left behind by Puabi, got away, but just long enough to grab a gun. He then circled around and went to the girl who was struggling futilely against the much larger Inean. He was tearing at her clothes to toss them in the pile to be taken to Inea, and she would be taken to be a slave of the worst kind.

Amar-Sin fired the gun and struck the Inean hard enough for him to let go of Enhedu. She fell away and crawled as did other women, clutching at their torn clothes. He fired again and again until the Inean fell backward. Another Inean raced up and leveled his gun at the boy, and Amar-Sin aimed as well. His gun just clicked repeatedly, and he knew it was out of ammunition. The Inean grinned and fired. The boy's head exploded, and his body flew backward on top of the escaping girl. She screamed out and kicked him off her. She got up and ran away screaming, leaving half her clothes behind. The Inean went to chase her down but decided not to.

Enhedu ran across the field and over the hill, still screaming, and finally collapsed when she crested the hill. She rolled down the other side and just lay in the tall grass, gasping for air. She stopped screaming as she fought for her breath. She had become close to Amar-Sin in recent months, and now he was gone. She lay in the grass and cried until she heard something moving in the tall grass. She quieted and listened. Then she peeked up and saw it was a wild sahu. It waddled over to her and sniffed. Then, it wandered off towards the village. She heard more movement in the distance and peeked up again. It was the local militia heading in. She realized she had little clothing on and ripped up some grass to hold against her. The officers reached her, and one gave her his coat. He instructed her to head back to their camp, and she did after they passed by. Soon, she made it to the trees, and she heard gunfire on top of gunfire. Next, she heard the shrill sound of Inean laser guns returning fire, and this continued for several minutes. Soon, the Inean transports took off and headed for space.

Enhedu arrived at the camp, where a few people were cooking. One of the women helped her to a tent and got her some army fatigues. They fit, and she vowed to join the militia to get revenge for Amar-Sin, who died saving her. The boy was a true hero, and she would let people know about it.

A few hours later, the fighters returned to camp, but only half of the fifty who went out. The Ineans were getting better at responding to the Ardonnarian rebels. They brought back over forty others who wanted to join the fight, including Puabi's mother, Shubad, who found the girl, hugged her, and cried.

They ate, and when it had gotten dark, they broke camp and headed northwest towards the military base at Idimmu. Here, they would rearm and await instructions from General Asar in the mountains.

Idimmu base had been raided by the Ineans, and they had destroyed much of the base. However, the militia had hidden cases upon cases of small arms and ammunition underground, where the Ineans could not find it. It would take days to return to the base, and there was the constant threat of the Inean patrols crisscrossing the countryside.

Commander Utu of the militia fighters was on the radio with one of General Asar's officers. He was informed of the Ineans going on killing sprees to retaliate for the troops they had lost between the attacks in Ninki and Samuqan. The Ineans were broadcasting around the planet that they would kill a hundred Ardonnarians for each of their people killed. Utu was informed that the Inean death toll was over one hundred fifty and to be prepared for strafing runs by their patrols. Utu decided to break up into small groups and head back to Idimmu. Asar's officer agreed and wished them luck.

The fighters traveled by night and rested at daybreak.

Enhedu told Shubad about Amar-Sin's sacrifice. Commander Utu offered to praise him to Kur and did as Utui crested the eastern hills.

Three days had passed, and they came up to the military base at Idimmu. Commander Utu held the group back while he sent scouts up to the base. They were concerned that the Ineans may be lurking about, waiting for them. Many hours later, they heard gunfire from the base and then quiet for several more hours.

Utu's radio crackled, and he pulled it from his pocket. "Go ahead."

"Sir, the base is secured. There were a few Ineans here, but we cleaned them out. As far as we can tell by our scanner, there are no more," the voice wavered over the static of the radio.

"Very good. We will move out when it gets dark again," Utu said.

"Very good, sir, out."

Utu put his radio back in his pocket and turned towards his platoon leaders. "I want the platoons broken up. Let's say about ten to fifteen in each building. That way, if something goes wrong, we will be spread out."

"Yes, Commander, we will split up our platoons," they each said, nodding, and then they dispersed.

Enhedu was with one of the lieutenants, and he was showing her how to handle a gun. He would show her more when they got to the base. There, she would be able to actually fire the weapon and learn how to toss grenades. She looked forward to it. She was slowly being consumed with revenge and wanted to kill the Ineans. Amar-Sin would be avenged.

TWENTY-FIVE

PUABI WALKED along the darkened corridor at the end of a long day towards her room. Outside her room was Bel. He leaned against the wall with his hands behind his back as she approached. He straightened and held out his hands when she got close. In them was a potted plant about to bloom. Puabi grinned, took the gift from him, and opened the door.

"May I come in?" he asked.

"Oh, if you must," she said with a grin. Bel followed her into the room and closed the door behind them. It was against the rules for her to invite him in, but now that he asked, she allowed him to enter her room.

In the distance, Gula was walking down the corridor and saw the exchange and stopped. He was on his way to talk with her about how he felt, but he was too late. Bel had the courage to ask her when he could not. Even with the months in open space between colonies, he could not muster the courage to ask her to be his, and now it was too late. He watched Bel close the door as he approached. He stopped by the door and listened. They were laughing. He put his head down and walked away. He cursed softly to himself.

Inside, Puabi placed the plant under a UV light on the table by the bed. She opened a bottle of water and poured some on the dry soil. She put the cap back on.

"I couldn't wait until you got off shift to see you," Bel said as he took her hands in his.

"Me neither," she said. She raised her head to receive his kiss. He hugged her, and they sat on the end of the bed and kissed for a few minutes.

"What would you like to do tonight?" he asked as he pushed away slightly.

"Um, I didn't think that far ahead," she said while glancing at the clock by her bed. "It is late."

"We could just eat then," Bel said, studying her for a moment.

"I'm not that hungry, and I'm exhausted. I want to stay here tonight."

"That works for me," Bel said, and he leaned in and kissed her again.

They fell back on the bed, which was forbidden by their culture before marriage and could land them both in trouble with the high priest of the base. Neither was thinking of the rules at the moment. He put his arms around her and brought her on top of him while kissing. Then they rolled over again with him on top of her. He began kissing her neck and reached up to begin unbuttoning her shirt when she pulled away.

"Bel, I'm not an Eastern girl. We should not be doing this," and she slid out from under him and got off the bed.

"I, I'm sorry. I don't want to offend you, but I really do like you."

"I like you, too, but I am a follower of Kur, and this is wrong. You should go. I'll see you tomorrow."

He got up off the bed and fixed his shirt. "You are right. I apologize. Are we okay?"

"Yes, we are fine. We can meet for breakfast, which is coming very soon. You should go now," she said.

He leaned in, and they kissed one more time. "Good night."

"Good night," she replied and smiled at him. He left the room, and she locked the door. She walked over to her bed, reached into the drawer, and pulled out a thick book with thousands of thin pages that were heavily worn. She sat cross-legged on her bed and meditated with the book open, and she read several pages she had read a dozen times before. In fact, she had read the collection of books by Kur many times over the years. Especially on long flights between colonies, she would end up reading whole chapters in one sitting. After some time, she put the book away and stripped off her clothes. She placed the clothes in the sonic clothes washer and headed for a brief shower.

Water on the moon base was strictly rationed, and each shower was allowed two one-minute bursts of water each night. One was to wet the body so you could scrub, and the second was to rinse, and that was all anyone got. It was better than a month prior when showers were allowed only once a week due to two of the purification plants being out of commission. Now, two out of three plants are running, and the third should be back up and running by the end of the week.

She exited the shower and dried off, brushed her teeth, combed her hair, and went to bed. She would dress in the morning and start it all over again.

That night, she dreamed about Gula and the two of them on the *ShuBuré*. In her dream, she kept asking him why he wouldn't commit to her, and all he did was talk about their home village of Samuqan, saying he would when the Ineans were gone.

The next morning, she sat on the bed and said a blessing over the book of Kur, and then she got dressed.

TWENTY-SIX

DAGAN RAN across the gym in shorts and a snug-fitting shirt. She had left her robe on the bench by the door with her sandals. She stopped, turned, and planted her feet firmly while putting her fist out. It connected with Zuttara's chin, and they both fell to the rubber mat. He rolled her over but slipped and ended up punching her in the mouth. She kneed him in the groin, and he fell over while she jumped up and placed the heel of her bare right foot against his Adam's apple.

"I think I win," she said with a widening grin. She wiped blood from her swelling lower lip and studied it for a second too long.

"Ugh," he said, but then he swung his leg out and knocked both her feet out from under her, and he rolled out. She fell back to the mat with a thud, and he quickly pinned her down, bringing his face very close to hers. "Not so fast," he said, and he brought his face closer until their lips touched. He kissed her, and she did not refuse. He leaned in again while a voice in his head was yelling at him. "*She's a priestess, you idiot. You can't kiss her. You could be forced out of the camp for thirty days,*" but he did not listen to that voice as their lips touched again, and he pressed himself against her. She brought her arms up to his head and then around his waist. Soon, he rolled over, and she was on top, and the long kiss continued.

Soon, she pulled away, "Is this part of the lesson as well, Zuttara?" she asked while panting.

"I wish it was. We shouldn't do this. I'm sorry, Dagan. I don't know what came over me." He pulled out from under her, and as he was getting up, she swung her leg out. His feet flew out from under him, landing him back on the mat with a thud. She then pounced on him and brought her lips to his. They kissed for a long moment.

"I don't think this lesson is over," she said with a grin.

"Priestess! What are you doing? The sacred rules?" he said in a panicked voice while struggling to slide out from under her.

"Our society says that I cannot kiss you, but the word of Kur says nothing about it. As I have explained before, our society has twisted, added, and taken away from the words of Kur to the point where people are confused. They read the great books but still follow the high priests, knowing full well that Kur did not pass down many of these rules imposed on us. So I hope you have an open mind to the truth," she said with a grin as their noses touched.

"If I didn't, then we would not be here, to begin with," he replied, and he embraced her, and they kissed again for several seconds.

Soon, they got up, and he looked at the clock on the wall. "I have a meeting with General Asar and President Aanepada very soon, so we should get going." He reached up and wiped more blood from her swelling lower lip. "Sorry, I hit you."

"It wasn't intentional," she said while getting up. "You are right; we should get going, though." She went over to a large mirror on the wall, and she was taken aback by how she looked in regular clothes. Outside of her private room, she had to wear the robe which covered her from head to toe. She also saw Zuttara watching her as she walked towards the mirror. His eyes never blinked. She knew it was the clothing she wore. She was embarrassed by what she saw, but it also felt good to break out of the priestess garb for once. She studied her face when she got to the mirror, and Zuttara was now walking up behind her. She was tall for a woman, and he was about the same height.

He placed a hand on her shoulder and reached around and touched her swollen lip.

"What are we going to do about that?" she asked him while turning towards him. She placed her hands on his hips while he did the same. It was a new experience for her, and, for once in her life, she was not sure what the right thing to do was.

"I think we could hide some of it with makeup, but the swelling, I do not know," he stated.

"Let me gather my things and see you later," she said and then pulled away. "Tomorrow, same time?"

"Yes."

She didn't say anything else. She pulled the robe over her head and brought it down over her. She tied the rope around her waist and fixed her long, wavy, blond hair by tucking it inside the robe. She pulled the hood over her head and left the gym.

Zuttara stood and stared at the door, thinking to himself. He was falling for a priestess of Kur. He already kissed her and touched her while training her to fight. If the high priests found out, or Aanepada, who treated her like a daughter, he could face a firing squad for sure. He knew he was falling for her, and he knew that spelled trouble. He finally started walking for the door and gathered his things to leave the room.

TWENTY-SEVEN

ZUTTARA ENTERED the room after having showered and changed his uniform. In the room, President Aanepada sat at the head of the table with General Asar to his left and Dagan to his right. Several other military leaders and scientists filled the seats around the table. There was one empty seat, which was next to General Asar and across from Dagan, who kept her hood pulled over her head and her head down. He could not see her fat lip, but he knew it was there. Zuttara pulled the chair out and sat while pulling the chair to the table. He placed his binder on the table with a thunk and flipped it open. "Sorry I'm late," he said with a glance to the president, who stared at him for a moment. Did Aanepada know about him and Dagan? No, he was sure if the president knew he had kissed her, then he would have ripped him to pieces by now. Zuttara had to block it out, but he was afraid of the consequences of kissing the priestess, even though she did not object and had returned the kiss. That would not matter based on their cultural rules.

Aanepada glanced at the clock and sat up in his chair. "Shall we get started?"

Everyone nodded, and Aanepada glanced toward Dagan, "Priestess Dagan, will you open this meeting?"

"Yes, Mister President." She stood but kept her head bowed. Her long, wavy blond hair fell to both sides of her face, hiding her swollen lip for now. She opened the thick book of Kur's writings to a page she had previously marked and cleared her throat. "May the God of our fathers and of their fathers look down upon this gathering and bless what we have assembled to do. May Kur, the one true God of the Ardonnarian people, give us wisdom and guidance as we fight the evil Mullas that have come upon us from the sky. Mullas that murder and rape our people. May Kur bless our struggle and see us to victory." She paused and opened the bottle of wine in front of her, and poured the wine into a silver goblet. She then held the goblet up with both hands. "The symbolic blood of Kur, who foresaw this great calamity and promised that whoever should drink of his blood would have redemption upon his return." She took the cup, too, took a sip of the wine, and held the cup out before her. "The blood of Kur strengthens us who believe and live by his holy words. Praise be to Kur."

The others murmured. "Praise be to Kur."

She passed the goblet to Aanepada, who took it and held it out while keeping his head bowed. "The blood of Kur strengthens us who believe and live by his holy words." He took a sip and said, "Praise be to Kur."

The others repeated, "Praise be to Kur," he passed the cup to General Asar, and it went around the room until all had taken a sip of wine.

Once the cup made it back to Dagan, she looked in the goblet, and there was a little wine left. She then held out the cup, "Kur's blessing is upon this gathering and all who go forth from this room." She took the cup and gulped down the rest of the wine. She then placed the goblet on the table and sat in silence for a minute while everyone sat quietly with heads bowed. "Praise be to Kur," she said and lifted her head slightly to see the others, especially Zuttara, who seemed nervous.

The others replied. "Praise be to Kur," and they raised their heads.

Aanepada looked around the room. "Thank you, Priestess Dagan. Ummani, you called this joint meeting between our government, military, and science divisions, so you may as well start us off."

Ummani stood while clearing his throat. He was one of the lead scientists working on a prototype bomber. He wore a white lab coat and walked with authority towards a large whiteboard. The man was in his sixties and showed the wear of having little sleep and living on rations. He was a balding, older man with pale skin, having not seen the sun in months. What little hair he had was messy, and he had the beginnings of a rough beard. "Thank you, Mister President." He then turned to the whiteboard on the far wall facing Aanepada. He tapped the screen, and several pictures of three different ships popped up and rotated on the screen. He stepped to the leftmost diagram and pointed. "We have seen many of these craft flying about the planet lately. They are Inean long-range transports. They are very fast interstellar ships capable of flying between Ardonnar and Inea in a matter of a few weeks. The second picture is one of our transports used to ferry supplies around our solar system," he said while stepping aside to show the image of the craft rotating on the screen. "And lastly, what do you get when you combine the two ships into one?" he stepped to the side further so everyone could see the rotating image of the long-range, high-speed bomber that was at their base on the moon, Anaru. "You get a hybrid ship capable of striking Inea with our most lethal urukii warheads." He pressed a button on the side of the screen, and now the images changed to show the insides of the ships as they rotated. First, peeling off the layers of the hull to show the structural ribbing and then stripping off that to show the insides. Everyone in the room was impressed by the third ship, which housed six nuclear launch tubes down the middle of the craft.

General Asar sat up straight and addressed Ummani. "How many of these hybrids do we have?" he asked excitedly.

"We only have one so far. That is why I am here. We need to

build at least twenty-five of these craft to have a chance of carrying out the mission," Ummani said.

"What do you need us for? I think I speak for everyone here; get going," Asar said.

"Well, we need resources. People, supplies, urukii warheads, antimatter fuel, and the list goes on and on. We only have a limited supply of raw material on Anaru, and we need several supply ships worth to have a chance to build enough ships."

"When is the next CME coming?" Aanepada asked.

Kashurra, who was a thin, gray-haired scientist with thick, dark-rimmed glasses, turned towards Aanepada and then glanced at his notes. "It looks like another twelve days, sir."

"Can we load enough materials to keep you going in that short of time?" Aanepada asked.

"Yes. We have two cargo ships loaded, but the big concern is our location on Anaru. The Ineans frequently park their ships just a few zag above the base, and we have to stop work and shut down until they move away. It is only a matter of time before our cover gets blown. I suggest we ramp up on Uggae. It is far enough from the Ineans to avoid detection, and that is where we are producing the bulk of our antimatter fuel anyway."

"Antimatter fuel, isn't that very dangerous stuff?" Aanepada asked.

"Yes, that is why we use the distant moon orbiting Idpa."

"I see. Can we get the ships off Ardonnar undetected? They are quite big and bulky. Even with the Inean sensors, I would think even they could detect them," Dagan asked quietly.

Aanepada looked at her and wondered why she was suddenly being withdrawn and quiet. It was not like her to be so.

Kashurra replied to her. "We have covered their hulls in absorbent foam, and turned off all transponders, and shielded several internal systems. I think we can get them through. Besides, the timing of the next solar flare puts them on the other side of the planet, behind Duggae, so we have Ardonnar and Anaru to use as shields as well."

"Good," she replied and went back to making notes. Aanepada

noticed the knuckles on her left hand were scuffed, and the skin was broken on a few of them. He made a mental note to ask her about it after the meeting.

Aanepada brought his attention back to Kashurra. "Transfer operations to Uggae as soon as possible, but I want us to continue manufacturing on Anaru as a backup plan or as a diversion if needed."

"Understood, sir."

"How long will it take to produce the twenty-five ships needed for this mission?" Asar asked.

"I would estimate, if all goes according to plan, one to two years," Ummani said as he changed the graphic on the whiteboard to show a timeline of events.

Several in the room groaned. "Two years?"

"Do we even have two years left?" Dagan asked, still without looking up, and now Aanepada was getting annoyed. It used to bother him when she kept asking questions, but now it bothered him that she wouldn't look up. She was bold before.

"If, and that is a big if, the Ineans continue their current strategy, many of us think yes. However, if the Ineans decide it is time to wipe us out, then we may have only days," Kashurra said.

"Great, how many will die during this time period?" Zuttara asked.

Dagan finally glanced up. "We can't go two years. Women are being raped and taken away. Children are being taken away to who knows where. They could be eating them for all we know. The old people are just being killed, along with the men in the streets by the thousands every day, it seems."

Aanepada finally spied her swollen lower lip and the black mark which now covered part of her jaw. He felt himself becoming angry that someone may have hit her. But why? he wondered.

"I cannot think of any way to speed up the construction without making mistakes and without the Ineans figuring it out," Ummani said while turning back to the whiteboard. "I am open to suggestions as to how we can speed this up."

"We need to speed this up," Aanepada said, and he turned to

General Asar. "Help them in any way you can. Make sure the troops and militia in the field continue to poke holes in the Inean plans to slow them down. If we can take down more of their transport ships, then maybe the people leaving the planet will slow down."

"Yes, Mister President," Asar said while making notes.

"There is one more thing, Mister President," Ummani said.

"Go ahead, Ummani."

"Our long-range antennas have been picking up signals from our outer colonies. It has been a few years since we had contact with them, and the transmissions are just coming in. They are wondering why there has been no contact," Ummani said while he cleared the whiteboard.

"Can we contact them to tell them to stay away, and they are on their own for the time being?" Aanepada asked.

"We can get a focused hyper channel beam off of Uggae, which they should receive in a week. But there are two problems with that. The first is that the Ineans might realize we have other colonies and attack them. The second is the hyper channel beam could easily be picked up by the Ineans if they have a ship in the area, and the focused beam could tip them off as to the direction to go in." Ummani said while sitting back down.

"I see. If we do nothing, then the Ineans will realize we have colonies, and simple mathematics will dictate how far by the time it took to get a message here. If we do something, then the Ineans might realize our plans. I would say the chance justifies protecting our colonies. At least a warning to prepare them for a possible invasion, and they can hide. Or set up an early warning system. We should transmit an encrypted message with all of what we know so far and hope for the best. Also, include your schematics on the new ships." Aanepada sat back and pondered his plan. "Kashurra put it together and transmit the information to Uggae for immediate transmission once the next CME strikes. The Ineans will be blinded for a brief time."

"Yes, Mister President. I will get right on it."

Aanepada glanced at General Asar, who nodded. "Captain Zuttara, please come here."

Zuttara got up and walked towards the president, who stood beside his chair. Zuttara stood at attention and faced the president.

"Captain, I won't mince words here or take much time, and possibly at a later date, we could make it more official. However, General Asar and several others feel that it is time to give you a promotion."

"That is not necessary, Mister President."

"For the people, it is. As of now, your new rank is major," Aanepada said. Then he opened a small wooden box. He reached in and removed two round buttons. He added one to each shoulder in line with the others he had already. Aanepada then shook his hand while everyone in the room clapped.

"Major Zuttara, thank you."

"Thank you, sir," Zuttara replied with a firm salute.

Aanepada continued standing. "I think that is all. Get the cargo ships loaded and waiting. Get the communication loaded and ready to be sent, and hopefully, we will hold up long enough to hit them hard." He held his hands up and closed his eyes. "Praise be to Kur."

"Praise be to Kur," everyone else in the room stood and said.

The room began to empty, and Zuttara glanced at Dagan, who kept her head down and started for the door.

Aanepada watched her until she reached the door. "Priestess Dagan! I want you to stay for a minute."

She stopped but didn't turn, "Can I come back?"

"No, I want to talk with you right now."

Zuttara watched as he gathered his notes, but he took too long, which drew the attention of Aanepada.

"Zuttara, do you have something to add?" Aanepada asked.

"No, sir. I was just thinking of a way to speed up production, but I have nothing. Excuse me, Mister President," He nodded and left the room with a glance at Dagan as he walked past her.

Dagan approached Aanepada and stood before him with her head angled down. "Can I assist you, mister president?"

"What happened to you?"

"I don't understand?"

"Remove your hood and look at me."

She flipped her hood back and looked up at him, and he saw the bruise on her jaw and the swollen lip where it had been bleeding.

"Who did this to you?" he demanded.

"I can not say, Aanepada," she was afraid of what he would do to Zuttara and her for breaching the laws. If she were not Aanepada's adopted daughter, she would be cast out and forbidden to enter the temples ever again. Zuttara would be whipped and cast out as well. Both would be disgraced.

"Tell me right now who did this to you so they can be punished in accordance with our laws," he demanded sternly.

"I will not tell you because it is not what you think."

"Then tell me. You hold onto a lot of secrets, Dagan, and I need you to be forthcoming with me. We need to rely on you. As a priestess, you are sworn to tell the truth."

"I am telling the truth. It is not as it appears, and none of Kur's laws have been violated."

She went to turn away from him, but he gripped her arm. "Who is he, and why do you protect him?"

"I will tell you only if you promise, as my president and former priest yourself, that you will not harm him in any way."

Aanepada sat and faced her for a long time, which made her uncomfortable. "You really like this person?"

"Yes."

Her blunt answer caught him by surprise. He half expected her to say no or avoid the question. He looked into her eyes and decided to trust her.

"Okay, I promise not to do anything to him. Now sit and tell me what is going on."

She pulled out the chair and sat facing Aanepada. She looked him in the eyes and leaned forward. "I have been having dreams and visions for the past few months where I end up fighting the Ineans. They come to this base, and I fight them off with several others. The dreams continue, and I am on a ship outrunning the Ineans, and then there are bright flashes on a planet that is not ours. I think it means we do destroy their planet."

"So, how did you get hurt?"

"I know nothing about fighting, so I asked Zuttara to train me."

"What!" he screamed while pushing out of his chair.

"You promised to leave him alone. I forced him to help me. This was an accident. Nothing more!" she screamed back while pointing to her face.

"That is sacrilege! You will stop this at once," he demanded.

"I will not because Kur is directing me. I know he is. If I stop, then it might mean we don't survive," she said while lifting out of her chair to face him.

Aanepada sat back. She had never yelled at him before or taken such a stand on anything except when she wanted to enter the priesthood. "I don't know how we are going to keep this from the high priests. If they find out, it will be a disaster for all of us."

"Zuttara is my trainer. He is going to finish training me, and then if the dreams are true, then I will be prepared to do whatever Kur directs me to do."

"I know nothing of this."

She stared at him for a moment. "Don't be mad at me. Deep down, you know I am right. Look at how you found me when I was little. Consider my journey into the priesthood and where I stand now. I am right where Kur wants me to be. I need your support in this. It means a lot to me, and I was afraid to tell you because of how you would react."

He stood and faced her. He looked to make sure the door was closed and hugged her. "You don't make me mad. Maybe grit my teeth, and you raise my blood pressure, which the doctor said I need to control, but you have a fire that I nor anyone can control. I just ask that you be careful." He released her and started for the door.

Dagan watched him leave the room, and then she pulled her hood over her head and walked out as well. She went to her room to meditate for the rest of the night.

Aanepada went to his office and began composing his message to the outer colonies. It pained him to tell them to stay away at all costs and to prepare for a possible invasion. He struggled with the wording, and, over time, a pile of crumpled paper began to grow around the already-filled wastebasket. It was deep into the night when he finally finished what he wanted to say to them. He would include it with Ummani's data-filed message that would go out from Uggae when the inner planets and the Inean fleet would be engulfed in the next CME.

TWENTY-EIGHT

ON THE MOON, Anaru, workers dragged the completed prototype bomber deep into a protected cavern should the Ineans come snooping around. Four more were already under construction inside the hollowed-out cavern while Inean battleships flew just a few zag overhead. General Innin frequently had to stop production to avoid detection from the Inean sensors. It was nerve-wracking, to say the least, as workers shut down their equipment and waited for the all-clear, which frequently did not come for hours. This delayed production and added time their planet did not have.

Puabi sat at a control panel in one of the new bombers and programmed the guidance systems, which was a quiet job. Bel walked up behind her and put his hands over her eyes. She grinned. "Guess who?" he asked.

"Um, General Gurtna?" she said, and she turned to face him.

"Not quite," he said while embracing her, and they kissed.

Gula stood off in the distance, watching them inside the cockpit of the bomber. His stomach lurched when they kissed. It was supposed to be him, but he had waited too long. He shut down his computer and walked away.

Bel presented Puabi with another gift. This one was a box of sugar treats, which were hard to come by. She thanked him and opened the box. She shared some with him. Soon, his comm beeped. He kissed her again and rushed off the bomber. Puabi put the box of candies away and went back to programming the guidance system.

A few hours later, Bel was in the mess hall with several other pilots agonizing over their rations.

"I'll be glad to whip these monsters and get a real home-cooked meal," one of them said while forcing down something that resembled meat cubes in brown gravy over soggy toast.

"I think sahu dung would be better than this," the one next to him added. "Why are you so happy, Bel?"

Bel glanced up from his rations and wiped his mouth on the cloth placemat. "Well, I'll tell you, but you have to be quiet about it. There are some people around here who would not like it."

He had their attention, and they all leaned in to hear what he had to say.

"I plan on making it with Puabi tonight. I have been working on her all day," he said.

One of them pulled back slightly and put his fork down. He pointed at Bel. "Don't do it, Bel. She is a Western woman with deep Kurian beliefs. If you hurt her, there are a dozen or more on this base that will kill you, including the General."

"Don't worry, she wants it. All Western women want it. They simply don't know how to navigate certain rules. Rules I can show her how to break and get away with it," Bel added.

One of the pilots quickly added. "Bel, you are making a mistake. You better rethink this for your sake."

A third pilot chimed in. "I heard she and Gula were already committed. If you mess with her and he finds out, you are a dead man."

Bel finished his meal and placed the remains on the tray with the utensils. "Gula doesn't scare me. He had his chance and blew it, from what I heard." He picked up his tray and got up out of the chair. "Tonight, men, I will make history."

"Yeah, see you with a flag draped over your coffin in the morning," one of the pilots said, and they all laughed.

Bel walked away and discarded his dishes. He left the room to clean up for his date with Puabi.

A few hours later, Bel knocked on Puabi's door. She opened the door, and he stepped in. He kissed her again and hugged her. She returned the embrace and returned the kiss. She guided him to a pair of chairs by a table. On the table, a candle was burning, and there were two plates placed with spoons at the side of the plates. In the center was the plant he had given her the previous evening, and the chairs were positioned side by side.

"Please sit," she said, and Bel sat in one of the chairs.

Puabi went over to the dresser and pulled out a box that was wrapped in clear plastic. She handed it to Bel. "Open it," she said with a grin.

Bel took his pocket knife, cut the plastic off, and then opened the box. "It's cake. How did you?"

"I have friends, too," she said as she sat beside him. "Well, are you going to cut it?"

He thought about what the pilots had said about being in a casket in the morning, and then he grinned. "Absolutely," he stated. He then cut the square chocolate cake with green frosting, which signified the first harvest of the year, which was in the seventh month of Kiam on their thirteen-month calendar.

Bel gave her the first piece, and then he took his. He took frosting on his finger and smeared it on her nose. She giggled, and then he licked it off. She returned the favor and licked the frosting off him. They ended up kissing, and he felt it was time to make his move. He slid his hands down her back to her rear end with no resistance from her. "Western girls – huh, they are all the same," he thought to himself as his tongue probed her mouth. His hands came up, and he guided her to the bed, where they sat and kissed again.

He had one hand behind her and the other on the side of her face. He brought this hand down the side of her neck and then down the front of her shirt and between her breasts. Still, she did not resist. "Time to go for it," he thought. He reached up and undid the top button and then the next. Her hands came up and grasped his, and she pulled back.

"Bel, no," she said.

"Puabi, the Ineans could bomb this base at any time. You can't tell me that you would want to miss out on one of the blessings of Kur in this life because of some archaic protocol. I like you. You like me. There is no better time," he said while staring into her eyes. He then took her hands and placed them on her lap, and he went back to the buttons on her shirt. He undid the third and then the fourth and kissed her again. He pushed her back onto the bed and reached for her unbuttoned shirt.

Puabi slid out from under him and pulled her shirt together. "Bel, I can't do this. I'm sorry." She turned from him.

He got up off the bed and came up from behind her, wrapping his arms around her. He pulled her hands down and kissed her neck and ears. He undid the last button and gripped her shirt again with both hands and started to pull it off her. She started to resist him again, but he held her tight. She closed her eyes and thought of Gula. She pretended the hands on her body were his, but it did not work. They were not Gula's, and Bel was not her love but a substitute to fill a void in her life. She so much craved Gula that she was pretending Bel was him as he pulled her shirt off her shoulders while kissing her neck and ears. She pulled her arms tight to her body, stopping him. Finally, she opened her eyes as his hand slid down to the button on her pants and unsnapped them. She could not do this. This is not how she thought it would be with Gula. It was not right, and she grabbed his hands.

"Bel, stop!"

He did not, and now she was struggling to get away as he undid the next button of her pants. She managed to break free enough to swing her elbow into the side of his head, and he let her go. "Get out!"

"But, you should not hold onto Kur so strictly. It makes life boring, and you will miss out on a lot of this life," he said, thinking there was still hope.

"I said get out! And here, take this with you." She grabbed the plant he had given her and threw it at him as hard as she could. It smashed against the door as he went to open it. He turned and lunged at her while she fumbled with the buttons of her shirt. She turned and planted her knee in his groin, and as he was going down, she swung back with her foot, which still had the hard-cased work boot on it and connected with his jaw. He fell back and rolled to his knees.

"Okay, fine. I will leave, but I will get you for this," he spat blood toward her and went for the door. He opened it and kicked the broken plant into the hallway on his way out.

Puabi went to the door and locked it, and then she sat on the edge of the bed, clutching her shirt, and cried.

After some time, there was a knock on her door. "Go away!" she yelled.

"Puabi, it is Gula. What is wrong?"

She sniffed and got off the bed. A quick glance at the mirror said it all. Her face was red, along with her eyes. "Give me a minute."

She rushed to the bathroom, splashed water on her face, and toweled off. She fixed her shirt and went to open the door.

Gula stepped in, "What did he do to you?"

She guided him into the room, and they sat in the chairs. "Please, don't."

"What happened, Puabi?" he asked while placing his hand on her shoulder.

"He tried to force himself on me. I kept telling him no, but he would not listen. So I hit him, and then he left."

Gula pulled her to him as she began to cry again. He held her as he tried to control his anger. "This is all my fault."

"Why is it your fault?" she asked.

"I should have asked you a long time ago."

She punched him in the chest. "Yes, you should have."

"I didn't know if you would say yes."

"Say YES? I would have jumped up and down for a whole month while saying yes, you fool."

"I'm sorry. Puabi. I am a fool."

"Finally, you agree with me," she looked at him. "Is that official, or was that a practice run?"

He looked at her for a moment and then got up. He grasped her hands to help her up. "Puabi, will you..."

The lights dimmed, and an alarm sounded. Gula went to pull away, and she gripped his hands. "Oh no, you don't. Finish what you were going to say first."

"Puabi, will you accept my vow of betrothal?"

She jumped up and down, "Yes! Yes, yes. Finally, after how many years?" She hugged him, and then the second alarm sounded.

They ran from the room and headed out towards the flight deck to see what was going on. There, they saw one of the new bombers with smoke billowing out from the cockpit. It was the bomber she had been working on hours before. The general walked up to them.

"Looks like the navigation computer had a short in it," General Innin said.

"That idiot," Puabi mumbled.

"You know about this?" Innin asked.

"Cushik!" She cursed, "I had a fight with Bel, and he vowed to get me. It just so happens that I programmed that nav-com earlier today."

"We need to get to the bottom of this right away. Gula, go find Bel and bring him to me," General Innin said as the technicians put the fire out.

"My pleasure, General," Gula said with a salute, and he left the flight deck.

Puabi walked to the bomber and into the cockpit to survey the damage. She sat in the seat and started touching wires that crumbled in her hands. "Duga!" she huffed. "I'm sorry, General. I will take this apart and fix it tonight so it doesn't slow us down tomorrow."

He patted her on the shoulder. "Take a break and get a fresh start in the morning. It is not your fault. Bel has a history of anger problems. The only reason he is here is because we need good pilots," the general stated.

"What else has he done?" she asked.

"Well, he murdered another pilot ten years ago. The evidence was shaky, and he got off on some technical clause. He has been in many fights. That's the shortlist."

"Why is he here then?" she asked.

"Like I said, he is a good pilot. One of the best, and we feel he is worth more than his baggage."

"Wish I knew that a few days ago. I would not have gotten involved."

The general stared at her for a moment. "You got involved with him?"

"Yes, but I ended it tonight."

"Did he threaten you?"

"Yes, he did. He said he would get me," Puabi replied with a slump of the shoulders.

"Take it seriously. We'll keep him away from you as best as we can. I might send you to Uggae on the next transport. You can work with that team and be away from him."

"Why not send him away, sir?"

"I can keep an eye on him here. There is no one to watch him on that moon."

"Understood, you should send Gula, as well. He is also in danger."

"And I just sent him to find Bel."

The general left the bomber and Puabi alone and went with a handful of officers who were armed to find Bel. They searched well into the night and found him in the last place anyone thought he would be: his quarters. Gula woke him and took him to the detention cell, where General Innin came and brought him to an interrogation room.

Gula called for Puabi to attend. She arrived several minutes later, and the general began questioning Bel about the incident. He had not been arrested at this point, but the general trusted Puabi more than Bel and wanted to put him away.

General Innin leaned over Bel in an intimidating posture while he tapped on a folder with dozens of pieces of paper in it. Bel did not know what was on the paper, but the general did.

"So Bel, tell me about Puabi," Innin asked.

Bel squirmed in his seat slightly. What did the general know? He wondered. He glanced at the folder Innin continued to tap his fingers on.

"You could answer anytime now, Bel."

"Yes, General Innin. Puabi is a good pilot, sir."

"That isn't what I was asking, Bel," Innin asked while getting directly in front of Bel's face. "Tell me about you and her," he snarled.

Outside the room, Puabi watched through the one-way glass and was nervous. What would he say? Would he go into detail? Gula stood beside her and watched the general interrogate Bel. She knew that if Bel went into any detail, then Gula had every right to retract his commitment to her and never speak to her again. She cringed as Bel smiled and looked at the mirrored glass.

Gula saw her cringe and knew there was more about this than she would ever tell him. He watched her out of the corner of his eye, and he watched Bel, whom he was beginning to hate for touching Puabi.

Bel's grin widened, and he turned to face the general who had stepped aside. "Puabi puts eastern women to shame, and then she tosses me out like garbage."

Puabi put her head down in disgust. "That isn't true," she mumbled.

Gula stood by her but was becoming concerned about what actually happened between them.

General Innin was not amused and slapped Bel across the face. "I want the truth from you!"

Bel brought his hand to his face to rub the sting out of his reddening cheek. "Fine, I tried to have sex with her, and she threw me out. How did you know?"

"I can tell the difference between an Eastern woman and a Western. She is by far a daughter of Kur and would have tossed you out long before anything would have happened." He gripped Bel's face with one hand and tilted it toward his. "Did you threaten her, and did you rig the nav-com to burn up?"

Bel laughed, "Is that what this is about?" He laughed again, which brought a sharp smack across his face from General Innin. "I said I would get her. I did not define what that meant."

"Did it mean sabotage of the nav-com?" the general probed, and he was growing increasingly impatient.

"Absolutely not, General, you have to believe me," Bel said as he spun in his chair. "I will get even with her, but that hurts us all."

In the other room, Puabi looked up at the window. "Duranki! That means I screwed it up." Duranki was a curse word worse than any other and not used on the Western continent, and definitely not by Western women.

"Puabi!" Gula said with a gasp.

"Sorry, but if I fried that console, then yes, duranki!" she said while watching the interrogation in the next room.

"You better pray to Kur for saying that," Gula stated in disgust.

"I will, after I fix that console," she turned and headed for the door.

"Where are you going?" Gula asked.

"To fix the mess I created and get us back on schedule," she said with a twist of the doorknob.

"He could be lying."

"No, Gula, I saw his eyes. He was telling the truth. He did not cause this. I did. Now I must fix it."

She exited the room and went back to the flight deck to rewire the control panel, which would take her until the wee hours of the morning.

The interrogation continued, but Bel did not offer any useful information at all. Finally, the general released him and went to talk with Gula. "What do you think?" he looked around. "Where is Puabi?"

"She left to fix the transport. She blames herself for that."

"What *do you* think, Gula?"

"I'm not sure if he's lying or telling the truth. My gut says he is lying."

The general stared through the glass at the now-empty interrogation room. "I think he knows more about the nav-com, as well. We'll watch him over the next few days."

"Understood, General."

"Oh, and Gula, stay away from him. I see the looks between you and Puabi and know this could become personal. So stay away from him."

"Yes, General. It already has," he said. The two men left the room and headed in opposite directions.

The next day, just before dusk in Kurdash, Puabi entered her quarters and stripped. She stepped into the shower and began chanting to Kur for forgiveness over her weakness with Bel. The purification ritual required running water, so the shower would have to do on the moon, Anaru. She turned the water on and made sure she was soaked. She chanted again. Then, she gathered her clothes and washed them as well to cleanse them. She put the clothing aside and turned the water on a third time to cleanse her body one more time. After she finished praying to Kur, she stepped out and hung her clothes over a heater to dry them. She went and sat on her bed and ate the half loaf of bread she had picked up at the mess hall. She also drank some water. She praised Kur again and slipped into bed. She reached into the drawer beside the bed and took out the book of Kur. She read for hours while condemning what she had done with Bel. She could not help but think of what the consequences would have been if she had allowed things to go further.

The cleansing was done at dusk based on the location of the great temple in Kurdash. It was to be done for seven consecutive evenings, and after that time, the body would be considered clean.

The clothing the person wore would also be washed at the same time. This was typically done in a flowing river, but the only water flowing on Anaru came from a shower nozzle. The cleansing process also involved reading Book Nine of Kur, which dealt with purification and repentance. She would have to read this daily for seven days as well.

Another aspect of the purification was that the unclean were not allowed in the temple and could not be blessed by the high priest during this time.

The next morning, she went to the Mess Hall and ordered bread and a glass of water. Then she sat at a table to the side of the room near the wall-sized video screens, which displayed a view of the moon's surface.

Gula entered and gathered his rations for breakfast, and then he sat across from her. "Where did you rush off to last night?" he asked.

"I had to perform the purification ritual," she said as she bit off a hunk of bread.

"I see. Bread and water for a week must be tough."

"Not really. Have you tasted your rations yet?" she smirked. "Not as tasty as what was here a month ago," she said.

"Tasty is not one of the words I would have chosen to describe these," he replied while poking at the food on his plate. "Can I have some bread?"

She broke a piece off and handed it to him. Then she finished hers. "Time for work. I have three more nav-coms to program."

"Have you figured out what happened to that other one that burned up?" Gula asked, having not seen her much since that night.

"No. It looks like the circuit board was installed backward, but that is impossible. It would never have booted up if that was the case."

"So it looks like sabotage then?" he pried.

"Yeah, maybe. I can't explain it," she said while brushing the crumbs off the front of her uniform. "See you later?"

"Yes, later," Gula said, and he watched her leave the room. He wanted to ask her why she was performing the purification ritual if she did not have sex with Bel. She was obligated to tell him if she had, but he had no idea how to broach the subject. He decided he had to trust her. He had known her since they were children, and she was a woman of integrity and conviction. She followed the teachings of Kur to the letter, and that was good enough for him. As far as he knew, she was probably repulsed by Bel and felt dirty. He would hold onto that reason for now.

TWENTY-NINE

DEEP IN THE MOUNTAIN HIDEAWAY, President Aanepada and General Asar met in private to discuss who would fly these ships. Many of their pilots were missing and presumed dead at this point. Even if they had pilots, the new ships were different from anything they had ever flown.

"Mister President, I had a lengthy conversation with one of the pilots on Anaru who helped design the navigation systems with a team of engineers. She has put together a test we can administer to our forces in the field to see if there are people who can fly these bombers to Inea and back.

"Who is she?" Aanepada asked.

"Her name is Puabi. She was the pilot of the *ShuBuré*."

"I have heard of her. Do you think this test will work?"

"Yes. Besides, she has given us schematics to build a simulator for people to train on here before being sent to the moons."

"How would you get the test out to the field and the potential candidates here?" Aanepada said while glancing at the general's proposal.

"We would send it as an encrypted file when we do our weekly check-ins. The platoon leaders would have everyone they felt was qualified take the test and send the results to us. I can put together a staff to analyze the data and request people from the field," Asar responded with enthusiasm.

"How would you get them here?"

"Unfortunately, Mister President, we would have to rely on them to walk or hitch rides from all across the planet."

"That would take time, Asar and the Ineans may figure it out. Worse yet, if this test falls into their hands, then we are sunk," Aanepada said with concern.

"Once a platoon takes a test and transmits the results to us, then the information automatically deletes from their computers, and we will have to rely on people to keep their mouths shut if they are captured. I don't see a better way, sir."

"Neither do I." Aanepada got up and walked around the room. He stared at the whiteboard, which was blank right now. He pressed a button, and the diagram of the new bomber came up on the screen. He studied it for a few seconds. "Get teams building two simulators and get the word out for your pilots, General. Hopefully, we can find enough close to home to fill the fifty positions."

"Understood Mister President. I will get the word out and have our engineers building the simulators right away."

"That will be all, Asar, and may the blessings of Kur be upon your task."

"Thank you, Mister President, and may the blessings of Kur be upon us all," he said with a bow.

"Yes, all of us," Aanepada said, and he bowed to Asar.

THIRTY

DAMOK-SAI WANDERED about the bridge of the *Nikstra*, watching the transports ferrying Ardonnarian slaves to the *Pavitra*, which had just returned from Inea. Damok-Sai was under pressure to double the number of slaves sent back to the Inean home world. He was now converting a second and third battleship for this purpose. The "Chanak," which was damaged by the Ardon nuke, was repaired, and the "Nivrutti." It would be weeks before these ships could be sent back with the high-priced cargo. He left the bridge and headed towards a meeting with his field commanders on the planet.

He and his field commanders had assessed the Ardonnarian threat. They determined that the Ardons were not a threat to destroy any more ships now that the Ineans instituted security measures. The only threat was on the ground, where the Inean soldiers found the Ardonnarians unpredictable and deadly on a small scale. However, Damok-Sai had hundreds of nuclear weapons at his disposal that he could launch in minutes, leveling the entire planet. This would be his trump card should the Ardonnarians launch a major offensive. He had already destroyed two cities, Suen on the eastern continent and Anshar on the western continent. He knew that was why the Ardons took to smaller confrontations. He also knew that Ardon nuclear warheads were missing, many of them.

Multiple field commanders had noticed troop movement but not on a mass scale, a few from here and a few from there all over the planet. All were heading towards the western continent. The field commanders wanted to eliminate them, but Damok-Sai did not see them as a threat and concentrated their efforts on selecting the best slaves to be sent to Inea.

"Damok-Sai, we should bomb them if we come across rebels heading to the western continent," one field commander stated. The others agreed.

Damok-Sai stood facing the windows with his back to his field commanders and pondered the option. Then he turned around and walked up to the table. "Their number is small," he said while staring at each one of them. "I want. Correction. Emperor Sankar wants us to step up transporting these slaves to Inea."

"As you know, the Emperor has requested a doubling of the harvest, and we do not have the forces to chase random rebels and keep his deadline. Besides, like I said, their number is small, and they are scattered. So if they choose to launch an offensive and take back a city, then we can destroy that city with the press of a button right from here," he laughed in a deep rumbling roar, and the others joined in as well.

After several seconds of booming laughter, Damok-Sai regained his composure. "Keep an eye on them to see where they are going. There must be one location where they are controlling the planet's forces. If we watch, maybe we can find out where it is." He leaned closer. "Don't waste time doing this. We can destroy them at any time when the Emperor gives us the go-ahead."

"Yes, Damok-Sai," the field commanders said in unison.

"So, we are done here. We need to double our shipments to Inea quickly. Besides, the sooner we ship them all off this rock, the sooner we can finish them off. Now go," Damok-Sai said with a wave of his hand, and he turned back to the window to watch a flock of birds go by.

THIRTY-ONE

RECRUITS BEGAN ARRIVING after two weeks and remained trickling in for another four months. The simulators were not finished when the first group arrived. The group immediately entered the classroom to learn about basic flight, mathematics, and the various systems they would need to operate. Asar had others oversee this process while he concentrated on planetwide raids to slow the Ineans.

The simulators were mock cockpits with navigation controls only, for now, so the trainees would not get confused by all the buttons, switches, and displays they would be confronted with in the real bombers.

Deep in the mountain was the firing range. Here, Zuttara brought Dagan for her first lesson in shooting. He handed her a small pistol and had her aim it at a target in the distance. She aimed and pulled the trigger, and the bullet went wide into the rock wall with a spray of small pieces of rock.

"Okay, stand with your feet apart for balance and hold your arms out, but don't lock your elbows."

He stood close behind her and placed his hands on her shoulders. She wore her brown robe today and had the hood down for now, and he knew that was all she had on. Until now, he did not think of it, but working with her in recent weeks had brought him closer to her, and now he was having thoughts any man would have when working with such an attractive woman. He leaned close to her so he could smell her hair, which smelled nice to him. He spoke in her ear. "Now look at the notch at the top here with one eye. You can close the other for now and line it up with the pin sticking up at the end of the barrel and aim them at the center of your target. Now pull the trigger."

She did, and the gun kicked back slightly in her hands, but she hit the bull's eye seventy pana away. She turned her head slightly to make eye contact with Zuttara, and she grinned at him. She leaned back slightly against him as well. She liked the feel of him behind her, and she was beginning to have thoughts about him as well. Oh, if the high priests heard of this, their heads would spin around. She had vowed a life of celibacy when she joined the priesthood, but she was sensing that she may have to fight that in the future. As far as she knew, there was nothing in the writings of Kur to prevent her from having a relationship with a man. For now, though, she would fight the urges as best as she could and learn all she could.

"Nice shot. Now try it a few more times," Zuttara said while stepping back.

She fired off a dozen more rounds, and all hit the target on the far side of the room.

"Impressive. Let's try something bigger." He walked away for a moment and brought back an assault rifle. He showed her how to hold it and then helped her place her hands on it. He felt her skin; it was soft and warm to the touch. Then he stepped back.

She fired off a few rounds and tore up the target across the room. Next, he handed her an automatic rifle. He stood behind her with his arms around her, showing her how to hold this rifle. "Remember to press it against your shoulder like this and sight it with your left eye."

She pressed back against him, and her long, wavy blond hair

was in his face. His cheek was against her ear as he talked her through, firing the automatic rifle.

"Now pull the trigger and release," he said.

She squeezed the trigger, and pow! The gun fired and slammed into her shoulder, pushing her back into Zuttara. The bullet went wide of the target and buried itself into the rock, spraying larger bits of rock out of the wall.

"Wow!" Dagan said with a glance at Zuttara. His face was right in front of hers, and he got the urge to kiss her as their noses touched. Their lips touched, and they kissed again. He eventually pulled back, and she turned to face the target. Their bodies remained pressed together, and neither cared.

"Wow, is right," he said. "Try planting your feet further apart now that you have a feel for the kick of the automatic." She did as he instructed. She aimed and fired the gun again. This time, she stayed firm, and the bullet hit the target.

"Do that a few more times," he said, and he stepped back.

She fired off several more rounds and got a better feel for the gun. She hit the target more times than not.

"Now, the fun part," Zuttara said, and he reached over her shoulder and flipped a switch on the side of the gun. "Now hold on and press the trigger, but hold it for a couple of seconds."

She took a deep breath and let it out. She sighted the target, pulled the trigger, and held it. The gun went off in rapid-fire mode, sending over fifty rounds toward the target while the gun pounded her shoulder. She released the trigger as a wisp of smoke rose from the barrel of the gun.

"Nice job, most of your shots hit the target. Now take all of the guns to that table, and we are going to take them apart and clean them for tomorrow."

She gathered the three weapons and took them to the table, where Zuttara showed her how to take them apart, clean them, and reassemble the weapons. Afterward, she kissed Zuttara and pulled her hood back over her head. She left the room, and Zuttara got the targets ready for his next group to train. His next class would pick up the spent casings and reload them.

. . .

Later that day, the High Priest, Kasua, cornered Dagan in the food line. "Priestess, several of us are concerned with your activities, which seem to be taking time away from your studies."

"I don't know what activities you are talking about, High Priest Kasua," she replied. She then pushed by him with her food tray and headed for an open table.

He followed.

She sat, and he sat across from her. "You have been spending time with Zuttara. You must realize the implications if you are involved with a man," he snarled at her. He did not like her because she raised too many questions that pitted the High Priests between the true writings of Kur and what their society believed. This annoyed them because they could not respond to her without admitting the hypocrisy of what they had been teaching. So they followed her and watched her for anything to use against her. Their goal was to have her removed from the priesthood. Kasua now had something to use against her.

"Tell me what the impropriety is, Teacher of Kur," she said while cutting the sandwich she had selected.

"You tell me what you are doing."

"I don't feel I need to answer to you. Kur is the one to whom I must answer," she said while taking a modest bite of the vegetable sandwich while a drop of dressing rolled down her chin. She wiped it off while he responded.

"Don't play your games with me. Now answer the question," his voice rose in frustration.

"I'm not playing games. I obey the writings of Kur, and, according to Kur, I have done nothing wrong except irritate you, which, last time I checked, is not a crime. If you have seen me *do* something that violates Kur's teachings, then please let me know. As of now, you are the one playing games and are in violation of Kur's word."

Kasua was getting steamed now. "I am not in violation of Kur's teachings, Priestess Dagan." His rising voice drew the attention of others in the area, who turned to see what was going on. "You have been having relations with that man, and it must end now!"

Dagan wiped her mouth as she put the sandwich down. She swallowed and took a drink of water. "So, you have proof that I violated Kur's teachings. So give me the sordid details then." She folded her hands, placed her chin in them, and stared at Kasua while painting a smile on her face. This threw him over the edge, and he had to compose himself before smacking that grin off her face. "I am calling a meeting of the High Priest Council for first thing in the morning. You will be there to answer for your sins against the Ardonnarian people and your false beliefs in what the scriptures state."

"So, you have nothing, as usual, and you just want to waste everyone's time and effort while we fight for our survival against an overwhelming enemy."

"Be there," he said. He threw his food down, and he pushed out of his chair with a glance at the people watching him.

"Oh, I wouldn't miss this for anything. Tell me, Kasua, do you get tired of losing against me. You have to admit it is getting old. Why don't you give it up?"

He walked away without responding, but he did hear her and knew she was a tough fight. However, this was the first time she smacked him down in public. Many in the room watched the exchange. They saw Kasua's face getting redder as he walked away. Dagan, well, Dagan was confident, and she went back to her sandwich, which seemed to taste better now. She sat back and enjoyed the rare desert that the cooks had put together, then chased it down with the ice-cold water. Despite their plight, life was still good, she thought. She opened a smaller version of Kur's writings and read for quite some time.

The room emptied and started to fill again. Dagan closed the book, cleaned up her dishes, and left for her room.

The next morning, she arrived at the temple hollowed out of the rock in the mountain. Support beams crisscrossed the room to support the rock ceiling above. Facing her were three High Priests and President Aanepada, who was the leader of the people and also a High Priest himself. The presidency consumed much of his time, and he no longer practiced.

Kasua stood when she entered and pointed to a seat in the middle facing them. "Sit there," he said sternly. She grinned at this, thinking he was still licking his wounds from their previous encounter.

"You think this is funny?" he yelled at her, which only supported her belief.

She said nothing as she knelt down at the railing and bowed her head. She said a prayer to Kur for guidance, and confidence flowed over her. She got up and sat in the chair facing the hostile panel.

"Priestess Dagan, you have been brought here to answer charges of impropriety regarding your actions with Major Zuttara. How do you respond?" Kasua stated while still standing. The others watched him, hoping he knew what he was doing. All of them, except for Aanepada, had gone several rounds with her and had not fared well at all. She was smart and knew the writings of Kur forward, backward, and sideways.

"Let's hear your charges first," she said, straight-faced.

"Fine, Priestess. The first charge is that you have had romantic relations with Major Zuttara, which is against Ardonnarian code of conduct for a priestess. You have also signed a declaration of celibacy when you joined the priesthood. Do you deny this?"

"Sounds like three different questions. Which one would you like me to debunk first?" Dagan asked while folding her arms across her chest.

The others groaned. She was going to mop the floor with him, and he didn't know it yet.

"Just take them in order and quit stalling. Your fate is in my hands," he growled. His face was getting red again.

"Be careful of your blood pressure, Kasua. What is the definition of romantic relations based on our culture?" she asked and quickly answered before they could respond. "If we are on the eastern continent, romantic relations can be construed as giving a gift of a beverage or helping an elderly woman across the street. Is that what I am accused of?" She paused briefly, "Or is it a Western definition that can be as simple as touching a person's hand with thoughts of more. Are you capable of reading my thoughts?" she grinned at Kasua. "Or why are we going to base this on cultural rules when we aspire to the writings of Kur, which says what on the subject? Anyone?" No one spoke. The others were afraid of her, and Aanepada was there only to make sure she did not tear them up too badly. "Is it because in all those pages, Kur says nothing on the subject? So I have to ask why, if it is true, why is it an issue anyway?"

The panel groaned. Two of them wanted to hide, and Aanepada knew this was not going well for Kasua.

"You also call into question the declaration of celibacy I signed many years ago. Have you ever read what that document says? Let me read it for you," and she produced a piece of paper from her pocket.

Kasua waved his hand towards her, "It won't be necessary to read that for us." He was now getting a feel for this woman, and she was making a fool of him.

"Oh, I don't mind at all. Perhaps we can all learn something today. Let's see, this must be what you are talking about right here. Paragraph seven. '*A priestess of Kur in accordance with Ardonnarian laws shall not have reproductive relations with a man during her priesthood or enter into marriage unless approved by the highest priest in power.*' I could go on, but the rest is just as cold and boring as that. So, have I had such relations with Major Zuttara or anyone else?"

Kasua went to speak, but she cut him off. "Provable violations, not hearsay," she said.

Kasua closed his mouth.

"Kur says nothing in regard to these actions. We are taught at the great temple in Kurdash to follow the teachings of Kur and forsake the rules of this world, but yet you have tried to use the rules of this world to trump Kur's teachings. Why do you embrace this world so much at the expense of what you have sworn your life to?" she looked them each in the eyes, and each one turned their gaze away from her. Her stare burned them and scared them. "I will tell you that Major Zuttara has been a perfect gentleman while he has been teaching me how to fight should the Ineans come here. This is in full compliance with the teachings of Kur and should not be an issue. And if, and that is a big if, I should choose to enter into a relationship with Major Zuttara, then I would still be within what Kur has taught. I say this to prevent another meeting like this."

"Priestess Dagan. We do understand your position, but you must understand one thing. While you are correct in saying that we must look to Kur first, we are still of this world and need to set an example to the people we are to serve," one of the elder priests said.

"I agree; however, we can do that without compromising our beliefs and adopting rules that have nothing to do with what Kur expresses in his many books. I feel this is why society on the eastern continent was falling apart, and it was coming here before we were invaded," she said with a glance at Kasua, who was fumbling for his chair. He was not well, and she could see it.

"I have one more question, Priestess Dagan. Why are you training to fight the Ineans?" one of the other elders asked.

"I feel that we need every ablebody to fight and defeat them. I believe it is my calling." She kept an eye on Kasua, who was now sweating as he pulled his chair out. He was in obvious pain. Dagan got up and stepped over the railing, which brought a shocked look from the other elders and Aanepada until they realized what was happening. She gripped Kasua and helped him to the floor. "Someone get a doctor!" she stated firmly, and Aanepada raced from the room.

Kasua had his hand on his chest as beads of sweat rolled from his face while grimacing from the pain.

"Don't worry, Kasua, doctors are on the way. Do you take any medication for your heart that we can give you for this?" she asked.

He nodded yes.

"Where is it?" she asked.

He tried to point to his bag on the floor beside his seat. One of the elders went for it and dumped it out on the table. He poked through it until he found the gray bottle. He read the label and dumped out two silver-coated, soft jelly pills. He handed them to

Dagan, who placed them in Kasua's mouth and made him swallow them. The elder priest handed her a cup of water, which she poured into Kasua's mouth to rinse them down.

A few minutes later, the base doctor raced in with a nurse and Aanepada behind her. Dagan yielded to the doctor and stepped back.

"I take it that we are done here?" she asked.

"We are done here," the elder said.

The doctor and the nurse helped Kasua from the room and brought him to the infirmary so he could recover from his heart attack, his third in the past year. He would recover from this one, as well, but he would insist Dagan was the cause.

THIRTY-TWO

PUABI WAS in her seventh day of the purification ritual. It had been a week of bread and water only. A week of rededication to the teachings of Kur and a week of odd looks from some of the other pilots and from Gula. She checked the clock, and it was now dusk in Kurdash. The week was now over, and she went to her quarters to perform one final act.

She entered her room and turned the light on. She stripped off her uniform. She retrieved the book of Kur and sat on her bed cross-legged. She opened the book and placed it before her, held her hands out, and recited the final passages of the ritual. She concluded with a prayer for her and her people.

She opened her eyes and put the book away. Next was a quick shower, with soap this time and a fresh uniform. A few minutes later, she was done and headed out the door for dinner with Gula, real food for the first time in a week. She looked forward to it and the company.

Puabi entered the mess hall and looked for Gula, but he was not there. She could not wait, and she stood in the short food line and gathered a heaping serving. She looked around, and still no Gula. She huffed and headed for a table and sat. She nibbled at her food, waiting for him, but it was getting cold, and she couldn't wait any longer. She finished off the mound of food and even discreetly licked the plate. She sat and waited a little while and then eventually left. She walked back to her room and heard of a confrontation on the flight deck involving Bel. She instantly knew the other person was Gula. She turned around and headed for the flight deck. There, she found General Innin with Gula. Two guards had Bel with his hands tied behind his back. Gula was pleading his case with the general, who did not seem to be buying it. All she knew was that Bel had blood trickling from his nose, which was probably broken, and a black eye. Finally, General Innin motioned for the guards to take Bel away, and then he turned to Gula, who snapped to attention.

"Gula, I want you to stay away from him," the general stated.

"Yes, sir, but he needs to stay away from me as well because I won't back away from him. He is a detriment to our efforts, sir," Gula stated.

"You leave me no choice then. I am sending you AND Puabi to Uggae to head up the construction of the ships there. Things are running a bit slower there, and I need someone with your determination to light a fire. I am sending her to make sure he does not have an opportunity to act on his threats." The general stated with a glance to Puabi, who entered his line of sight. "I want you both on the next transport out of here, which is in a few days."

The next Inean-induced Solar blast occurred a day late, which was becoming a pattern lately. The storms appeared to be slowing, and one cycle was missing altogether. They knew time was running out, and sooner or later, they would not have them to use for cover. Their strength had been waning, as well. Some speculated that Utui had been severely weakened by the constant shedding of plasma and mass for more than two years now.

Innin did manage to ship six transports loaded with supplies and personnel to Uggae, including Gula and Puabi. This would solve two of his problems. He would get Gula and Puabi away from Bel, and they would also get that base's production up to par. Granted,

Uggae was further away from Ardonnar than Anaru, and supplies took longer to arrive, but there were ample resources to draw from already, and there should have been no lag in production. Each moon was tasked with producing twenty-five bombers to attack Inea, and their schedule was tight. Each day, thousands of Ardonnarians died at the hands of the Ineans, and thousands more disappeared altogether. Their population had been severely diminishing along with normal deaths and a planetwide sharp decline in birth rates due to the war. It would become known as the missing generation.

THIRTY-THREE

GENERAL INNIN SAT with several technicians while observing the Inean fleet on the large monitors suspended from the rock ceiling. They had been taking notes on their movements, and he noticed patterns in how the ships interacted together. He also noted some changes lately, which he was preparing to advise the generals on the ground with President Aanepada.

"Comm, open a link to Antum base, please," General Innin said as he studied the colorful graphs on the large monitors.

A young woman turned to Innin. "Comm opened, sir."

"Antum, this is General Innin. Is the president and his staff waiting?"

"Yes, we are here, General. Go ahead with your report," Aanepada stated.

The camera panned back to show the room. Aanepada was seated at the head of the table and was flanked on either side by his military leaders.

The other side of the monitor showed the general hunched over a keyboard with a few technicians behind him. Also behind him were some monitors displaying Inean ship movements. It was also dark on the Anaru base in an attempt to conserve as much energy as possible.

"Okay, Mister President. We have noticed several changes in the Inean fleet as of late, which you will be interested in. First, they are down a few ships. The original invasion fleet was twenty-five ships. We got a lucky shot off destroying three of them several months ago and damaged two others. Those two have been used as ferries, probably bringing people and products to their home planet. The exit trajectory seems consistent with that flight plan. That leaves them with nineteen battle-ready ships in orbit."

"That is still a formidable force, General Innin," General Asar stated.

"Yes, it is General, but there is a catch. We feel they are running low on fuel. With all the trips back and forth to the surface over the past two years, and as far as we can tell, there has been no refueling of these enormous ships," Innin said.

"What are you saying, General?" Aanepada asked.

"I'm saying that they have obviously implemented conservation mode. If we could devise a plan to make them burn more fuel, such as chasing drones out of the system or something similar, it may help us when it comes time to attack Inea. They may not have enough fuel to get those ships back home."

"What if they send a refueling tanker?" Asar asked.

"Then we have to nuke it. We must take the risk if that happens. We can't let those ships refuel at all costs. But I don't think they will. The Ineans are so obsessed with stripping this planet that they may be making another tactical mistake," Innin said.

"Good work, General," Aanepada said, "We will work on a plan to strike any refueling vessel that may arrive, and we will also work on a plan to make them waste fuel."

"We are losing our secure window right now, General Innin. Sit tight and keep your eyes open. Asar out."

The connection closed with a crackle, and then the screen went black. "Okay, people. Let's set up some high-speed missiles with nukes to attack the Inean ships if we need to."

"We should set up some decoys as well, sir. To lead them astray if we need a diversion," one of the others added.

"Get on it, but don't take away from our bomber production. We need them space-worthy as fast as possible."

"Yes, sir." The officers saluted the general and left the room. The general went back to watching the Inean ships on the display. There was something he was missing.

THIRTY-FOUR

ANZILLU AND ENANATUMA got in a small wooden boat as dusk was setting in. He checked the power meter on the dashboard and was satisfied with the battery's charge. Next, he checked his plastic-covered map and his compass to set the right course. He shoved the map and compass in his jacket pocket and looked forward as Enanatuma pulled on rain gear to keep her dry from the rough ocean. She passed him one as well. He pulled on his rain gear and started the solar-powered electric motor while Enanatuma untied the boat from its mooring. The boat pulled away from shore, and dozens of others followed them. They went out into the choppy ocean toward the Hamata island chain, which was about as high up in the northern hemisphere as you could be before running into the polar ice cap.

Meanwhile, the under-powered motor whined with each wave they encountered. They had been traveling for over a month towards the Antum base. Now, they had to cross a cold, rough ocean and not be detected by the Ineans.

They had left with others from the Ninki area and trekked along the northern coast of Nin, mostly at night, until they came to the port city of Tiit, which was the northernmost port city on the eastern continent. Here, they crossed to the coast of the northern land mass, which was mostly covered with the northern ice sheet. They needed to get across the Kaspu mountains before the snow season kicked in, or they would be in trouble. They made it past the mountains and followed the western coast northward and around the bay, recruiting dozens of people to fight the Ineans on their way.

Now, they were in a boat heading into the open ocean in search of an island in the dark and in rough seas. Hundreds more piled in boats and followed them into the dark. The next morning, they discovered the first island and made shore by midday. They rested and continued their trip once it got dark again.

They went northward in the boats around the island and then headed northeast into the open ocean in search of island number two. As the night progressed, the clouds thickened, and the wind picked up. By the time they made landfall, a cold, windswept rain had soaked them to their bones. They quickly pulled the boats up onto the beach and made camp. Several of them lit fires and used branches and oars to prop the boats over them to keep the rain and wind off them. All wore plastic rain gear, but it did nothing against the cold, arctic wind driving the rain into them. Many huddled together under their boats by the fires. The storm lasted two days and finally blew out towards the North Pole.

Anzillu and Enanatuma headed back out with the others right behind them before dusk. The next island was further out and would take five to six days to reach. The solar packs had recharged the batteries even in the dim light of the storm.

A week later, they made it to the coast of Sikkuru, a large land mass to the west of the western continent. They found a diesel-powered truck in an abandoned town, which looked like the handiwork of the Ineans. Many buildings were wrecked, and rotting bodies were scattered about. They got the truck running and found fuel for it. Some of the women checked the local shops and found boxes upon boxes of winter gloves, boots, jackets, and thick clothing. Once it got dark, they continued traveling across the continent. It took over two weeks, all in the cold rain and wet snow, as the seasons were changing. Finally, they made it to an ocean port with boats that would take them across to the volcanic island of Isatum, which means land of fire. After another two days in a small, under-powered boat, they landed on Isatum Island.

The ground was shaking, and smoke spewed from the high rocky peaks as the twin volcanoes came to life after being dormant for over a hundred years. They knew they needed to hurry across before it erupted. The last time it did, the lava from the twin peaks blanketed the entire island in just a few days. The smoke and ash spread around the globe in weeks, causing a cooling of the planet that lasted three years. Those were difficult years, as crops failed across the entire planet.

The travelers found other vehicles and managed to get some running with the help of the local people. Eventually, they were on their way, and the local people followed them, realizing they all needed to get off the island before it blew. The ground shook frequently from the magma flowing beneath their feet, and everyone in their growing group knew their days were numbered as the smoke and ash plumes became denser.

Five days later, they closed in on the easternmost volcano while small rocks and ash fell all around them. Rocks dented the roof and front hood of the vehicles while progress slowed. Many of the wind-shields were broken. Anzillu and Enanatuma needed to cross the other side of the volcano and find a boat that would take them to the western continent quickly. The ground was shaking constantly now, and it was hard to drive as the roads buckled with each wave. Finally, the ash got into the electric turbines and destroyed them despite the presence of a filtering system. The fine, sharp ash worked its way into the turbines and tore up the precision blades.

Anzillu and Enanatuma dampened rags, held them over their faces, and left the vehicle. Small rocks pelted them from above. They ran to the next village, which had been abandoned recently. There were no boats. They ran from building to building in search of boats, but all they found were more diesel trucks. Anzillu got them running as the ash blanketed the ground. He sent Enanatuma back to get the rest of the people. She ran into them after only a mile as they ran to catch up with her and Anzillu. They turned and raced into the town and got the rest of the trucks running as small fiery rocks fell from the sky. The volcano was erupting, and they were just a few miles from the lava dome. They piled into the trucks and headed north for the next village as the trucks were pounded by the rocks being spewed by the volcano. The trucks sputtered as they entered the next town, and it was do or die at this point.

They raced down to the docks and found boats. Large fishing boats, which took little effort to get running. The ground stopped shaking, and the volcano belched one last puff of smoke and steam. Everyone breathed a sigh of relief that the worst was over. However, their elation was short-lived as the ground beneath their feet heaved up. The ocean began to recede, and the volcano exploded. They were not in the clear yet, as fiery rocks began to fall all around them. They pushed away from the docks and pushed the throttles of the boats to full open. The boats lumbered away slowly, and many kept looking back at the disaster catching up with them.

Lightning crackled in the black ash clouds overhead, and the wind picked up. It was daytime, but it was dark as night. No sunlight could pierce the ash clouds. They watched the lava flow down the mountain and engulf the village they had vacated moments before. The lava flowed into the ocean and seemed to be catching up with them. There was speculation in scientific circles that, with a few more eruptions, the island would become part of the western continent. The way the lava was flowing into the ocean it could be this time.

The lava began to recede as they closed in on the western continent, and landfall was made a few hours later. Ash and smaller rocks still fell all around them and on them, but they ran into the next village and took cover with the few people who lived there.

A few days later, the eruption let up. They wrapped themselves in extra layers and covered their faces to protect them from the harsh environment that winter and volcanic fallout brought. They braved the brutal conditions and continued walking. It was slow going as the travelers trudged through a snow and ash mixture until they could find enough vehicles to take them to Antum, which was still two thousand plus zag away and involved crossing the

Humbaba mountains in winter to get to the base. It would take nearly another month to reach Antum as the snowline progressed southward with them.

Anzillu sent the bulk of the people east towards Utuk, where the army would come and take them to be trained. He and Enanatuma continued to the Antum base and joined others who had also scored well on the test given. They could see the entrance to the base in the mountains and waited for dark to approach.

Several hours later, in the middle of the night, they walked up to the main gate, which was concealed in the rock face of the mountain. Two guards saw them and let them pass through to where other guards took them to meet General Asar.

THIRTY-FIVE

DAGAN AND ZUTTARA were in the gym late. She had worn her tight shirt and skintight shorts under her robe to the gym but took the robe off once inside. Zuttara looked at her in her skintight outfit, and he was turned on by it. "You are making this difficult, you know."

"What do you mean?"

"You know what I mean, look in the mirror."

She glanced in the mirror and chuckled as her face turned red from embarrassment. "Maybe it was my intent, Zuttara."

He stepped up behind her, kissed her neck, and then placed his hand on her stomach while she watched in the mirror.

"What's our next lesson?" She asked as his other hand came around and embraced her. He kissed her neck and then her ear. She liked it when he touched her, and she was falling in love with him. Oh, if the elders of the temple could see this, she wondered. "Zuttara?" she said while tilting her head for him. She did not make it easy for him to pull away from her.

He finally did pull back from her neck. "Yes, we will practice more hand-to-hand combat tonight," he said as he stepped away and collected his thoughts. He then came up behind her and grabbed her. She spun around and kicked him and flipped him over her shoulder, and he dropped to the rubber mat with a thud. She spun back and dropped on him, placing her elbow to his throat, but stopped short of actually thrusting her elbow into his Adam's apple.

He smiled at her. "Very good."

"I had a good teacher," she grinned back and kissed him on the lips.

He then flipped her over and pounced on her. He sat on her and pinned her arms to the mat. "Now, how do you get out of this?"

"You are enjoying this, aren't you?" she grinned at him.

"You have no idea," he replied, glancing down at her breasts.

She saw him look at her chest, and she made her move. She swung her knees up, hit him in the kidneys, and pushed him off her. She then hit him in the kidneys again with a punch, and he rolled over in pain as she sat on him, bringing the palm of her hand to his throat. Stopping just short of injuring him.

"That was," cough, "not bad. I think I need to wear padding from now on."

She got up and extended a hand to Zuttara, helping him to his feet.

He walked over to the closet on the far wall and pulled on a padded vest and helmet. He then slipped on forearm pads and walked back towards Dagan. She laughed at him. "Do I play too rough for you, Zuttara?"

"Yes, but I don't mind at all. Now come at me kicking and swinging. I want it fast, just like we practiced."

He took a stand with a fake gun in hand. "Come and get me before I can shoot you."

She raced forward and swung her leg, taking the gun out of his hand as he squeezed the trigger. Without skipping a beat, she swung and hit him in the head, and she quickly spun around with another kick to the head. She fell back and rushed forward with repeated punches to the stomach and kidneys. She finished him with a knee to the groin. He put his hands up as he dropped to his knees. "I think you pass," he gasped as he brought his hands to his groin. Even though he was well-padded, it still hurt.

"Sorry, need help?" she asked as she offered him a hand.

"Sure," he replied, offering his hand. She took it and helped him up again.

"How about dinner?" he asked as he walked slowly towards the closet to put the padding away.

"I thought you would never ask," she stated with a grin.

"Let me shower, and I will meet you there in half an hour," he said.

"Do you plan on sitting on ice?" she laughed.

"Thank Kur for padding," he said.

"I will see you there then," she said, and she headed for the door but stopped short and went to get her robe. "That would have been a disaster." She pulled the robe on and pulled the hood close to her head. She opened the door, peeked out, and left the gym.

Zuttara waited outside the mess hall for Dagan, and she arrived a few minutes later, wearing her usual brown priestess robe tied at the waist with a length of rope. She had the normal open sandals and probably nothing else, he surmised. She grinned at him and led the way into the mess hall, which was pretty crowded with the new people arriving from the eastern continent. There were large groups of locals surrounding the new arrivals as they told of their harrowing trek by the twin volcanoes on Isatum Island. They got in line and grabbed their trays. The line moved slowly, and the cooks were telling people to eat small portions as the food was dwindling quickly.

Dagan and Zuttara both took small portions of food and two tall glasses of water with ice. They searched around and found a table off to the side. People watched them go by, curious about why a priestess was with a man. No one could explain it, and many pointed. Zuttara saw some of the whispering and pointing and was concerned that this public meeting was a bad idea. There would be too much speculation, and most would have it wrong.

They made it to their table, and he sat across from her. She bowed her head, and he bowed his as well. After a minute, she had finished her prayer to Kur for their dinner. She lifted her head and took a bite of mashed yellow squash. Zuttara leaned in, "I don't think this was a good idea. People are watching us."

"Really? Well, let's see what they do now." She stood and leaned towards him. She placed her hands on each side of his face and tilted his head towards hers, and she kissed him on the lips. Nearby, a tray dropped, and when she sat back down, she glanced around and saw one of the high priests glaring at her. She smiled at him and went back to her dinner. "So, looks like you have your work cut out for you with all these new trainees," she said while glancing around the room.

"Are you going to get in trouble?" Zuttara asked as he glanced towards the high priest who remained standing several feet away, glaring at them.

"With him? No, but the others might have a rabum once they find out." With a mouthful of food, it sounded like waybum.

Zuttara laughed slightly at the way she said rabum with a mouth full of food.

"What is so funny?" she asked.

"Just you, you're funny," he said.

Zuttara glanced at the high priest, who was still staring at them. "He is beginning to creep me out."

"Try working with him. He is awful to deal with. If it isn't perfect, he goes crazy, and everyone runs and hides."

"Except you?" Zuttara asked.

"Except me. I go nose-to-nose with him, and it drives him crazy. I think if he had not taken the sacred vows, he could easily kill me," Dagan said.

"He probably wants to."

"Oh, no doubt at all about that. I'm sure he has thought about it and maybe even planned it, but to murder and be under the sacred oath means you are put to death as well. I'm sure no matter how much he wants to be rid of me, he doesn't want to join me there."

"That's a safe bet."

Many in the room had gone back to their conversations and forgot about Priestess Dagan and Zuttara for now. Even the high priest eventually stomped away, not wanting to make a scene in the crowded mess hall. He would deal with her later.

Two of the travelers sat with Dagan and Zuttara. Anzillu extended his hand to Zuttara. "Captain Anzillu and Private Enanatuma, sir."

"Major Zuttara and this is Priestess Dagan," Zuttara said while grasping Anzillu's hand firmly.

"So we start training tomorrow?" Enanatuma asked.

"How old are you?" Zuttara asked her.

"Old enough to get revenge for my mother and sister and my friend that those animals took from me," she snarled while stabbing her dinner harshly.

"Fiery one you have there, Anzillu," Zuttara stated with a concerned tone.

"You have no idea," Anzillu replied with a glare at Enanatuma.

"I'm getting the picture. Who is your father?" Zuttara asked Enanatuma.

"The former leader of Nin, Ur is his name," she said with disgust at mentioning her father.

"So that would make you pr.."

"Don't ever call me that P-word. It does not apply to me," she growled.

"So I see. Well, this is the wrong place for P-word people anyway," Zuttara said as he gathered his trash. "Enjoy your dinner."

Zuttara made eye gestures to Dagan, and they both walked away.

"She's a character," Dagan added once they were far enough away.

"Reckless liability, if you ask me," Zuttara exclaimed softly.

"Perhaps. What now?" Dagan asked as they entered the corridor, leaving the stuffy mess hall behind them.

There were dozens of people in the corridor, so he could not ask her what he really wanted, which was to go back to his room or hers for some private time. So they walked along quietly until they arrived at her room. He knew it was a bad idea. All it took was for one person to see him going into a priestess' room for the trouble to begin, but he was contemplating whether the risk would be worth it.

They stood there in awkward silence until the corridor was clear, and she glanced up at him. "I want you to come in, but you can't. It is too dangerous right now."

"I know," he took her hands in his. "Tomorrow, same time at the firing range?"

"I'll be there."

He released his grip on her hands and walked away. She waited for him to turn a corner, and she walked into her room. She was startled when she turned the light on to find the high priest in her room. She held the door open to ensure she had a quick escape if needed. "What are you doing in my room?" she asked firmly. "This is highly improper!"

"Look who's talking about what is proper! You push too hard, young lady, and make a mockery of what Kur wants from us!"

"I..."

"Shut up! For once in your life, shut up. Listen to what others have to say," he yelled. "I know you are very smart and see things differently. I understand this, but our people look to us for spiritual inspiration and guidance, especially now. And what do they see in you? They see a priestess making a fool of herself with a man. That's what they see. I don't care about your interpretation of Kur's writings. I agree with most of your arguments, but now is not the time to be pushing this. Not now. Our people need us to be a rock for them during this war for our right to survive as a species. Now, get your act together. Do not set foot in the temple until you have made your decision, and it better be the right one." He walked past her and left the room. She released the door, and it swung shut while she stood there thinking about what he said. She went and sat on her bed, bowed her head, and prayed to Kur the entire night.

After fighting sleep the entire night while praying to Kur, Dagan got off the bed and removed her robe. She went into the shower, stood before the mirror, stared at herself, and cursed. She turned the knob on the wall and waited a few seconds for the warm water. She stepped under the steaming spray. She had made up her mind under that shower, and now she had to put it in motion. The high priest was right. She had made a spectacle of herself the previous night, and while at the time she did not care that people pointed at her and Zuttara, she was now embarrassed. She would refrain from public displays and concentrate on helping the people come to Kur as their race struggled to survive the Inean invasion.

However, she still had dreams about fighting the Ineans and knew she would have to fight. This led to her other decision, which was to continue training with Zuttara. This would not be easy, as the high priests would be watching her every move. Any private training would be cause for question. The last part was the toughest. She needed to hold back on her feelings for him. She knew this would be difficult, and if it weren't for her vows to the priesthood and to Kur, she would have already taken him to her bed. It did help her understand the pressures that Eastern women were under.

She finished showering and toweled off. She brushed her hair and brushed her teeth and finally pulled on a fresh brown robe. She tied it at the waist, slipped into her sandals, and left the room in search of the high priest.

Zuttara held class in a deep cavern of the mountain with a dozen new recruits. Behind him were the simulated cockpits of the bombers they would be flying. At the controls were two of his best trainees from the previous group who would be assisting him.

In the group were Enanatuma and Anzillu, who stood side by side as Zuttara lectured. One of Zuttara's helpers handed them booklets with details on all the controls, which they would have to study to the point of knowing them inside and out. He explained to them the importance of learning these controls and passing the simulation tests.

He finally broke them into two groups, one group for each simulator. One at a time, they tried flying the bombers while the instructors sat in the copilot's seat and instructed them. Each person crashed within minutes of taking the controls. Zuttara was unfazed by this. His first group crashed and burned just as quickly. Next up was Enanatuma. Zuttara watched the young girl as she settled into the pilot's seat. He expected her to crash just as the others had. She attached the five-point harness and gripped the controls. The copilot instructed her to bank right and lean on the thrusters as they flew towards an Inean ship, which was displayed on the large monitor that had replaced the windshield. She leaned right, and the simulator banked for her on its hydraulic pistons. Soon, they were taking fake fire from the Inean ship, and the simulator shook with each impact. She worked the throttle and the steering thrusters, made it past the Inean ship, and got away. She was the only one to do so.

The instructor was impressed and programmed a more challenging scenario, which included two Inean ships racing toward them as they headed for Inea. She angled between the ships while taking fire from them and putting them in the crossfire. The simulated Inean ships stopped shooting for the moment and retrained their guns to the point where the bomber was supposed to emerge. Enanatuma saw this and leaned on the vertical down thrusters, then punched the forward thrusters. The bomber dropped away from the Inean ships and sped off.

Anzillu strapped in next and made it through the first run but was blown up on the second simulation. He cursed and glanced at Enanatuma, who grinned.

THIRTY-SIX

THE NEXT SOLAR storm was late, and many in Aanepada's military were concerned they had missed their window of opportunity to escape the planet under the cover of the Inean-induced solar bursts. Months passed as the pilots trained, and the builders on the moons of Uggae and Anaru put the finishing touches on the long-range bombers. Most of the ships had been fitted with the new multi-warhead urukii rockets, which were capable of destroying the Inean home world.

A new problem had cropped up on the distant moons: there was no food left. What little supply they had had been rationed and now was gone. They were days away from starving to death, and still, no solar flare came to hide the transports and cargo ships from Ardonnar.

Aanepada met with General Asar and his staff to discuss launching the ships anyway, and all agreed it would not help. The Ineans would intercept the slow cargo ships in minutes and destroy them. He even entertained the idea of launching urukii rockets at the big ships as a diversion, but still, it was not practical. They would have to wait and hope for a solar storm to hide their flight away from Ardonnar.

. . .

In the command center, Aanepada stood and watched the large display hanging on the wall. At the same time, Enir, now the senior solar observer, ran calculations that turned into a three-dimensional model of the star Utui.

Enir tilted her head towards the president, who leaned towards her. "Sir, computer models suggest a disturbance on Utui. I think a storm is brewing by the data stream from our remote stations." She could not speak with any certainty, as most of their stations had been destroyed by previous storms. All that was left was one on the moon, Anaru, and one on Nisaba in orbit around Ardonnar. Neither of these could give a view of the back side of the star and left much to interpretation. They had close calls recently with no storm activity.

"Should we ready the transports and cargo ships?" Aanepada asked.

"Start getting ready. I won't have a firm answer for at least forty-eight hours. And if a storm comes our way, then we may still have six hours before it does. Besides, the Inean ships are not on the move yet."

"If it does," he said.

"Yes, if it does," she replied.

"Okay then, I will alert the teams and have them prepare," Aanepada said.

"I never thought I would say this, but pray to Kur for a big storm," Enir stated as she ran a new calculation.

Aanepada patted her on the shoulder and walked away to confer with General Asar and Major Zuttara on the readiness of the new pilots.

The next day, Enir tracked down Aanepada with a printout in her hand. "Mister President, this one looks real. We expect the storm to be here in eight hours," she said excitedly.

He got up from the long table along with General Asar. "That is great. General, get the ships loaded and ready." He turned to Enir. "Are the Ineans on the move yet?"

"They have moved a few ships already, but one has broken away and is now heading towards Duggae, which is on the other side of Utui."

"What are they up to?" Aanepada asked.

"We should follow that ship with our scope on Duggae. Maybe they figured out what we are up to." Asar said with a glance to Enir.

"We will track the ship as best as possible, but once the storm strikes those sensors, we will lose it," Enir said, and she turned for the door.

Aanepada looked up. "Enir?"

She stopped and turned to face him. "Yes?"

"Keep us posted on the solar storm and that Inea ship."

"Yes, sir," Enir replied before turning to walk out of the room.

A few minutes later, she was in the command center and staring at the data coming in from the observatories on the two moons. The data was setting up like the first CME to strike the planet three years before. It had the same intensity as the one that destroyed their electrical grids and turned their world back three hundred years, setting the stage for the Inean invasion of their planet.

She charted the storm and displayed the animation on the screen as General Asar walked up beside her. "Looks like a bad one," he said while staring at the screen.

"It will be a test for the new electronic shielding that was installed in all the spacecraft," Enir stated while typing more data into the computer.

"Where is the Inean ship?" Asar asked.

"Taking a trajectory that will take it around Utui towards Duggae."

"They are retrieving the device that is causing the problems. This is our last chance off this rock," he stated. He turned quickly and exited the room.

Soon, people were scurrying all about the base as Asar loaded more cargo ships to be launched. He was sending everything they had ready to the two moons. It was now or never.

. . .

Zuttara had his pilots gearing up. Once they got to the two moons, they may have to take the bombers out, even though some were not ready for real flight. If the Ineans saw them leave, then the pilots may have to launch early. He sent teams to several transports. Some were heading to Uggae, and the rest were heading towards Anaru. He knew the transports would be launching soon as the level of activity on the flight deck was becoming frantic.

Soon, the large doors on the side of the mountain would slide open, exposing their base to a cave just below a waterfall. The wall of water rolling down, coupled with the mist off the rocks below, obscured the entrance. Hopefully, the Ineans would not be watching. There were two dozen ships now on the flight deck. Technicians ran large hoses to two new ships that had been wheeled out. They attached the hoses to the pylons on each side and transferred the highly volatile fuel to the tanks. While trucks pulled up beside the cargo ships, the workers, men, and women transferred crates from hand to hand into the ships. They were quickly stacked and tied down as red lights began to flash around the deck. The ships would be blasting out of the mountain very soon, and time was running out.

The Ardonnarians had not sent this many ships out at one time before, and this would test their ability. Each ship had twenty seconds to build up thrust and fly off the deck because the next ship in line would be warming up.

Zuttara guided his pilots to their respective transports and patted each on the helmet as they went past him. A pair of high priests stood there as well and said a quick blessing as each pilot went by. Everything was happening fast now, and nobody had time to think or get panicked. The first transports engines ignited, and the ship bolted off the deck at full speed. The next ship got off the deck but swayed slightly, and one of its pylons struck a rock on the side of the cave as it flew out beneath the waterfall. The next ship took off and lumbered as it struggled to get off the deck. It was overloaded with food and supplies, many of which would end up on the bombers going to Inea. It finally cleared the deck and dropped down slightly as its wings slid out to catch air. Once the craft was moving fast enough, it gained altitude. The next ship took off and then another, but they were taking off too slow, and word came down that the storm was passing.

Asar was at the command tower above the flight deck. "We need to launch two at a time!" he barked. The technicians controlling the ships on the deck started babbling commands. The next two ships lined up and went out the opening while the next two pulled up and took off. It was going well until two cargo ships lumbered off the deck. The ships kept bumping against each other's fuel pylons while they went out the opening into the waterfall. The ship on the left clipped the rock wall as it passed the opening, swung out, and hit the other ship, which veered off and dropped down. The cargo ship on the left over-corrected and swung wide into the rock face. The port side was scarred by a jagged rock, and the ship began to spill fuel down the side of the mountain. The ship lifted and headed for space, and the hot exhaust from the main engines ignited the fuel flowing down the mountain. Fire burst up the side of the mountain. Two more cargo ships took off as the ship that was on the right finally gained some altitude and was nearly struck by another cargo ship taking off.

All the ships got off the ground and into space. One of the cargo ships, the one that lost half its fuel, flew through the fire of the CME and headed for Anaru instead of Uggae. Even then, it might not make it.

Zuttara went to the control tower as the doors closed to get information on their ships. The news was good for the most part, and so far, all the ships had evaded the Ineans' sensors.

The nervous voice of a woman pilot crackled over the speaker on the wall in the flight deck command center. "Antum base, this is transport, Ishtar. We have a fuel cell breach. We will have to redirect to Anaru."

"We copy that Ishtar. Redirect to Anaru," Zuttara stated as he was joined by Dagan, who had been quiet lately. Zuttara had noticed the change in her, and he wondered if one of the High

Priests had finally gotten to her. He needed to ask her, but they both had been extremely busy the past several days.

"Is there trouble?" she asked.

"One of the transports struck a fuel cell on a rock when it exited the flight deck. It is redirecting to Anaru," Zuttara explained.

"That leaves Uggae short on pilots and supplies. We will have to send another ship to them," she stated.

"Not enough time. They will have to make do with what they have out there," Zuttara said. He felt fingers probing for his, and he intertwined his fingers with hers for a few seconds. Then she pulled away.

"I will be in the command center with the president and general," she said with a wink. His mind was at ease for now, knowing she still had feelings for him.

"Antum base, this is transport Ishtar. We are running out of fuel from our leaking fuel cell. We are cutting power and going to coast it in from here."

"Ishtar, we copy that. May the power of Kur be with you."

Anzillu took over the controls of the last transport heading towards the gas giant Idpa to get a feel for the craft. Once seated and strapped in, he pushed the throttle forward, and the engines roared to life, bringing the ship up with the rest of the ships heading for Idpa, which would be used as a brake to slow the transport as they looped towards the small, frozen moon Uggae. The craft flew through the dissipating fire cloud to keep the Inean sensors from detecting them on their flight. After a half hour, Enanatuma walked up behind Anzillu and placed her hands on his shoulders. She kissed his neck and grinned at him. "Can I fly it now?" she asked.

He turned his head and gave her a peck on the cheek. "In a little while. I kind of like this, and besides, we have two full days flying, so you can have a chance."

"You just want to have all the fun," she said as she lightly bit his ear.

"Hey, easy now. I'm still your superior officer," he said with a grin while checking his instruments.

She patted his shoulder. "You're just jealous because I fly better."

Anzillu was more than twice her age, and when they first met, he did not like her at all. He felt she was a spoiled princess whose father was leading the Eastern people down the wrong road. After nearly two years, he had learned who she really was and that she did not share any of her father's views and politics. He glanced over his shoulder as she walked away and admired her rear swaying back and forth. She was a fighter, and she was pretty attractive, and he was taken by her.

Enanatuma had a crush on Anzillu since the beginning, and now it was full-fledged love. She was hoping he would ask her to marry him, but she knew he was preoccupied with beating the Ineans. She wanted the same for her mother, sister, and friend, who were certainly dead now. She agonized at how they died, based on reports of how brutal the Ineans were.

Puabi sat at the controls of the newest fighter while her stomach rumbled from lack of food. Their food supply had run out two days prior after they had been on severe rations for the past month. All they had was water melted from ice found on the distant moon. One more day before the cargo ships would arrive. It would not be a minute too soon.

She programmed the navigation console as she had done dozens of times in recent months, and she sat back in the pilot's chair while the program ran and stared out the window. Outside the bomber, dozens of workers crawled about the new fleet of ships, which were in various stages of construction. Welders sprayed sparks as they joined steel beams and hull panels together. She looked at the rock ceiling a hundred feet above the deck. Steel girders crisscrossed to reinforce the rock. Large lights hung from the ceiling, illuminating the flight deck where the bombers were being constructed. She stared out at the large, spinning fans hanging from the ceiling, blowing the warm air back down to warm the deck. Puabi glanced down at her computer, and the file transfer was nearly done. She returned her gaze out the window at the bombers, and she knew their task was almost completed.

The computer beeped that the files had been transferred. Puabi glanced down, closed the window on her computer, and entered several commands. The control panel lit up and went into its diagnostic test. She removed the cable connecting her computer to the control panel. She performed the diagnostics and watched the monitor as the flight simulation played out. After several minutes, she powered down the system and sat back in the chair.

Puabi drifted back in time to when she was a young girl in Samuqan. She sat in a chair on her front porch, waiting for notification from the space fleet regarding her application to enter pilot training school. Her mother was hoping against it while her father sat with her. He had been a pilot when the Ardonnarians expanded beyond their solar system. He knew the ships she would be flying were much safer than the rickety tin cans he flew.

Racing down the dirt road was Gula. He was waving a piece of paper in his hand as he turned the corner by the post to their walkway and up to the porch. "I'm in!" he panted.

Puabi took the paper, read it, and hugged him. "Congratulations," she said while her father patted him on the shoulder.

"Did you get yours?" Gula asked after catching his breath.

"No, not yet," she said while pulling away.

"You will. I know it," Gula said.

Puabi jumped back to the present as a hand touched her shoulder. "What?" she said as she spun around quickly.

Gula retracted his hand. "Sorry to scare you. Where were you?"

"Oh, thinking about better times."

"Yeah, I think everyone has been doing that lately. Hopefully, we will get back to those times again," he said while sitting in the copi-lot's seat.

"You've been crying?" Puabi asked while reaching for him.

He stared out the window at the activity. "A few months ago, the Ineans raided our village. Many were killed and taken," he said while trying not to look at her.

Puabi went to him, a sense of fear gripping her, and she threw her arms around him. "Tell me."

"Your father fought them and actually killed a few of them before an Inean shot him. Your mother got away, but no one knows where she is. Some say she is with the rebels. Both my parents and brother fought with the Ineans and are dead as well."

She hugged him while he broke down. Tears started to roll down her cheeks.

"We have to win this war," she sobbed. A few seconds later, after she composed herself, she continued. "What happened to the two children we left with my parents?"

Gula sniffed and guided her to sit on his leg while she kept her arms around his neck. "Amar-Sin is dead, but he died a hero. He saved Enhedu from the Ineans."

"Where is she?" Puabi asked while staring out the window.

"She is a pilot. She is under the guidance of Major Zuttara and is on her way to Anaru."

"She can't be old enough. Is she?" Puabi asked as she searched her mind for the girl's age.

"Not really, but she is capable. Besides, we can't be picky. Our population is dwindling, and if we don't fight back now, then we won't be able to," Gula said.

His words hurt, but she knew it was true. She kissed him and got off his lap. She fixed her uniform. "We should get back to work." She sniffed as she gripped Gula's hand. She grabbed her portable computer with her other hand. They walked out of the transport, kissed, and went in opposite directions.

. . .

Gula walked down a corridor towards the command center, thinking about their losses in Samuqan and that there was no way life would be the same. Aliens have invaded their world and have been murdering their people for three years. There was one long-shot hope of turning the tide of the war, but he knew that one mistake could ruin their chances and bring their race to extinction. The thought was overwhelming.

Gula pushed open the steel blast door and entered the command center. This one was much smaller than Anaru base in orbit around Ardonnar. However, it was much newer and had a larger cavern where the ships were hiding. Deep in the moon was the particle accelerator, which was producing antimatter fuel for the bombers. It was the only place in the Utui system where the Ardonnarians could build a large enough ring to yield sufficient antimatter to fuel the fifty ships being built for a trip to Inea and, hopefully, back.

He walked up to a young man who sat at a console monitoring all spaceships in the area. All of the Inean ships were marked as red dots, and all but one were in orbit around Ardonnar. The one lone ship was on the other side of Utui and appeared to be slowing as it entered a close orbit to the star. There were several other ships in flight heading their way and were flagged as green dots. Those green dots were getting close, and so far, no Ineans were chasing them.

"Time until those ships arrive?" Gula asked.

The young technician covered his mouthpiece and glanced up at Gula. "The ships should be here in about ten hours if all goes well."

"Let's hope so. I'm starving," Gula said while staring at the monitor.

"Yes, sir. Everyone is."

Gula started to walk away when General Ningal walked into the command center in search of Gula.

"Gula, supplies, and pilots are on the way. I trust that we are closing in on completion of our ships?" the general asked.

Gula sensed a tenseness in the general's voice that he had not noticed before. "Yes, sir," Gula saluted. "Is there a problem, General?"

"Until those pilots arrive we are sitting telals. There seems to be concern about what that Inean destroyer is doing on the other side of Utui. It is the first time in nearly three years that they have done something that was not consistent with what we had observed from their behavior," the general stated.

"Let's hope we get those ships staffed, loaded, and out of here before the Ineans come snooping," Gula said as both men walked out into the corridor.

"We still have several weeks of work to finish the last ships," General Ningal stated as the men turned a corner. Two large blast doors slid open as they walked up to them, and they walked onto the flight deck. The general paused a moment to take in the view. Nearly two dozen bombers finished, loaded with fuel and packed with six nuclear rockets with multiple warheads each. All they needed were pilots to fly them and food.

Several hours later, the first of the supply ships flew past the gas giant, Idpa, and used its atmosphere to slow down. The cargo ships swooped outward towards Uggae at a greatly reduced speed. Technicians raced across the flight deck as red lights flashed. Soon, the air would be blown out of the large chamber, and the large rock doors would slide open. Next, the lights began to pulse, indicating less than a minute left, and a technician in the booth above the flight deck was ordering everyone off the deck. As the last person raced through the blast doors, large fans kicked in and pulled the air out of the large chamber. Dust and papers kicked up. After fifteen minutes, the large rock-covered doors slid slowly open, revealing the flight deck to open space. The first of the cargo ships ignited their thrusters and hovered a few feet above the moon's surface while blasting dust and dirt about the opening. Then, the ship moved through the large opening and flew to the far side of the flight deck. The next ship followed them in, and this continued until all ships were inside the hollowed-out cavern in the moon.

The large doors began to close, and then red lights started flashing alongside the yellow ones. People waited anxiously behind the blast doors, eager to get to their ships. They were tense, company was coming...

General Ningal and Gula hovered in front of a large monitor against the rock wall in the command center. On it was a red dot moving in their direction. It was the Inean ship that was hiding behind Utui. Their secret was up. They had been found out, and now an Inean warship was heading their way.

"How long until that ship gets here?" Ningal asked, his voice obviously tense.

Gula stood with hands on his hips, waiting for the reply as Puabi walked up beside them and stared at the large screen with the red dot turning past Duggae, the innermost planet in their system, and making a beeline towards them.

"I would say twenty hours at best, sir," the technician replied, typing numbers into his computer, which confirmed his assumption. "Nineteen hours, forty-three minutes, to be exact."

Reality had set in. The Ineans knew the Ardonnarians were up to something out on this moon. Now, they were coming to investigate.

"Cushik!" General Ningal cursed, and he turned to Gula and Puabi. "Get those ships loaded and staffed. You have six hours."

"But General! There are six unfinished ships between the finished ones and the large doors. Three can't be flown at all. Plus, it will be forty minutes before the deck pressurizes." Puabi stated what the general already knew. At this distance, there was a way to sneak off the moon and hide from the Ineans, but it would have to be soon. Once the Inean ship was closer to the moon and could use the combined sensors from their fleet, that window would close fast.

Aanepada stood in the command center deep in Laarsa mountain base. Antum was the official name of the base. He was joined by several people as they watched the red dot pass by the planet Duggae and head towards the moon, Uggae, orbiting Idpa, one of the distant gas giant planets in their solar system. It was about the same distance as Saturn in Earth's system.

General Asar watched and wrung his hands at what it meant. Dagan stood with the president, and Zuttara walked up and stared at the screen.

Dagan knew what it meant. She also knew the Ineans were coming here as well. She had seen it.

Asar turned towards the rest. "We need to be ready to launch at a moment's notice. I want all crews suited up and ready. I want all fighters on Anaru fueled and staffed at all times. Things will escalate now, and we can not afford to lose any fighters. If the Ineans destroy our fleets, then we are done. There is no hope."

"Understood, General," Zuttara said. He turned to walk away, but a hand clamped down on his wrist. He went to pull away but realized whose hand it was. It was Dagan's.

Dagan turned to face him and the general. "We will be successful. Kur has shown me."

"Not now, priestess," Asar hissed and turned to face the monitor.

"Yes, now," she fumed. "Now more than ever, we need to have faith in Kur. I AM a priestess, and he has shown me the victory that will be ours. However, we must also be prepared and vigilant. We need to be able to pounce on any opportunity at a moment's notice," she stared at the general for a moment. "Now we should pray. All of us," she said firmly.

Everyone in the room bowed their heads. Dagan looked around and saw everyone was waiting for her. She cleared her mind and spoke loud enough for everyone in the room to hear. "Blessed Kur, you have brought this time upon us. It is the appointed time for us to rely on you to guide us through this difficult time and to guide us to victory as you have prophesied so long ago. Our ships are ready. Our people are trained. We await the opening that you will give us to carry out this difficult mission, and defeat the Ineans, and reclaim our planet. It is time to put an end to the horrific death that has plagued our people for so long now. Please look upon us with favor and guide us to victory. Amen," she lifted her head and looked around. "Now, let's go fry the Mullas."

Asar glanced at her. "I will say amen to that."

Zuttara grasped her hands in his. "I have to go," he said with an apologetic look.

"I know. I will see you later." Dagan said, and she let him go. She watched him exit the room, and she turned her attention to the red dot slowly moving toward the moon Uggae. She also noticed that Aanepada was quiet. "Is there a problem, Mister President?" She asked while touching his hand.

"I'm okay. I am just worried about those people on Uggae."

"Are you sure that is all?"

He paused a moment and then turned towards her. A tear welled up in the corner of his eye, and he wiped it away. "I was thinking about Kilar. That's all."

"It has been over three years since she died. A lot has happened since then," Dagan added. She was concerned about him.

"I know. I'm being selfish. Millions have died since then, but all I can think about is her."

"It is quite understandable, Aanepada. She was your daughter. She died getting you out of harm's way and is a hero."

"If only I..." he began.

"Don't do this to yourself. You had no way of knowing that the solar storm that pounded this planet was caused by those aliens. There was no way of knowing until it was too late. There was nothing you could have done," Dagan stated firmly. She was becoming concerned about him all over again.

He had fought through depression while trying to lead his people through the worst disaster in their planet's history. He owed his life to Dagan. She saw him through it. She was beside him the entire time, and she was still there watching out for him. He wrapped his arms around her and hugged her. "I really love you, Dagan. I consider you my daughter," he wept while squeezing her.

"I know, I know. I consider us family as well, and I worry about you," she hugged him back.

"I have had visions from Kur. He has spoken to me as well, and I know what I have to do next." He pushed the hood of her robe back slightly, kissed her on the forehead, and started to walk away.

Now, she was scared. What was he going to do? And she followed him to the door. "What did he tell you to do?"

"I can't say. Just don't be worried," he said with a forced grin. He turned and walked out the door. She watched him go and followed after him at a distance.

The lights over the blast doors turned green, and the workers pushed them open and raced onto the flight deck. They had the impossible task of transferring all the supplies to the fighters, getting the crews set and suited up, and clearing the deck so the completed ships could get away, all in less than five hours.

Gula stood in the middle of the deck with his clipboard and grabbed two workers. "I need both of you to help me."

They both stopped and stared at the project they were heading for, then back at Gula. Gula took several pages off his clipboard and handed each of them several pages. "Go to those transports and get these people for me right away."

The two workers went to the transports as people filed off them and waited in groups.

"I need Damkin, Enki, Erra, Maqatu..." and he rattled off name after name while his assistant began to do the same. Dozens of pilots separated into two groups while crews dragged the unfinished fighters out of the way.

The noise level was deafening as large cranes lowered cables that technicians attached to the finished fighters so they could be lifted up and over the unfinished ones and placed by the opening in the side of the crater. It was a painfully slow process, and Gula kept checking his watch. It seemed time had sped up, or they had slowed down. Either way, he was not confident they could launch in time.

The two technicians Gula sent to gather the pilots returned with two large groups. Gula took the pages from his helpers. "You can carry on with your duties. Thank you."

Gula turned to the pilots and looked at them. Some were old. Some were way too young to be flying a bomber on an interstellar mission. But it was all he had. "I am Commander Gula. I am in charge here, so let's cut right to it. As you may know, we have an Inean battleship heading our way, and we suspect they know about us."

There was a murmuring among the new pilots.

"Quiet down! There is a lot to do. I need crews of three for each ship," he barked. He began pointing at people. "You, you, and you get to that bomber. Next three, go to that one," and he did this until no one was standing in front of him. He then looked about at the frantic running about on the flight deck. He spotted a dozen men struggling as they pushed an unfinished bomber to the side of the flight deck. He raced over to help push the bomber across the deck. The craft was heavy, even though the moon's gravity was only a fraction of Ardonnar's.

A large crane wheeled over and hovered over a finished bomber. Its cables dropped down and clanged against the hull of the ship. Gula grabbed a cable and fed the hook through the metal loop bolted to the hull. He gave the thumbs up, and the crane struggled to lift the fully loaded bomber, but it did. Next, the crane operator, who sat up high in a glass box, guided the bomber and crane towards the large doors.

Gula glanced at Puabi, who was racing his way, and then at his watch and cursed. *Not enough time.*

THIRTY-SEVEN

DAMOK-SAI WATCHED the large display on the bridge of the *Nikstra*, which had swung around Utui to retrieve the solar disruptor. The ship's sensors detected dozens of metallic objects exiting the fiery cloud as it dissipated well beyond Ardonnar. "Sensors control; what are those objects?" Damok-Sai growled as he stepped closer to the large screen in the hope he could distinguish them himself.

"Commander," the sensors operator said with a deep hiss. "Those are ships."

"Where did they come from?" Damok-Sai snapped.

"They came from the planet. I can not trace their origin. However, they are not ours."

Damok-Sai growled his displeasure. "They are up to something! Track those vessels. I want to know where they are going."

His Helmsman turned to Damok-Sai. "Sir, we will have to break orbit around this star to maintain sensor lock on them."

"Very well, break orbit," Damok-Sai stated.

The large ship had been slowing to retrieve the star disruptor, but now it lumbered up to speed and flew around Utui and headed towards the inner planet Duggae for a speed boost to the outer planets.

Damok-Sai was under pressure from the Inean leader Sankar to pull the star disruptor away from Utui. He was concerned that the constant bombardment from Utui would destroy the probe. Sankar wanted to use it at another location once the people of Ardonnar were eradicated. He was growing anxious to complete the takeover, which was now taking too long, and he had enough slaves to maintain a steady supply on Inea. He did not want too many so he could keep the price high.

The ship headed past Duggae and used the planet for a speed boost to slingshot itself to the outer planets.

"Notify the fleet to train sensors towards those ships and track them," Damok-Sai stated as he continued to stare at the dots on the main screen. What are they up to? He wondered to himself.

Over the hours, Damok-Sai and his crew tracked and followed the Ardon ships as they flew past the gas giant Idpa and landed on the moon Uggae. Damok-Sai grinned and turned to his Helmsman. "Set course for that moon and bring speed up."

"Yes, sir, course set, and we are bringing speed up slowly to limit fuel consumption," the navigator said. He then throttled up, and the ship began to rumble and shake.

"Time until intercept?" Damok-Sai asked eagerly. He had been waiting for a chance to blow something up, and it may as well be an Ardon rebel base.

"Will take us twenty hours before we are within striking distance," the navigator replied.

"Get our fighters ready and get our special nuclear rockets ready," Damok-Sai wrung his hands over the prospect. "Alert me when we get close. I will be in my chambers having my way with a couple of their slaves," he laughed and walked off the bridge of the *Nikstra*.

Deep in the *Nikstra*, the crew fueled two full squadrons of fighters, and the pilots went through their preflight checks. There were a few issues with some of the fighters, but the deck crew had plenty of time to repair them as the large ship lumbered toward the distant moon.

In other parts of the ship, other members of Damok-Sai's crew armed several nuclear missiles to use on whatever facility was found on the distant moon. Once armed, the large Ineans wheeled the missiles to the launch tubes. Others swung the large cylindrical door open while the first group pushed the missile on its rollers into the tube. The last one pushing removed the steel cover from the main engine nozzle, and he closed the large round door with a spin of the wheel, locking the door in place.

Another Inean programmed the launch computer.

Later that day, the *Nikstra* went in close to the gas giant Idpa, using the planet's atmosphere to slow the ship and conserve fuel. The ship slowed as it headed towards the moon, Uggae. This was necessary because all of Damok-Sai's ships were low on fuel and could not afford to waste any. Another reason why only one ship was sent to the moon.

The ship rumbled and shook as it hit the atmosphere, slowing to a low enough speed to enter orbit around the largest of Idpa's moon. Damok-Sai ordered the ship to orbit the moon a few times to take readings and isolate targets. Soon, his sensors officer turned to him.

"Commander. I am picking up strong energy readings from inside the moon. I think they are enriching antimatter!"

"All of our preliminary probes said nothing about these people having that capability!" Damok-Sai exclaimed while walking over to the sensors console for a look. Sure enough, he recognized the tell-tale signs of antimatter creation. The customary ring of energy of a particle accelerator buried deep underground.

"Sir, I am picking up several smaller power signatures in a cavern below the surface. Look here," the officer said.

"I can see that!" growled Damok-Sai.

"I don't think they know we are here. There doesn't seem to be any other activity."

"They have surprised us for the last time. We must destroy this base," Damok-Sai returned to the center of his bridge and faced forward. "Tactical, feed all target coordinates to the nuclear controls."

"Yes, sir. One moment," the technician said.

The sensors officer turned to Damok-Sai, "Sir, there is an opening forming in the side of a large crater!"

"What?" exclaimed Damok-Sai. "Put it on the main screen."

The technician transferred his sensors to the main screen, and a close-up of the crater appeared on the main screen. They all watched as two large rock doors slid open and two ships approached the opening.

"They are coming out to fight! Bring us to a safe distance and launch missiles!" Damok-Sai commanded.

The ship angled away from the moon and ignited its engines, taking it to a safe distance from the moon. As it did, Damok-Sai ordered the missiles to be launched. Several bright streaks of flame flew from the *Nikstra* and headed toward the moon. The missiles detonated just above the surface and, in a blinding flash, obliterated the surface of the moon where the base was. Several nukes exploded, caving the structure in and collapsing the antimatter ring.

The Ineans stood up and tilted their heads toward the ceiling and howled in victory as bits of rock and twisted metal flew by the *Nikstra* as it went around the moon for protection.

Several hours later, the debris from the moon settled down, and the *Nikstra* approached the collapsed military base. In the rubble, they could make out several ships and equipment, all melted and twisted among the rock. Damok-Sai sent several transports to the surface to check out the debris.

Ineans wearing space suits exited the transports and began close-up scanning of the debris. The space suit clad Ineans sent the data back to the *Nikstra*. Damok-Sai was becoming more pleased with the destruction.

"*Nikstra*, we are picking up a strange power signature down here," one of the Ineans stated as he swept his scanner out before him.

The *Nikstra*'s sensors officer watched his screen turn red as data flew across his terminal. He turned towards Damok-Sai in a panic.

"Sir!" he didn't have to say anything else as the flashing message appeared on the main screen for all on the bridge to see.

"Bring those transports back here!" Damok-Sai barked as several sensors turned red.

The sensors officer spun around, "Antimatter bombs are about to go off, sir!"

"Full thrusters now!" commanded Damok-Sai.

The ship pulled away slowly as the transports lifted off the surface of the battered moon.

"I'm detecting detonations deep in the moon, sir!"

"Helmsman! Get us out of here!" barked Damok-Sai as a blinding flash occurred behind them.

"Incoming shock wave!"

"Brace for impact!" the communications officer yelled into his microphone for the whole ship to hear.

The wave hit the *Nikstra* from the rear and sent everyone flying about on the ship. Alarms sounded throughout the ship, and then the large vessel was pounded from astern by rock and debris from the moon that had been blasted off. There was a warning of a second impact, which struck the ship's main engine port, causing an explosion. They had been hit by one of the transports, which exploded on impact. The *Nikstra* groaned as it started to spiral towards the gas giant. The Emperor's finest ship spiraled out of control towards the crushing atmosphere of the planet, Idpa.

Damok-Sai got up slowly, stumbled to the Nav-con, and fought the controls to bring his ship under control. He held the two control sticks and fired the thrusters to bring the ship back under his control, but it still spiraled toward the planet. Soon, the large planet, which was bigger than Jupiter, filled his view screen. More alarms going off on the bridge. Fire alarms!

His Helmsman staggered back and took the controls from Damok-Sai, and started entering commands. "Main engines are not responding!" He entered more commands. "I need fuel from the main engines to the thrusters!"

"We won't have enough to get back to the fleet!" his assistant yelled back.

"Back to the fleet! I need it so we don't crash into the planet," he screamed in his deep hissing voice. "Transfer fuel control NOW!"

The technician did as the *Nikstra* hit the upper edges of the planet's atmosphere. New alarms going off now, and Damok-Sai was screaming to turn them off.

The Helmsman steadied the enormous ship and managed to pull out of the atmosphere, putting the ship into a low orbit. "Low orbit established. We will need to get the main engines back up soon so we can break away from this planet."

"Good. Status report!" Damok-Sai yelled.

Several of his officers all spoke at once with their damage reports, and Damok-Sai growled at them.

Then, each gave their report one at a time.

"We have lost our portside main thruster nozzle and quite possibly the entire engine. We only have ten percent fuel left in our reserves," one officer stated.

"My report is incomplete," one officer began and stopped as Damok-Sai growled at him. He continued. "We have structural fractures all over the hull. It will take some time to reinforce the hull before heading back out. The stress of leaving orbit could be enough to destroy this ship."

"Fires are under control and should be out soon. Then we will assess the damage." A third officer stated.

Damok-Sai turned to the last one, "Casualties?"

"At least fifty, but there are areas of the ship we have not heard from yet. I'm sure it will go up," the medical officer said with a sharp tone. "You talked about surprises?"

"Enough out of you!" Damok-Sai yelled as he reached for his knife but discovered it was not tucked in his belt. He looked about as did the others on the bridge, and Zammani, who had just walked onto the bridge, picked it up. He held it up so that everyone on the bridge could see it. "The Emperor will be pleased, no doubt, at your report of this incident, Damok-Sai. His finest warship wrecked in a foolish adventure."

Damok-Sai growled at him while lunging to retrieve his knife.

Zammani stepped away while holding the knife towards Damok-Sai. "Give me that knife now."

"So you can kill me with it? I think not Damok-Sai," and with that, he tucked the jagged knife with dried blood crusted along its blade into his belt. "I think the Emperor would want to see this and possibly use it to kill you with it," Zammani growled at Damok-Sai and walked off the bridge.

"Fix this ship and get us back to the fleet!" Damok-Sai bellowed, and he left the bridge. Some thought he was going after Zammani.

THIRTY-EIGHT

AANEPADA WAS with General Asar and Zuttara, and they stared at the monitor on the wall. Aanepada cleared his throat. "Did our ships and people get off that moon in time?"

"I don't know, sir. We lost contact with them hours ago. The Ineans were jamming all frequencies as they got close," Asar said.

"Do you mean to tell me that we may have lost this fight without even getting one ship off?" Aanepada steamed.

"I think that General Ningal would have launched whatever he could before the Ineans got there. I hope they all got out," Asar replied.

"Mister President, I know General Ningal, and he would have launched everything he could and most likely found a way to get them all off that moon," Zuttara added.

"I hope you are right, but I don't like this silence coming from them."

"I understand, sir. We will keep listening," Asar added.

"How soon before the bombers on Anaru are completed?" Aanepada asked.

"A few more weeks, as long as those animals don't find the base," Asar replied.

"Have them ready to fly at a moment's notice regardless if they are done or not."

"Yes, sir," Asar and Zuttara stated together.

Aanepada huffed and walked out of the room. He winced in pain and brought his hand to his chest as he stumbled into the corridor. He began to sweat a little and leaned against the wall until the pain subsided. He was glad Dagan wasn't there. She would have forced him to see the doctors.

THIRTY-NINE

TWO WEEKS HAD PASSED since the Ineans attacked the Ardonnarian base on Uggae, and so far, there was no retribution for the damage inflicted on the *Nikstra*, which had not returned yet. Aanepada knew better than to think that the Ineans would not hold his people responsible.

There was still no word yet from anyone who was on Uggae; nothing but static on all frequencies. Aanepada and his staff were fearful that they were dead. Three hundred people gone without so much as a stray radio signal or etlutu signal, which was similar to Morse code.

Another concern was the distant moon Uggae. The exploding antimatter containment vessels buried underground near the accelerator ring had blown a tenth of the moon away with such force when it exploded that many of the large pieces flew into space. The rest of the moon was fracturing from the gravitational tug of Idpa and the other large moons as it orbited. The moon was expected to crumble and break up soon. Even from Ardonnar, telescopes had photographed large fissures opening across the entire moon. The hope was that Idpa would absorb the moon when it did fly apart, but some computer models showed that some of it could fly into space and eventually fall in towards Utui, passing the orbit of Ardonnar at some point in time. It could be years, could be centuries, but the threat did exist. So Aanepada had a team of scientists working on all the projections and watching the moon.

Work on Anaru progressed; there were twenty-four ships completed, and the last bomber was nearly finished. They anticipated the next solar blast to come tearing through any time, and they would launch their attack on the Inean home planet.

Two Inean ships had broken away from the fleet, leaving the remaining ships vulnerable from the ground. With three ships destroyed in previous attacks, the *Nikstra* limping back, and now three ships ferrying Ardon slaves to Inea, the fleet was getting thin and low on fuel. The refueling tanker had not arrived as promised, and Damok-Sai's invasion fleet ran the risk of running out of fuel and drifting away at the very moment when he feared the Ardonnarians were preparing to attack.

The two ships headed out in opposite directions. Both began low-level scans of each moon, planet, and asteroid in the system. Neither ship bothered with Nisaba and Anaru. They were too close, and the Ineans figured if there was activity on either moon, then they would have known it by now.

The Ineans took nothing else for granted. They bombed every asteroid base and planetary base they came across as they explored the solar system.

FORTY

THE *NIKSTRA* DRIFTED BACK into orbit around Ardonnar and joined the rest of the ships. The ship had exhausted all of its fuel and needed the assistance of two other ships to slow to a stop. Afterward, the two ships locked onto the *Nikstra*, and crews transferred fuel to the damaged ship.

Damok-Sai met with his other captains and ground commanders to plan their response to the Ardonnarian attack.

Damok-Sai paced along the full length of the windowed wall, which went from the floor to the ceiling in the large room. His officers sat around a large oval table. No one dared to speak, knowing full well how explosive Damok-Sai could be, regardless of whose fault it may be, including his. Finally, he stopped by the largest window, which was in the middle, and he stared out through the three-inch thick glass at the planet below. "We have a problem," he said as he spied the moon Anaru hovering in orbit on the far side of the planet.

No one spoke. All kept their eyes on him and waited for the inevitable outburst.

Damok-Sai surprised them by speaking in a normal Inean voice.

"These Ardons have capabilities that we did not realize when we invaded. They have highly advanced nuclear weapons, and they can enrich antimatter for spaceships. Plus, they can destroy an entire moon while we are on the surface, pulverizing it to dust with an antimatter bomb."

He turned from the window and faced the group of captains and field commanders, who kept their eyes locked on him, each with a hand on the dagger strapped to their belt. "I want to know their next move, and I want to know where they are operating from... And I want to know now!" he growled while wringing his hands together.

"What are our limitations, Commander?" one of them asked.

"None! Do whatever it takes to get it out of them. I am sure someone in each village has been in contact with a central government, and I am sure they know where they are hiding."

"Do whatever it takes?" another questioned.

"Yes, have your ears stopped working, or are you having trouble processing the simple command?" Damok-Sai sneered.

Damok-Sai changed his tone slightly. "What is the status of our cargo ships and our fuel tankers?" he asked while turning to the large window again to watch technicians in spacesuits extending a large hose to the *Nikstra* to transfer fuel to his ship. It was embarrassing for him that the pride of the fleet had to drift into orbit with help from other ships. However, no one dared to say anything, at least within earshot of him or his loyal following.

One of his officers cleared his throat and stood facing him with a hand-held tablet in his hand. "Sir, two of the cargo ships will be here in one more day. The fueling tanker is still weeks away. They are so slow in getting fuel from Inea to us. I would recommend in future invasions that we bring a tanker with us and have several launch weeks apart to keep a steady supply available to us."

"I think we are fine for now," one of the ship captains added.

"Fine?!" Damok-Sai's clerk exclaimed. "Fine? These Ardons have shown themselves to be quite resilient, and if they knew what our fuel situation was, then they could attack us at will. They obviously have the weapons and possibly ships to deliver the bombs. So to say we are fine is an obvious and potentially deadly error on our part."

The captain got up and went towards the clerk. "You! Do not speak to me that way. Do you understand?"

Damok-Sai watched the exchange out of the corner of his eye.

"Do you understand me?" the captain asked again while reaching for a knife he kept in a holder on his belt.

The clerk, who was as ruggedly built as an Inean could be, would have nothing of this captain. He stepped towards the captain while reaching for his own knife. The others in the room moved out of the way, expecting a blood bath. The two Ineans closed in on each other, snarling and spit dripping from their fangs. A knife flew between them and stuck in the tabletop with a loud knock. Everyone glanced in the direction the knife came from, and Damok-Sai was walking forward. He grasped the captain's hand and squeezed it until he dropped his knife. Then he growled at his clerk, who stopped, glanced at Damok-Sai's knife stuck in the table's top, and had a thought that was quickly squelched by Damok-Sai's growling. The growl was loud enough to shake the thick glass in the windows and cause ripples in the mugs of ale on the table.

"My clerk is correct. We can not trust these Ardons. We can expect them to pounce on weakness, and they do have the tools to do so. We can not let on that we are in trouble, or we will surely be in trouble then."

The captain bowed towards Damok-Sai, retrieved his knife, and went back to his seat. He was angry at the two of them and vowed in his mind to get them. Once an Inean made up his mind to kill somebody, it was usually done swiftly and with large amounts of blue blood being spilled.

The clerk went back to his seat, thankful that his leader found his opinion acceptable but upset that he was not allowed to fight the captain. He could have beaten him, which would have improved his standing in the fleet. He knew the captain would be coming for him now, and he planned on being ready for him.

"I want those cargo ships unloaded and supplies distributed to all ships in the fleet, and then I want them loaded with the Ardon slaves. If we can turn around these cargo ships, then maybe the Emperor will send us his blessing in fuel or order to finish these animals off once and for all," Damok-Sai said, and everyone in the room tilted their heads toward the ceiling and howled while praising Emperor Sankar.

"I also want information about where these Ardons are hiding and what their plans are. I want it within two days from this time. You may go now."

All his field commanders and captains looked at their clocks that hung like an ornament from their collars to mark the time. Then they saluted Damok-Sai and exited the room in haste. No one wanted to be around Damok-Sai any longer than necessary.

Once the field commanders landed on Ardonnar, they wasted no time rounding up people to question and, hopefully, torture. They would not be disappointed.

One field commander, Laraak, was barking orders to his soldiers while stepping off the transport from the *Nikstra*. "I want one hundred of these animals captured and brought to the town square in one hour. I want them stripped and bound very tightly and painfully. Now go to it!"

His troops checked their guns and headed into town to gather the unsuspecting Ardonnarians for Laraak's amusement. He might even get some information for Damok-Sai in the process. He longed to get rid of the Ardons so he and the rest of the Ineans could stake their claim to this planet.

Laraak exited the transport in precisely one hour, and his soldiers did not disappoint him. Before him were a hundred Ardonnarians stripped bare, with their hands and feet tied very tight. The ropes were cutting off circulation to their hands and feet. Many struggled against the tight ropes.

Laraak walked up to one of the prisoners with his assistant beside him, ready to take notes. He studied the middle-aged man for a moment, and he grinned while saliva dripped from his fangs. "Nice to meet you," he growled.

The man was not impressed and spit on Laraak. Laraak laughed and took his knife from his belt and cut the man's ear off, and he screamed. Laraak put his knife away as blood began to ooze from where the man's ear was.

"Now that we know each other, I need information," Laraak asked while speaking into the man's good ear.

"Go to Tari!" the man stated loudly.

"Lead the way because that is where you are going as well," Laraak stated while some of his soldiers laughed. "I want to know where your government is hiding," he said while whispering into the man's injured ear. He brushed up against the open wound, and the man flinched away.

"I will not talk. You will have to kill me."

"Oh, you will talk because death will not come for you, but you will wish it." Laraak nodded to the soldier standing beside him.

The soldier reached forward, took the man's left hand, and snapped two of his fingers sideways. The man cried out in pain but managed to not give any information.

"If you do not know what I want, then simply tell me who does know, and I will make the pain stop," Laraak stated while looking out at the other prisoners for a reaction. A lot of the women cried, as did the children that were captured. They knew the Ineans would kill them anyway, so they vowed to keep quiet.

"Tell me, who will know?" Laraak yelled as he held his sharp, jagged knife under the man's chin with enough pressure to break the skin, and blood began to trickle down the long blade.

"I don't know anything," the man gasped.

"That is too bad for you," Laraak thrust the knife through the man's throat and sliced through his esophagus and carotid arteries. He nearly severed the man's head as he held the knife in that position while the man gasped his last gurgling breaths. Then he pulled the knife away, and the man's body collapsed to the ground in a cloud of dust with a thump.

Laraak looked out at all the frightened faces, and he chose his next victim. "I want that one next."

A soldier grabbed the middle-aged woman by the hair and dragged her to him. She kicked and screamed, but it was useless against the large Inean. He brought her to Laraak and held her.

"Tell me," Laraak paused while he studied the woman. "Where will I find the government hideout?" he said in as soothing of a voice possible from a rough alien.

She began to cry. "I don't know. Really, I don't. You have to believe me!" she pleaded.

Laraak looked at her for a moment. "I do believe you," and he grinned.

She began to feel she was going to be spared. In a brief moment, that thought was gone as he buried the knife low in her abdomen and sliced upward. She really did not feel it until a burning sensation overcame her, and she looked down to see her insides starting to ooze out of the long, deep cut. The Inean let go of her, and she dropped to the ground. Her last effort was trying to stuff her intestines back in until the blood loss overcame her, and she fell backward and died.

"That was dramatic!" Laraak said to one of his officers, and they both laughed. "Let's walk down the line to see who might have the information we are looking for."

Both of them walked to the far end of the line and killed the first four people without asking any questions. Laraak simply took his knife and gutted them with no care at all, and their bodies crumpled to the dirt. They came to the next one in the line, a teenage boy who was shaking in fear and urinated on Laraak as he stood in front of him. Laraak looked down at his wet boots and grinned at the boy. "Do you know what I am looking for?"

The boy nodded nervously. "Yes, yes, I do."

"Excellent. Tell me what you know."

A man next to him turned to the boy. "Don't tell them, he'll kill you anyway."

The boy looked at the man next to him. Laraak's rough, hairy hand clasped his chin and turned his head back to him. "Don't listen to him. I won't kill you for helping us."

The boy glanced towards the man next to him, who kept shaking his head. "They are in Mount Laarsa," he offered.

"Where is that?" Laraak asked with a widening grin.

"In the Humbaba Mountains west of Delondra," the boy stated to the moans of everyone near him.

"Good, very good," Laraak said with a nod to the soldier next to him. "I will take this boy away. Take care of the rest while I question him further."

Once Laraak had the boy inside the shuttle, the soldiers pulled several of the women from the lines for themselves and massacred the remaining hostages.

Laraak had the boy sit down in one of the cold metal chairs. "So, tell me, who in your village is in contact with the government in Laarsa mountain?"

The boy squirmed against the cold metal seat and then looked up at the large Inean who hovered over him. "Um, there is Akkadi. He is the local priest, and he has been talking with a general. I can't remember his name."

Laraak handed the boy a glass of cold water, which he guzzled down quickly. "Good?"

"Yes."

"Here, have a warm biscuit," the Inean offered the boy a fresh, warm, steaming biscuit, which he ate quickly.

"Thanks, it is the first thing I have had in days."

"I know. Food has been scarce, even for us. I hope that changes soon for both our peoples," Laraak said while sizing up the boy.

The boy, Oueili, glanced up at the Inean, "Why do you kill us?"

Laraak stepped back and got down on one knee to face the boy eye-to-eye. "We have to in order to get the answers. We want to preserve both races. Let's face it, your planet is dying, and we need to help you get to your new home. However, many of you insist on fighting us. We are only here to help." Laraak looked at the boy, who nodded as he looked around for more food. "I will get you more food." He then got up and looked at the soldier standing off to the side, nodding. Laraak stepped off the Inean shuttle while the soldier tied the boy to the chair.

Zammani, who had been following every move Damok-Sai had made over the past few months, sneaked away to his quarters and plugged a portable transmitter into a port in the wall by a small desk. He leaned over a chair, which was pushed partially under the desk, and began typing commands into the transmitter.

He had established a link to the *Nikstra*'s main communications array and was now in the process of locking a channel to General FarQue on Inea, who was in charge of the invasion fleet.

Zammani tapped his rough fingers on the desk while waiting for the status bar to creep along the bottom of the screen on his transmitter. After a minute, the status bar turned green, and the fuzzy image of the fleet general appeared on the small screen.

"What is it, Zammani?" FarQue growled.

"I have to report about the latest failures of Damok-Sai."

"What is your report," FarQue replied with a slight roll of his eyes. He had placed Zammani on Damok-Sai's ship for this very purpose. However, Zammani had taken it personally since Damok-Sai had attacked him on his first day. FarQue's motives were self-serving as well. His father was one step down from Sankar's inner circle. FarQue knew if he could bring down Damok-Sai, he might bring down Damok-Sai's father, Manava, clearing the way for his own father's climb to the inner circle. If he were successful, then it would bring him close to the Emperor and possibly influence the Emperor or determine who would be the next leader of Inea.

"As you know, Damok-Sai has been reckless with the *Nikstra* and has nearly destroyed this ship. The ship is heavily damaged and out of fuel. We have lost hundreds of his Emperor's finest soldiers policing this planet while he obsesses over these Ardon women..."

"Yes, yes, we know all this, but I want specifics. The Emperor won't open an inquiry on generalizations, especially with Manava in his close circle. I need details, facts, and something to wedge between Manava and the Emperor," FarQue stated as he adjusted the way he was sitting.

"Yes, of course, general. He has just sent his field commanders to the surface to expedite the collection of Ardon women for shipment back to Inea while our fleet flies on fumes."

"Yes, yes, go on," FarQue said impatiently.

"General, his obsession clouds his judgment. He has, at any given moment, four of these women in his quarters. It is to the point where their blood is seeping under the door and running down the corridor. He spends so much time in there that the ship captains are calling more and more of the shots. He leads with his dagger, not with his father's skills as a commander."

"Okay, so he enjoys the fruits of this planet. We can't hang him on that," FarQue growled and leaned towards the camera.

"He underestimates these Ardons. They continually attack us, and each time they do, they succeed. And each time they attack, he seems surprised. He has given them a chance, and the Ardons take advantage every time..." Zammani glanced away for a second and then turned back to the general. "I don't think he wants to defeat these people and lose his addiction."

"Fine, that will be enough. I will contact those who have the authority to bring him in. I have your written report as well as the reports from two other field agents. FarQue out."

FarQue didn't mince words; he needed what he needed, and that was it. Now, his arduous task was to convince the council to bring Damok-Sai in on the next flight to ask him about his intentions for the Ardons and his fleet, which was on the edge of defeat should the Ardons choose an all-out confrontation.

FarQue stepped away from his desk and looked out his windows overlooking the city of Sabitta, the Inean capital. He viewed the steel and glass buildings rising hundreds of stories into the cloudless sky. Hundreds of small craft flew about the city in between blinking buoys, which hovered in the sky, marking travel lanes for the thousands of craft in flight. A mass transit train zipped by below his window on its magnetic monorail towards the capitol building, which was the tallest building in the city, rising a hundred-fifty stories from the ground. It was shaped like a slender pyramid and came to a point nearly a half mile up. FarQue spied the Capitol building and grinned. He walked back to his desk and picked up a black folder with all of his evidence against Damok-Sai. He closed the door behind him and made sure it was locked. He was off to present his case to the Emperor himself. He entered an elevator and went down to the ground floor. He walked by a pair of Ardon slave women who were chained to the reception counter in the center of the large room, giving them a glance. He noticed their hollow, dead eyes and knew they were a gift for some high-ranking official; it was then that he knew his case had to be solid. He had to admit he had sampled the goods and found them to be quite addictive. Under different circumstances, he would not mind owning a few for himself.

The woman's eyes followed him out the door as another Inean male approached the counter.

The Inean behind the desk pointed to the women. "Those were delivered for you by a courier from Manava's office, fresh off the last transport that arrived a few hours ago."

The Inean clerk handed him a slip of paper, which he stuffed in a pocket in his pants. He then unhooked the chains from the counter and walked back to the elevator with the two women walking behind him. "Should I call for a cleanup crew?" the Inean behind the desk asked before the other got away.

"No!" he stated and then turned back. "I plan on making these last a while. I was told if you are easy on them, then they will last a short time at least." He started back towards the elevator and turned again to the Inean behind the desk. "Do you know what they eat?"

"I don't, but I can find out and have some sent to your office."

"Do that," and he continued on to the elevator, which took him and his two slaves up toward his office.

. . .

FarQue entered the capital building and got past the security guards just inside the doors. The leadership of Inea had changed frequently in the past hundred years by assassination and hostile takeovers, and Sankar was not taking any chances, knowing there was a price on his head. Inea had a bloody history, and the current leader knew he was unpopular, with many groups vying for a chance to kill him and his council and take control of the planet. Many did not agree with how the Ardon slaves were distributed. Several were calling for slave farms where the Ardons would be bred on Inea to boost the supply. Others did not like that the Ardons were still alive and warned of repercussions, especially since word got out about how the fleet's flagship had nearly been destroyed.

FarQue was a frequent visitor to the capital building and breezed through security. He entered the elevator and went up to the top suite, which was the Emperor's floor. As the lift went up, FarQue rehearsed in his mind how he was going to present his case. A few minutes went by, and the lift slowed and stopped. The doors slid open, and he was greeted by two armed and armored guards. They recognized him and stepped aside to let him pass.

FarQue stepped into the open room, which was all glass. Sankar wanted a view of the entire city and countryside from his office, and it was the best view in the city. The Emperor sat at his desk, which was on a rotating platform, so his view changed as it went around. Around the platform sat a dozen Ardon slaves, Sankar's very own personal collection. Because he was so rough with them, they had to be refreshed every few days. Any who survived were handed down to his staff.

FarQue paused a moment and then continued on to a single chair facing Sankar. He walked up as Emperor Sankar looked up from his desk. FarQue bowed, and Sankar motioned for him to sit. FarQue sat and kept the black folder in his hands.

"You have information regarding Damok-Sai's poor handling of the Ardon takeover?" Sankar asked in a rough but decidedly pointed tone.

"Yes, Your Majesty. I have everything in this folder right here. I regret having to do this, considering Damok-Sai is under my command, and he is the son of your closest council member, Manava. However, our fleet is at stake and quite possibly our conquest of the Ardon planet."

A few of the women cocked their heads to listen in. They had learned enough of the Inean language to know what was being said. They had hope that their military was inflicting damage on the Ineans and had a chance of victory. This gave them a slim hope of being rescued, despite how the Ineans treated them.

"Let me see your folder, FarQue," Sankar asked, thrusting his large, rough, hairy paw out.

FarQue handed it to him without hesitation and quickly retracted his hand.

Sankar pulled the folder open and removed the contents. Inside were dozens of pages of typed reports and several memory disks. He took the first memory disk and placed it in a slot on the terminal, which sat on top of his desk. He watched the video report from one of FarQue's field agents. He studied it for a short time and then removed it before it had finished. FarQue was concerned that Sankar was not interested.

Sankar then scanned over several pages and looked up at FarQue, "Are all of your reports as detailed and incriminating as this?"

"Yes, they are."

Sankar went to speak but held back as two armed soldiers walked his way. One of them spoke up, "Sorry to interrupt, Your Highness, but it is their feeding time. Shall we take them away?"

"Yes, please do, and clean them up. Some of them stink."

The two soldiers bowed to Sankar and untied the women from the hooks on the floor. They gathered them up and led the women from the room to be fed.

Once the soldiers were gone, Sankar turned his attention back to FarQue. "I will convene the panel at once to discuss these claims. I trust all of these people are available for further questioning?"

FarQue nodded, "They are. I can have them on the next ship if you would like."

"Yes, I would like."

Sankar glanced back at the data in front of him. "Is there anything else, FarQue?"

"No, Your Highness."

"Then why are you still here!" Sankar growled.

FarQue rose from the chair, bowed to Sankar, and turned towards the elevator while the two guards parted to let him through. The doors opened, and he entered the elevator.

FORTY-ONE

AANEPADA STOOD at the head of the table, overlooking several of his top military personnel. "It is time, my loyal council, to put our plan in motion. We are due for another of these solar storms, and it may be the last chance we get. The Ineans have stepped up their hostage-taking and their murderous rampages, and our people are becoming more fragmented across the planet. We cannot delay because there might not be anything left to save if we wait." He then glanced at General Asar, who nodded and stood.

"I would like to thank everyone who put forth their best efforts on this difficult achievement without any intervention by the Ineans. I find our luck in this amazing. Either they are very stupid, or we are very lucky." He paused a moment to glance at his notes. "However, now we must implement our plans and pray to Kur that there are no mistakes. The next solar storm is due in three days, and here is what we hope to happen. Anaru and Duggae will be in opposition, which will provide us with a perfect distraction. As the storm hits the planet, we will launch the remaining ships from here towards Anaru. Once the ships are safely on approach to Anaru base, then we will detonate charges and launch missiles from Duggae. This should draw some of their ships away to investigate. Once they begin to move ships towards Duggae, we will launch fighters from the ground armed with EM pulse canons that will disable their remaining ships. Once the Inean battleships are disabled, then we will launch from Anaru towards Inea. We are hopeful that this will delay the Inean ships investigating Duggae, allowing us to slip away."

"Excuse me, General," Dagan said while looking up at Asar. He had grown painfully accustomed to her questions. Many in the room still struggled with a priestess asking questions at a military meeting. She was consistent, however, and she did ask what everyone wanted to know, so grudgingly, they let her speak. Even Aanepada gave up trying to restrain her. Asar looked at her. She continued, "What if the Ineans don't take the bait?"

Asar knew it was something they all wanted to know. "There is a small facility on Duggae which we will remotely open from the ground. Once we launch a few missiles their way and give the illusion of fighters coming from the opening, they will respond. If, for some strange chance, they do not investigate, then we will launch urukii missiles at them. That should get their attention."

"Won't they launch fighters themselves to take on our bombers?" Dagan asked.

"We are hopeful that the EM pulse weapons will fry their electronics and ground their fleet. They seem to be susceptible to EM radiation like we were in the beginning. We believe that is why they hide behind the planet each time Utui belches," Asar said.

Dagan seemed satisfied with his answers and glanced at Aanepada, who seemed distant.

Asar continued speaking. "We have to be prepared for an Inean ground assault, which will probably involve urukii missiles should our fighters inflict significant damage to their fleet."

"General," Dagan lifted her head once again and made eye contact with Asar, "is it true that the Ineans are running low on fuel? And if so, how will that affect our plans? Can they land these enormous ships on the ground?"

Asar looked at her for a moment and wondered how she knew so much while a few in the room groaned. "Those are all valid questions. It appears that some of their ships are low on fuel, which might help our bombers get away. We have seen them transferring fuel from one ship to another recently. We assume they are balancing their resources. Also, we do not think those ships can land. They are too large, and their engines are underpowered to achieve enough thrust to lift off the ground. With that said, we can expect any attack by the Ineans to come from space."

Aanepada glanced up. "So everything is in place. We just have to wait for the next solar storm?"

"Yes, Mister President," Asar stated.

"Every possible scenario has been taken into account?"

"Everything we know about these Ineans has been tested. We are ready."

"Very well then, everyone is dismissed," Aanepada stated as he got up slowly, catching a look from Dagan, who was concerned for him.

His advisers filed out of the room, but Dagan lagged until she was alone with Aanepada.

He sat back down, "Dagan, I'm glad you stayed behind. Come, sit with me."

He sounded tired.

"Is there something wrong with you?" she asked with a concerned tone.

"I'm tired, Dagan."

"We all are," she replied.

"Yes, but not like this. I cannot go on much longer."

"What are you saying?" she said while gripping his hands in hers.

"I don't have much time left. I am almost done with the fight."

Dagan got up and hugged him. "You have to go on. The people need you."

"No, they need a strong leader to take them to victory over the Ineans and to rebuild our society." He paused for a few seconds. "Look, since Kilar was killed, I can feel my life being sucked out of me, and the only thing keeping me going is you. Kur has a plan for me *and* for you."

She gave him a quizzical look.

"You know what I am talking about. Kur is with you."

"Who would you pick? Asar is a great military person but is not spiritual, and our people need that as well," she said as she thought through a list of potential candidates. She pondered some of the high priests, but none of them had any leadership skills.

"Who I would pick and who Kur would pick are different people. However, Kur seems to be pointing to a particular person to take over. Which is beyond our control," he said while holding her hands.

"Well, who is Kur saying should be our leader?" she was getting frustrated at being kept in suspense.

"Kur is pointing to you."

She was flabbergasted. "You are kidding me, right? And you constantly gave me a hard time when I butted heads with the elders and high priests. None of them will accept me as a leader," she stated while pulling her hands away.

"It is not up to them to choose. It is up to me, and I choose you based on what Kur tells me."

"Well, I think you must have bumped your head on something. You need to quit getting down on yourself and lead our people out of this mess." She said with a widening grin. "You had me going there for a minute."

"I'm not joking. You need to prepare to assume the presidency. There are many things you need to know," Aanepada said while getting up from his chair as his knees popped and cracked.

"No! You are the leader. You can teach me these things later," she said with a trace of fear and remorse and a little anger thrown in.

"There is no later. Look at me. I am old. No leader has been in office past his hundredth birthday, and mine was last year. My body is failing."

"No, no, no, we won't talk of this," she hugged him more to hide the tears welling up in the corners of her eyes.

"I have been a father to you since your original parents died many years ago. But you have to realize that I won't be here forever." He gripped her arms and held her away so he could see her face.

She exhaled and made eye contact with him. "Kilar's death was not your fault."

"I know that, but it does not change the way I feel." He studied her for a moment. "Your whole life has been one test after another to bring you to this moment, and I can understand your fear. However, you need to embrace this and take charge like you have always done."

"We have never had a woman leader. Besides, Kur warns of a woman leader in the end, which leads to great destruction, and this needs to be done through the people, and..." She rambled on until he interrupted her.

"These are unusual times, Dagan. Yes, the people should have a say, and they will once we get our planet back, and we can eliminate the threat from the Ineans," he paused. "You are young and determined. It is time for a lot of changes."

She slowly nodded her head. "I will do it," she said softly.

With that, he hugged her firmly.

"When will all this take place?" she asked.

"Very soon. I need to teach you a few things first."

He took her hand and placed a sealed envelope in it. "After I am gone, read this. It will open your eyes."

"What is it?" she asked.

"It will answer many questions you have, but you must promise not to open it until after I am gone."

"Don't talk of such things."

He started walking for the door. "Come, walk with me."

She got up, and he guided her from the room into the corridor.

FORTY-TWO

AN INEAN PLATOON entered an abandoned Ardonnarian military base to secure the nuclear rockets they had found on a previous visit. They walked up to a single door on a large metal building with no windows. Beside the door was a much larger door for trucks to enter. As the Ineans walked up to the door, they noticed something was wrong. The locks had been blown off the doors, and the small walk-in door was creaking in the light breeze. One of the Ineans continued forward with a hand-held scanner and slowly opened the door. Many Ineans had been killed recently by booby traps set by Ardonnarian rebels, and they had learned to look before rushing in. Many Ardonnarian field officers reported back to Central Command in Antum that the Ineans were learning their ways, and soon, their tricks would no longer have the deadly effect they currently did.

The Inean stepped into the large building once he felt it was safe. When he was satisfied that there were no traps inside, he waved the rest of his team in. They were concerned about who might have been there. The locks the Ineans placed on the doors could not be blown off with normal explosives. Someone had access to more powerful explosives and how to use them.

They walked over to the crates where the warheads had been stored, and all they found were busted wooden crates and foam packing noodles that blew about the floor.

"How many were supposed to be here?" The team leader hissed at his subordinates.

"At last check, there were over forty warheads stored here. Most had multiple nukes."

"Gurrack!" their leader cursed. "Damok-Sai will have our heads if he knows these are missing."

"We have to report this!" one of his soldiers stated. He turned to face his commanding officer when he heard a click. His eyes went wide as his commanding officer pulled the trigger, and the middle of his body blew out from him. He crumpled to the floor.

Does anyone else think we should report this? The Inean growled while staring at each member of his team.

Everyone agreed that they should keep this quiet.

"Now we have to find the people who took these and kill them. Start looking for anything that might give us a clue as to who took them."

His soldiers scattered, looking for anything that would give them a clue. They found nothing useful and left the building.

One of his officers spoke up. "We should go check the next town. The people might know who took the nukes."

"Good idea. Let's go interrogate them and maybe have our way with a few of them," the Inean grinned. He turned towards their transport, and the rest of his group followed.

An Inean cargo ship settled on the main street of Belit-Sheri as dozens of people scattered into buildings. A hundred armed Ineans spilled out of the craft and began clearing the rubble from the street as a much larger craft slowly thundered toward the ground. A strip mining ship settled onto the brick avenue and sunk down slightly. The hot exhaust from the engines rippled across the bricks and shattered the few windows that had remained intact after the disaster of the first CME to impact the planet more than three years ago.

Two large doors opened on the rear of the craft between the four large engines. Large trucks rumbled out and rolled along the street in search of raw materials to take back to Inea. Many of the Ineans walked ahead of these trucks, tossing trash out of the way and tossing metal, glass, clothing, and anything else of value to them in the large bins that hung in front of and off the back of the trucks.

Some of them pocketed rare minerals like gold and silver, especially when they came across a decaying body. They picked whatever they could from them and discarded the rotten bodies. They could sell whatever they took as long as the soldiers in charge did not know about it. Otherwise, they would have to turn over the goods to the officer in charge.

FORTY-THREE

DAMOK-SAI WAS on his bridge while a sleek Inean transport swung around Ardonnar and headed for his ship. He was puzzled at the unannounced ship and was concerned that FarQue was doing a surprise inspection of his fleet.

His communications officer glanced his way. "Commander, General FarQue is hailing us."

"Establish a connection, Puzur-Si," Damok-Sai stated as the transport turned and headed for the landing bay. It was a ship similar to the one stolen by Puabi and Gula months ago. Damok-Sai still had not accounted for the craft. None of its locator beacons could be found or traced.

"This is FarQue. We will dock in three minutes. Be ready for us. Connection out."

Damok-Sai growled at his crew. "Get the ship ready for the fleet general right now!" He punched a button on his chair. "Landing bay! Clean up your mess and open the doors for the General!"

"Landing bay is ready, Commander. Opening the doors now," the flight deck controller said immediately. He also despised Damok-Sai and had secretly planned a takeover of the ship.

Damok-Sai growled and exited the bridge. He quickly made his way to the landing bay. He was concerned about this visit. He wasn't sure why, other than the string of strange setbacks and delays, which he conveniently blamed on others.

The elevator opened to a long, wide corridor that went the entire length of the five-mile-long ship. He hopped on a motorized cart and sped off towards the hatch for the flight deck. The flight deck was off to either side of the large ship about two miles from the bridge. He arrived in minutes and entered the flight control tower in the *Nikstra*, which overlooked the entire flight deck. Inside were rows upon rows of fighters and various spacecraft. As he entered, the General's ship had just cleared the large doors, and the doors were sliding closed. The ship reached the end of the flight deck just below Damok-Sai in the tower, and he turned around to face the large doors it had just passed through. Crews in pressure suits raced out with a pressurized tube that they attached to the side of the sleek transport while its antimatter engines powered down. Hot exhaust still rippled from the engines as air slowly filled the flight deck.

Once the tube was attached, FarQue exited the craft with three other Ineans. Even by Inean standards, none of them looked happy. Damok-Sai gulped to himself. He knew there was going to be trouble. He exited the tower and headed for the next elevator to meet up with General FarQue and his other guests. He knew this would be a short meeting as the General's crew remained on the transport, preparing the craft for departure.

The elevator doors opened, and FarQue was standing, facing the doors so no one could enter or exit the elevator. "Commander Damok-Sai, you know the emperor's son, Commander Talakya?"

"Yes, I do, General," Damok-Sai replied cautiously.

"Good, come with us to your quarters so we can discuss the future of this mission," FarQue said.

FarQue pushed his way onto the elevator with the rest of his group crowding in with them.

"My quarters, General? Ah, they are too small. We can use the strategy room just down the corridor from my quarters."

"No, Damok-Sai. Your quarters will be fine. Take us there now," the General hissed.

"Yes, General. We will be there shortly," Damok-Sai replied.

Damok-Sai stood, crammed in the elevator, thinking of an excuse for what the General would find in his quarters once they got there. *Gurrack!* He swore to himself. One of his crew had just delivered several Ardon women to his quarters. How would he explain that? He was now panicking. There were no rules against an occasional indulgence. However, what was in his quarters would prove more than a passing indulgence.

The elevator door opened, and he guided them to a waiting cart. He sat in the driver's seat and sped off towards his quarters after they all got in. Damok-Sai searched for an excuse to avoid his quarters without appearing to be an intentional diversion. He had nothing. The cart sped forward towards his doom.

After a few minutes, Damok-Sai, FarQue, Talakya, and the others skidded to a stop and spilled out of the cart at the entrance to the elevators. Damok-Sai stepped in front of one of the doors, and a few seconds later, it slid open. He stepped in, followed by the others. He tried his hand at idle chit-chat with FarQue. "General FarQue, why the unannounced visit?"

FarQue said nothing as he waited for the elevator to stop climbing, which it did a few seconds later.

Damok-Sai guided them to the Commander's suite, which was directly below the *Nikstra*'s bridge. FarQue noted the traces of Ardon blood on the door frame and the traces of blood on the floor, which seemed to trail away from the door in dried streaks that had been poorly cleaned.

Damok-Sai took a deep breath and opened the door to his room. He walked in as if nothing was wrong; however, General FarQue walked in slowly, taking in the scene before him. There were four naked Ardonnarian women clustered in the center of the room, tied by their hands from the ceiling to a central pole in the middle of the room. They had been gagged and stared at the approaching Ineans with wide eyes.

FarQue looked at them and then scanned the perimeter of the

room. Along the entire length of the room were other women. "What are those?" he asked of Damok-Sai.

"Ah, General. I am glad you asked. I was going to send these to the Emperor as a gift. I feel he would find these to be quite profitable," Damok-Sai replied with a widening grin.

"What are they, dead?" FarQue pressed as he was becoming more impatient with the Commander.

"One of the biggest complaints I hear from Inea is that these animals don't last long and cost a lot of money. We have found a way to preserve and display them long after their initial usefulness has passed. The Emperor could sell this service so our brothers can display their hard-earned denar's worth longer."

FarQue walked up to one of them and touched it. It was a brunette woman when she was alive, but now she was stuffed and displayed like a hunter would display a prized bear or deer in their den. "These are preserved? Never heard of such a thing."

Damok-Sai joined FarQue as he studied the detailed workmanship. "We discovered this process in the Ardonnarian history books from deep in their past. It seems they used the process to preserve kings and rulers for all time."

"How long do they last?" FarQue asked.

"Hundreds, maybe thousands of years. We really don't know."

"What of this one? Why the ornamentation?" FarQue said as he stepped up to a well-preserved young woman.

"You have a keen eye, General. This one was my favorite. She was the daughter of the eastern leader Ur. Her name was Kanpar. She was a wild one, probably the best at satisfying me," Damok-Sai said with a grin.

"Interesting, what of those hanging in the center of the room?" FarQue asked as he turned and walked towards the women hanging around the pole. The women cowered away at the large Inean as he studied them closely.

Damok-Sai stared into the eyes of one of the women. "Well, General, after I exhausted them, then they would join their friends lining the wall."

"Cut these down now and prepare them for preserving. If it is to be a gift for the Emperor, then they should not be defiled by you first." FarQue stated, and he turned towards Damok-Sai.

"Yes, General," Damok-Sai replied as he motioned for two guards who stood by his door to walk forward. "Take these down at once and bring them to Balakumar to be prepared for the Emperor."

"Yes, Commander," they both replied. The two large Ineans cut the ropes and dragged the women away.

"You will have no more contact with these Ardon women. They are clouding your judgment on this mission," FarQue said. "Now we have other business to discuss."

"As you wish, General."

"You are being recalled by the Emperor to answer questions about delays and loss of his finest soldiers here. Talakya will take command of the fleet while you are gone."

"Recalled?" Damok-Sai asked in disbelief.

"Yes, gather what you need and get back to the transport. We leave in one hour."

"Yes, General. I will be ready."

A few weeks later, Damok-Sai was guided to the presidential tower and brought to Emperor Sankar's suite high up in the tower. The last time Damok-Sai was here was over ten years ago when he was first put in charge of the invasion fleet, which had seen unmatched success until now.

The doors of the elevator slid open, and Damok-Sai stepped out along with FarQue and two guards. He was guided to stand before the Emperor.

Sankar stood to face Damok-Sai, and Damok-Sai bowed to him, "Emperor Sankar, it is a pleasure."

Sankar adjusted his black robe, which was decorated with many military medals and awards. "I cannot say the same, Damok-Sai. I have been reviewing the case against you, and I am quite upset with what I have been told."

"I would like to know what has been said about me, Emperor. I have concerns that I have been set up by a crew member who can't fight me directly, so he has to take the cowardly way to get rid of me."

Sankar looked down at the pile of paper in front of him, which was turned over so Damok-Sai could not see what was on them. He then gathered them all up and stuffed them into a zippered folder. He started for the elevator. "Bring him."

FarQue guided Damok-Sai towards the elevator and joined the Emperor to the bottom floor, where his closest council members waited.

The elevator door opened, and two guards standing outside stepped forward to open the large wooden doors as the Emperor approached. The large doors opened with the slightest creak, and Sankar nodded to the guards as he passed them. The guards hissed at Damok-Sai when he passed, which led Damok-Sai to wonder what he had done that was so awful.

Sankar sat in his usual chair at the center of the long table, which was elevated a few feet above the main floor. He was flanked by six council members on each side. Manava, Damok-Sai's father, sat next to Sankar and to his right. He glared at his son when he was brought forward by FarQue.

The large wooden doors behind them closed with a bang, and Sankar stood. Everyone else in the room who was not already standing stood as well. "This won't take long. Let's begin."

He sat back down and was followed by everyone else except for Damok-Sai and FarQue.

"The accused will step forward," Sankar stated, and FarQue pushed Damok-Sai forward.

"Damok-Sai, it is well known that you are third in line to the throne of Inea behind myself and Manava. We are quite saddened at what you have done on this latest mission to destroy and conquer the planet known as Ardonnar. Your incompetence has left us no choice in this manner."

Damok-Sai, smelling a rat, snarled back at the Emperor. "What manner is that?"

"You have been reckless with our finest battleships. How many have you lost? How many are critically damaged, including the pride of our fleet, the *Nikstra*," Sankar bellowed.

"That is not my..." Damok-Sai did not get a chance to finish, as FarQue placed his jagged knife harshly to Damok-Sai's throat.

"Not your fault? Is that what you were going to say? The evidence says otherwise." Sankar got up out of his chair and leaned towards Damok-Sai. "Your obsession with these Ardon women has consumed you and clouded your judgment. Hundreds upon hundreds of our finest soldiers have died in your quest to satisfy your lust for these creatures!" he screamed as spit flew from his mouth.

"You keep sending me cargo ships to fill with them for your own pleasures, but yet every request I put in for fuel comes up empty. My ships are running on fumes, and how do you expect me to defeat them if I can't launch a ship? We have had to rely on fuel from our nuclear rockets to keep the warships moving."

"Those ships are filled, and then those animals are sold for profit to fund your escapades, Damok-Sai. You have not received fuel because we have not received any requests for fuel."

"What? I have sent requests daily for fueling ships and have been told they were on their way." Damok-Sai then turned towards FarQue. "You have told me those tankers were on the way just the other day."

"You never sent me any requests, Damok-Sai," FarQue said with an unknowing look on his face.

"I have sent you written requests, FarQue!"

"I know of no requests for fuel. Now be quiet!" FarQue growled.

"Records show that your captains had requested fuel from you, but your orders were to farm these animals as quickly as possible so you could take over as emperor," Sankar stated.

"That is not true at all!"

"We have several witnesses, and captains have come forward and given their stories. That is beside the point. We now have information that these Ardons are building weapons to defeat us because we did not finish them when we had the chance. We are now sending a fueling tanker to fuel your fleet at the request of Talakya, and then we will level the planet once and for all," Sankar stated.

"What about your precious Ardon slave women?"

"We are farming them here. It is a slow process, but you have been good to send us a wide variety of ages, so we will have a constant but limited supply of them, which will keep the price up," Sankar said, and he sat back down. "Let's get back to you, Damok-Sai."

Damok-Sai, sensing a set-up, spoke up quickly to defend himself. "My field commanders have found the secret Ardon military base in the mountains. When we left, they were planning an assault on their stronghold to get rid of them once and for all, and we can still take the planet."

"Yes, we know. That is underway as we speak," Sankar stated.

"We also destroyed their fleet of fighters hidden in a moon orbiting a gas giant in their system."

"Yes, we know about that as well. We also know that the *Nikstra* was nearly destroyed in the process," FarQue added this time. "The fact that these animals could build this fleet under your nose is proof of your incompetence, Damok-Sai."

"I've heard enough," Sankar stated, banging his fist on the table. "The council has read all the statements. You have heard from Damok-Sai directly. His failure has put our fleet in danger and has cost the lives of thousands of our finest warriors." He paused a few seconds. "Commander Talakya is now in charge of the fleet and is in the process of removing the Ardon's ability to fight. He will deny their right to live, and the planet will be ours very soon. No more of our finest warriors will be lost in this failed adventure now that we have strong leadership in charge. I recommend to the council that Damok-Sai be executed for crimes against Inean interests. I am looking for a unanimous vote, but my mind is made up."

All the hands went up except for Manava, Damok-Sai's father, who was next in line to be leader. He just forfeited that chance to save his son.

"Manava, I am disappointed in you," Sankar stated. "It doesn't matter. There are more than enough votes to carry out the sentence," he turned his look to FarQue. "Take the prisoner away."

"Yes, Emperor Sankar," FarQue stated with a bow. He grasped Damok-Sai by the shoulder and nodded to the large Inean soldiers who stood by the door. The soldiers walked forward and took Damok-Sai away.

"Manava, these poor choices your son made are partly your fault. You encouraged this behavior and his lust for these animals. You will relinquish any line to the leadership you may have. You will turn over all profits made from the sale of these Ardon slaves, and you will leave the council in disgrace for your role in this," Sankar stated.

"Who will be next in line then to the throne?" Manava asked.

"If you must know, EmuQue. The father of FarQue. He has paid his way to your seat."

"You may as well kill me as well, Sankar. I will not live in disgrace."

"As you wish," Sankar replied with a wave of his hand. "Guards, take Manava to be with his son."

Manava stepped away from the council table and walked towards the guards with his head up. The guards took him away.

"EmuQue, the ascension seat is available."

"Thank you, Emperor Sankar." EmuQue rose from his seat at the far side of the table and took his place next to the Emperor.

"Excuse me, Sankar," EmuQue said. "I think it would be best to send Manava to the slave mines for the rest of his life. It would be the ultimate punishment. Death is so easy and simple."

Sankar pondered this for a brief moment. "You are right. To the slave mines, it is."

The coliseum near the presidential tower was filling fast as the news spread of the impending execution of Damok-Sai. The platform, which was used to auction off Ardonnarian slaves, had been cleaned of human blood and repainted for the event. It had been many years since the last high-level military official had been executed, and Sankar was expecting a huge crowd. He had chosen to charge admission, which would cover the cost of sending antimatter fuel ships to Ardonnar. The same antimatter ships FarQue had held back so he could frame Damok-Sai and remove his father from the council. He feared Manava and Damok-Sai, as their power with the people was growing too strong. His plan had worked perfectly. His next move would be to get rid of the remaining council members and secure his line as Emperor.

The crowd started filing into the coliseum, and they were a boisterous bunch. Thousands lined up and filled the seats. Sankar looked down from his lofty suite at the coliseum and grinned at the lines leading to the entrances.

FORTY-FOUR

SANKAR'S SON, Talakya, was at the head of the large table with the captains of the fleet seated on either side of him. They faced him while he read information off his tablet. Talakya, who was a tall, rugged Inean, rose up from his chair and walked around the table while looking at each one of his captains. Once he reached his seat again, he placed his hands on the backrest of the seat and remained standing. "As you know, Damok-Sai has been recalled to Inea to account for his failures in securing this planet."

Many in the room grinned and voiced their pleasure with the decision as Talakya continued. "My father, the emperor, has placed me in charge of this fleet with the explicit instruction to finish the job."

All of the captains howled their approval and voiced it was about time.

Talakya continued. "Our first task in this is to remove the Ardon military base in the mountains. Normally, we would just send in nuclear missiles, but I am interested in capturing and interrogating them to find the extent of their plans. So, we will invade the base with that in mind. Once we gather whatever information they have to offer, then we will attack the planet and wipe them out once and for all."

The captains voiced their approval at this and howled towards the ceiling.

"I want Captain Dasak to coordinate efforts with the field commanders on the ground. I want three full units to attack the base and gain control. I suspect we will lose some of our finest warriors in this attack, but in the end, the Emperor will reward the families of those who sacrifice themselves on this mission."

The captains again howled towards the ceiling.

"Captain Dasak? You will coordinate with my adviser on all the details of their base. There appears to be only one entrance to and from the base, but it is heavily fortified and will be your toughest challenge. You need to get in the base without collapsing the entire mountain into it before we get what we want." Talakya looked around the table. "Any questions?"

"What if they launch an attack during this raid?" one of the captains asked, knowing his ship was very low on fuel.

"A fierce animal that is cornered will attack when it is threatened, and these animals have had three years of Damok-Sai's incompetence to prepare. I am sure they are waiting for us to strike so they can fight back, so plan on it."

"What is your timing for this attack?" one of the others asked.

"Within two weeks. It will take us that long to quietly move everything we need into place without arousing suspicions," Talakya said.

"So this won't be a full assault then?" the first captain asked.

"No, not yet. We want to take the center of their operation, learn where all their resources are, and then systematically remove them. Don't forget, the Emperor wants this planet inhabitable immediately. Which means we won't be carpet bombing with nukes. We will use them when necessary."

Talakya looked around the table again. "I know the battleships are low on fuel. I have Sankar's promise that the fueling tanker is on its way. However, we will launch this attack before it gets here, so we will have to economize our resources until it arrives."

"Why not wait for the tanker?" a captain asked.

"Rumor has it that the Ardons are planning to attack anyway. Therefore, we need to eliminate their central command before then, which is why we must attack them now. Any more questions?"

"What about the slaves we are sending home?"

"The last three ships will be leaving in a few days. We will attack after they are out of the system."

"I heard we are shipping the men as well this time? Why the change?"

"Sankar has set up slave camps on Inea. He plans on raising these animals there. The men will work the fields and mines while providing reproductive services to grow the population for the Emperor."

"I find this dangerous. If their population gets too big, it could pose a threat in the future," one of the captains stated.

"There are controls in place. First, the embryos will be altered in the womb to produce mostly females. There will be one male for every two hundred females, and they will be scattered. Once we have moved beyond a generation or two, then they will learn this way of life and forget where they came from. We don't see it as a problem. Any more questions?"

No one answered.

"Let's take this world!" Talakya growled.

FORTY-FIVE

THE COLISEUM WAS PACKED and getting restless as Sankar made his way to the balcony above the coliseum. He walked out, flanked by two heavily armed guards. He waved to the crowd that stood and howled when he did so. He raised his hands, and the crowd quieted. "Fellow Ineans! This is a sad day and a glorious day!" he yelled, and the crowd howled in a deafening roar. "One of our own has failed us, but our system of justice has prevailed!"

The crowd roared again.

The executioner stepped forward wearing his black leather hood and robe. He looked like a poor excuse for a professional wrestler. "Bring out the prisoner!" the executioner yelled over the roar of the crowd.

A side door swung open, and four guards brought a chained Damok-Sai into the coliseum. The crowd howled and threw bottles and rocks at him. Luckily, the guards were in full body armor. Damok-Sai growled back at them as he was guided onto the platform where a rope with sharp spikes hung in a noose from a pole high above. The guards positioned Damok-Sai beneath the noose and lowered it down and around his neck while he tried to bite their hands. The guard pulled the noose tight, driving the sharp spikes into Damok-Sai's neck. Blue blood oozed out around the spikes. The rope was tightened, removing all slack. One of the other guards tied a rope to the chain around his ankles. Then, the guards stood back and waited.

Sankar stepped closer to the edge of the balcony. "Damok-Sai, son of Manava, you stand convicted of treason against your fellow Ineans and against the rightful conquests of our military. Your punishment shall be death by hanging."

The crowd growled its approval.

"Do you have any last words before the sentence is carried out?" Sankar asked from above.

"No, Your Excellency," Damok-Sai growled as the spikes bit into his neck.

The crowd was working itself to a fever pitch now as several fights broke out and sharp objects hurtled at Damok-Sai. Chants of "Kill him! Kill him!" repeated over and over.

Sankar grinned from his perch, "Damok-Sai, your peers have spoken. Kill him!"

The executioner grabbed the rope tied to his ankles, and he gave it a tug, pulling Damok-Sai's feet out from under him. The spikes dug into his neck further, and more blue blood trickled down his neck onto his body. He fought the noose, but all it did was tighten around his neck, eventually blocking his airway. He gasped as he began to taste blood in his mouth. The spikes dug further into his neck, and he began to lose feeling in his feet as one of the spikes bit into his spine.

The crowd was cheering as his vision began to fade. He was about to black out when the four guards who escorted him to the podium pulled out their knives and stabbed him repeatedly. Blue blood began to splatter on the floor. The executioner stepped forward with his long knife with a curved point as the guards backed away. He held it up to the crowd, who went wild. He then thrust his knife low into Damok-Sai's abdomen and sliced it upwards. His intestines began to spill out as the crowd cheered.

Damok-Sai died and was left hanging.

After several minutes, Sankar stepped forward. "Bring out the next prisoner!"

Four more guards walked in with Manava in chains and brought beside his son to face the angry mob.

"Manava, son of Akul, father of Damok-Sai, you have been charged with aiding Damok-Sai and plotting to overthrow my leadership. You had requested death, but that is the easy way out for you. Instead, you will be sent to the mines of Bauzimu on the moon, Adhideva. There, you will live out the remainder of your life picking Urbab from the rocks with your bare hands."

"No! Just kill me now!" Manava screamed.

"Take him away!"

The crowd cheered as the guards dragged the struggling Manava away.

The guards returned and began cutting Damok-Sai down. They looked up to see a large transport descending towards the tarmac outside the coliseum. A fresh shipment of slaves from Ardonnar had just arrived. While his body was removed, several others raced out with high-pressure hoses and sprayed the platform clean by blasting it with high-pressure hot water.

FORTY-SIX

AFTER WORD HAD SPREAD throughout the Inean fleet of Damok-Sai's execution, Talakya met with Captain Dasak, who had sent out several high-level fighters to scan Mount Laarsa for details of the Antum base. It would be the first of several missions to probe the base for access and escape routes. Talakya and Dasak both watched as detailed images began to assemble on the large view screen on the bridge of the *Nikstra*. The base and its entrances were well hidden, but now the Ineans knew where to look thanks to the teenage boy who had given Laraak the detailed information in trade for his life.

They watched as camouflaged trucks approached the base, and Dasak ordered one of the fighters to zoom in on the trucks.

The fighter turned and headed back towards the mountain while zooming in on the trucks rolling along the dirt road towards the dense forest that was between them and the entrance to the mountain. The images opened on the monitor while Talakya and Dasak looked at each other. The trucks were loaded with heavily armed soldiers and what appeared to be the missing nuclear warheads: one in each truck with the pointed end sticking out of the rear of the canvas-covered vehicles.

"So, now we know where the missing warheads are going," Dasak said, walking closer to the big screen, which extended from the floor to the ceiling for a better view.

"The question remains, are they all here, or are they scattered around the planet waiting for us to make yet another mistake?" Talakya asked.

"We might be able to scan that mountain for any signs of radiation. It may give us an idea of what is there," Dasak said.

"Do all your scans. I also want small teams on the ground looking for any early warning systems, trip wires, remote detonators, and mines and to closely monitor their activities," Talakya said. Then he gripped Dasak's arms tightly, pulling him closer. "Tell them to watch, but do not engage yet. Do not let the Ardons know we are watching, understood?"

"Perfectly, Commander. I will have boots on the ground before nightfall in that location," Dasak said.

"And, I want hourly reports on whatever they find. I don't care how small."

"Yes, Commander."

"You may go back to your ship," Talakya said.

Dasak bowed towards Talakya and left the bridge of the *Nikstra* while Talakya continued to study the detailed images on the giant view screen. He was troubled by what he saw. There was only one reason he could think of for all those nuclear warheads heading into the base, and that was the Ardons had a way of delivering them to the Inean fleet to destroy the fleet. Or at least they thought so. This troubled Talakya, and now he was reconsidering a nuclear assault on the mountain, which he had taken off the table days before. He could allow nothing off the ground for the fleet's sake.

Aanepada hovered over a technician while he studied data from the remote tracking stations. Beside him were Dagan and General Asar.

"What is it, Rabishu?" Aanepada asked.

"It looks like the Ineans know we are here, sir. There have been several pings from our outer rim of sensors around the mountain, and all are Inean. I think they are studying the mountain for a point of entry. I have also noticed high-level flights crisscrossing the mountain the past few days."

The news hit them all in the pit of their stomachs, prompting Aanepada to sit down. "So, this is it?" he thought.

Dagan stepped behind him and placed her hands on his shoulders. "It is time. The eighteenth book of Kur is about to pass. We have to pray to Kur, and he will take us through this. I would prepare our attack. Things will surely unfold quickly now." She spoke while staring at the monitors in front of them.

Aanepada reached back with his left hand and patted the hand she had on his right shoulder. The pain in his chest returned, and he knew his time was almost done. He prayed to Kur that Dagan was ready. He had to let it be. It was out of his hands now.

Aanepada stood again but slowly. "Any indication of a CME soon?"

Enir, the senior solar scientist, turned towards him. "There is nothing to indicate a solar disturbance in the next forty-eight hours, sir."

"We will have to consider launching without the cover of the solar storms, Mister President," General Asar said while he studied the president. He knew something was wrong. Asar liked Dagan, but he did not trust her to be the next leader of Ardonnar, at least under these conditions.

"It is out of our control, General. Kur has spoken through the prophets, and we must prepare all of our people to retake our planet. Everything is in place and waiting for the order, and I am giving that order now." He leaned on the chair in front of him. "We are now in prelaunch mode. Everything should be fueled, loaded, and ready to go. The launch order will come within the next day, maybe within the hour." He slumped more while the pain in his chest worsened.

Dagan reached into his pocket and retrieved the bottle of nitro-glycerin. She opened the bottle and handed him two of the silver tablets. He glanced at her with a questioning look. She forced a grin. "I have noticed you sneaking these, and I know what they are for. So please sit, Mister President." She turned to Asar, "General Asar, could you get the president a glass of water?"

"Yes, right away," he replied. He hurriedly walked away.

"Dagan, give the order."

"Yes, Mister President. People!" she spoke firmly. "Prepare all ships and crews for launch!"

People turned towards her for a second and then realized she was now in charge. Many hesitated, unsure of the title they should use to address her. President did not quite fit. Some fell back on her given title and used it instead. "As you wish, Priestess," they replied.

FORTY-SEVEN

OVER THE NEXT FEW DAYS, Aanepada, General Asar, Dagan, and several others monitored the Ineans carefully, probing the Ardonnarian defenses to mount Laarsa. The Ineans were getting closer to the entrance, and Aanepada's officers watched as more Ineans began to close in. Invasion of their base was imminent. Inean fighters continually flew over the base at high altitudes. Aanepada knew they were scanning the mountain, and he knew the Ineans were searching for any means the Ardons could escape the mountain base. He had also gotten word from an automated outpost that a larger Inean ship had entered the system. It was over two days away, based on its current rate of deceleration. Visual scans revealed that it was unlike the other warships orbiting above them. This ship was large, with dozens of large hexagonal balls with what appeared to be electromagnets all over them. Asar was under the impression the magnetic tanks held antimatter and a lot of it. Long-range scans from their outposts on a distant asteroid studied the ship for weakness. If they could rupture one of the magnetic orbs, the explosion could rip a small planet out of its orbit. It was an attack that would have to happen far from Ardonnar.

"Mister President," Rabishu stated with a glance over his shoulder.

"What is it, Rabishu?"

"Looks like the Ineans are massing for attack from two angles. But it looks like both groups are poised to enter the main gates."

Asar piped up. "The first group storms the base and takes control, and the second group comes in and gathers information."

"So, we get everyone out of here, and we blow the base," Dagan said. She leaned forward to view the topographical map on the screen with all the red dots getting close to the base's entrance.

"Prepare all fighters for launch. Prepare all transports for launch as well. Is everything in position on Anaru?" Aanepada asked as the pain gripped his chest again. "*Not now!*" He thought to himself.

"All fighters are ready. Transports are loading as we speak." Asar replied. He listened to his headset and glanced at Aanepada. "Anaru reports all ships are ready. They also report our diversion on Nisaba is ready."

"Excellent. Any word from Gula's group?" Dagan asked.

"They are waiting for our orders," Asar said with a questioning look towards her.

"We could have them bomb that antimatter ship and destroy it. That would create quite a diversion," Dagan said.

"Yes, it would, but it would have to be timed perfectly with all of our other attacks," Asar stated.

"I think they can do it," she replied.

"The magnetic spheres are heavily armored, Priestess."

"A concentrated attack on one of them is all we need to rip that ship apart. Even a solid jolt might be enough to break some antimatter free," she replied while studying the troop movements outside.

"I don't..." Asar began but stopped when Aanepada turned around. He was sweating, and his face was white.

"Do as she says. It will work," Aanepada said, and then he turned around.

"Yes, sir," Asar said, and he turned away to contact Gula about the plan.

. . .

Gula had led the bombers away from Uggae under the shield of the gas giant Idpa when the Inean warship *Nikstra* closed a few months before. The bombers, along with the cargo ships, took up residence in the giant planet's atmosphere above its magnetic poles. It hid them from the *Nikstra*'s sensors long enough to detonate an anti-matter bomb deep in the moon, nearly destroying the *Nikstra*. Puabi wanted to finish the Inean ship, but Gula held her back along with the others. If they had destroyed the *Nikstra* and word had gotten back to the rest of the Inean fleet that ships were lurking out by Idpa, it could have had disastrous repercussions for Ardonnar. It was best to keep their existence a secret.

A supply depot had been erected under the ice on another moon orbiting farther away from Idpa, where food, water, air tanks, and the remaining antimatter were stored for their trip to Inea. The crews had already been in space for a few months, and some were suffering from space sickness brought on by the cramped quarters, rushed training, and the very low gravity of the little moon. Gula was becoming concerned and had planned to shuffle some of the crews around to pair up weaker pilots with stronger ones. He might not have a chance now. He received orders to prepare to attack the Inean antimatter ship heading their way. He sat in the crowded cockpit of his lead bomber and plotted the attack. They would wait for the large ship to pass Idpa, which it would in about twelve hours. He chose a small attack force, leaving the bulk of the bombers hidden behind a small, rocky, frozen moon on the opposite side of Idpa.

Two officers entered the control room of the Antum base carrying a large crate. They opened it and distributed automatic weapons. Dagan held out her hand, and one of the officers looked at her briefly until she grew impatient and took it from him. He had not come to grips yet with an automatic-wielding priestess of Kur.

Dagan checked the weapon, installed a magazine, and clipped

two more to her belt. She set the safety and slung it over her shoulder. Then she looked around at everyone who was watching her. "What?" She said with a shrug. Everyone went back to what they were doing.

Asar turned back to Aanepada after a few minutes. "Gula is planning to use a small attack force to destroy the Inean ship as it passes Idpa in about twelve hours."

"Twelve hours? I don't think we can hold out for twelve hours. The Ineans are advancing as we speak," Aanepada stated.

"It would give them the best chance of surprise if we can hold out that long, then we can launch everything at once and hopefully overwhelm the Ineans with attacks from several fronts," Asar stated.

"We will hold them, General," Dagan said as she gripped the large-caliber automatic rifle firmly in her hands.

"You! Make sure you are on one of those transports!" Aanepada said to her.

"You make sure that you are ahead of me, Mister President."

"But..." Aanepada began.

"But nothing, sir," Dagan and Asar both said in unison.

Aanepada went to reply but chose not to. *"Two against one,"* he thought.

FORTY-EIGHT

INEAN FIELD COMMANDER Laraak squatted behind a shrub several hundred yards away. He studied the entrance to the Ardon military base, which was buried in the mountain. The doors were built of reinforced steel with thick concrete abutments. So far, no Ardon troops had been spotted, and he was confident that their surprise attack would be successful. He was joined by several junior officers. "Sir, the rockets are ready."

"Understood," Laraak stated. "Any word from Talakya?"

"None, sir. We believe he is waiting for the refueling ship to get here before executing the attack," the junior officer said.

"Idiots! How far away is the ship? You know our cover could be blown by then!" Laraak fumed.

"It is two days away."

"Two days!" Laraak exclaimed with a growl. "Pass me the radio!"

"Yes, sir," the officer handed him the secured radio to the *Nikstra*.

"This is Field Commander Laraak. I wish to speak with Talakya." He paused as the voice on the other side spoke to him. "Fine, I will wait." After a moment, he spoke again. "Commander

Talakya, why are we waiting! My personnel are in place and ready to attack, and we have the element of surprise on our side!"

Talakya spoke over Laraak's headset. "Field Commander Laraak, our ships are low on fuel, and we cannot take the chance."

"I understand, Commander, but if we surprise them, and we can, then they won't be able to launch an attack. If they had that capability, then we are sure they would have struck by now," Laraak stated.

"I will take your concerns under advisement. I will respond in two hours. Talakya out."

"What a fool!" Laraak stated as he tossed the radio back to his junior officer.

"What did he say, sir?"

"We wait and hope not to get spotted."

Dagan watched the screen and turned to Rabishu, "What are they doing?"

"I don't know. Maybe they are waiting for the antimatter ship to get here first."

"We can't let that happen. Can we do something to bring them out sooner?"

"I thought it was a good idea that they waited?" Rabishu asked.

"It is, but I don't like them setting the pace for this," she replied.

"I agree. I will look for ways to stir them up. So in eleven hours, we can start the fight," Rabishu said, and Dagan gave him a nod of approval.

Talakya walked onto the bridge of the *Nikstra* after spending the past hour conversing with General FarQue and his father, Emperor Sankar. The topic was the timeline for attacking the Ardon base. Talakya was convinced that waiting was the best option, but FarQue and Sankar wanted to put an end to the Ardonnarians as soon as possible. Talakya was overruled. The attack would commence in two hours.

"Connect me with Field Commander Laraak," Talakya growled.

"Yes, sir, Laraak is waiting."

"Laraak, you may launch your attack in two hours from now. I trust you will find that satisfactory?" Talakya stated. He knew it was a mistake not to wait for the refueling tanker, but the Emperor and the general both decided from nearly one hundred light years away what was best.

"Thank you, Commander. It will be a glorious victory for the Emperor," Laraak stated.

"Don't thank me, I think it is a mistake and we should wait. It has been three years since this invasion began. What is wrong with waiting two more days until we are at full strength? But the Emperor and General FarQue both want a faster timeline. Talakya out."

The connection clicked off, and Talakya stepped towards the view screen and stared at the planet below. "Prepare all ships for attack!"

On the ground, Laraak talked with his missile crews, who were miles away with their short-range missiles with high-yield warheads pointed at the fortified main entrance to the base. The missile crews rechecked their settings and ensured the launchers were concealed among the thick trees so the Ardonnarians could not see them.

Laraak then called up his infantry and got them into position to rush the entrance once the doors had been blown off.

Inside, Aanepada and the others watched the red dots moving around, and they knew it was only a matter of perhaps minutes before the attack would begin. Flight crews stood ready as the fighters would be first out of the base, followed by the transports that were bound for Anaru or perhaps the small, frozen moon orbiting Idpa.

FORTY-NINE

TWO HOURS of staring at the computer displays and suddenly activity. Two explosions rocked the base as the missiles struck the thick steel doors that had been pinned on all four sides into the concrete and steel sides, floor, and roof. The doors held as the Ineans began moving forward. Soon, they stopped when they realized the doors held. Laraak cursed when he saw the buckled doors still in place. "Radio! Give me the radio!" he growled as his junior passed him the radio. "I need another two missiles NOW!"

"They know we are here. We have to get in there!" His junior officer said as two more missiles rocketed into the doors with thunderous explosions. Dirt, bits of concrete, and rock showered down on Laraak and his soldiers. Once the smoke and dust cleared, they could see that the doors still held.

Laraak cursed and grabbed the radio. "I want a battlefield nuclear warhead on the next missile, and I want it now."

"Are you sure, Laraak? You are too close!" the rough voice crackled over the portable radio.

"Yes, send it in."

"On its way!"

They heard the missile launch. A split second later, there was a crash and a blinding flash followed by a fiery wind that bowled Laraak and his soldiers over. Trees snapped off and fell over. Laraak pulled on his goggles and opened his eyes. Even with the goggles, it was still bright from the explosion, but the doors were gone. "Head in! Head in!" He screamed over the radio, and his forces staggered towards the blazing pile of rubble.

In the command center, Aanepada ordered his people out. "They have gained access! Everyone to the transports!" he yelled.

"Should we launch?" one of his officers asked as he checked his weapon.

"No, not yet. I want them to think we have been surprised. Just a few minutes," Aanepada stated while he started towards the door with Dagan and Asar.

They reached the door as Ineans spilled into the corridor above and slowly made their way towards them. Soon, bullets flew toward the advancing Ineans, and laser pulses streaked toward Aanepada's soldiers. There was little cover in the corridor, and many soldiers fell as the Ineans advanced.

Aanepada took his gun and began firing from the doorway toward the Ineans. Asar did the same as the two men blocked Dagan from getting out. The firefight was fierce. The Ineans stepped over the bodies of their fallen soldiers and advanced. They were now twenty feet away when Aanepada was hit in the hand by a laser pulse. The pulse burned through his hand completely. He cried out in pain and dropped his gun in the process. He gripped his hand, which was now bleeding. He leaned forward from the pain in his hand and the growing pain in his chest. He was hit again in the shoulder, and he fell to the floor.

Dagan cried out and started for him, but she was held back by Asar. She then took her automatic rifle, planted her feet, and began shooting up the corridor. She struck one Inean. His body jumped several times from the impact, and he staggered and fell. Asar replaced his clip and stepped out into the corridor. The Inean troops had thinned, and he drilled several of them. Dagan followed him out and kept firing up the corridor. A few Ineans made it to them, and one grabbed her. She tried to hit him with the butt of the gun, but he swatted it away. With one hand, he gripped her throat, squeezing off her air, and with the other, he tried to rip off her robe. Asar saw this and watched as Dagan stabbed him in the abdomen and sliced him up to his ribs. He released her. Asar shot the Inean repeatedly until he stumbled and fell to the ground.

Dagan fell to the floor, gasping for air while searching for her machine gun. She found it as several laser pulses buzzed by her and burrowed into the wall, spraying her with bits of rock. She turned and began firing with her eyes closed as a hand clamped down on her shoulder.

"Time to go!" Asar yelled as he pulled her up.

She opened her eyes, but they were full of grit, and she could barely see. She saw Aanepada's body on the floor. "He comes with us!" and she gripped his good hand and began to drag him while firing her machine gun up the corridor at the next wave of Ineans coming in.

"Dagan! We can't do this! Leave him. He is dead."

"No, we must take him!"

"There is no way!" Asar yelled.

"Cushik!" she swore. She released her president and her adopted father. Tears began to run down her cheeks, washing the grit from her eyes, and she saw the next wave coming at them. There had to be thirty of them with lasers drawn, firing at them.

Asar dragged her around the corner, and she regained her balance. They turned and raced down the corridor with guns blaring over their shoulders. Then they turned again, and they were on the flight deck.

"Launch everything!" Asar commanded. He and Dagan spilled into the last transport, and a soldier closed the hatch.

The fighters exited the launch bay first. Two at a time, with each pair practically with their noses in the engines of the front ships.

Asar reached the cockpit and punched the radio. "Anaru Launch! Nisaba! Launch Nisaba." He reached forward and entered a new frequency. "Gula, this is Asar. The base has been penetrated. Attack the Inean fueling ship!"

Gula's crackly voice came over the transport's speaker, "On our run now."

Asar turned the radio off and fell forward as the transport rocked from the Ineans lasers striking the transport.

The transports in front of them blasted away, rippling turbulence from their engines over Asar's transport. A split second later, their engines ignited, and the ship lurched forward with streaks of Inean lasers chasing them out through the waterfall before them.

Once the ships were out of the base, the fighters broke away and engaged the ground troops. As they swooped low, the fighters fired dozens of air-to-surface missiles that burrowed into the ground and then exploded, sending dirt, rocks, trees, and Ineans flying through the air. The next wave sent air-to-air missiles that air-burst just above the Inean troops on the ground, killing them in magnificent fireballs while the Ineans barely managed random return fire. The fighters turned toward space as the Ineans sent their own fighters toward the transports.

Asar watched the display fill up with dozens of incoming Ineans. He knew it was time and gave the order. "Anaru, engage!" He placed a hand on Rabishu's shoulder, "Blow up the mountain."

"Yes, sir. Detonation in five...four...three...two...one," and he flipped the red switch on his hand-held trigger, which was connected to the transport's console via a coiled wire. Even at thirty miles above the surface, the flash behind them was blinding as a lone nuclear bomb detonated deep within the mountain, and the mountain crumbled in upon itself.

"Shockwave in ten seconds," Rabishu stated.

"Prepare for impact," Asar said as he held on.

"Should not be bad, sir."

The Ardonnarian fighters flew past the transports, and soon, missiles launched from under their wings at the incoming Inean fighters. Several hit their targets, and the Inean ships began exploding. The Ineans launched next, and missiles screamed in as the transports turned and headed for Anaru. The lead fighters launched hundreds of flares to confuse the Inean missiles, and it worked. Most detonated when impacting the flares. Only a few got through, and a pair of fighters broke away to take those missiles out while the rest of the fighters destroyed the Inean fighters with the next salvo.

On the moon, Nisaba, several small explosions blasted rock away from the surface, revealing IPBM (Inter Planetary Ballistic Missile) silos. The tubes opened. Large rockets exited trailing flames from multiple engines and raced from the tubes on their way to the Inean fleet.

The Inean warships turned and ignited their large engines, which were low on fuel while launching their fighters. The large ships lumbered up to speed as the IPBMs jettisoned their first stage, ignited their second stages, and gained speed.

The Inean fighters headed towards the rockets as the Ardon fighters passed the IPBMs to engage the Ineans. Two squadrons of fighters exited Anaru base and headed towards the Inean fighters, and the Ineans were confused. They had to take out the IPBMs before they reached the fleet.

The Ardon fighters engaged the Ineans. However, this group of Ineans was much better. Several Ardon fighters were destroyed, and the Ineans made it through the first wave. They fired their missiles at the IPBMs.

The second stages of the Ardon rockets burned out, and the Inean fighter pilots began to grin that they could destroy them easily. Their grins were quickly dashed as the nose cones of the IPBMs blasted off, along with the outer shell of the rocket, revealing seven other rockets within. There were six in a circle, with the seventh in the center. The seven rockets fell away from the spent second stage and ignited their engines. The rockets raced off toward the Inean fleet. The rockets spread out and locked onto their targets. The Inean missiles could not lock on and flew off harmlessly into space.

The Ineans turned back and tried to catch the missiles before they reached the warships, but it was too late. The Ardon fighters cleared the path and quickly turned away, and the nuclear rockets hit their targets. Thousands of megatons of explosive power destroyed the Inean engines, and the next group blasted the landing bays. Several ships exploded. A few broke apart, and only three got away with minimal damage. The *Nikstra*, Manikya, and the Onkar headed off towards the refueling tanker, which was now nearing the planet Idpa.

The Inean fighters turned their attention to the Ardonnarian fighters, which now headed towards the moon, Anaru.

The Ineans watched twenty-five bombers blasting away from the moon. They set a course toward Idpa. The Ineans assumed they were going to attack the antimatter ship, and the Inean fighters could only watch them go. Between the Inean fighters and the bombers were the Ardon fighters, and now they turned to fight one more time.

Talakya was on the bridge of the *Nikstra*, facing the front view screen, which displayed the image of General FarQue. He was in shock at the news, but Talakya was screaming at him for pushing his quicker timeline. "We lost ten of the Emperor's finest warships because they ran out of fuel! I warned you about this! We did not surprise these animals! They surprised us. It was your poor leadership that has led to this humiliating defeat at the hands of animals we had ample opportunity to defeat three years ago!"

"Do we still have the capability to destroy their planet!" FarQue growled as he pondered the consequences of this loss.

"Yes, but we need to refuel these ships before we do anything. From now on, I am calling the shots because no one in upper command has any idea of what we are facing!" Talakya fumed.

"That will get you executed, Talakya. I don't care if your father is the Emperor."

"If we are still alive, you can come to get me; then that would prove me correct. Right now, we are refueling our ships and then turning back toward the planet to finish the job. Talakya out," he made a slashing motion across his neck, and the screen turned back to viewing the stars in front of them. "Time until we intercept the fueling tanker?"

"Three hours, sir," one of his junior officers replied.

"Time until we run out of fuel?"

The same officer replied. "Two hours ten minutes."

"Wonderful. So we will stop in two hours and wait." He growled. Talakya looked around his bridge, "Status of our fighters?"

"Fighters have engaged the Ardon animals at the moon, Anaru. Both sides are taking casualties, but several dozen ships got away and are heading towards the gas giant."

"They could be heading for one of their colonies, or they are going to attack the fueling ship!"

The junior officer turned to Talakya. "I thought that at first, but they are angling away from the tanker. They are up to something else."

"We can take them later, once we are fueled and the planet is rendered uninhabitable," Talakya stated.

"I don't think so, sir. If that is the case, then they are on the wrong trajectory. They have changed course again, and it looks like they are now going to head out of the system. I think they are heading towards Inea," the junior officer said while studying the graphic on his computer.

"WHAT! Why would they do that?" Talakya screamed.

"They are bombers, sir. I think we found all those missing nuclear warheads. Look at these energy readings from those ships."

Talakya stomped over and looked over the officer's shoulder at the screen. "How did they do that? They are going to bomb our home world. No one has ever done that in recorded history. Get me, Sankar, immediately!"

"Yes, sir. Sir, I am receiving a message from the fueling tanker Shripal. The Ardons are attacking them. These ships came from a frozen moon orbiting the gas giant."

"What? Damok-Sai said he destroyed those ships. Another lie!" He stomped back to the center of the bridge. "Put their sensors up on the screen!"

"Yes, sir."

The three-dimensional image displayed the Shripal in the center and the gas giant Idpa to the far side with six small dots heading towards the Inean ship.

"Get me the captain of that ship!" Talakya growled.

The image of the rough-looking Inean appeared on the screen in the corner. He had a patch over his eye, much like a pirate. He was dirty-looking as well.

Talakya stepped closer. "Captain, what countermeasures do you have?"

"We have several decoys we can deploy, and we have one fighter squadron that we are preparing to launch to attack those ships."

"Attack them before they launch their missiles. They have multiple warhead capabilities that will overwhelm your fighters and decoys." Talakya stated as he watched the tiny dots closing in.

"We are launching fighters now," the Inean captain replied.

Talakya watched the tiny dots leaving the Shripal and arcing towards the Ardon bombers. The Ardon bombers were getting closer, and then they engaged. Talakya listened in as the Inean fighters launched missiles towards the Ardon bombers, and a few hit their targets. The bombers returned fire and launched countermeasures to attract the Inean missiles, which were inbound.

The Ineans destroyed three of the six bombers while only losing two of their fighters, but the Ardon ships were getting closer to the antimatter ship. The Ineans swung around and raced up behind the bombers, and having used all their missiles, they began shooting their guns. The Ineans pulverized the rear of the Ardon ships, and another one exploded.

The remaining two bombers spread out, and Gula had no choice but to commit more bombers to the run.

One of the remaining bombers lost an engine, and the pilot was having trouble holding the craft steady, but now he was in range. He checked his sensors, and the Ineans were on top of him. He flipped the cover up that blocked the red toggle switch underneath. He flipped the switch up and pressed one of the red buttons beside it. There was a loud whoosh behind him, and he saw the missile streak away. One of the Ineans took off after it, but the others remained locked on him. They began firing their weapons again at the cockpit. Bullets pierced the hull and sprayed the interior of the cockpit. The air began to leak out with a hiss, and the pilot flipped his visor down to contain his air supply. He continued to struggle with the ship and launched his remaining missiles. He got them all away as a bullet punctured the hull and crashed through his helmet and through his head. He lost his vision and control of the craft. It began to spin out of control and broke up a short time later.

The missiles raced towards their target as the Ineans continued to shoot at them. One missile exploded, but there were still five others, and soon, the nose cones blew off, exposing the multiple warheads. A few seconds later, the warheads flew off the rocket and spread out as they screamed towards the Inean antimatter tanker.

Impact was imminent, and the crew of the Inean ship abandoned it in the last shuttles. They hurried away as the first missile struck and exploded, but the ship did not. Then another and another, and suddenly, the antimatter containment broke down, and the ship exploded in a fireball the size of a small planet. The Inean shuttles and fighters were incinerated in the shock wave while the Ardonnarian bombers had turned back long ago.

The shock wave engulfed a small icy moon and was so strong the moon shattered and flew apart, sending pieces as small as a grain of sand and chunks larger than a city flying through space in all directions. A cheer went up through all of Gula's ships, and then they focused on the three remaining Inean warships.

The remaining bombers and now fighters from Anaru attacked the *Nikstra*. They wanted this ship, being the flagship of the Inean fleet. It would be a crushing blow to the Ineans to destroy it, especially while the other two lagged behind.

The Inean ships turned back to the planet. They had to destroy the planet before they ran out of fuel and were destroyed themselves. Talakya set a direct course for Ardonnar, and they went full throttle. He knew the ship would be destroyed, but he needed to launch his nukes before that happened.

Gula took charge of one group of fighters, and Anzillu took charge of the other group from the frozen moon. Zuttara led the fighter group from Anaru as they closed in on the *Nikstra*.

Talakya sent out every fighter he had. The Ineans outnumbered the Ardonnarian fighters three to one, but each of Talakya's fighters barely had enough fuel to engage. His fighters initially began firing conventional guns.

Fighter pilot Nigissu headed towards the Inean fighters as the front of his fighter took fire from the Ineans. Several bullets smacked against his windshield, leaving small craters in the thick glass with spidery cracks extending outward for a few inches. He veered off to avoid taking more fire, but the bullets followed him. He held his hand on the joystick and swerved side to side while keeping his thumb above the firing button in the center of the joystick. He needed to get closer before shooting at the Ineans because his guns could not take large magazines, and he was flying alone like all the other fighters.

The Inean kept spraying his fighter with bullets, and his windshield was beginning to crack further. Nigissu reached forward and pressed a button on his control panel, and two steel panels slid across his two-part windshield to close it off. He watched as Inean bullets dented the shields, and he turned on his heads-up display.

Zuttara was talking in Nigissu's headset, ordering the pilots to begin firing at the Ineans. Nigissu pressed the button on his joystick, and he could feel the large-caliber machine guns pulsing away beneath his feet. He watched his display as the Inean began dodging him. He kept angling the joystick to follow the Inean until he passed him, trailing a stream of fuel, and then the Inean began spiraling out of control and out into open space.

Nigissu and a few of the others locked their small missiles on the *Nikstra*, which began firing its cannons at the small fighters. One fighter was hit and was vaporized. Another fighter was grazed by the large-caliber cannons and had to turn back to Anaru with its starboard nacelle, leaking rocket fuel for the thrusters.

Nigissu and the others locked onto the *Nikstra*'s cannons and fired their small missiles. A few seconds later, small explosions rocked the *Nikstra*, disabling their cannons.

It was now Nigissu and two other fighters clearing a path for a pair of bombers flown by Enanatuma and Anzillu as they led the charge for the *Nikstra*. They flew below the reach of the Inean cannons, and the large ship rotated to lock onto the bombers.

The *Nikstra*'s main engines flared out after burning the remaining fuel reserves, and now the massive ship hurtled towards a collision with Ardonnar. The impact was sure to burrow a deep crater in addition to the nuclear warheads destined for key cities.

Zuttara and Anzillu realized what the Ineans were doing, and now the race was on to destroy the ship before it was too late. The bombers got closer, and they noticed launch tubes opening on the underside of the warship. The telltale nose cones of nuclear missiles poked out of the tubes. It was only a matter of seconds before launch, and neither Zuttara nor Anzillu felt they could destroy all of them.

Suddenly, two rockets blasted away from the *Nikstra* and headed for the planet. Then two more, a few seconds later. Anzillu and Enanatuma had no choice. They launched their IPBMs at the *Nikstra* while yet another two rockets pulled away from the *Nikstra*. The IPBMs struck the *Nikstra* while Anzillu and Enanatuma turned away and raced towards the nuclear rockets, screaming toward their planet. The *Nikstra*'s engines exploded, and the ship began to tumble towards the planet. The next two rockets launched from the *Nikstra* exploded in their launch tubes, fracturing the ship in half with a blinding explosion. Several smaller explosions rocked the ship, causing it to break up further.

Anzillu fired two missiles at one of the rockets and then targeted the next one and fired. Enanatuma did the same, and now it was a race against time. The Inean rockets entered the upper atmosphere as the missiles caught up. Four of the rockets exploded high in the atmosphere, but two got through and headed toward cities on the eastern continent. One of the rockets turned sharply to the west as the other headed northward towards the eastern city of Kulaba. A few seconds later, the city was engulfed in a nuclear fireball. The other missile raced along the ocean towards the largest southern city of the western continent, Sakanu. A few seconds later, all Anzillu and Enanatuma could do was watch in horror as millions of people lost their lives.

The two bomber pilots were brought back to the present when warning alarms sounded in their cockpits. Fragments of the *Nikstra* were getting too close to their bombers, and both pilots bolted away as the *Nikstra* entered the atmosphere in a blazing fireball from the ship slamming into the atmosphere. The ship burned up as it tumbled toward the planet at thousands of miles per hour. Finally, the remains crashed into the Lugal Ocean off the coast of Belit-Sheri.

Other fighter groups took on the last two Inean warships and damaged them, while the Ineans launched their nuclear rockets towards Ardonnar. Soon, the miles-long ships entered the planet's atmosphere and began blazing through the atmosphere. Ardon fighters took out several of the missiles. The Manikya crashed into the eastern plains of Shuruppak, and the Onkar crashed into the Kaspu mountains near the planet's equator. Three nuclear rockets got through the Ardonnarian defenses, and one crashed into the Kibrat-Ati, which was south of the destroyed city of Suen. The others hit their targets, vaporizing the cities of Ninazu north of Sakanu, which was already burning, and the other hit the city of Kungzu.

The Inean fighters ran out of fuel and were easy targets now for Ardonnarian pilots.

FIFTY

WHEN THE BATTLE WAS FINISHED, all the remaining Ardon ships returned to Anaru except the twenty-five bombers heading for Idpa. Those ships would be stopping at the small, icy moon to retrieve the antimatter fuel for their trip to Inea.

The fighter pilots raced from their fighters and bombers once the flight deck pressurized on Anaru and began cheering their victory.

General Innin walked out onto the flight deck as soon as it was pressurized to greet the pilots and assess any damage taken. He was not smiling when he was greeted by Anzillu, Zuttara, Gula, Puabi, Enanatuma, and many others who were dancing around.

"Why are we dancing while our people are suffering on Ardonnar?" Innin bellowed. Everyone stopped dancing and gathered in front of him. "Four of our cities have been hit with Inean urukii missiles, and quite possibly millions are dead. We need these bombers repaired, refueled, and on their way to Inea as soon as possible. We will celebrate when the Inean threat is completely removed from the universe. Think about the countless societies that they have erased from the galaxy forever. Possibly billions upon billions were slaughtered at the hands of these butchers. We have sent twenty-five bombers to Inea in the hope of leveling their planet. It is a journey across a hundred light years of space with minimally trained pilots and untested ships against what is more than likely a formidable and waiting enemy. The odds are against our success. We have more bombers here that need to get underway to help them out. We also need to get to the surface of Ardonnar and help the millions who are hurt and fight the thousands of Ineans who are on the surface raping and murdering our families." He paused a moment and then finished, "We will celebrate when our planet is ours again." He stepped back as General Asar and Priestess Dagan walked onto the flight deck.

Asar stepped beside General Innin. "General Innin is correct. Our hardest work is in front of us. However, we must come to grips with some changes. Our president, Aanepada, died today as the Ineans stormed Antum. The president, whose health was failing, stood his ground and killed several Ineans in a firefight that would have made the most hardened warrior proud. He went down on his last breath, shooting the enemy."

His words resonated hard with all the fighter and bomber pilots. Some broke down and wept at the loss of their leader. He waited for the pilots to compose themselves, which took a few seconds.

Asar continued, "President Aanepada left us with a hard-working leader who fits the model of our historic leaders. This person went out of her way to try and save Aanepada while gunning down many Inean soldiers. Even while an Inean had grabbed her, she fought him and eventually got free, and the Inean died. She has an unorthodox style and has a habit of ruffling feathers, but I am happy to present our new leader, Priestess Dagan."

People clapped in approval but were in shock that a woman was the leader of their people.

Dagan reached up and pulled her hood back with scuffed and bloodied knuckles. She faced the group, revealing a black eye, and several gasped. "President Aanepada raised me from a small girl when my parents were killed many years ago. I considered him my father over the years, and he has put his dying trust in me to lead us out of this nightmare. Once we are safe, I will call upon our people to elect a new leader and council. I feel that is the best way to establish the will of the people."

Everyone clapped at her remarks.

"Finally, we must get these bombers on their way to back up the ships already en route to Inea. The fighters need to return to the surface of our planet and begin recruiting for an inevitable Inean retaliation. The facility on this moon must begin producing more fighters for when that happens." She looked around at all the faces. "Now let us bow our heads and thank Kur for our victory and pray for the loss of life from the Inean attacks today. Let us pray in silence and take as long as you wish."

Everyone bowed their heads, and no one spoke. The sound of machinery in the distance and the air vents was the only noise heard. After a few minutes, a few looked up and walked away while others took more time. After several minutes, everyone had filtered away, leaving the generals and Dagan alone.

Asar finally spoke. "We should go to the planet and establish our base of operations."

Dagan looked up finally and wiped a tear from her eye. "Do the Ineans still hold Delondra?"

"Yes, but their numbers are small. We can take it back," Asar said while glancing around the flight deck. "Zuttara, I want you to get these ships heading to their proper destinations and then head to the surface. We will take Delondra first."

"Yes, sir!" he saluted and walked away, barking orders.

"Priestess, what should the people call you?" Asar asked.

"Priestess is fine. This leadership role is only temporary. I don't want to be called president because I was not elected by the people but appointed," she replied.

Several hours later, Dagan, Asar, Zuttara, and several others boarded a shuttle and headed for the planet. Their goal was to take back the city of Delondra and establish the capital once again. Asar was in communication with troops on the ground, and they estimated there were about a thousand Ineans in the capital. Just about all had fallen back to the presidential tower, so flushing them out would not be easy. It would involve many casualties.

Dagan held Zuttara's hand as the shuttle flew towards the planet. It was the first time in weeks they had been together, and it would only be a few minutes before they would be separated once again. They flew wide around the city of Sakanu, which was a flaming pile of rubble for miles around. Very little of the city could be made out. There were no more skyscrapers, as far as they could tell. Millions were probably dead or dying, and there was nothing Dagan or the others could do about it. Their mission was to retake their capital and kill the Ineans.

Dagan pulled out the sealed letter that Aanepada gave her before he died, and she opened it. She took a deep breath as she unfolded the letter and prepared to read it. She had no idea what was there, but the contents would prove shocking.

She began to read:

My Dearest Dagan,

Over the years, I have held onto deadly secrets, and you deserve the truth, especially now as you lead our people through their deadliest struggles.

You have been in search for answers regarding the death of your parents. Here is the truth.

Many years ago, a new group of followers was founded in the east. Shortly after, a small group was founded in Delondra, which I joined to investigate. What I found was horrible. These were not followers of Kur but of Nergal. They were a powerful group that infiltrated the government at all levels and worked their way into the priesthood. They convincingly mouthed the teachings of Kur but swore allegiance to Nergal. You have done battle with a few of them already, and you will do battle with them in the years to come.

Your parents were naive when they joined the group in Delondra. However, when they discovered what the group represented, they tried to leave. They took jobs on distant asteroids to hide from The Order and protect you. The Order found them. Soon after, I heard of a plot to kill them and tried to stop them, but it was too late. Months went by, and I discovered that a young girl living in a box in an alley, wearing ripped and soiled clothes and begging for food, was their daughter. I adopted you, and The Order threatened to kill me for taking you in. Threats were made against my family, and I was told that I had traded all of them for you.

I lived in fear for years over this because I knew they would carry out the threats. Soon, my wife died of a rare cancer. Shortly after that, I received a package from this group claiming responsibility, including details that only the doctors and I knew. Then, my parents were killed by a suicide bomber. Again, The Order claimed responsibility. I received another letter years later claiming my brother would die on a remote outpost on a distant planet from the flu. I didn't think anything of it at the time because my brother was uninterested in space exploration. Months later, I discovered he was on a transport to one of the outer colonies. I tried to warn him, but he ignored me.

Kilar's death? The Order has not laid any claim to her death. Maybe it was Kur punishing me for my weakness in dealing with The Order. I don't know, but since you're reading this, Kur may have given me the answer.

In closing, your battles with the Ineans are just preparation for a much tougher battle against your own people. In a closet in my office in Delondra is a small box. In it is a list of loyal cabinet leaders and priests that shun The Order. The names will surprise you. Align yourself with them, stay focused, and may the blessing of Kur be with you.

Dagan wiped a tear from her eye and folded the paper. She shoved it in her pocket and stared out the window. Several minutes later, the shuttle landed a few miles away from Delondra.

There were diesel troop carriers and trucks with heavy caliber machine guns waiting for them when they landed. They all piled in and headed around the city to where their forces were. It was just a few miles through the tree cover, and there, General Asar assessed what he had. It was a bunch of farmers, basically. But he had thousands, and they were armed and trained by several dozen real soldiers. They would have to do, he thought. "Commander Utu, what is your plan?"

"General, Major Zuttara," he said, snapping to attention. "We have three access points to the tower. This will be a three-pronged attack with a twist. The twist will come first. We will have fighters firing gas grenades and smoke grenades into the building. Then we will send a third of our troops into the access tunnels below the tower and work our way up while another third storm the front doors. The last group will be airlifted and set on the roof to work their way down. We will have to go room by room, which will take hours."

"What will you do with prisoners?" Zuttara asked.

"We don't plan on taking any," Utu stated.

Zuttara checked his sidearm. "Excellent. If you need me, I am ready."

"Thank you, major, but your job is to protect Priestess Dagan," Utu said with a bow to her.

Dagan looked up. "I don't need protecting." She held up her automatic machine gun, then she wrapped a belt around her waist loaded with replacement magazines. "I'm going through that front door with group 'B.'"

"Priestess, I object to this!" Zuttara exclaimed.

"I know, but you know there is no stopping me."

Asar butted in, "What is our timeline?"

"We will be underway in a few minutes. The longer we wait, the better entrenched and more difficult the Ineans will be to kill," Utu stated.

"Very well. I will monitor from here," Asar said while he saluted Utu.

"Thank you, sir. Major, you may as well take group 'A' into the tunnels, and I will lead 'C' to the roof. Priestess Dagan, you may lead group 'B'. Let's go."

As they walked away, Utu handed them radios and pointed to the leaders of each group for Zuttara and Dagan. They split up and went to their groups. Everyone bowed as Dagan went by, and, as the new leader of the people, that would be the first rule she would abolish.

Dozens of vertical take-off (VTO) planes landed, and Utu waved his group to load up. Zuttara waved him to the troop carriers, and Dagan did the same.

Zuttara's group was the first to roll out, then Dagan's. Utu waited for them to get ahead so they could all attack simultaneously. As the trucks rolled on towards Delondra, which was now in sight, dozens of fighters streaked by to the cheers of the troops. It was the first time in almost four years that they had control of their air space. This was their first major ground offensive, as well, of the war, and morale could not be any higher.

The fighters launched their missiles, which smashed into the presidential tower, shattering the large windows on their way through. The missiles exploded and filled the building with noxious gas and smoke.

Hundreds of Ineans came spilling out of the building, and several fighters turned and made a run for them. The pilots switched from missiles to machine guns and flew low with their guns firing. Bits of asphalt and chunks of bricks kicked up with each bullet that struck the ground. Many bullets hit their targets, some multiple times, as the Ineans were mowed down in the palace square.

The fighters turned again and made another run at the building and fired more gas and smoke missiles from the top of the tower down to the middle. More Ineans came running out and took cover. Some had shoulder-mounted rockets, and others had laser rifles.

"Alpha group, come in from the west. Beta group, come in from the east and draw their fire while we hit them from the rear," the lead pilot stated over the radio.

"Affirmative," a random voice said over the radio.

The fighters split into two groups and made their runs. The Ineans were now confused and did not know which group to attack, but they had another problem. Dagan's group arrived and was one block away from the tower. They started running along the rubble-strewn streets while the few human residents scurried into buildings.

They made it to the square as one group of Ineans stood to fire their shoulder-mounted rockets. Dagan gave the Order to fire.

The Ineans had no idea what just happened as one whole group was cut up and fell to the ground. Her troops stormed in and took the rockets, and fired them at the other group of Ineans. The ultimate in humiliation, getting killed with your own weapon. Her group went from car to car for cover as they flushed the Ineans into the open. The Ineans laid their weapons down, knowing they were defeated. Dagan had no use for prisoners, and she gave the Order. Her troops were more than willing to comply and killed the Ineans who had just surrendered.

"Let's make sure the square is secure and set up a perimeter. Then we go in," Dagan ordered. She heard Utu telling the fighters to pull back while they did the drop. She saw the fighters fly away as the VTOs flew in and landed one at a time on the roof of the presidential tower.

Dagan heard Zuttara's voice on the radio. His group was storming the tunnel, and they were taking laser fire. She ordered her troops to close in on the front doors, and she led the way. She had seen this event in a dream put in her mind by Kur. She knew the fight was far from over, but they had to take it to the Ineans, who had dug in by now. She looked up as several of Utu's men rappelled down the side of the tower, and through the smashed windows, the rockets had blown out. She heard gunfire from above and knew they had engaged the Ineans.

On the moon, Anaru, the remaining bombers were fueled and loaded. General Innin had one last meeting with his squadron leaders in the middle of the hangar bay. "We have just received word that the first group has gone to hyperspace speeds and are clear of Utui's system, so each of you will have five ships in your groups. I wish I had more information on what awaits you at Inea, but I plan for them to be waiting for you. All I can suggest at this point is fly high over the plane of their system and then drop down as fast as you dare and bomb them to oblivion."

"Yes, sir!" they exclaimed. They saluted General Innin and headed for their respective bombers. All the other pilots boarded, and Innin exited the flight deck as the red warning lights began to flash. Soon, the large doors opened, and the bombers took off for their mission to Inea. The second wave, Innin hoped, would just mop up for the first wave.

Innin sent the remaining fighters to the planet to assist in killing the many Ineans scattered about the planet.

Back on the planet, the three groups assaulted the tower and killed the Ineans. The Ineans did manage to kill many of the Ardons in the fight as well, but in the end, the Ardons prevailed. It took well into the night to flush each one out and clear the building. They cleared anything Inean from the building, and Dagan went to the president's office for the first time in years. She walked in and broke down for a few minutes, and Zuttara had to console her until she managed to compose herself.

"These are your offices now," he said.

"No, these are the president's offices. I am only a temporary leader," she said, wiping a tear from her eye. "Aanepada hoped to see this day. Now he won't," she said as another tear rolled down her cheek.

"He does see it through you. First thing tomorrow, we get the word out that we have taken the capital back, and we will be swearing you in as our new leader."

"Okay, but I have to do something first."

Zuttara was puzzled as she walked over to a closet that was locked. She took the machine gun off her shoulder and pointed it at the lock. She fired several rounds, and the lock flew off amid splinters of wood. She slung the weapon over her shoulder and opened the doors. Hanging there was Aanepada's red robe, along with a small box.

Zuttara walked up beside her. "What the Tari?"

She reached into her pocket and handed him the letter Aanepada had written her. She took the robe from its hook and placed it in front of the blown-out window. She took her machine gun and shredded it with bullets. Not being pleased with that, she lit it on fire and watched it burn.

She went back to the closet, retrieved the box, and opened it. Inside were a few scraps of paper and a pendant she wore as a child. It was a pendant her original parents had given her. She clutched it and cried.

FIFTY-ONE

THE FIRST BATCH of bombers cleared the Ardonnarian system and began feeding antimatter to their main engines. The controlled explosion in the mix chamber generated an enormous amount of energy, which was directed to two high-powered cannons. Each was mounted at the front of the nacelles on either side of the sleek ship and faced forward. Each plasma cannon was aimed at a point in front of the craft, and the energy released from the cannons focused on this point, tearing a hole in space. The resulting wormhole would close the distance between the Ardon system and the Inean system. Instead of taking dozens of years to travel the distance, it would now take only a few months.

Each ship flew into the wormhole created and ignited its waste fuel engines. The waste fuel would be created from the antimatter explosion and vented out the rear of the ship via conventional rocket nozzles, creating propulsion through the wormhole. It was fast and efficient.

A few weeks into the journey, one of the pilots was about to inform the fleet commander, Maqatu, of an impact on the port nacelle, which housed the antimatter fuel. The woman pilot watched her containment readings fluctuate as she fumbled with the radio's controls.

"Commander Maqatu, this is Messani. We have hit something."

"Is there any damage?" his reply came a minute later.

"Our containm..."

Her voice gave way to hissing on the radio and was then replaced by the sound of alarms. There was another bright flash as another bomber exploded. The second bomber bore the brunt of the first one exploding next to it.

"All ships spread out and drop out of hyperspace!" Maqatu demanded as he watched two of his ships obliterated instantly.

Once out of trouble, Maqatu tried to calm his remaining pilots, but it would not be easy. Everyone was on the same frequency, and their voices chattered over one another, so he could not understand them.

"People, people! Calm down. Let's go over what happened here. We have access to each ship's data recorder, so let us analyze what happened."

Maqatu turned the radio off, and he studied the data from the first bomber explosion. He saw one of the hull sensors resonate, indicating an impact, and right after, the containment field began to fluctuate. It was a one-in-a-million shot, but something hit the bomber. Probably a small rock in space, but that did not fit the scenario of a wormhole. There should not have been anything else in there with them. His only conclusion was that something fell off one of his other ships that were in the lead.

Maqatu ordered his ships to inspect the hulls of each other and report back. Nothing was found. He was hoping to find a missing panel or large bolt hole where a bolt had been, but nothing was missing. This concerned him because they had never flown this small of a craft at such speeds. Even ships like the *ShuBuré* had thick hulls and shields protecting sensitive components of the larger ships against most objects, but they did not.

After a few hours of studying the data, Maqatu came to the conclusion that there had to be some debris that had entered the wormhole with them, and there was nothing any of them could do.

"All pilots, let's get underway. I want all ships flying in as wide a pattern as possible, and hopefully, this won't happen again. If it happens again to your ship, then immediately fall away from the main group. We will continue to study this while we head to Inea," Maqatu stated.

He then sent a coded message back to Ardonnar.

One after another, the bombers tore open a wormhole and took off. Their concern now was whether they had enough ships to complete the job.

FIFTY-TWO

A FEW DAYS LATER, word got out that the Ineans had been defeated. Tens of thousands made their way to Delondra for Dagan's swearing-in ceremony. The presidential plaza was cleaned, and the windows on the facing side of the tower were repaired. The rest would be repaired over time. Food vendors set up their carts, and food was brought in. No one had money, so everything was free until the economy could be rebuilt. The square filled to capacity, and the crowds spread into adjacent streets. The balcony was repaired, and the military presence was strong. A wall of armed soldiers stood between the tower and the people. Hundreds of troops roamed the streets, and hundreds more filtered through the crowd. They didn't expect trouble, but if trouble happened, it would be squashed quickly. The hours ticked by as the crowd grew. The sun was warm, and vendors went up and down the street handing out water, sandwiches, and other food to anyone who needed it.

At high noon, General Asar walked out onto the balcony and waved to the crowd, which went crazy, cheering. He let them go on for a few minutes, and then he held his hands up, and they quieted. "People of Ardonnar!" he yelled. "We have successfully removed the Inean threat from this planet!" The people screamed, yelled, cheered, and pumped their fists in the air. He let them cheer again for a few minutes. "Everyone here has been affected by this disaster. The entire planet has been affected. Our climate has been altered by these beings. Our cities were ravaged, and many were destroyed by urukii bombs. Millions upon millions have been killed, and many more are missing, stolen from their homes and families, never to be seen again." The crowd was quiet. "Our president, Aanepada, gave his life fighting these animals to his very last breath, and he has given us a temporary leader to see us through this crisis." The cheering rose up again. "I present to you, Priestess Dagan." The crowd cheered. Some were reserved at cheering because she was a woman. It had been hundreds of years since a woman was a leader, long before the Great War.

Dagan stepped out, and most of the crowd went wild. She pulled her hood back and smiled at the thousands of people. She finally held her hands up, and they quieted. "People of Ardonnar, we are gathered here today to claim victory." The crowd went insane with cheering. She held up her hands, "but it is a cautious victory. As we stand here today, we have sent bombers to Inea in the hope of destroying their planet." More cheers. "However, we must be careful not to get lulled into complacency. There are still small pockets of Ineans on our planet that need to be dealt with, and we must concentrate on them. We also need to rebuild our society from the ground up. It is a task that will not be easy, nor will it be quick." The crowd cheered. "We also must prepare for alien races such as the Ineans. We need to build faster and better-armed spaceships."

She raised her hands for the crowd to settle down. "As we speak, military engineers are working with General Innin on Anaru to equip the moon base to handle the larger warships and to begin construction as soon as possible. I want to be prepared the next time the Ineans or any hostile race looks our way." The crowd cheered. "We plan on having twenty of these ships built within three years." She paused as the sun broke through the clouds and shone on the people again. "Closer to home, we will build up our ground forces and rearm." Dagan looked out over the crowd and at her notes and decided to wrap it up. She was beginning to sound like a typical politician, and that was the last thing she wanted.

"We have many more plans that we will roll out over the next several weeks, but I won't bore you with them today. I will say, in closing, that once the threat from the Ineans has been eliminated, we will hold proper elections and let you, the people of Ardonnar, decide who will lead our race into the next chapter of our history." The crowd cheered. "Now, let us pray to Kur for the millions who have died and are among the missing."

She bowed her head along with all the people, and there was silence. "Oh, Great, Kur, you have guided us to victory over the evil mullahs from Inea against incredible odds. Please take care of the millions who have died and watch over the many that are missing. Bring them all home to you. We also pray that you will see us through rebuilding our society and protecting our people from future invasions by such hostile and evil forces. Blessed be Kur. Amen." The people all around her and in the streets below all chimed in, "Blessed be Kur. Amen." She looked up and grinned, "Let's celebrate."

Music began playing, and it was truly a party atmosphere.

FIFTY-THREE

THREE MONTHS HAD PASSED, and the first wave of bombers closed in on the planet of Inea. Long-range scans displayed heavy spaceship traffic around the planet, and some of the ships were large. It appeared to be a fleet of Inean warships massing for an attack.

The leader of the first wave, Commander Maqatu, was discussing strategy with his other pilots. He studied the three-dimensional model of Inea in the cramped confines of his lead bomber. "The only way I see that we can get by those ships is to surprise them, and the only way I can see that is possible is to send half the ships around the moon to draw them off while the rest drop down into the system at the highest speed possible."

"I think we can drop in at near light speed to their front door. I am scanning for orbital debris, and there is not much. I have to assume that they cleaned up the space around their planet decades ago so they would not run into it as well. I am panning out to see how far the clear zone extends. This might work," lead pilot Labritui stated. He was also Maqatu's wingman.

"If we do this, then we will have to split the group soon so we give the impression that each force is independent, should they figure it out," Radjni said.

"I understand. So are we in agreement on this attack?" Maqatu asked.

All of his pilots chimed in and said yes.

"Okay, then this is how we will split up. Once we separate, there will be no more radio communication because they will pick it up." Maqatu gave the breakdown of the two groups, which now comprised twenty-three ships. They had lost two during the three-month flight when the antimatter engine of one bomber lost containment and exploded, taking out the ship next to it. After that incident, Maqatu gave the Order for the ships to spread out and closely monitor the containment systems. One other bomber had a problem, but the pilot was able to shut it down in time and repair his magnetic containment line to the antimatter injectors. He was able to catch up and rejoin his group after a few days.

Fourteen ships broke away and headed towards the Inean system after working out the final details and timing of the attack. Maqatu led this group towards the Inean moon, Adhideva, where they would fly in low and utilize the moon's gravity as a speed boost to approach Inea without engines. Hopefully, giving them a few additional seconds of surprise before the Ineans discovered what was happening. Maqatu felt deep down that the Ineans may already know they were coming, and they might be flying into a trap. He did know deep down that this was a one-way mission, but he did not tell his pilots that. He assumed they knew already.

Events would happen quickly now as Bahuvah, Inea's sun, was growing in their front windows, and the pilots had to turn on their sun filters so they could see.

Maqatu continued to plot their course and adjust their timing. He expected to be behind the moon in twelve hours and engaged with the Ineans minutes later. He knew the second group would be dropping in twenty minutes after that, and Gula's bombers would be arriving the next day. If nothing else, his job was to weaken the Inean defenses and leave it up to Gula to finish the job. However, Maqatu did not like to leave it up to the second group. There were too many things to go wrong, too many unknowns, and far too many Inean warships against their little bombers.

Maqatu's bombers dropped out of hyperspace and cruised behind the moon. Soon, they were taking groundfire, but their ships were moving too fast for the Inean guns to lock on. They spread out using the moon's gravity to catapult past the moon and towards Inea, where the big ships loomed. The Inean fleet turned and started in their direction as the bombers closed the gap quickly.

"Open bay doors and target those warships!" Maqatu ordered as he broke radio silence. "Prepare to fire on my command."

The Ineans began launching missiles toward the bombers. Two missiles hit and destroyed two of the bombers. Now, they had twelve. More missiles raced in, and another bomber was destroyed.

Maqatu had no choice. They were going to be slaughtered. "Launch rockets!"

Several of the rockets blasted away and headed toward the Inean warships, and some of the warships turned away, but it was too late. Several of the nuclear rockets hit their mark. Three of the Inean ships exploded into blinding fireballs as the nuclear warheads exploded and broke the antimatter containment fields of the Inean ships. The combination of nuclear warhead and antimatter sent a shockwave that blew all ships off course. Several more missiles headed in, and now they only had seven bombers.

"Launch the next wave at those ships, and then launch the rest of your rockets towards the planet. All planet-bound rockets should have population density data loaded by now from the scanning computer," Maqatu stated as he launched everything he had left. He turned his bomber towards an Inean ship that had broken through. He said a prayer to Kur and aimed at the missile array under the Inean ship. He programmed his antimatter containment to shut down seconds before impact.

The rockets raced in and destroyed several more Inean ships. A handful of rockets broke through the Inean defenses and headed toward the planet. As the Ardonnarian bombers ran out of ammo, they resolved to the fact that this was it, and the rest of them followed Maqatu's bomber.

Maqatu's bomber struck the Inean ship as it was launching the next wave of missiles. The bomber exploded and blew a massive hole in the ship as its missiles went wild, striking another Inean ship and destroying it. Another bomber followed Maqatu's in and broke the Inean ship in half with its antimatter explosion; the pieces fell towards the planet. Soon, the ship broke apart and burned in the atmosphere. Its flaming hull eventually crashed into fields, leaving a crater several zag wide.

The rest of the bombers slammed into the Inean ships, destroying one and severely damaging others. The whole attack was over in minutes, and none lived to see the urukii rockets strike Inea. It would be the worst attack on Inea in hundreds of years and the first by an alien race.

While the Ineans licked their wounds, the rest of their ships converged and began repairs. The lull would not last long as the next wave dropped down, firing almost everything they had at the planet. Some of the rockets were destroyed, while most made it through.

Once in the atmosphere, the rocket nose cones flew off, revealing the multiple warheads. A few seconds later, the banding let go, and hundreds of warheads flew away in multiple directions as the Ineans had difficulty locking on to the warheads. Seconds now from detonation, several Inean fighters tried to ram the warheads. Some were successful, but now the warheads tumbled toward the planet as the guidance systems tried to regain control.

On the ground, Inean radio broadcast the attack and ordered all of their people to take cover. Ineans on the ground panicked, as their planet had never been attacked by a race they had tried to conquer. It didn't matter anyway, as city after city vaporized in nuclear fireballs, even the Ineans had never seen the likes of. City after city crumbled and disappeared as the shock waves spread out in all directions, burning up everything and everyone in their paths. Vast clouds of fire and debris lifted into the sky, blocking out the light from Bahuvah.

Labritui turned his attention to the remaining Inean ships and had his bombers launch their rockets at them. He lost three of his nine ships due to Inean missiles, and he knew that they needed to clear out more of these ships before Gula's strike force arrived to finish the job. He aimed his rockets and fired them at the ships along with the rest of his bombers. Realizing their ammunition was running low, Labritui ordered his bombers to turn about and head for the moon. He was unsure if there was a military base there, but he knew that whatever was there had to be destroyed. He flew in and launched his last rockets, all three of them at the base below. As he did, hundreds of fighters came racing out of tunnels in the ground, and now they were in a dog fight with no bullets.

"All ships, prepare to shut down your antimatter containment as those ships get close and pray to Kur for your soul."

As the Inean fighters raced in, they must have realized what the Ardons intended and broke away at the last minute as the Ardon ships exploded. Only a few Inean ships were destroyed in the process. The Ineans turned towards their home planet and headed down to help out in the disaster.

Smoke, dust, ash, blazing fires, and radiation began to engulf the Inean planet as the last remaining warships sent their fighters down to aid in rescue. Several hours passed, and the Ineans were confident that the attack was over. The Inean leader, Sankar, ordered all ships to the ground to aid. Inean ship after Inean ship headed down to the planet, leaving the space around their world unprotected.

Outside of the Inean capital, Sabitta, which had so far gone unscathed, thousands of Ardonnarian slaves working in the fields began to cheer as they saw the mushroom clouds rising from a distant city. Several Inean soldiers ran to the fields to collect them, and the slaves turned on them with pitchforks and shovels. The Ineans were not prepared for the attack, and many fell, both Ardonnarians and Ineans. The Ardonnarians outnumbered the Ineans ten to one, and it took many of the slaves to finally defeat them on the ground. The Ineans were much larger and stronger than the Ardon-narians.

The Ardonnarians ran from the field as the large warships swooped over the plain with a deafening roar and rush of wind that knocked them over as they tried to run. Suddenly, one of the Inean ships exploded in the air in a blinding flash of light, followed by a boom that had enough force to lay trees over and blow the Ardon-narians to the ground.

Minutes later, other missiles began falling from the sky, and Gula's bombers had arrived.

Gula's bombers dropped down on Inea from above the orbital plane of the planets. This minimized the amount of debris and small frag-ments they would have to fly through. This made it possible to fly at hyperspace speeds almost to the end.

The bombers engaged small fighters, which began to overpower Gula and his bombers. He gave the Order, "Launch all rockets, except one each, towards the planet."

All the bombers launched the rockets, which lumbered slowly away from the bombers. Then the big engines fired, and they streaked away towards Inea. Just about all of them made it through the Inean defenses and entered the atmosphere. Soon after, the nose cones blew off, and the multiple warheads separated and headed off towards their targets.

Sankar stood in his office and stared out the windows at the city in the distance, which was burning. The mushroom cloud had dissi-pated some as it got caught up in the planet's jet stream, which pulled the burning, radioactive cloud to the east.

Sankar was joined by his council, who began begging him to take cover as there was a flash above the city. They all stepped toward the window and looked as the Ardonnarian slaves bowed their heads and began chanting to Kur. Sankar looked at them, and then he saw the rockets streaking towards him. There was a blinding flash above Sabitta, and he exchanged looks with his council. The building they were in shattered, and they were vaporized, along with all the inhabitants of the Inean capital.

Gula's bombers turned their attention to the moon, Adhideva, which was also sending up fighters. He lost another ship, and the rest were taking damage. He led the rest of his team to the moon and launched their remaining rockets. Quickly, they sped off as the moon exploded, sending chunks of the rocky moon towards Inea.

The ships raced away and stopped outside the system when they had lost the last Inean fighter. Several of them were too damaged to go on.

Gula held a roll call. He had twelve ships left and thirty-six pilots. Four of those ships would not make it back to Ardonnar. "Enanatuma, what is the status of your ship?"

"Gula, we are losing power. I don't think we can keep containment much longer!" she replied frantically.

"I want your team to suit up and head to Anzillu's ship," Gula stated.

"On our way," she stated nervously.

"Enan, I will pull up close and open our airlock," Anzillu said as he fired his thrusters. He and Enanatuma had been lovers, and the three-month space flight separated by the vacuum of space had created a longing that both hoped to quench soon. He called her many different names, and Enan was one of his pet names for her. He was thankful that her ship was not destroyed. However, it did take a nasty hit to the starboard pylon, which housed the craft's anti-matter, and there was no need to take chances. Eventually, the containment would fail, and the ship would explode.

"Gula, we are picking up objects coming our way from Inea!" Ayla said. She was Gula's backup pilot, which made Puabi very jealous. Gula spent many nights talking with Puabi about how Ayla was getting involved with their other pilot, but it was not enough to ease her concerns. He knew this would be a test of their relationship, and some nights, he wished he had never gotten involved with her. He also knew they had three months before landing on Anaru.

"Understood. We need to get underway quickly, people!" Gula stated over the open channel to all his ships.

After several minutes, Gula's ships got moving again, but now the remains of the Inean warships were breathing down their necks. Three large ships followed them as they went to hyperspace. The Ineans lost them, but they knew where they were going. The Inean commander set course for Ardonnar. His mission was not to engage the Ardons but to destroy their planet. The Inean ships were loaded with nuclear warheads, enough to destroy the planet five times over.

The planet of Inea was in flames. Every city had been blown away by the Ardonnarian cluster nukes, leaving craters where they had been. Fires spread from the cities to the suburbs from the scorching wind whipping across the planet. The sky darkened from thousands of tons of debris blown up into the atmosphere. An Inean warship broke up as it twisted and fell through the atmosphere at thousands of miles per hour. Its antimatter containment breached, and the resulting explosion leveled half a continent while displacing a fifth of the planet's atmosphere. The scorching, thousand-zag-per-hour wind leveled the rest of the continent. Millions of Ineans ran from their homes, dodging debris falling from the sky, and boarded buses that were taking survivors to the mountains. Many were struck down by steel beams, chunks of concrete, and thick sections of glass from the cities miles away.

Hours later, as the planet rotated, fragments of the moon, Adhideva, that had been blasted away, began to fall towards the planet. The blast was caused by the suicide explosions of the Ardon Antimatter fuel cells. The fragments, some as large as a building, burned through the atmosphere and crashed into the ground. Some landed harmlessly in open fields or the oceans, but others crashed into populated areas.

FIFTY-FOUR

MONTHS LATER, the Ardon strike force that had obliterated the planet of Inea slowed as it entered their home system. Their antimatter fuel was almost gone. Their food had run out the day before after living on rations for the past month and a half. Their water supply had an odd flavor due to being recycled too many times, and the air supply was stale at best. Their nerves were on edge after living in cramped quarters for the last three months after doubling up for the journey home. Fighting and bickering over nothing of importance were common. They slept in shifts, typically at the feet of whoever was flying the bombers. While humans are social beings, time alone is also a requirement, especially for Anzillu and Enanatuma, who longed for just five minutes to be alone together. It was just not going to happen on this leg of the mission. To top it off, the three Inean warships inched closer to them with each passing day and were almost within range to start shooting.

Gula had spent much of the last few weeks studying the Inean warships and was in contact with General Asar and General Innin, who were waiting for them.

The bombers flew past the orbits of the outer planets, which were on the other side of Utui and flew in towards Idpa. At this point, Idpa was out of the way as it had moved in its orbit away from Ardonnar, but it was still on Ardonnar's side of the star Utui. This would be beneficial if they could lure the Ineans away from their direct course to Ardonnar. So far, the Ineans did not change course. They needed a reason to deviate, and Gula had an idea of what it would take.

Gula slowed his bomber while the others continued on towards Idpa. He sensed that they knew it was a trap, yet they continued towards Ardonnar. He turned his bomber and headed towards the lead warship, which did not pay any attention to him. He then fired his last two missiles, which struck the large, heavily armored Inean ship harmlessly. "Ardon Control, this is Gula. The plan failed. The Inean warships are still heading towards Ardonnar, and I estimate they will be there in a few hours."

"Gula, this is Asar. There is nothing else you can do. Get your people to Nanshi base and help them get off the ground."

"Confirmed Ardon Control. Good luck, General," Gula said, and he clicked off his comm. He fired up his engines, swung around, and aimed his bomber towards the outer moon of Idpa.

Nanshi base replaced the base that was on the moon, Uggae, which had been destroyed. The Nanshi base was very limited in capability and capacity, but the Ardonnarians did manage to tuck nearly forty fighters into the deep cavern of the icy moon. The rest of his bombers would be there in half an hour. He would be there shortly after that.

As Gula's bombers closed in, dozens of targets took off from Nanshi. The fighters were away and heading towards the Inean warships. This gave Gula and his people a clear landing, which they took advantage of.

The bombers flew low above the icy moon and found the opening that was waiting for them. The bombers landed and slid across the ice and finally parked on the far side of the hollowed-out cavern made of rock and ice with steel reinforcements. The cavern slowly pressurized with air, and they got the green light after a few minutes. They staggered out of the bombers and breathed in better air. Many collapsed to the ground, and some even kissed it. It was the best air they had had in months. They struggled against the weak gravity of the small moon and finally made it to the entrance. Anzillu had his arm around Enanatuma's shoulders, and she was kissing his neck. Puabi wrapped her arms around Gula, and he returned the embrace for more than a minute. All those nights of cursing getting involved with her because she was jealous of his copilot were forgotten now. She was soft and warm in his arms. After a few minutes, they continued in for their debriefing, which would be short.

Others had paired up as well, and it looked like a couple's night at the local club.

The pilots entered the control center, and several technicians monitored the advancing Ineans and the Ardonnarian ships in flight, who were now in a race to catch up before those warships made it to Ardonnar.

There was plenty of chatter over the speakers as the fighter pilots talked among themselves.

Once the pilots were out of the hangar, technicians raced out and began refueling the bombers.

The Inean ships slowed as they swung wide of the moon, Anaru, and Nisaba, knowing full well that the Ardonnarians were capable of anything. Once past the moons, they broke formation, which was a tactic the Ineans typically did not use. The Ineans preferred a two-dimensional frontal assault, but from the choppy reports put together by survivors of their encounters with the Ardons, they had to change their tactics. One ship went to the left of the planet, one went to the right, and the last one spun around to face Anaru. They were prepared, and General Innin knew he was dealing with a different enemy this time. They had lost billions of lives. Their planet was bordering on being uninhabitable, and raiders from their own colonies were descending upon Inea to scavenge what they could.

Innin watched as the ships spread out, and he called the attack. Missiles launched from Anaru and Nisaba and headed towards the three ships that were prepared for the incoming attack. Small missiles streaked away from the warships and destroyed many of the incoming Ardon missiles. Then, fighters exited the warships and went after the remaining missiles.

Innin sent out the second wave of missile attacks as the fighters began swarming Nisaba and many more headed for Anaru. There would be no surprises this time, as Innin sent up all his fighters from Anaru, and they engaged the Ineans. The Ineans had the upper hand in firepower and in sheer numbers as they overwhelmed the Ardonnarian fighters.

"Get me, General Asar," Innin asked one of his officers as the Ineans began to pound the Anaru base with conventional warheads. Dust and small rock fragments fell from the ceiling. The lights flickered, and the monitors went out and came back on.

"Sir!" The communications officer yelled over the drone of the explosions above them. He handed Innin a headset.

"General Asar, we are getting pounded up here. You better launch everything you have on the ground and put it up in space and get Priestess Dagan to a safe location; Delondra is not safe."

"We concur, General Innin; we are moving the priestess as we speak. We will attack them from the ground, and we..."

In the city of Delondra, the warning sirens wailed, and Dagan was ushered from the presidential tower by Zuttara in haste to a waiting transport. He pushed her in against her protests, and he closed the hatch as the transport lifted off the ground quickly, sending all who had just boarded to the floor. The transport arced harshly, and then the pilot hit the thrust levers. Anything not held down, like Dagan and Zuttara, was sent to the rear of the craft with a thud.

"Are you okay, priestess?" Zuttara asked as he helped her to her feet.

"Yes, fine. Where are we going again?" she asked. At first, she thought about the mountain base, but that had been destroyed months ago.

"The mountains," he said as he guided her to a chair and helped her buckle in.

"But that was destroyed months ago!" she stated.

"That base, yes, but we have been building another one," he said.

"It can't be finished this quickly."

"No, far from it, but it is safer than being in a city right now. The Ineans are interested in two things: high body count and taking from us what we took from them: their world."

"Maybe it was a mistake destroying their planet."

Zuttara held her hands in his. "Don't ever think that. If we did not attack them when we had the chance, then they would be here with more ships than this. This way, we have a chance. The other way, we did not."

The pilot looked over his shoulder. "We have incoming missiles from the Inean ships!"

The connection from Ardonnar to Anaru was severed as the Ineans hit the antenna array hidden in the side wall of a crater facing Ardonnar.

"Sir, the Ineans are opening their launch tubes," another officer stated.

"Sir, we have launch detections on the ground. Dozens, no, wait, hundreds of urukii rockets are heading into space," another stated.

"Sir, we have hundreds of fighters leaving the ground and heading up," yet another officer said.

"This is it, people. We have everything up. Now it is up to Kur to see us through this," Asar stated.

In space, hundreds upon hundreds of targets swarmed about. It was a dogfight to end all dogfights as Ardonnarian fighters ganged up on the Ineans. Two to one, three to one, and a few went four to one as the next salvo of nuclear rockets headed towards the Inean warships. The Inean fighters tried to break away to take out the rockets, but the Ardonnarians kept chasing them and keeping them busy. It was starting to turn in their favor as the Ineans launched their own nuclear rockets toward the planet.

The wave of fighters from Nanshi arrived and went after the Inean rockets, firing their own missiles at them. Many of them exploded, but a few got through and made it into the atmosphere. Several fighters went down and continued to lock on until one exploded over Delondra. The fighter was vaporized, and the city below was blown to bits and engulfed in a nuclear fireball. Other Inean nukes made it to the ground and destroyed three other cities.

Most of the people had been evacuated from the cities over the past few months, but the damage to the planet would be extreme as the fireballs slowly rolled up into the atmosphere.

Innin watched in horror as the Ineans began destroying cities, and all three ships were still intact. "Launch our urukii rockets!" he bellowed as he saw the Ineans lining up for another launch.

The floor rumbled with the thrust of dozens of rockets pushing away from the small moon and heading into space. They arced towards the battle, which was beginning to thin as fighters from both sides took heavy losses. One of the ground-based rockets hit its mark as one of the ships was launching its nuclear rockets towards the planet. The ship exploded in an enormous fireball, which destroyed the rockets taking off. A rocket from Anaru struck another Inean ship, and it exploded the same way. Now, there was one left, and it still had enough firepower to level the planet and make it uninhabitable forever. It broke away from the battle and headed for the other side of the planet. Ardonnarian fighters pursued it while the Inean fighters chased after them.

The Inean ship was now out of reach of Anaru and Nisaba, so the fighters would have to destroy this last warship. It was reloading its launch tubes as it went behind Ardonnar. Innin knew if it launched, it could ruin their planet for generations to come, or worse.

"Sir, I'm picking up dozens of targets entering our system!"

Innin's stomach turned as he suspected it was more Inean reinforcements. He studied the screen and realized these were smaller ships; then he saw the IDs appear on the screen. A cheer went up around the room as more than thirty ships entered the system from Shullat. Dagan had reestablished communications with their colonies and sent them the plans to build ships to defend themselves. Now, those ships were closing in on Ardonnar and the last Inean warship.

More fighters came up from Ardonnar, but these would be the last. There were no more fighters, no more nuclear rockets, no more anything other than ground troops, but that was useless for this battle. There were no more fighters on Anaru or Nanshi. All that was left was the thirty ships coming in from their colonies and a handful of antimatter bombs in the hangar, but there was no way of delivering them to the Inean ship. Then Innin had an idea as he watched the last of his space-born fighters destroyed. There were still dozens of Inean fighters swarming around the Inean warship to protect it as they prepared to launch their rockets.

Innin looked at the dots coming in and realized there was not enough time. He swallowed hard. "Load the antimatter bombs into the transports. I need five volunteers for a suicide mission."

Every hand went up across the control room. Innin picked five people to fly the transports into the Inean warship. "May the blessings of Kur be with you and your families," he said as he put his right hand on each of their foreheads. Each bowed their head and said, "Praise be to Kur, and victory will be ours."

They all left the control room. Two women and three men headed for the landing bay, where technicians were loading the antimatter bombs into the transports. The pilots strapped in, and the deck cleared as the doors were blown off to allow the transports a quick exit. The transports flew off the deck and into space.

The Inean fighters saw the transports leaving Anaru, and all turned to head them off. Several minutes went by, and the Ineans closed the gap quickly. The fighters flying high above Ardonnar took off for space and headed for the Inean ship as the launch tubes opened. The Inean fighters turned when they realized that it was only transports flying in and went to engage the fighters that were heading in.

Once the Ineans were in firing range, the Ardonnarian fighters swooped back towards the planet and waited for the Inean nukes to come down. Then, the transports were closer, and the Ineans were confused as to why transports were approaching in such a spread-out pattern. The Ineans attacked one with a missile, and it exploded in a blinding flash, briefly knocking the others off their flight plan. The Inean fighters realized what was on the transports, turned, and headed back to destroy them before they got any closer.

The Inean ship launched a half-dozen rockets as their fighters engaged the transports. One was disabled. Another was destroyed, and two got through and headed in while the fighters turned to get them. They destroyed another, and the first one got away and was close enough as the Inean ship started launching more nuclear rockets. The transport exploded at the rear of the Inean ship, which blasted off its engines and sent the massive ship tumbling out of control.

The Ardonnarian fighters attacked the nuclear rockets entering the atmosphere and destroyed all but one. It exploded over an eastern city.

The Inean warship tried to pull itself out of its tumble, but its thrusters were not powerful enough to quickly handle the large ship, and the ship began to tumble away from the planet.

The Ardonnarian colonists cruised in, and their home planet came into view. In the distance, a bright speck winked at them. The Inean ship continued to roll out of control as the fighters aimed for it.

General Innin had one more option and decided to use it. There were a few nuclear missiles on an asteroid in the direction the Inean ship was heading. He decided to use them, but that would mean he had nothing else to use should another ship attack. If this one survived, it would mean the end of Ardonnar as well. He had one of his remaining officers connect to the asteroid and program the missiles. He launched them when he was ready, but it would be a few hours before they would be in range. It was their last line of defense.

The fighters from the colony engaged the Inean fighters. Their numbers were equal, but their training was not. The Ineans flew circles around the colonists and destroyed most of them while only losing a few of their own. This brought the fighters out of the atmosphere, and they had to take on the Ineans, leaving the planet vulnerable should the Inean warship get itself under control. They took on the remaining Inean fighters and finally destroyed them. There were four Ardonnarian fighters left, and they were low on fuel.

Innin was barking orders in the ears of his pilots. "That ship has steadied and is turning towards the planet! Do whatever is necessary to stop them from launching!"

The pilots turned their ships and made a run at the gigantic warship. As they got closer, the warship began firing guns at them, and one was hit. Then, another burst as its fuel tanks were hit by a small missile. The last two darted about, trying to avoid being hit, and they flew under the miles-long ship towards the launch tubes as one of the missiles was exiting the ship. One pilot fired his guns at the warhead, and he struck the liquid fuel tank and the rocket exploded as it exited the launch tube, engulfing the underside of the craft in fire. He turned his fighter and headed straight for a launch tube that had a rocket that was igniting in it. He fired his missiles into the launch tube, and his fighter followed in as he detonated his remaining fuel reserves. The explosion was enormous, and several other warheads exploded. The last fighter flew around the ship and aimed for what he believed to be its command center or bridge. He flew into the large glass windows and exploded his fighter while praying to Kur, and the bridge of the Inean ship filled with fire. The Inean ship rolled away from the planet while it burned in space.

On the Inean ship, workers raced about trying to extinguish the fires that were getting dangerously close to the stockpile of nuclear warheads. Right now, the Ineans were flying blind as their bridge had been destroyed, and all they had at the moment was visual flying. Then, a rough Inean voice was hollering over the ship's speakers about incoming missiles. The big guns took aim at the missiles coming in from the asteroid. The Ineans picked off three of the five missiles, and two remained. Another was destroyed, leaving one. The last one was hit, but it was a glancing blow, and the rocket tumbled toward the Inean ship as it prepared to launch its final attack on Ardonnar. The rocket tumbled in and exploded just above the Inean ship as it was launching. The nuclear shock wave pushed the ship downward as the rockets were leaving the launch tubes. One of the rockets snagged a thruster cone and slammed the side of the launch tube, and the nuclear warhead triggered and exploded. The ship exploded into a fireball that engulfed it, and the rockets leaving it. The last Inean ship had been destroyed.

Innin looked around, and nobody cheered. It was him and a few others remaining. All of their pilots were dead. All of their ships were destroyed. All of their missiles were spent. All they had if the Ineans came again were handguns and ground troops. He didn't even have a transport back to the planet. There was nothing left.

FIFTY-FIVE

SINCE THE FALL OF INEA, many of the Inean colonies sent transports to Inea to grab whatever resources they could take. Almost all of them gathered weapons, food, and building materials. The colonists built up arms and took the few remaining ships back to their colonies. Some even took Ardonnarian slaves they had found. Many were sick and died, but others lived and were forced to reproduce to be used as slave fighters for the Inean's amusement. The Ineans built fighting arenas out of stone, similar to coliseums with human slave labor. These coliseums were very similar to the ones built by the Romans for gladiator fights. Here, the Ardon slaves fought to the death.

Soon, fights broke out between the colonies, and with no big warships from Inea to keep Order, the fighting grew fierce as they fought over the few resources between the planets. It was a matter of a few years before dwindling resources and constant fighting resulted in the Ineans killing each other off on their colonies, leaving the Ardonnarian slaves to fend for themselves. Most of the slaves had come from Ardonnar, while some of their offspring were born on these remote planets. Over the years, these groups would slowly grow on these harsh planets into independent societies. Many wrote what life had been like before the Ineans invaded their home world and preserved their history for their descendants. These people felt deep down that their home world was no longer there, and no one knew where it was.

Eventually, these societies grew into small colonies and then expanded to higher latitudes where they could grow food. Their numbers never increased very much on these harsh worlds, as the climate kept their food production to a minimum, and disease killed off half of any children born.

They persevered in the belief that they might be the last of their race and strove to survive.

FIFTY-SIX

ARDONNARIAN GROUND TROOPS rolled into Ninki under the leadership of Captain Anzillu in a quest to rid the city of a few Ineans that had been terrorizing the citizens. They went door to door searching for them after tips from several citizens that the Ineans were hiding in the city. It was a painstakingly slow process. After a few days of searching, Anzillu's troops finally found the Ineans. There were about twenty hidden in a few different buildings. The fighting was fierce, and Anzillu ended up face-to-face with one of them when his gun jammed. The Inean hit him, and he fell and then rolled to his feet. He pulled out his knife and started slicing at the Inean until he got help from another soldier, who shot the Inean in the face.

Anzillu fell to the ground, and the Inean fell on top of him with his knife drawn. Anzillu kicked the Inean off as the jagged dagger in the Inean's hand tore from his stomach. He yelled in pain and rolled on his back as blood gushed out from his abdomen. Enanatuma tore off her helmet and applied pressure to stop his bleeding, but the blood oozed between her fingers. She screamed out for a medic over and over as she watched Anzillu's eyes roll back in his head. He gripped her hand and tried to speak, but he could not talk. His grip loosened, and his hand fell to the side. She cried out.

As her back was turned, an Inean rushed from the building. He pulled a knife from his belt and raised it above his head. She heard the heavy stomping of his boots, and she turned quickly. He plunged the knife deep into her left shoulder, right next to the collar bone and in the opening of her bulletproof vest. She fired her gun point-blank into his stomach, and she screamed in pain. She held the trigger as a dozen rounds tore through his body.

The Inean fell on her, crushing her to the ground and pushing the knife clear through her shoulder. She tried to get up to help Anzillu, but the Inean kept her pinned down under his crushing weight, which made it hard for her to breathe.

A few seconds later, help arrived and pulled the Inean off of her as medics began working on Anzillu. She crawled over with the knife still deep into her shoulder as the medic shook his head.

"No! You must save him," she cried as she fought the urge to remove the knife which burned in the deep wound it had made.

"He has lost too much blood," the medic said.

"Take mine!" She pleaded, "I'm the same type."

"You need yours,"

"I said do it!" she screamed. "I'm not bleeding that badly."

The medic shook his head, knowing there was no reasoning with her. "Get them both to the truck and start IVs right away. Get Anzillu stabilized and then start a blood transfusion from Enanatuma as soon as possible."

"Yes, Irkala," the other medics replied as they listened to the random automatic rifles firing throughout the city.

They strapped Anzillu to a backboard and carried him off while Enanatuma strolled behind them, clutching her now useless arm. They got in the back of an open truck and started rolling towards the makeshift hospital just a few miles away while the medics worked on Anzillu.

One of the soldiers walked up to Irkala, "What do we do with the Inean bodies? Anyone know?"

Irkala glanced up at him, "We are to burn them except for two males and two females if we find any females."

"Why save them?" the soldier asked.

"General Asar wants the scientists to study them so we can find weaknesses we can use against them in the future."

"Yes, sir," the soldier saluted and walked off toward others in his group to deliver the instructions.

On the other side of the planet, Dagan and Zuttara walked through the woods outside the mountain base that had been established quickly in light of the recent Inean invasion. It was a clear and cool day as the leaves of the trees began to change colors with autumn fast approaching. They walked hand in hand for the first time in weeks, taking in the countryside and each other. As they walked, they heard a noise in the distance. The birds suddenly quieted, and then dozens of them took flight and headed away. A predator was approaching.

Zuttara pulled his hand away from Dagan and pulled out his pistol. Dagan removed hers from its holster and checked it while grasping a knife in her other hand.

They walked gingerly through the tall ferns among the trees. She stopped at a peculiar odor. One she had not smelled in a long time, but she knew instantly what it was. Now, there was a warm, rancid breath on the back of her neck.

"Priestess Dagan, I presume?" The rough voice asked with a snap of its forked tongue.

Zuttara inched closer but stopped in his tracks as the Inean pressed his jagged knife to her throat.

"I am Priestess Dagan," she replied while calculating her options.

"You are the one that ordered the destruction of my planet," the rough voice said as the knife pressed harder against her throat. "I will execute you now for crimes against the people of Inea."

Blood began to ooze around his blade as she felt it begin to slice her throat. She had one shot at getting out of this as she watched Zuttara's face. There was nothing he could do for her; it was all her. She gripped her knife tightly and angled it towards the Inean's groin. She plunged it into him and spun around, pulling her head out of his grip as he loosened his grip for just a second. She pulled the knife out of his groin with a twist as he lunged towards her. His knife grazed her arm, breaking the skin as it did, but she found her mark again as she thrust the knife up under his ribs with a scream. She spun around, picked up her pistol, and squeezed the trigger, slamming a bullet in between his eyes at point-blank range. The Inean was dead before he hit the ground. She turned at the commotion, and two Ineans had Zuttara cornered. She smelled the rancid breath of another Inean behind her. She turned and fired several rounds into his face, which erupted in flying bits of bone, flesh, and a spray of his blue blood. She turned and emptied the magazine into the two Ineans that had Zuttara pinned.

She raced to him and checked him over. He was fine, but his ego was not since Dagan had single-handedly defeated four Ineans. She hugged him as several troops arrived to help out. "It's all over. Get these bodies to Asar's doctors," she said as she helped Zuttara to his feet.

Later that day, word was beginning to spread about how Dagan defeated the Ineans in hand-to-hand combat. The soldiers embellished their story, and rumors began to build about how she was sent by Kur to save them from the enemy. Over the next few weeks, much would be written and spoken about her fifteen seconds of combat, but it was enough to solidify her as the next president of the planet. It was a job she did not want. She wanted to marry Zuttara, have children, and live a quiet life. The last part, she knew, would not happen now.

Gula and Puabi returned to Samuqan and found little left of their families or their village. It had been ravaged by the Ineans, so they took the few people remaining and headed southwest away from the destroyed city of Delondra. Here, they found a valley just to the south of the Akkad River where several others had put up tents.

Puabi looked at Gula. "This is the place."

He smiled back at her. "So it is."

Gula took charge and put together teams of people. Some went to the forests, cut trees, and trucked them back to the valley. Others planted short-term crops, and they prepared for winter at the equator. Others began building houses and other buildings.

Once the first house went up, Gula held a ceremony to dedicate their new village. It was named Tamora after the goddess of Kur. Tamora was once thought to be a mythical being, but research years ago had proven that she was a real woman and the wife of Kur in ancient times.

Soon after the first house went up, many more were built. Gula and Puabi married and moved into their new home weeks before she gave birth. Everyone in the village was nervous about the baby from all the radiation surrounding Delondra, but when the baby was born, all of their fears were put to rest. They had a boy, and he was healthy. They named him Suen after Puabi's father, which was also the name of a character Kur spoke about in his writings.

The months passed, and the village continued to grow. Gula was officially elected as governor of the village, while Puabi had another child, a girl named Zikia, after another legendary character from the books of Kur.

FIFTY-SEVEN

ENANATUMA WOKE up in the hospital with her shoulder bandaged and wrapped around her neck as well. She looked about and saw several others in the same room. She began to sit up, and a nurse raced over and gently pushed her back down onto the bed. "No, no, dear. You need to lay back and rest," the nurse said.

"Where is Anzillu?" Enanatuma asked.

"He is right over there. He is going to be fine."

"Oh, thank Kur," she said. She listened to the nurse and laid back in the bed. "How long was I out for?"

"Two days. We were becoming concerned because of the infection running through your system from the knife, but it looks like we got it."

"Great. How am I?"

"You will be fine. Just rest for now," the nurse stated.

The nurse smiled at her and went to another patient that required her attention.

A few days later, they were released from the hospital and went back to the city of Ninki. There, they found a house and got married.

Both stayed in the military while promoting Kur's writings to the Eastern people. Their efforts led to the rebuilding of the great temple in Kurdash. The last of the Ineans had been killed, and the planet and their people began to heal.

FIFTY-EIGHT

DAGAN PACED NERVOUSLY in front of the mirrors as she was fitted with a robe made of more than forty pieces of robes worn by previous leaders of Ardonnar over the centuries. She wrapped it around herself and admired how ugly it truly was, but it was a tradition, and it had to be worn. Once it was fitted, she walked out onto a balcony where Zuttara waited in full military uniform. In front of them was the high priest, Kasua, who leaned on a crutch with the sacred book of Kur in his shaking hands. His health was failing fast, and Dagan wanted him to perform the ceremony, even though they had bumped heads on many occasions. There was no one else she would have trusted to perform this. Besides, he was one of the few remaining who was on Aanepada's list, she found.

Beyond the balcony, thousands of people crammed the courtyard of the new presidential residence. There was nothing elaborate about this one. It was basically a small fort with towers at the corners and sentries manning the towers.

The crowd cheered as Dagan stepped out, and Zuttara grinned. She grinned back while Kasua rolled his eyes.

"Shall we get started, Priestess?" Kasua asked in his broken voice.

"Yes, by all means," she said, waving to the crowd, and then she turned to face Zuttara, grasping his hands in hers.

Kasua raised the ancient book above his head with shaking fingers. "Blessed be Kur!" his voice cracked.

Everyone present echoed his words. Then, everyone except for Kasua, Dagan, and Zuttara knelt down on the ground and bowed their faces to the ground.

The wedding was brief, and a large reception followed after. The people brought food to the feast and provided music, which consisted of stringed instruments along with various brass horns.

Eventually, Dagan and Zuttara arrived and were mobbed by hundreds of people. Several marines tried to keep them away, but Dagan allowed them to surge forward. She greeted as many as she could, along with Zuttara.

The party lasted well into the next morning. However, Dagan and Zuttara slipped away early on when given the chance, and the people partied on.

EPILOGUE

RADIATION CLOUDS BLANKETED the planet of Inea as thousands of Ineans huddled in caves surrounding campfires. Outside, radioactive snow fell while a few hunted a dog-like animal called a Champak. A Champak was a fierce animal that hunted in packs and attacked the Ineans in their own search for food. Soon, the hunting party returned with a few of the Champaks slung over their shoulders. They carved them up and skewed them over the campfires.

The Ineans started getting sores on their skin, and their hair fell out. Soon, their teeth began to fall out as well. After about six months, the Champak became hard to find as they died off from the radiation and the loss of their food supply. The Ineans turned to the remaining slaves that so far had lived through the ordeal and butchered them and ate them. The Ineans turned towards rodents and insects, which seemed to thrive in the radioactive world. Finding them was hard, as the planet was blanketed in snow from the nuclear winter that had gripped their world. The Ineans would have to pry up fallen trees and pick the insects out. It could take up to several hours to find enough insects to make a meal. Life for the Ineans was difficult, to say the least.

. . .

Several years passed, and the Inean population dwindled to the brink of extinction. They teetered on the brink for dozens of years and, in some cases, were one bad storm away from being extinct. After some time, the planet began to warm, and vegetation returned along with the animals. The Ineans started to multiply and spread across the planet. The Ineans had no leaders; instead, they consisted of small tribes that fought constantly over territory and resources.

Hundreds of years had now passed, and their tools got better along with their weapons. The battles and wars became fiercer, claiming more lives. After a few hundred years more, these tribes coalesced into three competing factions, which now could build tanks, rockets, and other weapons. Most of the designs had been taken from schoolbooks found in the bombed-out cities from the past. They began to relearn who they were.

After another hundred years, the Ineans had learned how to build nuclear rockets and now had the capability to wipe themselves off the planet as their wars threatened their existence. What they needed was a leader to unite their people.

Lord Marduk came on the scene and was considered a god. He stood a full foot taller than the average Inean and was stronger than any three put together. Everywhere he went, the Inean women fought over who would bear his next offspring, and, over the years, he had thousands. The Ineans flocked to him as he single-handedly defeated tribe after tribe. His battles became a legend, and then it became a religion to the Ineans. He united the Ineans, and their culture began to re-create the glories of the past. Legend stated that Marduk never died but went to be with the other Inean gods and would return when the Ardons were found. The Ineans, in a quest to have their leader return, became obsessed with finding the Ardons. Soon, they had ships heading into space. Soon after that, they began heading to other solar systems. They expanded into the galaxy, conquering race after race in their quest to find the Ardons. A thousand years after the Ardon war, their expansion brought them toward Earth.

They worked as one with a single focus: find the Ardons and kill them all...

ARDO TRANSLATIONS

COMMON ARDO WORDS

- An – god
- Awah – wolf-type animal
- Bulkrah – vulture birds
- Cacama – amen
- Cushik – swear word
- Duga – damn it curse
- Duranki – bad swear word
- Etlutu – type of Morse code
- Kur – God's name
- Melam – wheat
- Mulla – demons
- Nergal – devil
- Rabum – chicken
- Sahu – pig like animal
- Tari – Hell
- Telal – ducks
- Urukii – nuclear bomb

UNITS OF MEASUREMENT

- Pana = 1.5 feet
- Ima = 15 feet (yard)
- Zag = 1.3 miles

WEEKDAYS

- 1 – Ahtu
- 2 – Tidtu
- 3 – Serhertu
- 4 – Nasatu
- 5 – Wabatu
- 6 – Ezertu
- 7 – Sabitu

MONTHS

- 1 – Alal
- 2 – Edin
- 3 – Galu
- 4 – Nergan
- 5 – Rappi
- 6 – Gidim
- 7 – Kiam
- 8 – Lilit
- 9 – Eanna
- 10 – Leu
- 11 – Kish
- 12 – Alme
- 13 – Shinir

NUMBER

- Zero – Vour
- One – Tuam
- Two – Kilu
- Three – Girse
- Four – Gal
- Five – Baur
- Six – Nadi
- Seven – Tulu
- Eight – Amam
- Nine – Nidi
- Ten – Pur

ABOUT THE AUTHOR

Henry Eaton is the independently published author of science fiction novels including Siege of Ardon and The Inean Debacle. He has enjoyed science fiction for nearly his entire life, sharing the ever popular Star Trek and Star Wars, as well as other, less popular, works with his family. His work blends real world issues with the vast expanse of space to create stories that resonate from the first page to the last.

Visit his website at henryeatonbooks.com